CW00556049

The Wrong Things Right:

Ace's Wild

By Maxine Keith

This is a work of fiction. Names, characters, places, and incidents either are the product of the author's imagination or are used fictitiously. Any resemblance to actual persons, living or dead, events, or locales is entirely coincidental.

Copyright © 2020

First:

I do not own any rights to any of the songs that may be mentioned in this, or any of my other, books. Music is one of my muses and when a timeless song hits me at the right moment, it brings to life a character or a scene that has been stirring in my head. By including well-known songs by well-known artists, I am in no way attempting to do anything more than pay homage to great music and greater musicians who touch our lives and sometimes change our destinies.

Second:

I apologize for any and all of the grammatical and spelling errors in this story. I'm a simple dreamer who had a story to share. I hope the mistakes don't negatively impact your reading experience.

Thank you so very much for taking a chance and buying my simple little book. I hope, with all my heart, you'll love it and the characters in it.

I owe a final thank you to my dearest husband, without who this book never would have been published. He reminded me that I write to escape and to find peace, and others read to do the same. I hope this story will allow you a little time to escape.

Wrong Things Right, and it's follow up book Right Things Wrong, are meant to be read in order. These were written as one book and broken into smaller sections simply for publishing purposes. I beg of you to please read these books in order, as reading them out of order will cause confusion and disrupt the story line.

The Fast Saga:

Wrong Things Right: Ace's Wild   (Fast Series Book 1)

Wrong Things Right: Losing Hand   (Fast Series Book 2)

Wrong Things Right: Straight Shot   (Fast Series Book 3)

Right Things Wrong: Full House   (Fast Series Book 4)

Right Things Wrong: Queen's Run   (Fast Series Book 5)

Right Thing Wrong: Royal Flush   (Fast Series Book 6)

Promise or Threat (Fast Saga Book 7)

Picking Daisy (Fast Saga Book 8)

Racing Rayne (Fast Saga Book 9)

Look Me in the Eye (Fast Saga Book 10)

Chapter 1

Jez didn't miss much when it came to things. That was one advantage to sitting in corners at parties and not actually participating in them. So, in addition to watching her friend, Molly, flirt with a new and helpless guy; Jez saw the pathetic attempts of other girls who tried to get the attention of other boys. Some were successful, some not. Jez smiled and shook her head as one girl in specific walked away in a huff as her big, full curls bounced in opposite rhythm to her feet. The guy that she had failed to attract glanced over at his friend with an amused smirk, then his eyes drifted across the seas of faces landing on Jez's.

She had never seen him before, at least she couldn't remember if she had. He was tall, a full head taller than anyone else in the room, aside from the basketball players who were freakishly tall. This guy offered her a small smile, a slightly cocky grin that showed just a flash of white teeth. His head was shaved bald with a clean-shaven face and a nose that was perfect, even though it had a bump on the bridge where it had been broken a couple of times. His jaw was square and strong. She couldn't see the color of his eyes from across the room but they drilled into her making her uncomfortable. Jez's smile faded as she looked away, suddenly occupied with her red, plastic cup.

Even though she had looked away, Jez still felt the weight of his stare on her. It was heavy and made Jez tired. She suddenly wished Molly would come and take her home. But her friend was nowhere to be seen. Instead, another body drifted to her. He loomed over while Jez stared into the cup, fighting every urge to look up at him. She knew he was going to be mad. He always was when it came to her being at the same parties. Jez thought he'd be used to it after all these years.

"That better not be beer." Jordy's voice was dark and drew Jez's eyes up.

"Soda." She replied and held the cup up so he could see.

He looked at it carefully and then nodded. The slutty looking girl with him, someone Jez didn't recognize, tugged on his arm. He glanced at her and then looked back down at his baby sister. "Don't stay too late."

As he allowed the brunette to lead him away, Jez sighed. She loved her brother with no limits, but she was getting tired of his overly protective side. She took the last sip of soda and placed the cup on the floor near the leg of the chair. As she sat back, another red cup appeared before her.

"You look thirsty." The smiling face was exotic with dark hair and strong features.

Jez wasn't really thirsty but she took the cup to be polite. "Thanks."

"An ex?" The guy sank into an empty chair beside her. He crossed one leg over the other and leaned back confidently.

Jez allowed her eyes to glance over in the direction Jordy had gone but didn't reply.

"His loss. That plastic Barbie ain't got nothing on you. You're …. natural." He sat up and leaned toward her, elbows on his knees and eyes scanning her body.

Jez knew what he'd see. Natural was guy code for not real pretty, not real cute, not real ugly, but completely fuck-able. She was slightly overweight, with larger thighs and butt, a slight curve in at her waist that could only be seen if one stood directly in front of her, a chest that wasn't overly large, and arms that were not tone or skinny. She was no model, and not the typical beach baby one was accustomed to in their town. She hated being in a bathing suit, although most of her friends and her brother's friends were understanding and supportive. They complimented her when they could and stood up for her when they couldn't. They reminded her that her figure was not her fault, just the product of nature and a side effect of her situation. Most guys didn't see beyond the fat though. They didn't take the time to get to know her or understand why she looked how she did. They didn't care to. The only time she was ever even asked out was so someone could ask Molly out too. Jez had no misunderstandings, she knew she was the grenade of the group.

Even though this guy was eyeing her deeply, smiling as if he liked what he saw, Jez knew better. Her heart sank with the sadness and despair that came with her reality. She knew she shouldn't drink whatever was in the cup. There were at least five reasons that came to mind instantly. But in that moment, she didn't really care. As she lifted the cup to her lips, she caught the widening grin was spread across the guy's face. But it was the deep voice that came from just behind her that made her stop.

"You don't want to drink that."

Jez looked down into the cup. She moved it away from her lips. "And why not?" Her eyes flashed up over her shoulder to the voice.

Even though her heart raced a bit, she forced herself to be calm. It wasn't hard, she'd done it for a couple of months now. The very tall, bald man towered over her. Jez tried not to look at him, wide-eyed, as she took him in. Besides the incredibly handsome face, his broad shoulders and big arms were breathtaking. His black shirt was tight, but not too tight. She traced the thick black lines of the tribal tattoos down his arms. As she did, he smiled for a brief second, but then his eyes flashed to the seated guy opposite him. "Because the asshole spiked it."

The words hit her hard, and Jez looked down at the drink she had almost sipped. Stunned, she looked up at the dark man. "You're going to drug me?"

He opened his mouth to protest or defend himself but a flash of blond came out of nowhere and plowed into him and the chair, toppling both to the ground. As Jez recognized Jordy, he stood over the guy, pounding his fists into the stunned guy. "Don't you ever, fucking, come near my sister again." He said each word with a punch as if to nail the point home.

"Jordy, please." Jez cried out, standing quickly and then regretting it as the world tilted. A hand grabbed her arm and steadied her. She didn't bother to look at who had her, instead looking around for one of the group who could stop Jordy. It wasn't much longer than a second later before two blond guys dashed up and yanked Jordy off the badly bleeding boy.

"I don't ever want to see you around her again." Jordy thundered as his friends pulled him back.

"You got him, man." Ty, the short and stocker of the three said as the exotic looking guy charged off across the room and vanished into the crowd.

The third, a guy with hair so white it was almost the color of snow, patted Jordy on the back. Jordy looked at him. "Fucker tried to drug her." He pulled away from his buddies and grabbed Jez's arm. "Come on, we're leaving."

She quickly looked up at the tall man and smiled weakly. "Thank you."

Jordy was already dragging her across the room before she realized he had responded with "anytime."

Outside, Jordy shoved Jez into the cab of the battered pickup and slammed the door. As soon as he slid behind the wheel the lecture started, "I told you never, ever take a drink from anyone but the guys. You never know what's in it, Jez. And with everything that's going on, you don't even know if a safe drink would be safe for you. Jesus Christ, how many times am I

....." He continued to rant and rave, lecturing her on the importance of being safe around strangers the entire drive home. Jez only listened to half of it. She had heard it so many times before, she could almost say it verbatim.

Once home, standing in the safety of their living room, Jez kissed her brother's cheek. "I love you too. Good night."

His dark mood mellowed slightly and he sighed. "Rest well, Jez."

She smiled at him and padded up the stairs and down the hallway to her small bedroom. After changing quickly, she slid into the soft bed and tried to relax. For the first time in a long time, Jez allowed herself a smile as she drifted off to sleep with thoughts of a tall, bald, tattooed hero coming to her rescue.

Chapter 2

Jez woke early. The sun was rising outside of her window and lit her room brightly. She sighed and climbed out of bed. Jordy had left again last night after he made sure Jez was safely tucked into bed. She hadn't heard him come back. As she headed down to the kitchen to make herself some coffee, Jez thought about the day ahead. She had class, then her appointment. When that was done, she'd be too tired to do anything else. Hopefully, she'd manage to get some homework done. If not, that was on tomorrow's to-do list.

She dressed and collected her things. She was slipping on her flip-flops as a horn blasted from the street out front. Jez rolled her eyes and headed out the front door. Two steps, a fifteen-footstep cracked concrete walkway, and then a strip of dying grass. That was what she walked every day, it was one of the few consistencies of her life. Today the old green Buick sat in the street, engine growling like a tank. It was one of three vehicles that she expected to see. Behind the wheel, there was one of three smiling faces she knew would be there.

"Morning Pickle." He smiled.

"Morning OB." She smiled, pulling the seatbelt across her. He cranked up the music, some surf band that sounded a little too punk for her tastes, and drove off down the street. He pulled up in front of the college campus and stopped. Reaching over to turn down the radio, he stopped her from jumping out of the car with a raised finger. "What? I'm gonna be late."

"Jordy ..." OB started to say, but then stopped. He glanced around as he thought, but then returned his gaze to her eyes. "Have a good day, Pickle."

She narrowed his eyes at him, but let it go. She knew the three boys were tighter than friends and closer than blood. OB had a reason for not completing that sentence. She nodded. "Do you know who's picking me up? I have an appointment today."

His usual happy-go-lucky smile returned. "One of us will be here. Don't worry."

She nodded and pushed out into the warm morning air. Summer was coming to an end. These were the last few days of a heat wave that was predicted to wane. The meteorologists promised cooler weather soon. Jez hoped so. She hated hot days. They made her condition worse and made everything so much harder. Jez had to walk to class a little slower. She knew the deal. It had been a long, hot summer. She knew she had to be careful these last few days.

Jez was just pushing into the last corridor, walking close to the wall, when she spotted the tall bald head weaving through the crowded hall. He looked too old to be there, but then again, this was college and there wasn't much that didn't go. She watched as he smiled and waved at people, speaking to guys and leaning down to hug girls. When he glanced up the hall, Jez ducked inside the classroom and headed for a seat in the back row. She found her usual place, second seat in from the aisle with her bag set on the end seat to ensure no one sat there. She pulled out her notebook and a pen, an unlabeled bottle of purple liquid, and a baggie of pickles. While she waited for the class to begin, she snacked on the pickles and watched the others settle in. Just behind the professor, the tall bald guy slid into the room and then into an empty seat in one of the middle rows between three girls who giggled and tossed their hair stupidly. Jez pulled her attention from them as the professor started into his lecture.

Jez got through the two-hour class without too much difficulty. It wasn't a hard class if you did the readings and studied a little. Humanities were more about ideas than facts. But it was a lot of writing assignments and even more readings, and Jez was glad it was her only class for the quarter. Just two weeks into the nine-week class and she was already feeling a bit overwhelmed. As the class was dismissed, the professor called out her name and asked that she come see him before leaving. Jez slowed down her packing up so that the other students would be gone before she approached the front of the room. A small group of girls along with the tall bald guy, who was looking back at her, moved slowly to the doorway and then exited.

Jez waited for the professor to look up from the papers he was straightening. "Jezebel, I've been made aware of your situation and I wanted to let you know that I am willing to help you out as much as I can. If you need extra time or anything, just let me know, alright?"

Jez nodded. "Thank you. I appreciate that. I should be fine though. This is my only class this quarter."

"Well, just the same. Don't hesitate to ask for anything." He smiled and she realized how good looking he was for an older man. Distinguished and mature but not old. Jez suddenly understood why he was one of the more popular professors on campus.

"Thank you." She smiled and turned to leave. Jez walked straight back to the parking lot where she saw Ty leaning against the side of his late model VW bus. He had spent more time and money keeping it running. Nothing meant more to him than that bus, except maybe his friends.

"Hey, Pickle, I was about to come looking for you." He smiled.

He pulled the passenger door open for her as she said, "The professor wanted to talk to me."

She climbed in and fastened her seatbelt as he jogged around the front and climbed in. As he started the engine, he glanced over at her. "Everything OK?"

"Sure." Jez nodded and glanced out the window as Ty pulled away from the curb. She noticed a group of people standing around talking, one head higher than all the others. He was watching her curiously as Ty drove her from the parking lot.

They were halfway to the center when Ty turned down the radio and looked over at glanced over at her again. "So I met this girl at the party last night."

"Oh?" Jez smiled with a knowing look. Ty was always meeting girls everywhere he went.

"She's cute," He added.

Jez sighed, knowing exactly where this was going. "I'll cover your shift tonight."

"If you don't think you'll feel up to it, I completely understand." He rushed, concern coloring his face.

"I'll be fine. It's all good." He opened his mouth to say something but she raised her hand to stop him. "How many times have you had to cover for me? I can do this."

He smiled and relaxed a little. "You're a doll, Pickle. I'm just taking her to dinner and maybe down to the beach."

Jez replied with a soft laugh and a knowing smile. She doubted that was all they'd be doing, but she didn't say it. As much as Jordy, Ty, and OB pretended she was just their kid sister and pretended she was innocent, growing up around three boys had taught her a lot about guys. She had learned their code words and tells early on. Her education about life was all from a guy's point of view since she never had much of a mother figure. Her mother had left years ago, and the only female she ever had around was Ty's mom, who was nice but not overly motherly towards anyone.

Ty pulled up in front of the center and stopped. "Do you want me to come in?"

"Naw, I got this. Just make sure someone is here to pick me up?"

He rolled his eyes and chuckled. "Of course."

Jez hopped out of the van and walked through the automatic doors without looking back. She heard the van pull away as the door closed behind her. Guilt plagued her a little. Everyone but her brother and father thought her appointments were counseling sessions. She hated hiding the truth from them, but in the long run, she knew it was for the best. Better to be hated than pitied. She approached the small, circular desk and waited for the small woman to look up at her. "Good Afternoon, Jezebel."

"Morning," Jez replied, taking the pager that she was handed. Without saying anything else, Jez turned and walked down the long corridor. She allowed herself a moment to look at the paintings that hung on the walls. They were pretty still-life's and nature scenes, and Jez always liked looking at them when she passed. Approaching the elevators, Jez stopped to use the bathroom and then headed for the second floor. Another woman greeted her as she passed another desk, then settled in a small waiting room to be called back. It only took ten minutes before the pager buzzed and the location appeared on the tiny screen. Jez gathered her things and headed for the south wing. A nurse met her with a bright smile.

"Afternoon, Jezebel. How are you feeling today?"

"Good. How about you?"

"Perfect." The nurse was shorter than Jez and even more round, but her face was cute and shined with an inner light. "We're going to have you in a group room today. Is that alright?"

"Sure." Jez knew some patients didn't like the group rooms, but she didn't mind them. Sometimes it was actually nice to talk to others who understood.

The nurse led her back to the farthest room and pointed to the only available seat. Jez dropped her bag and plunked down. "Margie will be your nurse today. She'll be with you in a moment."

Jez pulled her highlighter and textbook from her bag, then sat back in the reclining chair. She knew not to get too comfortable until she was hooked up. While she waited for Margie, Jez looked at the other patients. A frail, older woman sat in the opposite chair. She was laid back and her eyes were closed as her meds pushed into her gaunt body. In the seat next to her was a middle-aged man who was in a deep discussion on his cell phone. He was dressed in business slacks and a button-down shirt as if he was on his lunch break. Jez absently wondered how that was going for him. Her eyes drifted down to the one sleeve that was pushed up and the IV needle that was stuck in his arm. She noticed the bruises that showed he was here often. She felt bad for him.

Jez allowed her eyes to fall on the older man that sat in the chair on the other side of her. He smiled at her as she took in his white hair and big brown eyes. He looked strong and healthy, and Jez couldn't help but wonder if his journey was just starting. "Hate to see a pretty young thing, like you, in here." His voice was a little shaky.

Jez smiled back to him and shrugged. "I don't have cancer. It's OK."

He gave her a curious look but didn't have time to inquire as Margie the nurse appeared before her. With a loud, fake southern cry, Margie called, "Jezebel."

"Hi, Margie." Jez smiled back. She hated the way Margie said her name but never said anything. It just wasn't worth it.

As the nurse pulled a rolling chair over, she took a seat and snapped on the blue rubber gloves. "How're you feeling today?"

"I'm good. A little tired." Jez said honestly. Then dropped her voice, and said, "I went to a party last night."

Margie's eyes smiled as brightly as her lips. "Good for you. Was it fun?"

"Not really. My brother was there and didn't let me do anything except sit in a chair."

Margie twisted her lips up. "So no cute guys?"

"There was a lot to look at, but no one for me." Jez laughed lightly as she tended to in order to cover what she was really feeling.

Margie took Jez's arm and turned it over. With a gentle pat, she said, "Someone will come along." Jez nodded but didn't express her doubts. Margie pushed around a little on Jez's arm and then tied a blue rubber band above her elbow. After pressing around a little more, Margie untied the strap and repeated the process with the other arm. Eventually, she settled on a vein in the back of Jez's hand. As she pushed the needle in, Jez bit the inside of her lip. "I hate to say this, Jezebel, but I think you might need a port soon. It's getting harder and harder to stick you."

Jez nodded silently. She was already aware of this. Her doctor had mentioned it at the last visit. They had an appointment scheduled for next week, when her dad was going to be home, to get his approval. Once the IV was in place,

Margie stood up and checked the chart as another nurse brought in the fluid-filled bags. Jez was surprised to see a clear one and a yellow one, and not two clears. Margie saw the look on her face and gave Jez a soft smile. "Your labs came back. The doc's not happy with the results. I'm sure he'll talk to you about them when you see him next."

Jez blinked back the emotions and forced a smile. In as cheerful a voice as she could muster, Jez held up her hand. "Filler up."

Margie shook her head with a slight smile and went about getting the bags hung on the pole. Attaching the plastic tubing to the first bag, she screwed it to the IV in Jez's hand. After making sure that Jez was good, offering a pillow, blanket, snack, and drink, all of which Jez declined for the moment, Margie left to check on her other patients. Jez looked up at the yellow bag hanging next to the clear one and reminded herself it was going to be just fine. Pushing away any nerves she had, Jez focused on the textbook she had sitting on her lap. Flipping open the book, she began to read the assigned pages, highlighting and rereading important information.

When both bags were drained into Jez, the nurse removed the IV and wrapped her hand in a bright pink, elastic wrap. She watched as Jez packed up and wished her a good day. Jez said she'd see them in a couple of days and then headed back out the way she had come. She was tired, as she usually was after her appointments. Getting fluids was supposed to help, but it always took a day to feel the effects. She walked slowly down the hallways and out to the front of the center. She had expected to have to wait a few minutes until her ride showed up since they usually weren't on time. But Ty was sitting in his van, talking with a pretty strawberry blonde in the passenger seat. Catching the movement, he jumped from his seat and came around to help Jez into the back of the van.

"How do you feel?" He said looking at her carefully.

Forcing a smile, she replied, "Awesome."

He gave her a look that let her know he wasn't buying it but didn't push. As Jez got settled into the back seat, he climbed behind the wheel. "Jez, this is Patty. Patty, Jez."

"Hey." Jez smiled.

"So, Ty tells me you're his sister." She smiled sweetly.

"Yep." It wasn't technically true, but close enough. The girl seemed sweet and she was pretty, and Jez wasn't up for getting into the reality of it with her.

"You sure you're up for taking my shift?" Ty asked as he drove them down the busy street. He had been glancing up at Jez in the rearview mirror for the past few minutes.

"Sure. I'm fine, really." When his eyes narrowed, she waved him off. "I just spent four hours reading my humanities text, and talking about my feelings." She added to help cover her lies. "My mind's fried. I'm good to work."

Again he gave her a doubtful look, but then Patty said something and he was distracted. The two talked all the way back to the store, where Ty pulled to a stop. Jez pushed the door open and called over her shoulder. "Thanks for the ride, Ty. It was nice to meet you, Patty. Have a good time."

She didn't wait for their response, but slammed the door and headed into the shop. The van pulled away with the typical bubbly rumble of a good running VW.

OB looked up from behind the counter surprised to see Jez pushing through the front door. "What are you're doing here?"

"I'm taking Ty's shift. He's got a date." She replied, glancing around the empty store. It was a small auto parts store that was as old as the community itself. It had been started by Jez's great-grandfather, expanded by her grandmother, and passed down through the generations. Her father was the one to run it until her mother left and the family needed more money to survive. Once the kids were old enough to survive on their own for short periods of time, he took a job on an offshore oil rig with his best friends, OB and Ty's fathers. Now the kids ran the store when their dads were offshore, and the fathers ran it when they were on dry land. Between the seven of them, it worked out well. They had hired one other to help out when Jez had become sick, and he worked the odd shifts and busy weekends. But today was a slow day, and Jez knew she'd be fine closing the store alone.

OB gave her an odd look. "A date? With who?"

"Patty? He met her last night at that party." Jez replied as she rounded the counter and headed back to put her bag in the office.

OB followed her back and stood in the doorway. "You want me to take the shift?"

"No, I've got it." She smiled, turning back to look at him. "Don't you have plans?"

He looked away from her for a second but then nodded. "Yeah, but I can cancel."

"I got it." She smiled and moved past him. He followed again as she crossed the edge of the back room and then back into the main store. When he leaned on the counter, still looking at her carefully, she turned back to him. "Really, I'm fine."

"You look tired, Pickle."

She shrugged. "I've got it. Go, have fun."

He still looked doubtful though. "Maybe I should call Jordy."

"I said I've got it." She moved in front of him and looked into his eyes. "I'm fine. Yes, I'm a little tired, but I'm fine. I got this. Go, have fun."

He still didn't look happy but he nodded anyway. He moved around her and grabbed a couple of things from below the register. Placing a kiss on her cheek, OB whispered, "Call if you need anything."

"I'm not going to bug you." She giggled and shoved his shoulder.

He laughed at her and headed for the door. "See you tomorrow, Pickle."

"Night." Jez walked the store floor when she was finally alone. It looked good. Sometimes the guys didn't do as much as they should, but today they had. The shelves were stocked and tidy. Labels faced out and the stacks looked neat. Jez checked and saw that she needed to dust, but other than that everything looked good. She found the feather duster under the counter and did the little bit of work. When it was done, she returned behind the counter. She reorganized the few things that she saw behind the scenes that needed it. After pacing a little bit, she decided to double check the time slips and then fix the following week's schedule. The dads were due back in three days, so they could pick up a few shifts, but Jez made sure to give them easier times or fewer days. She remembered her appointment and made sure that day was covered by someone else. Three customers came in that night, all needed just basic things that Jez could help with. Windshield wipers, oil, and air filters were easy things for Jez to research and gather. She was completely capable of looking things up and finding parts. It was the harder things, like troubleshooting or complex problems, that she couldn't help with. That was one reason why she usually took the quieter shifts or scheduled herself to work with one of the guys. Tonight was a good night though; quiet and easy.

The sun set and Jez watched it from the front window. When the sky was a deep ocean blue, she returned to the counter and checked the time. She could close in an hour. With a sigh, she began to get ready. It was a half hour until closing when the front door opened, ringing the small bell above the door. Jez smiled as she turned her head up to greet the customer. "Hi. How can I ...." She stopped mid-sentence as her eyes fell on the tall man.

His lips curved up when she stopped speaking, continuing to move toward the counter. "How can you ... what?"

Jez took in a breath and composed herself. "Help you. How can I help you?"

He chuckled. "I got it."

As he moved towards the back wall, looking at the various cans, jugs, bottles, and containers, Jez pulled herself together. She refused to allow him to get to her. Yes, he was cute, OK, more than cute... hot, sexy, dreamlike would be better words to describe him. And yes, seeing him in these multiple places was confusing and unsettling, but she was not going to let a player like him fluster her. She moved to the register and watched as he picked up a jug and walked over to her. He placed it on the counter and she turned it to see the barcode. "Do you need anything else?"

"Nope." He replied as she rang it up. He watched the readout and then pulled the money from his black leather wallet. He placed a twenty on the counter and she handed him the change.

"Have a good night." She replied pleasantly with her customer service smile.

He smiled as he picked up the jug. He moved to the door and called back, "You too, Jezebel."

She watched him leave, getting into a lush, classic black, 1970 Barracuda. She swallowed and let out a breath. Putting her elbow on the counter, she dropped her head in her hands. "He's trouble, girl, you gotta let it go." She spoke out loud, trying to convenience herself. The door chimed again and she looked back up, a forced smile on her face.

"Jez? You OK?" Her brother looked at her a little concerned.

"Yes, I'm just getting a little tired." She admitted.

He moved around the counter and put a hand on her shoulder. "Why are you working tonight?"

"Ty had a date. He asked me to work for him."

Jordy smiled weakly. "You know you shouldn't work on treatment nights."

She nodded and leaned into him. "I know, but I felt bad. You all work so much more than I do."

He placed a kissed on her head. "Go count out. I'll lock up."

She did as he told her, just like she usually did. Taking the register drawer to the back room, Jez counted the money and made sure it matched the receipt report. She made out the bank deposit and dropped it all in the safe. When she was done, she grabbed up her bag and met her brother in the main part of the shop. He had already shut off the main lights and flipped the closed sign. He wrapped an arm around her and pulled her close as they moved out to the door. He pushed her through the front door then went back to set the alarm. Jez waited by the truck until he came out and finished locking the front doors.

"Have you eaten?" He asked as he turned from the door.

"I'm not hungry." She replied.

They got in the truck and Jordy turned to look at her. "That's not what I asked. What did you eat today and when?"

It took her a minute to think. "I had pickles in class today."

"And that's all?" Jordy rolled his eyes with a sigh. "You haven't been eating much lately."

"I'm not hungry."

"You need to eat though."

"But I'm nauseous." She almost whined.

Jordy didn't reply but cranked the engine over. He drove them down the street, opposite direction of their home. Jez didn't ask where they were going. She already knew. She didn't argue either. It would be pointless. Two blocks down, he pulled them into the parking lot of a favorite diner and found a spot right next to OB's Buick and Ty's VW. It was just another typical night for them. As Jordy grabbed Jez's hand and pulled her along behind him, she noticed the other cars in the lot. A familiar looking muscle car sat a few spots down, as well as four other cars she recognized.

Jordy pulled her along as they entered and crossed to their usual booth. Ty and OB were already there, lounging and talking happily. As they approached, the two moved around and Jordy pushed her in. When Jez was seated, wedged in the circular booth between Ty and Jordy, she glanced around the diner. Jez saw several people she knew, some she didn't, and one that stood out like a strobe light to her. His bald head shining under the harsh fluorescent lighting and he leaned over to talk to a pretty blond across the table.

Jez turned her attention back to the group around her. Surprised to see them all looking right back at her. "What?"

"That's what we asked you," Jordy said.

"What did the doc say?" Ty asked.

OB leaned over and rubbed her arm. "Ty said you looked rough when he picked you up."

"I'm fine." She smiled.

A waitress came over and dropped a plate of food in front of Jez and Jordy, without them even ordering. The woman winked at them and walked away. But before Jez could grab up a fry, Jordy grabbed her hand. "You know we aren't buying this crap. Do I need to call the doctor?"

"I'm fine. We go see the doctor next week." She sighed, looking at each of the guys that she loved dearly. The worry was clear on each face. "I'm fine."

She smiled at them, trying to let them know that meant what she said. But Jordy held her arm tighter. "Jez?"

"We see the doctor next week; you can talk to him then." She said with a sigh. "Now can I eat?"

Jordy let go of her arm, and Jez dug in. While she focused on the BLT in front of her, she missed the worried looks between the ones she cared about. Jordy pushed his plate away, too worried to eat. This was what caught Jez's attention.

Looking up from her handful of sandwich, she sighed. Without a word, Jez sat down her food, wiped her hands on her napkin, and reached her arms around her brother's neck. "I'm fine."

"No, you're not," OB said in his flipped way. "You're more than fine. You are one fucking amazing girl."

It was exactly what was needed at that tense moment. Jez looked across at him and smiled, as did her brother. Ty started laughing and pretty soon the others were too. Jez picked up a fry and tossed it at OB, who caught it in his mouth. With a bright grin, he chewed it while the others laughed.

Jordy and Jez both ate then, with OB and Ty picking off their plate. When they were done, Jordy paid the bill. Jez gave both Ty and OB a kiss on the cheek, then met her brother at the door. He wrapped an arm around her neck and pulled her out into the night. They were both full and happy as Jordy pulled out of the parking spot. As he put the truck into drive, Jez looked up and saw a bald man watching them through the window of the diner, his expression unreadable. Once home, Jordy sent Jez upstairs to bed. She didn't argue much. She had grown very tired on the way home and was looking forward to crawling into her soft bed.

Three hours later, Jez awoke to her stomach cramping. It didn't take long for the cramping to turn to heaving. Jez just barely managed to get to the bathroom before she lost what was left of her dinner. She spent the next two hours emptying her stomach and wishing there was more to heave than just dryness. At two-thirty, she crawled back to her bed and fell back to sleep.

Chapter 3

Friday morning came quicker than Jez would have liked. Her alarm went off at six- thirty and she staggered into the shower. She dressed in jeans and a long t-shirt that hid her round figure. After making a pot of coffee, she shoved 2 bottles of a generic hydration drink into her bag, filled a travel mug with coffee, and headed out to work. It was her job to open the store on Friday mornings. The guys had to come in about mid-afternoon when their knowledge was needed to help the weekend warriors and make-believe mechanics who filled their weekends working on cars. So, Jez opened the store and worked the quieter morning.

It was only two short neighborhood blocks down to the family shop, but in the late summer morning heat, it might as have been a mile. Jez was weak and queasy when she unlocked the door, and moved to shut off the alarm. It took every ounce of her strength to push the gates back into the farthest corners of the wall. When it was done, she sank down to her knees and breathed, her heart racing as if she had run a marathon. It took her several long minutes before she had calmed enough to even think of moving. During that time, she was so very thankful no one was out front watching her. It was horrible enough to suffer through this alone, but to be embarrassed by having someone watch was five times worse. After a few minutes, Jez tried to stand, but fell to her knees. Her legs were still too weak to hold her up. Crawling across the floor, she reached her bag which she had dumped in front of the register. Pulling out one of the bottles of liquid, she cracked it open and downed half of it. It was still a little cool, and tasted amazing. She replaced the cap and took several more minutes to gather her strength.

As she began to feel better, Jez pushed herself up the counter and held on as she regained her balance. Just when she thought she was alright, the wave of nausea rolled over her and she had to rush to the closest trash can. Falling to her knees again, this time behind the counter under the cash register, she heaved up all the fluids she had just drunk down.

The nausea was passing when the bell of the door sounded. Jez wanted to cry, but instead grabbed the bottle of water that they kept under the register for her. She rinsed her mouth as quickly and quietly as possible, then rose slowly. She forced a smile and tried to hid her surprise as her eyes met the sapphire eyes that shined down on her. They were breath-taking, and not just because they were inside a tall, bald headed man with a strong jaw and muscular, tattooed arms that grew out of a jet-black t-shirt. His eyes lost some of their shine as he looked at her.

"Are you alright?"

"Sure. What can I do for you?" She lied as if her life depended on it.

His eyes narrowed but he didn't continue down that path. Instead he said, "My baby's making an odd noise. Is there anyone here who knows about cars?"

A smart-ass comment rolled through her mind, but she allowed it to keep going. "One of the guys will be in around eleven, but if you need help now, I can call someone in."

"Naw. It's OK. I'll come back later." He turned and started for the door, but then looked back over his shoulder. "You sure you're alright?"

"Never better." She widened her smiled. He looked at her darkly for a moment, but then turned and left, the bell ringing his departure. When he was safely out the door, Jez grabbed onto the counter tightly and sank to her knees. Hovering over the trash can, Jez debated the idea of making herself throw up again. In the end, she didn't. There was nothing left to heave. She rinsed her mouth with the room temperature water and then tied up the plastic bag. After resting a bit longer on the cool tile floor, Jez forced herself up. Walking slowly and using the walls, counters, and racks for support, she made her way to the dumpster out back to dispose of the bag.

Jez was alone in the shop for another two hours until her brother showed up. He wasn't in the best of moods. She could tell by the way he shoved the door open and the stomp of his boots on the tile. She looked up from her textbook about to ask what was wrong when he stopped short. "Are you alright?"

She smiled and shook her head. "Why does everyone keep asking me that?"

"Because you look like shit." He responded, slowly walked over to stand opposite the counter from her. "What's wrong?"

"Nothing." She shrugged.

He didn't buy it though. "Pickle, you have to tell me what's going on."

"Nothing. I'm fine, really." She insisted. Jez knew that if she told him the truth that he would make her go lay down, or worse, send her home. The queasiness was gone but the weakness was still there, she wasn't going to give in to it though.

He gave her a dark look but was stopped from arguing with her when his phone rang. He glanced around to make sure they were alone in the store before answering it. "What?" he snapped.

Jez watched as her brother's face darkened, fury growing in his eyes. He had a short temper, that was well known, and whoever was on the other end of the line was lighting the fuse.

"You're fired." Jordy said in such a soft, menacing voice it made Jez nervous. When he was finished, Jordy threw the phone across the room. It hit the wall and shattered into pieces. Jez watched him take a calming breath before turning to her. "Call OB and Ty. We need to rework the schedule."

Without a word, she picked up the store phone and started dialing. She said the same words to each guy when they answered. "Get in here. Jordy fired Tom."

While she made the calls, Jordy had gone over and picked up his shattered phone and tossed it in the trash can. His anger was calming by the second, but Jez didn't bother asking what had happened. She knew one of the others would ask and she'd just wait. It wasn't much later when the two guys pushed into the store together.

"What happened?" OB asked as Jez pulled the schedule from under the counter where they kept a copy.

As they gathered around it, Jordy sighed. "He fucked Brina."

Three words and everything became crystal clear. Jez moved over and leaned her head on his shoulder, while the other two nodded silently. It was a simple rule, a code of ethics between the guys that worked at the store. It was as old as store itself, having been one of the agreements and rules established when Jez's great-grandfather had hired his first employee, and every employee since. Each other's girlfriends, sisters, daughters, and wives, were off limits. You didn't make a move on a girl anyone else was seeing or lived with, even if they broke up or moved out. Tom knew this rule. He understood it clearly. He had worked with them for the past few months and it had never been a problem, until now. Obviously being with Jordy's ex-girlfriend had meant more to him than his job.

"OK, so …" Jez said moving the schedule around so they could all see it. "Let's divide up his shifts."

Tom's hours weren't all that much, so it wasn't hard. He mostly worked the weekends and overlapping shifts to help with coverage. They all agreed that those overlapping times could mostly be handled without two people. The only concern was the weekends, and Sunday evening when the dads were going to be coming home. Tom always worked that shift alone. It was every other Sunday night when the fathers came home. They wanted one night with their families, eating dinner and just spending time getting caught up. As they each thought about how they could handle it, the bell rang as a customer came in. Jordy and Jez looked up instantly. It was the tall man with the eyes that stabbed.

Without a word to him, Jez nudged Jordy. "His car's making a noise that he can't identify."

Ty looked back at the guy, then to her. "What are you psychic now?"

"He came in earlier. I told him one of you would be here later." She smirked.

The guy had stopped, eyeing the four of them without a word. Ty, OB, and Jordy gave up with their thoughts on the schedule and turned to him. But it was Jordy who offered the help. "Let's go have a listen."

As the four men moved back to the door, Jez called out an idea that came to mind. "Why don't we just close early that day?"

There was a collective look over their shoulders and a glance at each other, but they didn't respond. She had expected that. It would take a few minutes for them to think it through. They followed the customer out to the parking lot and Jez watched as they went through the process she watched daily, but still didn't understand. The bald guy started the car, and Jez could hear the rumble and roar as he revved the engine. Ty popped open the hood. The three looked down into the engine, as if it were a crystal ball that could reveal all the answers. They talked amongst themselves for a few moments, then the guy in the car cut the engine, and joined them. They spoke for several long minutes. There was some pointing and a little debate. Eventually Jez got tired of watching, and returned her attention to the following week's schedule. She crossed out Tom's name and made notes where the others had agreed to pick up his shifts. The dads would be around to help cover here and there also, but Jez hated to make them work too much. They worked 12 hour shifts while off shore, and they needed this time to rest. She used them to help with double coverage days and times when she knew people needed off, like when she had her doctor's appointment the following week. Jordy, her dad, and herself would all be off that day, but she knew her dad would need to work the following day to get his mind off the stress. It was a balancing act that was carefully composed. Not having

Tom around was going to make it a little more difficult for a while, but they'd make it work, just like always.

OB rushed in after a little time and jogged across the room, around the counter, and vanished into the storage room. He reappeared a moment later with a box and jogged back out to the others. Jordy glanced over his shoulder at his sister and she saw the anger had evaporated. Jez smiled.

It was a while later when the group of four pushed back into the shop. Jez grabbed the roll of blue paper towels from under the counter and tossed them to Ty, who was first through the door and caught the roll effortlessly. He pulled one sheet off and handed it to the others. Jordy pointed the bald man to the bathroom in the far back corner, and he peeled off from the group, who was coming over to Jez.

"OK, I think I've got it worked out for the weekend and next week. It's helpful to have the dads back but we are really going to have to find someone, or we are all going to be pulling a lot of shifts." She said. "The only day I can't figure out is Sunday afternoon. I can open, and then come back after dinner to lock up, but …"

"No. I'll come back and lock up." Jordy interrupted.

"But that still leaves about five hours." She sighed. "Maybe we should just close up for the day."

"You looking to hire? Cause I'm looking for a job." The four of them looked up at the bald guy who had rejoined them without a sound.

"You really looking for a job?" Jordy asked.

He nodded. "I just moved here a few weeks ago. I haven't found anything that doesn't involve food, and I refuse to flip burgers."

Jordy looked at the others. It was really his decision, but Jordy always liked to hear what the others thought too. Ty nodded once, and OB shrugged. "He knows about cars. That gives him one up on Pickle."

She wanted to defend herself but really couldn't. Jordy looked back over his shoulder at her. "Pickle?"

"If he clears background, why not?" She replied, hating herself for agreeing with them. Her eyes glanced up to the man, who was smiling tightly, as if he knew she would agree to it. She walked away without a word, taking her time and staying close to the wall as she headed to get the paperwork from the office. She moved slowly, listening to the discussion that was happening behind her.

"Before you accept, you gotta know the rules." Jordy said sternly.

"Rules?"

"Rule 1, no stealing. You pay for everything you take. Rule 2, be honest. If you need something just say so." Jordy explained.

"Rule 3, there is no messing with anyone's girl, past, present, or future." Ty added.

"OK, but I don't know which girls are off limits." The man spoke.

There was a group chuckle. "We'll tell you."

"Should I guess Jezebel is one of your girls?"

There was a moment of silence, and Jez desperately wanted to go look around the corner to see what was happening, but she held her ground, standing just inside the office doorway clutching the new hire paperwork. It was Jordy that finally answered. "Jez is off limits to everyone."

"Besides, a guy like you doesn't want a girl like Pickle." Ty chuckled.

"Sure, you got the pick of the liter, you don't want the runt." OB added lightly.

Tears stung Jez's eyes, but she pushed them back. She knew that they were right. A guy like that would never want her. And she didn't want someone like him either. He was too much like the rough necks her dad worked with. Taking in a deep breath and pushing away the last of the hurt, she returned to the counter. She set the paperwork and a pen in front of him. "Make sure you let me know what times and days you need off."

"I can work anytime." He said without thought as he glanced at the papers.

She narrowed his eyes. "Don't you have classes at the university?"

He shrugged as if they weren't important, and started filling in the small boxes on the forms. Jez glanced up to the others who were talking but watching as well. Jordy moved over and pushed Jez into the back room. His voice grew soft but not gently. "What happened this morning?"

"What?" She asked confused.

"He said he came in and you were sick. He asked if you were OK." Jordy had tossed his head to the man filling out the papers.

Jez sighed and rolled her eyes. "I'm fine. I was queasy after the walk in. What did you tell him?"

"I told him you were probably hung over." Jordy seemed honestly hurt. "And don't lie to me. I can't help if you don't tell me the truth."

"You can't help me anyway, Jordy." She responded sadly. "I got sick. It happens."

"How much?"

She thought about lying again but gave in. "Last night and this morning. I can't keep anything down."

"Were you going to tell me?" He was annoyed but more from worry.

"No." She smiled. "You can't help. We go see the doctor next week. We'll talk to him then."

For several long moments, Jordy looked at his little sister. She knew he wanted so badly to make it all better. He wanted to protect her but he just couldn't. How can you protect someone from their own body? "Will you at least go lay down and rest? You look tired."

"What about the shop?"

"We've got it."

"And the new guy?"

"I'll bring the paperwork back. You can do the checks after you've rested some."

Jez knew the conversation was pointless. He wasn't going to let her continue to work today no matter what. She knew she just needed to be happy he wasn't going to send her home. Giving in, like she usually did, she nodded and allowed him to help her into the back office. A cot was already set up, all they had to do was cover it with a clean blanket and fluff the pillow. Once she was down and resting, Jordy gave her a quick kiss on the forehead before leaving the room and closing the door behind him. With a deep breath, Jez closed her eyes and drifted off.

Chapter 4

Jez's eyes fluttered opened when she heard the squeak of the door. "Sorry Pickle, didn't mean to wake you. I was just going to use the computer."

She swallowed and blinked. Remembering where she was, Jez sat up. "Is that for the background? I'll do it."

"You rest, I've got it." Annoyed, she pushed up onto her feet, then immediately regretted it as she grew dizzy. Her legs gave out and she fell to the floor before Ty could get to her.

"Shit Jez. Damn it."

"I'm fine." She snapped, waiting for the room to stop spinning.

Ty stood over her waiting for her signal, and the door way filled with bodies. Jordy was in the lead with OB and the new guy right behind. She began to stand, Ty and Jordy reaching to help steady her.

"I'm fine." She lashed out and ripped her arms away from them. Jez looked down and yanked the paperwork from Ty's hand. She moved, a little unsteadily, to the desk and the laptop that sat on it. While it booted up, she waved them away. One by one they vanished from her sight, but as Ty and Jordy, the last two, made the doorway, she called out to them. "Don't tell him."

Both looked back at her. "He's going to figure it out eventually." Ty said.

"And eventually we'll tell him." She snapped. "But we don't know how long he's going to be here, and I don't want him or anyone else knowing unless they have to."

Jordy gave Ty a look. He nodded and left the room, while Jordy turned to his sister. "It's nothing to be ashamed of you know. People get sick."

Her icy stare drilled into him. "I'm fine."

"You'd really rather people think you have a drinking or drug problem then know the truth?" He quipped.

"If it keeps them from looking at me with those pity me eyes, absolutely. I'd rather be hated than pitied." She said. It was the same old argument they'd had before. Jordy knew he wasn't going to win, just as Jez knew people would find out eventually. No matter how much you wanted to keep something like this a secret, it always came out.

Jordy turned and left his sister alone to do her job.

Less than an hour later, Jez had done the background check. Everything looked good. Boone Kingston was the same age as the guys, which was three years older than herself. He seemed older than just twenty-two, but he had come from a rough background. According to the check she'd run, he had been born in Detroit but had moved around Michigan quite a bit. There were hints that he was related to an infamous family from New York, but it was all rumors. There wasn't much specifically on him, which said he was either very good at staying under the radar, or he had a past that was sealed. Either way, he needed a clean start. Jordy had already given his seal of approval, and Jez couldn't find any reason not to give him the chance. She made a note on the paperwork, and tucked it in a file folder. Moving slowly to the cabinet, she tucked the file into the right drawer, and removed Tom's. She made a red mark on it, and tossed it on the desk to deal with later. Using the walls to keep her steady, Jez moved out to the main room. Jordy was standing at the counter, listening as Boone spoke to a customer about oil filters. He seemed to know his stuff.

"So, you like him?" She asked Jordy as she leaned into him.

"I think he's going to work out." Jordy nodded. "He certainly knows his shit."

"How do you want me to schedule him?"

"Overlap him the rest of today and tomorrow. You open Sunday, give him the middle shift, and I'll come in to close. He can overlap the rest of next week." Jordy said.

"What about days off?"

Jordy glanced down and gave her an odd look. "How did you know that he takes classes at the U?"

"I've seen him around. He's also in my humanities class."

Jordy nodded. "Give him Tuesday morning, and all day Thursday and Friday off next week. We'll readjust after the dads leave."

Jez nodded. She moved down the small area to grab the marked-up schedule from under the counter where she had shoved it earlier. Boone had just finished with his customer as she moved up next to him. With a small smile, he glanced over at her. "Feeling better?"

"I'm fine." She replied habitually. Without another word, she turned and moved back into the office to finalize the schedule. She finished and sent it as an email to everyone, then printed four copies: one for the office, one for under the register, the third for her to take home, and the last one for Boone. She walked out and waited until he was finished with the customer he was helping. He took the paper as she held it out to him. "Let me know as soon as possible if you can't work one of the shifts you're scheduled for."

He glanced it over quickly. "Looks fine. Thanks."

She nodded her head and then turned away. But the bell rang above the door and loud laughter filled the store. She looked back and saw Ty and OB juggling drink cups and paper bags. They quieted as they noticed that there were other people in the store, and moved back to the store room. There was a work bench in the middle of the store room. It was used to rebuild pieces and parts of engines, as well as various other things throughout the years. The two guys dropped everything on the wood table and started sorting out the food. Jez knew she wouldn't be able to eat, so she moved back to Boone. "Why don't you go get something to eat."

"I'm fine. You go." He offered.

"Really." She smiled tightly. "Go."

Jordy had just finished ringing up the customer he had been helping and looked over at Jez and Boone. As if he understood what was happening, he called to Boone. "Come on man, you've earned lunch."

Boone opened his mouth and pointed to Jez, but Jordy cut him off. "She'll cover the store. Come on."

With a quick, slightly confused look at Jez, he followed.

Jez smiled at the customer who was now approaching the register. "Find everything alright?"

"Yep." He replied. She rang him up and watched as he left. Glancing at the clock on the wall, she knew it was going to start getting slower. They might have a few more people between now and closing, but dinner time was approaching and that meant things slowed down for a while. Jez grabbed the stool she usually sat on behind the counter, and pulled it to the doorway. As she sat on it, she positioned herself so she could see the store but also could be included in the conversation in the back room, if they wanted to include her.

Ty saw her, and brought her over a burger. "Here Pickle. Eat something."

"I'm not really hungry." She smiled and tried to wave it off, but he wasn't having it.

"You need to eat." He pushed, then physically placed the burger in her hands. Standing before her, he waited until she took a bite before returning to his place at the work bench. The guys talked about all sorts of things, Jez only half listened. Boone listened to the same kind of music the guys did, but he wasn't a surfer like them. They had similar taste in cars and girls. Jez focused on her burger as their conversation turned to a topic she didn't want to know anything about. She forced half the burger down, hoping it would stay there, then returned to the register as a customer came in.

The night wore on slowly. A few customers came in, some to buy things, others to see the guys. Two hours after she'd eaten, Jez had to rush to the bathroom to throw up the hamburger. When she emerged from the bathroom, Jordy stood waiting for her. He was not happy, but she couldn't tell if it was anger or concern that painted his face.

"You alright?" He asked.

She nodded feeling weak and tired again.

"Ty?" He called. But Ty didn't answer. "OB?"

"They're outside talking to some girls. Want me to get them?" Boone's voice replied.

Jordy sighed. "Naw. Thanks."

He grabbed her arm and pulled her towards the back room. "Go lay down. I'll get someone to take you home in a bit."

"I'm fine." She said.

Jordy's look was harsh, so she didn't argue anymore.

"I can take her home and come back, if you want." Boone offered.

Jez could see the conflict on her brother's face. He glanced out the front window just in time to see Ty and OB get into a car with a pretty brunette and a gorgeous blond. They tore out of the parking lot and away from the shop. Jordy looked back at her.

"Really, man. I don't mind." Boone offered again.

Jordy looked at him and then nodded. "If you're sure. Thanks man."

"I'll get my bag." She said, but Jordy stopped her.

"I'll bring it. You just go home." He pushed her toward the front door where Boone was already headed.

Boone started up the engine just as she slid into the passenger seat. Their only conversation was her explanation on how to get to her house. When he pulled up in front, he said, "I know it's none of my business, but your brother really seems to care about you. For his sake, you might want to lay off the partying some."

She nodded. "Thanks for the ride home." As she moved up the front walk, she heard the roar of his engine as he pulled away.

Jez showered and climbed into her pajamas. Not really wanting to go to bed yet, she lay on the couch and watched television until Jordy came in. He fell into the chair nearest the door and yawned. "I think Boone's going to work out."

"He's just like one of the guys already." She tried to keep the jealousy out of her voice, but he caught it anyway.

"What's that mean?"

"Nothing." She turned her attention back to the TV.

Jordy sat up in the chair, "Jez?"

With a sigh, she looked at him. "I got the 'you need to stop partying' speech when he brought me home."

"You were the one who didn't want them to know the truth, Jez."

"I know. I guess I just didn't think …" she said.

"Do you want me to talk to him?"

She shook her head. "No. Hate is better than pity any day."

"I don't pity you." Jordy said.

Jez sat up and stood slowly. "I don't want to talk about this anymore." She moved upstairs and closed herself in her room. The heaviness of the day was getting to her. She climbed under the covers, but as she relaxed she couldn't fight back the emotions. Tears rolled down her face and a sob racked her chest. Curling into a ball, she cried. At some point, Jordy pushed into her room. It broke his heart to see his sister in so much pain. He climbed onto her bed and pulled her against him, holding her tight until she cried herself to sleep.

Chapter 5

Jez woke to the sound of banging on her door. "Pickle! Pickle! Either get your ass up or cover up, because I'm coming in."

"Go away, OB." She called back, pulling the pillow over her head. She heard the door open and knew he had come in. "I'm tired, go away."

He grabbed her hand and pulled her into a sitting position, the pillow fell from her face. "No dice, Pickle. You're coming with us."

"But I don't wanna go." She whined.

"Too late kiddo," Ty laughed.

"Where're we going?"

"The beach, get your suit on." OB slapped her shoulder.

Jez sighed knowing she wasn't get out of it. "Get out so I can change."

OB turned and headed to the door, pushing Ty out of the way, as they vanished into the hallway. Jez got up and closed the door with a slam. Grabbing up one of her bathing suits from a dresser drawer, she headed into the adjacent bathroom to change. She covered her suit with a pair of cut-off jeans and a t-shirt. She met the guys downstairs in the kitchen where they were packing a cooler full of hydration drinks and snacks. They smiled up as she entered the room.

"Where's Jordy?"

"He's manning the shop so we can go play." OB winked as he grabbed up the cooler. Ty wrapped an arm around her neck.

"I should work so you guys can go." She said as Ty pulled her out of the house and to the waiting VW.

"OK," Ty replied as he pushed her into the back of the van. They drove her to the shop and pulled into a spot next to the muscle car she knew was Boone's. She jumped from the back and headed into the shop, feeling a little sad about working on a pretty day like this. Boone and Jordy looked up surprised.

"Um? What are you ..." Jordy asked confused.

Ty and OB followed her in, but it was Ty that spoke. "Pickle wants to work so you can come with us."

"Isn't that nice of her? What a great sister." Jordy smiled coming around the counter. He wrapped his arms around her waist and picked her up. She smiled and returned his hug, but then realized that he was carrying her.

"Where are we going?"

"You're going to the beach." He said as OB held open the door.

"But ..."

"Shut up Pickle." Jordy said with a laugh. As they moved to the van, Jez watched Boone step into the store's doorway with a smile. Jordy dumped her into the back of the van. "Go with Ty and OB, Pickle. Ride a wave, or ten. Refocus and pull your strength from the ocean. Dad comes home tomorrow."

Jez looked up, and even though her brother was smiling, she saw the pain and fear in his eyes. She knew that last night had been hard on him. He needed her to be strong. In a very soft voice, she nodded and whispered, "OK, Jordy, ok. I'll find it."

He slammed the door shut and they were off to the beach.

Ty and OB stayed close to Jez the entire time she was in the water. It was fun and she enjoyed herself. By lunchtime she was tired though, and she spent several hours laying on the sand, soaking up the sunlight. It felt good for a long time, but then, it didn't anymore. OB and Ty bounced back up the beach towards her not long after. "You feeling alright, Pickle?"

"Sure." She tried to smile, but even she had to admit it was weak.

"Time to go." OB nodded. They gathered up their things, OB carried the surfboards and Jez carried everything else. Ty carried Jez. They drove back to Jez's house where the guys dropped her off. "You guys are coming tonight right?"

"I'm sure Jordy's planning on it." Jez said, opening the side door of the van.

"You better show too." Ty pointed at her. "I got those pickles you like, and I'll be damned if I'm going to eat them."

She giggled. "Sea Salt and Cracked Peppercorn?"

He cringed at their name but nodded. "Yep. You'd better be there."

She slammed the door shut and sighed. Fighting against her body, Jez walked across the yard and pushed into the house. She waved at Ty and OB and they drove away. She closed the front door and leaned heavily against it. It took her several minutes to gain enough strength to climb the stairs, where she collapsed at the top, falling to her knees. Her head was starting to pound and swim, but she fought against it. Her heart raced but she ignored it and crawled to her bathroom. She ran a tub of water, while she laid on the cool tile. When the tub was full of warm water she pulled off her clothes and dragged herself in. The warmth helped cool her fiery skin but it took resting weightlessly in the water to calm her restless body. She eventually felt good enough to climb out of the water. She stood carefully, still unsteady, and drained the tub. She dressed in a loose sundress, and did her hair and make-up. Given a choice, she would have rather gone to bed, but she knew better. It was Saturday night before the dads came home, it was tradition.

She was about to head downstairs when she heard the front door open. "Jez?"

"Up here." She called, taking the first of the twenty steps. Unfortunately, it was on the third one down that her legs gave out and she tumbled down the rest of them, landing at the bottom of the case in a heap.

"Jez, shit, are you alright?" Jordy was right next to her.

"Ouch." Jez blinked and mentally checked her body. "I don't think I broke anything."

"Good, because I don't want to spend all night in the ER." He smiled. He looked her over and his smile faded. "You're going to have a nasty bruise though."

She touched her cheek where it was growing sorer by the second. With a sigh, Jordy helped Jez to her feet and got her to the couch. He vanished into the kitchen and reappeared with a bag of frozen corn.

"Here, put this on it. I'm going to go change." He ran up the stairs to shower and change. When he returned, he found Jez sitting in the same place holding the now thawed vegetables on her shoulder. He came and sat down next to her, looking cleaner. "Where does it hurt?"

She smiled weakly. "Everywhere."

He smiled and chuckled. "Well, falling down the stairs tends to do that to you."

"How bad do I look?"

"Um, … well, you have a great bruise on your cheek, and your arm."

"And probably my hip too." She added gently rubbing it.

He sighed and shook his head. "Do you ever do anything half ass?"

"Nope." She chuckled weakly. "Maybe I should just stay here."

"And miss OB's turn? No way," he smiled. "You'd never live it down. We'll come up with a good story."

He offered her his hand and helped her up. He helped her walk out the front door and one house down to where OB lived, across the street from Ty. The lights were on in OB's house and

Jordy walked Jez right up and inside. Ty and OB were standing in the kitchen discussing something. They turned when they heard the door close.

"What the hell?" OB said rushing over to look at Jez. "I swear she didn't look like that when we dropped her off."

"I know." Jordy said with a smile. "She was so excited I was home; she fell down the stairs."

"Jesus, Pickle." Ty shook his head.

"Can I just sit down?" She asked weakly.

"Sure, we're going to be outback." Ty turned and grabbed the closest high-backed chair. He carried it out back and placed it on the patio at the large glass topped table. The others were following and Jordy helped her sit.

"So what're we doing?" She asked confused.

"A new game." Ty winked and left, pulling the other guys with him.

Jez sat back and breathed against the pain. Ty brought her a bowl of pickles and placed several other bowls of snacks around the table. OB and Jordy carried out a cooler full of beer and ice. There was commotion as a group of people entered the house. Jez could hear the laughter of girls and at least one male voice. She sighed. Saturday nights use to be just the four of them hanging out and watching movies, but then girlfriends had started to join, and now there were more involved. Ty came out with his arm wrapped around Patty.

"You remember Jez?" He said.

"Hi Patty."

"Hey, wow, are you alright?" Her eyes grew big.

"Oh sure. I'm fine. It's nothing." Jez said with a wave.

Ty offered Patty a seat and then got her a beer. OB and a blond soon emerged from the house and found seats as well. They were followed by Jordy, a red head, Boone, and a strawberry blond. Someone made introductions around, and Pickle waved each time her name was mentioned but she didn't even try to remember their girls' names. Ty got Jez a red plastic cup before he took a seat across from her, and the others grabbed beers as they settled in at the table. They sat boy-girl with Jordy to one side of Jez and Boone on the other. It didn't escape Jez's realization that she was the odd one out. Ty explained the game, and they played several hands. It was a fun combination of rolling the dice and drawing cards to make a certain number. After a few hands though, Jez was having a hard time keeping up with it. Ty called for break and everyone agreed. The girls took off into the house to use the bathroom, and the three guys vanished to dig up some more snacks, leaving Boone and Jez alone together at the table.

Looking over at Jez, Boone asked, "Are you alright?"

She smiled half-heartedly. It hurt to smile too big. "I'm fine. Why?"

"What happened?" His eyes graced her cheek and fell on her shoulder.

"Nothing. I got clobbered today by a wave."

He narrowed his eyes, but didn't ask again. Ty, OB, Jordy, and the girls all returned and took their seats. They played several more hands, Jez sitting out each one. She snacked on the pickles after Ty and OB teased her about them, and drank her cup. But as the hour grew late, Jez grew more and more tired. The clock chimed midnight, and she was just about to excuse herself to go home, when the nausea kicked in. She closed her eyes and fought it off, but soon it was too much. She pushed away from the table and raced to the bathroom, bouncing off wall and doorways as her balance shifted. She just barely made it into the bathroom before she lost the pickles she had eaten.

When she was done throwing up, a soft knock came at the door. "Jez? You alright?"

"Fine." She called but the door opened and her brother pushed into the room.

"Aw, Pickle." He held her hair back as she puked again, then helped hold her up while she rinsed her mouth out. When she was done, he lifted her and carried her into the living room. Putting on the sofa, he whispered. "I'll be right back."

He walked out to the others and said he'd be back in a few moments. When he came back in, Boone was following him. "No, man, it's all good. I'm just going to take her home."

Jez stood and almost fell, so Jordy lifted her into his arm. As she rested her head on his shoulder, Boone watched. "You're sure she's OK?"

"She's fine. Just too much today." Jordy said and Jez nudged him, causing him to add. "She tends to not know her limits."

Boone opened the door and Jordy carried her out. As they crossed the grass, Jez looked over Jordy's shoulder and watched as Boone stopped and watched them leave. Turning her eyes back to her brother, she said, "I'm sorry."

"Hush, Pickle."

"Tell them I'm sorry."

"Enough Jez." He carried into the house and up the stairs, placing her in bed. "Rest a little bit, and then go brush your teeth and change. I won't be too late."

"Don't worry about me."

She offered him a weak smile, as he leaned down and gave her a quick kiss on the head. "Rest well, Pickle."

☐

Chapter 6

Jez got up early and headed to work. She felt tired and sore. The bruise on her cheek wasn't as bad as she had thought it might be, but the one on her hip was worse. But none of that really matter because her father was coming home today. She loved when her dad came home. It was hard too, since she tried to down play her condition, but just having him there helped her feel better. She had dressed in jeans and a plain t-shirt and done her hair and make-up to cover her bruises. She wanted to look nice for him, and the guys would pick her up on their way to the docks so she had to be ready. The morning was a little cooler so she had no difficulty as she made the walk and opening the store.

As was typical on a Sunday morning, not one customer came in until close to noon. Most of the young guys were sleeping or surfing and the older men went to church, so no one had time to stop until the afternoon. The first three customers bought oil and filters, and a fourth picked up lights. It was nothing thrilling or difficult, which made Jez happy. It was the fifth customer of the day that made her a little nervous. He was a loyal customer who came in at least once a month and spent a lot of money. Apparently, he was restoring a classic car that meant the world to him, and he always wanted to talk to a knowledgeable person, which Jez was not. As he pushed into the store, his shoulders sank when he saw her.

"Morning Jezebel."

"Good Morning, Mr. Morlick. How are you today?" She smiled brightly.

"Still alive." He chuckled. "I don't suppose your brother or dad is here?"

"No, I'm sorry, Mr. Morlick. Dad's boat doesn't dock for a couple more hours. Would you like …" She stopped seeing the black Barracuda pull up in front of the store. "Have you met our newest employee, Mr. Morlick?"

His eyes narrowed in thought. "No, who's he, or she, replacing?"

"Tom left us." She decided that was the safest answer. "And we hired a gentleman by the name of Boone. He's very knowledgeable, and he's coming in right now."

The elderly gentleman turned and watched the big, bald man walk through the door. Mr. Morlick turned his eyes back on Jez. "Knowledgeable by who's standards?"

"My brother's, and Ty, and OB." She offered. "If you give him just a few minutes to clock in, I'm sure he'll be able to help you."

Mr. Morlick grumbled but nodded as he wandered over to look at the newest accessories that were displayed. Boone was giving Jez a curious look as he crossed the room and rounded the corner of the counter. She followed him into the back room where he clocked in. When he was done, he turned to see her blocking the office doorway.

"That's Mr. Morlick. He's a very good customer."

"Got it." He replied quickly, his eyes flitting over her. "You feeling better?"

"Better? Oh, yeah. Sorry about last night." She shrugged and moved out of his way. She watched as he moved past, but then stopped and looked her over again. His eyes met hers and he looked like he wanted to say something.

"You look good; more alert, clean, sober. You should try it more often. You're pretty like this."

"Daddy comes home today." She said quickly with a heavy heart. It sounded bad, she knew. Like she was a daddy's girl, and unable to stay clean. It made her sound like a drug addict. As he moved into the store to help Mr. Morlick, she fell against the doorframe and closed her eyes. Hatred and disgust were better than pity, she reminded herself. He was incredibly hot, and had he just called her pretty? But he thought the worst of her. She convinced herself it was for the best. He wouldn't be interested in a girl like her no matter what. At least she was giving him a reason to stay away, right? No false hope for her.

"Pickle!" The voice called across the building. "Let's go."

With a smile, Jez grabbed up her bag and started for the front of the store. She paused just briefly enough to look at Boone, who was pointing at something in a catalog. "You good?"

"No problem." He smiled.

"Call one of us if you need anything." She smiled brightly, excitement filling her. "Good-bye Mr. Morlick."

"Say hi to your dad for me, Pickle." He replied absent-mindedly. Hearing him use her nickname made her giggle, and rush out to the large family van that waited for her.

The group was quiet and happy as they drove to the northern side of town to where the harbor was. Ty's mother drove the eight-passenger van that already held six. It would be a tight ride home, but not one of them cared. The dads would sit close to their families, holding their children and smiling, halfway across the ocean if that's what it took to get them home. When the van was parked, the group made the short walk to the edge of the pier to wait and watch as the boat came in. The pier was crowded with other families, all waiting anxiously for their loved ones. As the boat came into sight, the excitement grew and the joy was almost infectious.

As was usual, the crowd made way for the younger families and newly-weds to be reunited first. Next to leave the boat were the senior crew members, then the rest of them. The dock was half empty when the dads appeared. They were smiling and joking as they always did, just as much brothers and friends as their sons. Seeing their families waiting for them, the three men darted up to pull their loved ones to them. Jez was crushed between her father and her brother in a monstrous hug that left her unable to do anything but giggle.

After several minutes of hugs and kisses, the group moved towards the van and piled in. The ride back was filled with chatter about what was happening in each of the homes, Ty's sister and mother talking the most. Ty filled in here and there, but Jez and Jordy were silent. Whether or not anyone but their dad noticed wasn't clear, but that's the way it was. When the van was parked back on their street, the group separated. Aside from a few hours here and there at the store, the group wouldn't see much of each other. The boys would see each other more often during the week, taking a few hours here and there to surf together or hang out, but the dads needed space after their week entirely spent together. If they wanted to talk or needed each other, they knew where to find one another. And like all family, they'd be there for each other, but space was also needed. OB and his dad vanished into their small, one story home while Ty's clan moved into their larger two-story one. Jordy, Jez, and their dad walked the couple of yards down to theirs as well.

They had only gotten a few feet away when Dad pulled Jez to his side. "So, Pickle, how have you been feeling?"

"Good." She smiled.

The smile that he had since seeing them from the boat faded a little. He reached up and brushed the back of his finger across the bruise on her cheek. "Really?"

"She's had a few rough moments, but she's been doing good." Jordy cut in.

Dad nodded silently. He was always really good at reading between the lines. "So when do we see the doctor?"

"Tomorrow." She answered.

"Oh, hey did I mention that we fired Tom and hired someone else?" Jordy said out of the blue. Jez knew that he was just trying to get their dad's mind on a new subject.

"Why?" He looked over a Jordy curiously.

"Rule 3." Jordy looked sad, but covered it quickly. "This new guy is really good. I think he's more knowledgeable than Tom anyway."

"And better looking." Jez said out loud, then blushed as the two men looked at her. "I'm just saying that he's brought in a few more female customers recently."

Dad and Jordy both smiled knowingly as she blushed uncomfortably. Dad turned back and the two continued to discuss Boone as the trio headed into the house. Jordy ran Dad's bag up to his room, while Jez took a seat on the sofa. When Jordy had come back down, he looked at his two children. "Why don't we go by the shop, close it up, and then go out to dinner?"

Jez gave Jordy a worried look, but he smiled. "Sounds great, Dad."

"Good. Let me run through a fast shower to get the salt water off." He took the stairs two at a time, and vanished.

"Jordy?" Jez started to say quietly so her father wouldn't hear.

"It's fine, Jez. Just order something light. He's going to figure it out soon or later anyway."

Jez fell back in the chair. She knew it was bound to happen. Their dad wasn't stupid, but she had hoped to not burden him with everything on his first night back.

It wasn't twenty minutes later when they were driving the pickup down to the store. The lights were on and they could see Boone standing behind the counter talking to someone. As they parked he made the sale and rang up the customer. As the trio pushed into the building the customer was headed out. He was a regular and stopped to say hi. He complimented the newly hired Boone and wished everyone well before leaving for the night. The sky was a deep indigo when Jordy flipped the sign to closed and locked the door. Jez took the long way around the store, looking at the shelves and making sure the place was clear of customers, while her dad stepped up to introduce himself. By the time Jez stepped up to the register to print the nightly report and empty the till, the three men were involved in a conversation about cars that she didn't really want to listen to.

They continue to talk as she took the money and reports to the office to reconcile. Everything came out perfect and she made the deposit slip and put it all in the safe. When she returned to the main room, Dad was talking to Boone. They seemed to be hitting it off, and Jez smiled. Jordy came over and wrapped an arm around his sister's neck.

"I think Dad might have found a new son." He chuckled. A second later, he pushed her back into the store room. "Look while Dad's occupied, ..."

"I don't want to talk about this now." She said shaking her head.

"We need to." She tried to move away but he grabbed her arm and stopped her. "Look, we've got to tell Dad the truth, and we might as well tell the guys and Boone the truth too."

"No. We can tell Dad, later, after we get home. But we are not telling them. They can think what everyone else in this town thinks."

"Why do you do this, Jez? Why don't you want them to know? No one is going to think less of you because ..."

"Because I'm a drug addict?" She narrowed her eyes as the heavy footsteps approached. "I don't want to talk about this right now."

Jordy's eyes flashed up as Boone stepped into the doorway. He was silent for a moment, looking from one sibling to the next. "Sorry to interrupt, but your dad's waiting."

Jez pulled her arm the rest of the way from her brother's grip, and moved around Boone, keeping her eyes on the ground. She moved out to where her dad stood by the door and smiled to him. "Everything OK, baby?"

"Sure Daddy."

"Go wait by the car." He motioned, and she left the shop. She stood next to the truck as Jordy and Boone exited, followed quickly by her dad. The three climbed into the truck and Boone climbed behind the wheel of his supped up baby. Dizziness overcame Jez at one point and she put her head on her dad's shoulder. He patted her knee sweetly, but it was Jordy that took her hand and squeezed in support.

They pulled up in front of the restaurant and stopped. Jordy walked close to Jez even though she was putting on a good show for her dad. They had just about made it into the restaurant when the familiar rumble of a muscle car came up behind them. Jez looked up at her dad without even looking behind to confirm her suspicions. "Please tell me you didn't."

"I couldn't let the poor boy starve. Besides, I need to get to know him if I'm going to allow him to hang out with my kids." He smiled.

"You mean, hang out at your store." Jordy laughed, pushing his sister in through the glass door. The waitress waved them into a large booth. Jez situated herself between her dad and her brother, with Boone sitting on the opposite edge from her dad, in the circular booth. The waitress gave them a few moments, then took their order. While all the men ordered big meals, Jez stuck to a small salad. When the waitress walked away, her dad turned to her. "What's with the salad, Pickle? You're not on some diet, are you?"

"No, Dad, I'm just not very hungry." She sighed and rolled her eyes.

"Good because you don't need to diet." He looked at her sternly. "You're beautiful just the way you are."

Jordy and Jez looked at each other with wide eyes. In unison, they both said, "Don't you dare!" Just as he started singing a pop song. Jez put her head in her hands growing beet red as Jordy reached around her to cover his father's mouth. While their dad wasn't a bad singer, actually he was pretty good, but it was incredibly embarrassing in a crowded restaurant. As their dad wrapped up the first verse, he quieted. The people at the tables around them clapped and he stood up to take a bow, oblivious to the fact that he was embarrassing his family. As he took a seat again, Jez looked up from her fingers. Her eyes fell instantly on Boone's, who seemed to be enjoying this immensely.

When the other tables had returned to their meals, Jordy looked over at Boone. "So, now, when you see Jez in all her splendor, you'll know exactly where she gets it."

"It's not going to bother me in the least." Boone laughed.

Jez covered her face again and took in a deep breath. "You had to invite him." She looked up at him. "He used to think we were normal. Thanks Dad."

He chuckled. "Better he knows sooner than later. Boone, I'm sorry, but you've come to work for a crazy family. If you want out, please say so now. Otherwise, you just might go crazy like us."

"Crazy don't scare me, sir." He smiled.

They had a few more minutes of banter about being crazy, and then their discussion turned to other things. Surf, school, the store, OB and Ty, they discussed all kinds of things during the two hours they sat eating. Jez tried to stay silent, only adding in when she had to. She pushed her food around her plate and ate the tiniest amount possible. But she smiled and laughed along with everyone. She tried not to look at Boone too much, but when she did, she noticed he was watching her too.

When the meal was done, Boone offered to chip in but his offer was pushed aside. As they walked out to the parking lot, Jez stumbled and Jordy caught her arm keeping her upright. Jez smiled weakly at her brother, and notice Boone watching them carefully. Jez turned away and headed to the truck quickly. Jordy and his dad said good night to Boone, then they all went their separate ways.

Jez became nauseous on the way home and had to run into the house as soon as their dad got the truck stopped. She spent the next hour heaving in the bathroom. Wondering how she was going to explain this to her dad.

When she was finally done, Jez washed her face and brushed her teeth. She changed into her pajamas and went downstairs to get a bottle of water from the fridge. The house was dark and quiet, and Jez had hoped that everyone had gone to bed. She crept through the house but found her dad sitting at the kitchen table a bottle of whiskey open and a half full glass in front of him. He looked up as she came into the room.

"You OK, Daddy?"

"I'm good. But you're not." He said sadly.

She sighed and grabbed a bottle from the fridge. Taking a seat across the table from him, she asked, "What did Jordy say?"

"He didn't have to say anything. I know my daughter. I've seen you stumble, barely eat, get sick. I've heard the rumors, Jez. I know you are trying to make everyone think you're not sick."

Jez's heart grew heavy. "I just don't want…"

"I know, baby." He reached out and took her hand. "It's easier for people to believe you're like your mom."

"They almost expected it. I didn't even start the rumors, you know. I got drunk at one party, and then I kept getting sicker. They all just assumed …" Tears filled her eyes. "It's easier to just let them believe than to try to explain."

He clutched her hand tightly. "I'm sorry. I shouldn't …"

"It's fine, Dad. Really. As long as you and Jordy …."

"We'd love you no matter what." He smiled weakly. "What's the doctor going to say tomorrow?"

She shrugged. "I'm not positive, but it's not going to be good. They're having a hard time getting my IV in and I can't seem to keep anything down now."

"Are you falling more?"

She nodded, unable to verbally admit it.

He sighed, and took a big drink from his glass. "OK. I'll call and ask for some time off."

"No, Daddy, please don't. Let's see what the doctor says. Jordy and I have been doing really good."

"Good? Jordy's worried sick about you, and you are ..." He shook his head. "I need to be here."

"You need to work. We need the insurance and the money." She said honestly. "Ty and OB have been really helpful. They cart me around and watch over me. I don't think you could do a better job that those three."

He wasn't convinced but she pushed a little harder.

"Please dad, I'm already too much of a burden."

"You're my daughter. You are NOT a burden." He slammed his glass down on the table with such force she thought it might shatter. Tears overflowed his eyes which broke her as well, she got up and came around the table. Wrapping her arms around his neck, he pulled her down onto his lap, cradling her like he did when she was a little girl. Together they cried. After a few minutes, he pulled back and wiped his eyes with the back of his hand. "I'm sorry, baby. I should be stronger for you."

"It's OK, I don't want you strong. I want you to be my daddy." She smiled weakly. "Come on, things look better after a good night's sleep."

She got up and pulled him to his feet. She turned and put the cork in the bottle before walking him from the room and up the stairs. She kissed his cheek and pushed him into his room, where he stumbled to the bed. Jez wasn't sure that he wasn't asleep before he hit the mattress.

When she turned to head to her room, she found Jordy standing in his doorway. "He's not taking it well?"

"He wanted to take time off. We can't let that happen, Jordy."

He nodded. "I know. He's not good at this."

"Will you help me?"

"Don't I always?" He smiled, and it too was weak. The stress of all this was wearing the entire family down. Jez gave her brother a kiss good night and closed herself in her bedroom. After climbing into bed, she said a silent prayer for her family.

Chapter 7

They woke mid-morning and made a good breakfast, which Jez ate and then promptly threw up. They piled in the truck, made a quick stop by the store, and then headed across town to the medical center. They had to wait almost an hour before the specialist could see them. In the room, they took Jez's weight, which was down, and her blood pressure, which was low. The nurse smiled and reviewed a few things with her before leaving them to wait in the sterile room. Jordy and Dad looked nervous, but Jez made them smile when she started singing along with the music that was being piped into the room.

Eventually the doctor came in. He shook hands with each of them and took a seat in the rolling chair. He flipped through Jez's file and sighed. "Well, we're not exactly where I wish we were."

Jez nodded. "You're telling me."

The doctor was a kind, older man with white hair and soft brown eyes. He was one of the top neurologists in the city, and was willing to learn about Jez's condition. He smiled at her. "So what do you want to do?"

"You're the doc? What do you suggest?" Jordy asked, as he leaned up on his knees.

"I think it's time for a port." He said, looking at Jez's dad.

He nodded. "And will that help her be able to eat?"

The doctor looked at Jez narrowly. "You're not eating?"

"She throws everything up." Jordy answered for her.

"How long has this been happening?"

She shrugged. "A week, maybe two."

He took in a deep breath and leaned back, clearly not happy about this new development. He thought for a few moments, and then finally spoke. "Well, we have a couple of options. First, put the port in and see if that helps. I don't think it will, but it's the first step. Second, put the port in and a feeding tube. Third, would be the most sever, put the port in and hospitalize you until we can run some tests to see what's going on."

"So the port is not negotiable?" Her dad asked.

"Her veins are shot. The nurses are having a hard time getting an IV in, and with her going twice a week, and getting a banana bag and fluids each time, it's better to have the port."

Jordy and Dad's eyes both flashed to Jez, but it was Jordy that spoke first. "You've been getting a banana bag at each session?"

She looked away. She hadn't mentioned it, because she hadn't wanted them to worry.

"Since I know now she's not been eating, that explains the labs. I prescribed the banana bags when I saw how low her labs were." The doctor hadn't realized that the rest of the family didn't know about them.

"OK," Her dad finally said. "When can we get the port in? I leave on Sunday, and I would like to be here for it."

"It's a simple outpatient procedure. She'll need to rest for a few days after, but she should be fine to resume normal activities after three or four days." The doctor nodded. "Why don't I go see if I can get her in within the day or two?"

They watched the doctor get up and walk out, before Jordy spoke. "So what do we do about the food?"

"Let's give it some more time." Jez suggested. "Maybe I just have a flu bug or something."

"Feeding tube. I can't handle knowing she isn't holding food down, and I'd rather not have my baby in the hospital if I'm not here." Her father decided. Jordy agreed with a nod.

Jez wasn't in accord though. "If they put a tube in my nose, people are going to find out I'm sick. I don't want ..."

"You'd rather them believe you're a druggie?" Jordy snapped. It was the same old argument. "How are you going to explain the incisions from the port?"

"Accident." She responded bluntly. "They'll make up their own stories about how it happened."

Dad had had enough of this though. "No. Your health is a hell of a lot more important to me than your embarrassment, Jez. It's time."

Tears swelled in her eyes. "It will make me even uglier."

As the tears streaked her face, her father got up and wrapped his arms around her. "It's not forever, baby. Just until you can eat again. And any guy who can't look beyond a tiny plastic tube, to see your true beauty doesn't deserve you."

The doctor came back into the room then with a satisfied look on his face. "Well, we can get her in tomorrow afternoon. We can do it here, in the outpatient surgery ward on the fourth floor. You need to be here two hours early."

"So I'll need to cancel my infusions." She said, wiping her eyes with a tissue Jordy handed her.

"We'll get your fluids in there too." The doctor smiled. "You'll need to take the rest of the week off of school and work though. Will that be a problem?"

Jez looked at her father. "Is that a problem, boss?"

He smiled, and rolled his eyes. "Yes. Geez," then turning to the doctor he chuckled. "Give your kids an inch."

The doctor smiled sensing the teasing. "And this might be a good time for the feeding tube also. You'll be sedated so it's a good time to put it in as well."

Jez nodded, but didn't respond. She couldn't speak.

"OK, so I'll see you tomorrow at one."

"Will you be doing it?" Jez asked surprised.

"No, but I'll come see you." He moved back to the door. "Can't let my favorite patient go through this alone."

They thanked him as he left and then got up to leave also. On the way back through town, Jordy insisted they stop and get Jez a new pair of pajamas. Dad also needed some new long underwear. It was getting cooler on the rig and he didn't want to wait until the last minute this year. They shopped for a little bit, then headed home. Jez announced that she was going to school the next morning, since she was going to miss at least one class. They weren't happy but allowed it. Once home, Jordy and Dad went down to the shop to work while Jez laid down to take a nap.

When she woke, the house was empty and growing dark. The truck was gone but Jez knew where they were. It was the same place they always were. She slipped on her flip-flops, grabbed a hydration drink from the fridge, and headed down the block. As expected the truck sat in the parking lot, tucked along the familiar line of cars. Pushing into the brightly lit store, the tiny bell announced her arrival, and seven men turned to look at her, their expressions ranging from sadness to shock. She stopped as the door closed behind her and let out a breath.

Ty and OB were the first ones to move, racing over and wrapping her in a huge group hug. "Why didn't you tell us?" Ty demanded.

"You let us think the worst." OB snarled.

"I didn't want you to worry."

"And what do you think we've been doing for the past six months?" OB snapped. "Do you know how we've turned this town upside down trying to find the asshole who's been dealing to you?"

She had to roll her lips in to keep from smiling. "Why?"

"Why?" Ty repeated. "Why? Because we love you. Because we didn't, we couldn't …" He couldn't finish his thought and just pulled her tighter against him.

Then as the thought washed over her, she pulled back and smacked both guys on the arm as hard as she could.

OB looked stunned. "What was that for?"

"For believing the damn rumors."

It took a second, but soon all seven of the men were laughing. Ty pulled her close and walked her over to the group that was huddled around the counter. Ty's dad looked at her with smiling eyes. "Don't you worry about a thing, Pickle. We've got it all covered."

"And if you need more time, we'll figure it out." Boone spoke as if he was one of them. She looked up at his blue eyes and turned away quickly.

"What are you doing here?" Jordy asked, as if realizing for the first time she was standing before him.

"I woke up alone." She shrugged.

"You need to be resting." Her dad said sternly. "You're going to have a rough day tomorrow."

"I think I have the easy end." She smiled. "But I'll go home if you want me to."

There was a general nod and agreement, but it was Boone that once again spoke up. "If it's OK with you, boss. I can give her a ride."

"You were supposed to be off an hour ago anyway." Dad nodded. "If you don't mind, I'd feel better knowing she wasn't walking."

"Just let me go clock out." Boone said to her, then moved away from the group.

Jez looked at her father with an upturned eyebrow. "You know I can walk the two blocks."

"You haven't eaten in at least a week. You're falling daily. You're having surgery tomorrow. I'd take you home if I didn't need to get a few things done here. So take the ride, Pickle, and shut up about it." He instructed. Boone appeared beside her a second later and walked her out the front door. He held her door open and helped her in the car.

As he turned down the street, she looked over at him. "I don't want you treating me differently now."

He glanced over at her. "I don't know what…"

"Really? Would you have offered to give me a ride when you thought I was an addict? Would you have held my door open?"

He twisted the corner of mouth. "Yes, because it's the right thing to do."

She narrowed her eyes. "If you're trying to get in good with my dad, you already did. You don't need to be nice to me to do that. And if you're trying to get in good with Jordy, being nice to me isn't going to help. So let's not pretend. Don't be nice to me because you know the truth."

"Did it ever occur to you that I want to be nice to you? Did it ever occur to you that I might like you, as a coworker and friend?" He was quick to add the last part.

He pulled up in front of her house. "No, that didn't occur to me. Because I know guys, and I know that unless it's going to end with you getting laid, being nice isn't in your vocabulary. And since that's not going to happen, you can just drop the crap." She opened the door and stepped out into the night.

"I'm going to pretend that this new bitchiness is just because you're scared. And you know what, Jez, you don't have to be scared. They all love you more now than ever." He spoke loudly, and she slammed the door on his words. Turning in a huff, she stormed up the front stairs. She was digging her keys from her pocket when the darkness closed in around her.

Jez came to and realized she was sitting on the couch in her living room. A single light was on and Boone was sitting next to her, watching her with a worried look. A random thought came to her as she blinked him into focus. "How did you know where I lived?"

"What?"

"You knew where I lived and I didn't tell you. How did you know?"

He smiled uncomfortably. "I brought you home once before."

"And you remembered?"

"Yep. For some reason, I remember things that are linked with you." He seemed surprised to admit it.

"Like what?" She was so confused and tired.

"You look tired. Why don't you rest, Jez?" He stood up and moved a pillow under her head.

"Tell me something you know about me." She said sleepily.

He sighed and pulled the blanket off the back of the sofa. Covering her up with it, he said softly, "I know that you think people don't see you. But I do."

He brushed the hair from her face as she drifted off to sleep. He looked at the bruises that marked her. The one on her cheek, the many on her arms, there was even one on her ankle. He grew angry with himself for thinking the worst of her. He had bought in to the rumors that they were from shooting up, or getting beat up, or from falling while stoned. He knew what drug addicts looked like. He had experience with them in his past, and she was so clearly not one. She was just a scared little girl, fighting a battle that was too big for her to fight alone.

☐

Chapter 8

Jez woke to her alarm going off. She didn't remember coming to bed. The last thing she remembered clearly was being a bitch to Boone when he dropped her off last night. She felt bad about that and told herself that she would apologize when she saw him in class today. She wasn't sure why she had done it, aside from frustration and fear, like he had said.

She dressed and her brother took her to school. They didn't talk much beyond making arrangement for someone picking her up. He was focused on his own thoughts, and she wasn't sure she was strong enough to help him today. So she gave him a kiss on the cheek and climbed out of the truck as she headed off to class. She wasn't as early as she wanted to be, and another group of students sat in her preferred seat. With a sigh, she dropped her bag in a row three in front of them. She climbed the few steps and stopped, waiting for Boone to realize she was standing there. It took several minutes, but eventually he looked up with bored eyes.

"I just wanted to say I'm sorry for being a bitch last night."

"Whatever." He shrugged, then returned his attention to the buxom blonde next to him. Jez rolled her eyes and returned to her seat. When she sat down, she heard him say. "Naw, I work for her dad. He asked me to give her a ride home, so I did."

The blonde giggled and said something Jez couldn't hear, but she heard Boone respond.

"I was just trying to be nice. See, I can be a nice guy from time to time."

She giggled again, and Jez rolled her eyes. The professor came in and called the class to order. He lectured for two hours straight, and Jez tried her hardest to stay focused, but between the high-pitched giggles behind her, and the surgery ahead, her mind was definitely not on her school work. When the class was finally dismissed, Jez approached the teacher. During a quick discussion, she let him know that she would miss at least one class, and possibly more due to a surgery. He wished her well, and was about to give her the assignments, when Boone stepped up behind her.

"I can pass on the assignments and notes."

Jez spun on him. "Thanks, but I don't need your charity."

He looked a little stunned. "It's not charity. I told you last night that…"

"And today I'm just your boss's daughter. Thanks, but no thanks."

She smiled tightly and told the professor that she would email him when she was up to completing the work, then turned and stormed out of the room. She was halfway down the corridor when Boone caught up to her, grabbing her arm and spinning her around. "Look, I don't know what your problem is, but…"

"My problem is I don't like being a charity case. I don't want your pity. And I don't want to be used to pick up other girls."

"Fuck, I just can't win with you, can I?"

"No, I guess you can't. You want brownie points with me? You want to be my friend? Uphold the rumors that they're all spreading. Tell them I got trashed and you had to take me home. Tell them, that I'm off on a bender."

"If I do that, your brother will have my head."

She shrugged. "I guess then you need to decide who's friend you want to be." Without another word, she spun and stormed off down the hall to meet up with her dad and Jordy.

She was silent on the way to the clinic. The two men gave each other curious looks over her head, but she didn't want to talk about it. They had to wait several minutes before a nurse came to get her. While her dad stood at the counter filling in forms and answering questions, Jordy leaned over. "Are you alright?"

She smiled tightly back at him. "I'm fine."

He twisted his lips hiding his smile. "You're anything but fine. You're pissed. I haven't seen that look in a long time. Who pissed you off?"

"I don't want to talk about it." She said with a sigh.

"Something happen at school?" He pressed.

"I said I don't want to talk about it." She snapped, just as a nurse called her name. She stood up and reached out to use the chair arm to balance herself. Jordy reached out to her and helped steady her as well.

"We'll call you back as soon as we get her settled in pre-op." The pretty brunette smiled.

Jordy nodded and returned her smile. "Thanks. I'd like to speak to my sister before she goes under."

Jez rolled her eyes at Jordy and his highlighted tone on the word sister. As if it wasn't obvious that they were related. Jez followed the nurse down to the pre-op rooms. It was actually one room separated into eight compartments by hanging curtains. Jez tried not to look around her. She understood the value of privacy, especially when one didn't feel well. The nurse pointed her into one area, directed to her to change into the hospital gown, and left. As Jez changed, she was happy to see it wasn't your typical gown. She had a pair of hospital scrub pants and a top that resembled the top half of a hospital gown but that opened in the front. She folded her street clothes neatly and put them in the plastic bag that was provided, then climbed into bed.

Over the next twenty minutes, nurses and techs came and went. They gave her yellow socks, and a yellow plastic wrist band, to match the white one with her information on it. They hooked her up to a heart monitor, that beeped annoyingly in the background, pulse-ox finger monitor, oxygen tubes in her nose, and EKG leads. It took a good ten minutes to put in an IV, and they finally had to get the most experienced nurse to get it in, after eight pokes by others. Once they had a bag of saline pushing into her body, and she was practically tied down to the bed by all the cable, wires, and tubes, they allowed her family to come back to see her. Ty and OB joined Jordy and Dad much to her surprise.

"What are you guys doing here?" She asked confused.

"Geez, sis, we couldn't not be here." Ty said a little too loudly glancing at the nurse that was walking past.

Jez smiled at their kindness. "I hate having you guys see me like this."

Jordy reached out and rubbed her foot. "You look fine."

The siblings snickered at the use of the word that she had use all the time. Ty and OB just looked at each other confused. Dad took her hand in his, obviously worried. "Mick and Sam are in the waiting room too."

"Why? Who's watching the shop?" Jez asked shocked and confused.

"Boone's got it for a little while." Dad explained. "They're going to go back as soon as we know everything is alright."

"I'm going to be fine, Dad. Really." She insisted.

"There's that word again." Jordy pointed out with a knowing smile. She kicked his hand slightly with her foot but smiled at him.

"OK, it's time." The nurse said pulling open the curtain. Ty and OB each reached out and gave her legs a pat, while her dad leaned down and placed a kiss on her head.

"We'll be right here." Tears glistened in his eyes as Ty and OB patted his shoulders, moving him away.

Jordy stepped up and looked down at her. "I don't know how many times I've seen you like this, but it still sucks."

"I know. I'm sorry." She reached out and took his hand. "Be strong for Dad, OK."

He nodded, unable to speak. Placing a kiss on her head, he opened his mouth to say something but she stopped him. "I love you too."

He smiled weakly and walked away, following the other back to the waiting room.

The nurse smiled kindly as she stepped up to Jez's bedside. "Boyfriend?"

"Ew, brother." She said wrinkling her nose.

"Good big brother then."

"The best." Jez nodded.

They wheeled her from the room and into the waiting area for the surgical room. She had to wait for about ten minutes before the surgical nurses came to push her in. Jez couldn't see much of their faces as they spoke to her, but their eyes crinkled up at the corners when they smiled and explained what was going to happen. She didn't really follow the whole thing, but they promised to sedate her enough to avoid the pain but had to keep her semi-conscious for the procedure. Jez told them she didn't care as long as they drugged her enough. That brought a chuckle from the room. A tech she could barely see from the corner of her eye asked her to turn her head, which she did and they laid a blue paper tarp across her face. She felt the shirt being tugged away but the paper still covered her chest. It got cold just above her right breast as they cleaned the area. She hissed a little, and everyone stopped.

"Are you alright?" A voice asked.

"That's cold." She said completely serious, but again they all chuckled.

A man with hazel eyes stepped into her line of sight and leaned down. "OK, Jezebel, I need you to do something for me."

"What?"

"Relax."

She rolled her eyes. "Easier said than done, doc."

He smiled, but she could only tell by his eyes. "What do you like to do? What kind of music do you enjoy?"

"Um, don't tell anyone, but I really like James Taylor." She was surprised at her honest. That was a closely guarded secret after a stupid boy had teased her about it for months on end during middle school.

The doctor looked up and nodded his head to someone behind her. "Oh, what else do you like?"

"The ocean."

"Do you surf?"

"Yes."

"Ok, here's what I want you to do. I want you to take a deep breath in when I tell you to. Then I want you to close your eyes and picture the ocean. Imagine you are sitting on your board waiting for the next big set to roll in. OK?"

James Taylor began to sing about sweet baby James in the background and she nodded.

"Now, don't move unless we ask you too, alright?"

"OK."

"Deep breath and close your eyes."

Jez did as he asked. It was only a second later that the prickling filled her arm and moved across her body, filling every nerve and pore with a dullness that made everything feel better. Suddenly nothing mattered but the words that were being sung and the blue current that swirled around her.

Chapter 9

Jez was aware of the beeping sounds first. It was slow and steady, then grew more rapid, then slowed down again. Her heart felt funny, like it was racing and then not. It took a few moments but she could match the feelings with the noise. Fighting to open her eyes, she looked up into the worried eyes of her dad.

"Hey Pickle."

"Hi Daddy." She felt tired and her eyes grew heavy. The beeping slowed down again as her eyes closed.

"Jez, honey?" Her brother's voice was in her ear. "We need you to wake up. Can you tell us what's going on?"

She took in a breath through her mouth, but didn't open her eyes. "My chest feels heavy. And my heart … it's sprinting and then stopping to rest." The beeping rushed again, after a few minutes, it slowed back down.

"I know you're not going to like this, but we need you to step back out to the waiting room." A voice said.

"What's happening?" Her dad sounded upset.

"She's going to be fine, but her heart is reacting to the medication. We need you to step out of the way."

"I'm fine, Daddy. Go get me some coffee, please." Jez said weakly.

Darkness started to pull at her, but she heard her brother's voice. "Come on, Dad. That's her signal."

"What signal?" Dad's voice was getting angry.

"She doesn't want us to see this. Trust me, they're going to help her. Let's just step out for a bit."

"You have a signal?" Their voices were a little fainter. Jez slipped into the darkness.

☐

Chapter 10

Jez opened her eyes to the soft green room. Her brother and father sat in chairs side by side, facing her, although her dad's face was in his hands and her brother was staring at something across the room. Her chest hurt badly and she felt tired, beaten. "What happened?"

Both men sat up and looked at her, worry and relief covered their faces. "Hey Pickle. How do you feel?" Her brother asked, as her father reached out and took her hand.

"My chest hurts." She admitted.

"Your heart or your chest?" Dad asked to clarify.

Jez swallowed and tried to isolate the pain. "Chest, right side and up my neck."

They both breathed out. "That's the incision."

"What happened?"

Jordy got up and pressed a button on the bed rail. "Your system didn't like the stress and drugs. It sent your heart into a tail spin."

A nurse rushed into the room. Jez turned her head to look as the door opened and then regretted it as pain shot up her neck. "Ouch." She whispered and cringed.

"We can do something about that." The nurse smiled down at her kindly. Her eyes glanced up and she made a note on the chart she held in her hand.

"Is that smart?" Dad asked. "Giving her more drugs after all this?"

"A mild pain killer should be fine. But I'll check with the doctors to be sure." She smiled and left the room.

An itch started to form on her cheek and Jez reached up to rub at it. Her fingers fell on the tape and tubes. Eyes growing wide, she tried to feel where they all started and ended.

"It's not as bad as it feels." Jordy said seeing the fear in his sister's face.

She traced the tubes to her nose, one she realized was oxygen, the other vanished up her nostril. Moving back along the plastic, she felt one was taped down and the other wasn't. At the edge of her face, one tube went up the pillow and the other ran down and off the bed. "Jordy?"

"One's just oxygen. It will come out in a little while." He spoke calmly.

"The other?"

"It's the feeding tube we talked about with the doctor." He smiled.

Tears brimmed in her eyes. "It's in my nose, Jordy? How am I going to hide it?"

He reached out and took her hand. Looking right in her eyes, he smiled. "We don't. It'll be fine. I promise."

Their dad stood up and cleared his throat. "I'll go call the shop. Let them know she's awake." Jordy and Jez watched him leave the room, hunched with emotion. When he was gone, Jordy turned back to his sister. "You scare the shit out of us."

"I'm sorry." She sounded about five years old.

He smiled. "It's not like you had control over any of it. And I doubt it was much fun on your end either."

"I don't remember."

"Good." He nodded seemingly relieved about that fact. They sat holding hands and not talking for several long minutes until the nurse came in. She pushed a liquid into Jez's IV and she sighed as the pain subsided.

As the nurse was leaving their father was just coming in. "The doctor will be up to talk to you soon." She smiled.

"Thank you." He mumbled as they crossed paths. Taking a seat in the chair, he looked at his children. Seeing the calmness in his baby girl, he relaxed a bit as well. "They all send their love and best."

"What did you tell them?" Jez asked softly, enjoying the mellow feeling in her body.

"Just that you came out of surgery and we were waiting to talk to the doctor."

Jordy gave his dad a heavy look. "It's been hours. They didn't ask what took so long?"

"Nope." Dad's answer was short and to the point. Jez was on too big of a high to catch the look that passed between the two men. There was more to the story but neither one wanted Jez to hear about it right now, so they left the conversation where it was until they could talk privately.

The doctors came in some time later. Jez was riding high on a pain killers and time was distorted for her. But she sat the bed up a little and tried to focus on what the doctors were saying. One of the doctors was her neurologist, a second introduced himself as the cardiologist, and the third was the surgeon. They each talked in turn. The surgeon went over how well the actual surgery had gone. He complimented Jez on being a perfect patient, and how she had them giggling when she sang along to the music that was piped in. The neurologist then tried to explain how the stress of the actual surgery and the medication had pushed her body to its limits which sent it into overdrive. That was the cardiologist's cue to talk about what had happened with her heart. They all laid out the facts as clearly as possible so everyone understood, although Jez was still so loopy she didn't really care.

"So where does this leave us, Doctor?" Dad asked.

There was a collective discomfort to their stances, and they looked to each other, none seemingly wanting to be the barer of the news. Finally, it was the neurologist that spoke. "Jez," He reached out and touched her foot. "You're not going to like this."

"I hate when you say that."

"We'd like to keep her here for a few more days."

Jordy and Dad looked up. "Why?"

"She's in quite a bit of discomfort. She can't swallow any pain meds with the feeding tube. So it all has to be done through the IV." The neurologist said.

"I'm also very concerned about what her heart is doing. It's stable for now, but I'd like to keep an eye on it for a day or two." The cardiologist added.

Jordy and Dad looked at each other, then looked down at Jez. She was still processing what they were saying. "You want me to stay?"

The neurologist stepped forward with a gently smile. "For a couple of days. If all goes well, you can be home by Thursday night."

"And the tubes?" She touched the plastic taped to the side of her face.

"Let's just get through the next few hours, alright?"

Tears swelled in her eyes and she looked to Jordy. Understanding, he reached out and grabbed her hand. "It's going to be fine."

"But..."

"Shush." He stopped her, then a sparkle twinkled in his eye. "Rehab."

It took a moment for her to put the pieces together, but then she smiled through the tears that ran down her cheeks. She nodded with a weak smile. "Rehab."

The doctors looked at each other confused and then to Jez's dad, who shrugged just as confused. Jordy pulled a tissue from the box on the nightstand and handed it to his sister. As the doctors filed out of the room, the surgeon stopped and looked down at her. "You might not want to cry too much. It makes the oxygen tube gross." He winked at her and they filed out of the room.

Her dad and brother stayed for a couple of more hours but then she made them leave too. She claimed she was tired, but in reality, she was just tired of their worried looks. She also knew they needed a break. Neither did well at hospitals and both were getting antsy. She asked Jordy to bring her a few things from home if he came to visit her the following day, to which he gave her an exasperated look. They both gave her kisses and told her to call if she needed them. Jez agreed, but knew she wouldn't.

The nurse gave her another shot a little after dinner time, and left Jez to stare at the television. It wasn't long before her heart rate and blood pressure spiked and then plummeted. The doctors and nurses stood by her bedside watching the monitors and hovering with medications and equipment. They offered to call her family, hoping that having them near would calm her some, but she refused. The last thing Jez wanted was to worry them anymore than necessary.

It was a long, hard night. Sleep only came when her system crashed, and the shot of adrenaline her body pushed through to counteract her falling blood pressure woke her with a start. Her emotions ran the gambit as well. The lows made her tired and depressed, and the highs made her angry and hyper. By morning's light, she was physically, mentally, and emotionally drained. Her chest hurt but they were worried about giving her any pain killers for fear of setting her system off again. In the end, they just had her dissolve something under her tongue, and left her alone to rest.

Chapter 11

Jez woke to find Jordy sitting in the chair next to her watching television. "Hey."

He looked over a little surprised and smile. "Hey yourself. How do you feel?"

"Tired."

"You had a rough night." He said.

"Does dad know?" She sighed and felt the ache in her chest.

Jordy looked at the door and then down to her. "No. I suggested he take the store today so the other could have the day with their families."

Jez wanted to nod, but it would hurt too much. She knew that was the best place for him. Her father was a predictable man. He dealt with stress and emotions by working. He didn't like confrontation unless it involved a physical fight and preferred to live in denial when it came to emotional things. It actually worked out for Jez's benefit most times, since he left her alone and allowed her brother to raise her. "Please don't tell him. I don't want him to change the plans because of this."

Jordy reached out and too her hand. "Don't worry, Pickle. I got this. He'll be on that boat Sunday no matter what."

She smiled at her brother and he smiled back. She allowed her eyes to close as he turned his attention back to the television.

Jordy left a few hours later, giving her a kiss and promising to come back the next day. She nodded and stared at the television until the cardiologist came in to check on her. He seemed pleased that she was stable and pleased with the way she was healing. When she told him that her chest was still sore from the surgery, he offered her a few options to deal with the pain that weren't drug based. She agreed to try them. He told her that if she had two stable nights in a row, he'd release her. That helped Jez's mood, and she was in better spirits when the guys called from the shop later that night. She pictured them huddled around the speaker phone and smiled.

"Jordy won't let us visit." Ty said with a chuckle in his voice.

"Good, because I look like a freak show, and I would hate to give you all nightmares." She smiled.

"How are you feeling?" She recognized Boone's voice, although it held a little seriousness.

"When can we go surfing?" OB asked. "We've only got a few more days before the dads leave. We need to get out there."

She laughed. "I don't think they'll let me surf for a while, but let's plan on Saturday."

"Sounds perfect. Now to get the dads to watch the shop." Ty added.

"I'll do it." Boone offered, but then there was a slapping noise.

"No way man, you're coming with us." OB stated matter-of-factly.

"I don't surf."

"It's not about the surfing, man. It's about the experience." OB said dreamily. Jez smiled as she pictured that dopey face he got when he was trying to be metaphysical.

"It's about the hot girls in little bikini's." Ty chuckled. "Trust me, you don't want to miss it."

As they laughed, Jordy's voice came through clear. "How are you feeling tonight, Pickle?"

"Fine."

"Have any more…"

"I said I'm fine, Jordy." She snapped.

She heard the click as the receiver lifted and she knew she was no longer on speaker phone. "Bite me, Jezebel."

"Screw you." She lashed out. He waited in silence, then she gave in as she always did. "It hurts some, but they gave me some other ways to help. The doc says it looks good. He says if all goes well, I could be released on Friday."

"Ok." Jordy said softly. "I, …. Oh, wait a second, what?"

Jez listened as Jordy spoke to someone else. She couldn't tell who it was but when Jordy got back on the phone he said, "Would you be up to doing some homework? Boone says there's a paper or something due Thursday. I can bring your stuff by tomorrow morning. He said he can turn it in for you."

"Sure, that would be good. It'll give me something to do. I'm getting bored just laying here. Thanks."

"I love you, Pickle."

"Love you too." She heard the phone line click and she set hers down on the rolling table before her. She sighed and turned back to the program that flashed before her.

Just like clockwork, the nurse came in to check her vitals, and check her fluids. They changed her IV bags and her food bag. They checked and cleaned her incisions, allowing Jez to watch in a hand mirror. It looked horrible, but the nurse said it wasn't too bad. There was an inch long cut halfway between her collarbone and breast, another tiny one at her collarbone, and bruising from her throat to her nipple.

"The incisions look really good." The nurse smiled. "We normally don't see as much bruising, but with your medical history, I'm not surprised. It'll fade in a few weeks."

She redressed it all and handed Jez an ice pack to help with the pain. The room phone rang just as the nurse was writing notes on the chart, and Jez answered it. "Hello?"

"Jezebel MacIntosh? This is the front desk. You have a gentleman who would like to visit. He's not family, but says he's a friend."

"Um, I, um," Jez's eyes flashed up to the nurse. "I'm having my dressing changed. Now's not a good time."

"I understand. I'll pass the message along." The line clicked off.

The nurse stepped over. "I'm done you know. You could have ..."

"No, the only person I want to see me like this is my brother." Jez swallowed.

The nurse nodded, but Jez could see that she didn't understand. She wanted to explain but it wasn't worth the effort. The nurse left the room, and Jez readjusted in the bed. A few minutes later, a soft knock came at the door and a candy stripper popped her head into the room. "I have a delivery for you."

"Me?"

She smiled and came in carrying Jez's bag. She set it on the rolling table and pushed it closer to the bed. "The man who dropped this off was very good looking. He seemed disappointed he didn't get to see you. But he made me promise to bring it directly up."

"Thanks." She smiled.

The teenage girl hesitated before leaving the room. "Was he your boyfriend?"

"I don't have a boyfriend." Jez said pulling the zipper open.

"Oh." She sounded hopeful. "Those tattoos were so hot."

"Tattoos?" Jez looked up as the girl started for the door. "Was he bald?"

She nodded and her eyes sparkled. "Had that bad boy thing going on, but those blue eyes showed what a sweetie he really is."

"Boone? Why would he..."

"You know him?" The girl was almost high at the thought.

"He works with me." Jez said absently.

She bounced back to the bed. "Where? Do you think he'd…"

The girl's sudden eagerness to know more about Boone irritated Jez. "No. I don't think he'd be into you. You're not really his type."

Jez watched the girl shrink and felt a little bad. "Well, it was worth a shot, right?"

"It's nothing personal. He's just into..." Jez left the words unsaid, simply because she didn't know what his type was. She had seen him flirt with just about every type of girl imaginable, so this cute little thing was probably right up her alley, but the thought of it made Jez's stomach turn.

The girl was trying to hide her disappointment as she back to the door. "Well, have a good night."

"Thanks. You too."

Jez wiped a hand across her face, wondering where that flash of jealous had come from. As her hand moved over the tube that was taped to her cheek, she felt the familiar feel of pain and disappointment fill her. You're not his type either, Pickle. She told herself. Tears swelled in her. She reminded herself that she didn't like him. He was too … too …. much. Too much of everything and no matter what he said or did, he wasn't going to see her as anything but what she was, just one of the guys who worked at the shop. Jordy's little sister and a fuck up. And she didn't want his pity.

Jez pushed the rolling table away and rolled to her side. The pain in her chest flared but that helped give her a reason to cry. She would allow herself to cry over the physical pain, but she would not cry over anything else.

☐

Chapter 12

It wasn't until much later that night, when Jez was woken by a nurse coming to check her vitals, that she decided to see what the assignment was. She pulled the table back to her and opened her bag. She pulled free her laptop, notebook, and text. A small paper was stuck in pages of her book and she pulled it free. Written on a piece of hospital stationary was a note from Boone.

'Was hoping to stop by and say Hi, but they won't let me up. Call me if you have questions. 587-2361.' Instead of a complete signature it simply read B.

Jez looked at the note for another minute contemplating the meaning. She was trying to figure out if he really did want her to call, or did he really want to see her? Or was it just as meaningless as it sounded? Finally, she grabbed up her cell phone and entered his number in her contacts. They worked together after all. It could be helpful to have his number. Then, folding the note, she tucked it in her binder where she also found a piece of copy paper with that week's writing assignment. She had only done part of the reading, but it didn't seem too hard. She sat her bed a little further upright, and flipped on the over bed light. While her computer booted up, she flipped open the text and thumbed around until she found the group of pages related to the assignment.

The sun was rising when she finishing the last sentence. She hit grammar and spell check as the nurse came in to get her vitals. Smiling as she glanced down at the screen, she commented. "You must be feeling better. Not many kids would be doing homework in here."

"Can't get too far behind. Besides it gives me something to do." Jez replied, laying her head back on the pillow. She was tired now. "Is there Wi-Fi here?"

"Sure. Connect under guest and just accept the rules." She smiled and headed out of the room.

Jez followed her instructions and was able to pull up her emails easily. There were five from people she didn't want to talk to. Deleting them, she moved on quickly. Her professor had emailed her, wishing her a speedy recovery. The last new one was from Boone. Confused, Jez looked at the main inbox page. Boone's message sat directly above the only other one that waited for her reply. The bottom one was old, but untouched. She had never had the strength to read it. But seeing Boone's name right above Paulie's was pointed. It was like a warning. A red flag that made her heart beat harder. Jez closed her eyes and swallowed. Paulie was the past. Boone wasn't anything like him. Boone didn't even like her. They were just … just... She didn't know, but they weren't what Paulie was. When Jez opened her eyes, she clicked on Boone's message.

'Hey, hope you're feeling better. Don't freak out. I'm not stocking you. Jordy said this might be a better way to get ahold of you since they won't let me up at the hospital. Let me know if you have any questions about the assignment. If you want to email it to me, I'll print it and turn it in for you. I'll check emails before I leave, just in case. See you soon.'

Jez had to blink the tears from her eyes. The words 'freak out' and 'stalker' had punched her. But after reading the message a few times, she saw through them. He was trying to be helpful, and she had no reason to doubt him, yet. Without thinking it to death, she hit reply.

'Hi, thanks for my stuff. Sorry you couldn't visit. Would you mind reading over my paper and make sure I got the right point? If it's alright, go ahead and turn it in. If not, if I'm way off, let me know and I'll rewrite it. Thanks for your help. Hope everyone and everything is good. See ya.'

She attached the paper she had just written and hit send before she could change her mind.

Jez left her computer on but put the head of her bed back a little. She closed her eyes and drifted off to sleep.

☐

Chapter 13

Jez woke to the nurse talking to someone as she entered the room. She blinked and looked up to see Jordy's smiling face. "Good Morning, Pickle."

"Hey." She said sleepily.

"How'd you sleep?" He asked sinking into the chair next to her bed.

She thought with narrow eyes. "Did I sleep? I wrote my paper and emailed it to Boone to turn in for me."

It was then that he looked over at the computer. "You saw Boone?"

"No, he left it at the front desk." She smiled remembering the candy striper. "Just about gave the volunteer a stroke."

"I told him I'd bring it to you." Jordy said distractedly. She let him think a minute before asking about everyone else. Coming out of his thoughts he looked at her. "They're all good. They send their love. OB and his dad are about to kill each other already." He shook his head.

"Do you think they'll be like this forever?" She smiled.

"Until OB finds a girl that his dad likes, yep." They continued to talk. He filled her in on the girls that were hanging out at the shop, mostly because of Boone, which made her heartsick. She tried to hide it, but her brother could see right through her walls.

"He's not good for you."

"I know. And I know that he isn't even into me. And I don't care about him either. It just makes me sick to see girls throw themselves at guys like that." She rolled her eyes.

Jordy narrowed his eyes for a minute. "He'd use …"

"I said I know. I got it." She snapped annoyed. "I'm not good enough for a guy like him. He'd use me and toss me. He's a Paulie, I got it. I'm not pretty enough, I know. Just drop it."

Jordy's face was blank with shock. "What? That's not what I…"

"Drop it, Jordy, or leave." The monitor started to beep faster and she took in a deep breath to calm down.

He reached out and took her hand. Scooting closer to the bed, he looked at her high heart rate and back to her. "Hey, Pickle, I didn't mean you weren't good enough for him. He's not good enough for you."

"Drop it, Jordy." She said through clinched teeth. A nurse came flying into the room, looking up at the monitor. Her eyes looked down at Jez and then over to Jordy. "Go get some coffee."

Jordy nodded and left quickly. When he was gone, Jez pulled her knees up to her chest and curled around them, only to have her sore chest scream out in pain. Tears stung her eyes as she fell back on the bed.

"Take some deep breaths, and I'll be right back." The nurse rush from the room and Jez did her best to focus only on breathing. When the nurse reappeared, she pushed a needle into the IV and handed an ice pack to Jez. As she began to relax, the woman smiled down at her. "No one can get a girl as upset as her guy."

"He's my brother." Jez replied as the medicine kicked in.

"Even worse." She smiled and patted Jez's arm. As the nurse left, Jez over heard her speak to Jordy. "Be careful what you say to her. Don't upset her, alright? I've given her something to relax."

Jez was going to say something to them, but the medicine was calming her and making her sleepy. Jordy came in and took his seat again. Jez looked over at him. "Sorry."

"I love you, Pickle."

"Love you t…" she never finished the words as sleep pulled to her.

❑

Chapter 14

The nurse's touch woke Jez. "Sorry to wake you, but I need to pull some blood."

Jez nodded and blinked. The room was darkening, and Jordy was gone. "How long was I out?"

"A while." She smiled. "He said he'd come back later."

Jez watched while the nurse took her vitals and then the lab tech pulled blood. Before the nurse left, Jez said, "I'm kind of hungry."

"I'm sorry but you have a feeding tube. I can't give you anything to eat."

"I figured, but I haven't been hungry in a long, long time. Could you just mention it to the doctor when you see him?"

"Sure." She smiled. Jez watched her leave and laid there for a few minutes. She sat up carefully and stretched. Reaching for her IV pole, Jez took the short walk to the bathroom. She brushed out her hair and brushed her teeth. She tried to wipe off her face, but it was hard with the tape still on it. After using the toilet, she returned to the bed and flipped on the computer. A message waited from Boone.

'Turned in your paper for you. It was really good. Wish I could write like that. Maybe you could help me with the midterm. Hope you are feeling better. Everyone is asking about you.'

Jez forced herself not to read too much into the message.

'Thank you so much. I'm doing better. Hope to be out of here soon.'

She sent the message and pushed the computer away. She knew in her heart this was dangerous. It was just messaging, casual, friendly, just like she would with any other friend, but this wasn't any other friend. This was Boone.

Without thinking, she picked up her cell phone. Running through her contacts she found the one she looked for. "Jezebel!" The girl's voice was ear splitting.

"Hey Molly." Jez smiled.

"Where are you? Rumor has it you're in rehab. But I'm like no, not my girl. My girl don't do rehab."

Jez laughed out right. "Well, I am."

Her friend became quiet. "What are you getting off?"

"Doesn't matter." She responded.

"Are you OK?"

Jez thought about how she should reply.

"Bels?"

"No Molly, I don't think I am. As soon as dad's gone, can you come get me?"

"Are you sure you want that?" Her friend was very serious, more serious than she'd been in a long, long time.

"Yeah, Molly, I do."

"OK, you text me when you're good to go, and I'll be where ever you need me to be."

"Thanks Molly."

Molly was quiet for a little bit, then the line cut off.

"Who was that?" Jordy asked as he came around the corner into the room.

"No one." She looked up with a fake smile. "Just someone from school. How was your day?"

He sat in the chair and sighed. "Good, I guess. Dad's going to come by in a little bit."

"Cool."

"Yea, I thought we could play a card game or watch a movie or something."

She smiled at him. "Sounds good."

Jordy turned and flipped on the television, and settled into an old program. About an hour later the doctors came in. Today there were only two, the cardiologist and the neurologist. They stood smiling in the doorway until Jez looked up at them. "Hey docs."

"How are you feeling?" One of them asked.

"Good." She forced the smile. "I'm kind of hungry."

Jordy looked up startled. "What?"

"So, I heard." The neurologist said. "Your labs look really good."

"Can we take the tubes out?" She asked hopefully.

"How's the pain?"

"Better. The ice helps, and taking it slow helps too." She sat the bed up.

The doctors came closer and the cardio pulled the dressing off the incision. The bruising looked worse, but the actual cuts were cleaner. "They look good."

"You've got to be kidding?" Jordy said sitting up horrified. "It looks like you beat the shit out of her, doc."

"It's not unusual." The cardio said. "The bruising makes it look worse than it is."

"So, where do I stand?" Jez asked as the doctor replaced the bandage.

Jordy came over and placed a hand on her arm. "You don't stand, Pickle. You sit."

The doctors smiled. "If all continues to go well, I think you could leave tomorrow."

"And the tube?"

"I think we might be able to take it out tomorrow. I'd like to see how your labs look, but if they look good. We can take the tube out. But then you should stay in for another day so we can make sure you're able to eat."

Jez looked over at Jordy, who looked concerned. "And when she gets out, what are we talking about?"

"Slow and steady. Continue with the hydrations, if the labs are good we can drop the banana bags." The neurologist explained.

"So back to normal." Jordy relaxed a little.

"When can I go back to the beach? Surf?" Jez asked. "We made plans for Saturday."

"Not for a few weeks. I want the stitches out first. But you can shower starting tomorrow, as long as you keep them dry."

Jez smiled and nodded. Looking to Jordy, she said, "The boys'll be pissed that I can't go."

"They'll understand." He smiled.

"So, we'll do another pull later tonight. If you want the tube out, I'll come see you in the morning."

Jez nodded and smiled for real. "Thanks doc, docs."

They said good night and left the room. Jordy looked over at his sister and took her hand. "So, you'll be home tomorrow with the tube or Saturday without."

"Saturday." She nodded.

He nodded, and turned his attention back to the television.

At nine o'clock, the nurse came by to toss out Jordy and any other visitors she found. Jez was napping but woke when Jordy got up and leaned across to kiss her cheek. "Are you leaving?"

"Yea Pickle. I gotta go."

"Thought daddy was coming." She asked feeling a little thick.

"Me too. Something must have come up though." He smiled. "I have to work tomorrow but I'll stop by later."

"OK. Say Hi to everyone for me." She smiled and waved as her brother walked out of the room. The nurse did her thing, and then the lab tech came in. When they all left, Jez pulled her table closer and turned on her computer. Three messages waited for her.

The first was from Molly. 'Hi Bels, looking forward to taking you shopping when you are able. Miss hanging out. Hugs!' Jez skipped answering that one for now.

The other two were from Boone. 'Hey I just wanted to see how you were feeling. Jordy seemed quiet today. Hope all is well.'

'Hey, didn't hear from you today. Do you know when you'll be back? This schedule sucks.'

Jez thought about messaging him back, but didn't. Instead, she picked up her phone and called him.

"Hello?" He sounded unsure.

"Hey, it's Jez."

There was a shuffle of noise, and his voice softened. "Are you alright?"

"You don't like the schedule?"

He chuckled. She heard him draw in a breath, and pictured him smoking. "I don't like that you're not on it."

"I'll be back next week. The dads leave Sunday and I have to be back."

"I heard you weren't going to the beach on Saturday." Another drag on the cigarette.

She shook her head stupidly. "I probably won't get out until then."

"Why are they keeping you so long? Are you alright?"

"I'm fine."

There was a moment of silence and it sounded like he was walking. After a few moments, he stopped moving and his voice was normal again. "What's wrong?"

"Nothing's wrong."

"Then why have they kept you, and why are they keeping you until Saturday? I thought this was out-patient surgery."

"Things didn't go as planned." She said. "Everything's good though."

"You don't sound like it."

She bit her lip. "What do I sound like?"

"You sound like you're hiding something, Jez. Are you sure you're alright?"

"I'm fine."

There was an awkward pause. "Ok, Jez."

"If you can, ask Jordy to bring me the schedule and I'll make one for next week. Message me with the days you want off."

"Sure."

"I'll let you go." She said awkwardly. "Bye."

"Night." The line went dead.

Tears filled her eyes and she didn't know why. Rolling to her side, Jez allowed herself to cry, even if she didn't know why.

Chapter 15

There were footsteps outside her door, and Jez quickly brushed the tears from her cheeks. She grabbed a tissue from the box on the nightstand next to her. She wiped the oxygen tube and then her nose as the soft knock came at the door. "Jez?"

Confused and surprised she turned her head to the voice. He stood in the doorway, filling most of it, outlined by the bright hallway lights. "Boone? How'd you get in?"

He stepped into the room and closed the door behind him. "It's not hard."

"What are you doing here?" She asked as he crossed the dark room to her bed. She watched him reach up to the string that hung from the light above the bed. She turned her head down quickly just as he yanked the string and turned the light on. Her hair fell across her face just in time. Keeping her face down, hiding from him by her long hair, she asked again, "What are you doing here?"

"You sounded upset. I wanted to make sure you were alright." He said from right next to her.

"I'm fine."

"That's why you were crying, because you're fine." His statement was pointed. When she didn't respond, he put a hand on her arm. "Please look at me, Jez."

"No, I'm fine. It's after visiting hours. If you get caught, you'll get in trouble. You should go." She was rushing her words.

He reached out and touched the side of her head. "Please look at me."

She shook her head no, but she didn't fight him when he used a finger to move her chin. She didn't look up at him, but kept her eyes caste down on the white blanket. "I don't want you to see me like this. No one should see me like this."

"Like what? Hurt? Sick? Scared?" He brushed the hair from her face. "It's OK you know. We all get that way."

"Uglier." She whispered, eyes still cast down. "I'm ugly enough, no one should see me looking worse."

"You're not ugly." He said softly, pushing her chin up to see her.

She met his eyes for a moment. The rich blue pools so enticing and warm, they almost made his words believable. But Jez remembered herself and looked away. "You should go."

"Why do you push everyone away?"

Again, she didn't answer. She knew he was looking at her. He was seeing the ugliness, the tubes, the bruises, the bandages. She couldn't hide those, but she could hide her eyes. She could keep him out.

"Did someone hurt you so bad that you don't trust anyone but the three amigos?" He let go of her chin and she let it fall. His words stung with truth, but she didn't want to admit it. Tears pushed at her eyes again and she wanted so badly to swallow them, but they wouldn't go away. "You know; I just want to be your friend."

She took in a shuttered breath. The first tear fell.

"Just … I'll be there when you need me." He said, his hand barely touching her arm as he stepped away.

The second, third, and fourth tear fell. She fought to keep it in. She didn't watch as he moved to the door and pushed out it. She didn't look to see if it had shut all the way before the dam broke and she sobbed uncontrollable again.

At some point she drifted off to sleep, only to be woken up by a nurse coming to take her vitals. The lab tech came in and drew more blood. Both asked Jez if she was in pain. She lied and said no. The pain she was experiencing they couldn't help with. When they left her, Jez shut off the light and sat in the darkness holding onto the sheet with a death grip until sleep came.

Jez slept off and on most of the morning, only waking long enough to use the bathroom and get her vitals checked. It was late morning when a doctor came in and told her that they were going to remove the feeding tube. He explained that she would be on a soft food diet for a little bit, and finally real food for the last two. If she could keep it all down, then they would discharge her. If all went well, she'd be home for Saturday night diner.

Removing the tube wasn't pleasant, but didn't take long. They gave her ice chips to suck on until lunch, and she was glad for them. Not only did they taste amazing, who knew ice could taste so good, but the coolness felt good on her sore throat. Her dad showed up just as her lunch tray did, and he seemed pleased to see that she was going to get to try to swallow something, even if it was just broth and juice.

He stayed for an hour, uncomfortable silence filling the room for most of it. He handed over the next week's schedule and a copy of this week's for her to deal with. Finally, he stood up and took her hand. "You know I love you, right Pickle?"

"I know, dad. I love you too. And I'm sorry for all this."

"I wish I was better at dealing with all this for you." He admitted.

She smiled. "It's OK. Jordy and I do OK."

He nodded, then leaned over and placed a kiss on her head. "I'll be back tomorrow to take you home."

"Ok Dad." She watched him leave, a heavy feeling in her chest. She spent the afternoon making the following week's schedule. She checked emails to make sure Boone hadn't emailed her with days he needed off. He hadn't, and aside from the couple of days she wanted off, she made the schedule much like it had been the week prior. Each guy got two days off in a row, and the others worked eight-hour days, aside from her and Jordy who worked ten or more hours. She split her days off, making sure Jordy was working long days when she was off. It would keep him out of her business and give her some freedom. She was just finishing when Jordy showed up at the hospital. He smiled seeing her with one less tube.

"Hey, Pickle. Dad said you got to eat."

She smiled back. "Just broth and juice, but so far it's staying down. They said I might get some food for dinner."

He looked happy with this news as he plopped down in the chair. She handed him the schedule. "What's this?"

"Next week's schedule. Check it over please, make sure I didn't screw something up."

He looked it over and nodded. "Looks good. I'll take it in tonight." He folded it and placed it in his pocket. "Patty's been around a lot. I think her and Ty are really hitting it off."

She smiled. "She seemed nice."

"Cute too. Let's hope he doesn't screw this one up." Jordy chuckled. Something on the television caught his attention and he turned away from Jez. She was glad. She really wanted to know about Boone but couldn't ask. Jordy knew her too well, and would see right through her. They sat and watched TV for two hours before Jordy's phone rang. When he hung up he looked at her sadly. "Sorry Pickle. I've got to go. OB's ride broke down and he needs a lift."

"It's OK. Tell them all I say Hi."

"See you tomorrow." He placed a kiss on her head and escaped from the hospital.

When he was gone, she turned on her computer and checked her emails. There were still two messages in her inbox; one read, one not. She clicked on the read one from Molly and typed a quick response. 'Monday after my meeting. Can you pick me up?'

Molly's reply was quick. 'Perfect, there's a race and party at the Toro that night. Just text me where and when to get you. See you soon.'

Jez took in a deep breath and reminded herself this was what she wanted and needed. Toro's wasn't exactly what she had in mind, but it would do. She'd find exactly what she needed there. Hitting delete to the message, Jez told herself it would be fine, just fine.

Chapter 16

Jez ate dinner and while it didn't taste all that great, it stayed down. As did breakfast and lunch the next day. By mid-afternoon, Jez was anxious to get out. The pain in her chest was minor, more a muscle ache from the bruises, or tenderness from the incision. The nurse helped her shower and removed the stitches. They used a butterfly bandage to hold the larger incision closed during and after the shower. They recommended she keep it covered for a couple more days, just to make it not so obvious. The nurse also explained how the infusions would work with the new port. They told her it might hurt for a while but the center should use a topical numbing cream to help. She listened to all the advice and nodded when they handed her all the papers. She changed into her street clothes, the ones she had worn into the hospital the day of her surgery, then sat and waited for her family to come and get her.

The sun was setting when they finally showed. Dad was all smiles and Jordy was apologetic, but they collected her quickly. The nurse took the last IV out and they were on their way home. Except they didn't go home. Dad pulled to a stop in their drive, but Jordy took Jez's hand and led her over to Ty's house. She was welcomed with hugs and happiness as they pushed into the crowded backyard. The dads were bar-be-cueing and drinking beer, while the guys sat around the table doing the same. Ty's mom worked in the kitchen and waved Jez's attempts to help away. It was the usual family, plus one. Boone sat quietly watching the group as they interacted with each other. Jez tried to keep her attention off him, but she allowed herself small glimpses at him here and there. He seemed to be doing the same. Both working too hard to stay away from each other that when they did catch the other's eye, or accidently bump into each other, it was strained and stressful. Thankfully no one else seemed to sense it and the night went smoothly. Everyone was very aware of how much Jez was eating, or not eating, so she made an effort to eat as much as she could without making herself sick. When dinner was over, she mentioned to Jordy that she was tired, and he walked her home after saying good night to everyone.

Sunday came quietly. The dad's said their good-byes and headed to the docks with only Ty's mom to see them off. The guys split apart, one going to work at the shop and the others headed down to the beach. Jordy left strict instructions for Jez to take it easy at home. She was tired of taking it easy and spent much of the day doing housework and laundry. It needed to be done, and it killed the time until Jordy got home. Ty came over too and the three of them ate dinner and watched television until Jez got tired and went to bed.

As Jordy drove Jez to the center for her infusion the next day, she mentioned her plans to him. "Hey, Molly and I are going shopping and maybe to a movie today. I was also thinking of maybe crashing at her place."

Jordy looked over at her with dark eyes. "Molly? I didn't know you were still friends with her."

"Of course, I mean we don't hang out as much lately, but we're still friends. She's going to pick me up after this." She giggled at the silliness of his statement.

"I don't know."

"Really Jordy? Come on. I need some girl time. I need shopping and pedicures, and boy talk. I spend all day with guys, I need some girlie stuff." She smiled and looked at him with puppy dog eyes. "Unless you want to take me to do all that stuff with me."

"No." His eye widened, horrified that she would even suggest it. "But I don't want you staying over there, not so soon after getting out of the hospital."

"Ok, I'll come home, but it might be kind of late. She said something about the eleven o'clock showing of that new romance movie. I think it opens tonight."

"It's Monday, Jez. Movies don't open on Monday nights."

"They do when it has something to do with the date." She pulled her cell phone out and looked up the movie information. As he pulled to a stop in front of treatment center, she showed it to him. He looked at it but couldn't argue with her. Jez was silently glad she had taken the time to plan this out.

"OK, but come home right after."

"Eye, eye." She smiled and leaned over to place a kiss on his cheek. "I love you, bro."

"Love you too, Pickle."

She climbed out and headed inside to get her fill. She didn't need her usual amount since she had gotten so much in the hospital, and was finished early. She texted Molly, who met her two blocks over at a restaurant for lunch. They chatted about all kinds of things, but mostly Molly filled Jez in on what she had been missing. When lunch was over, the girls headed for the mall. They spent hours shopping and getting their hair and nails done. Not only did Jez buy the jeans and winter clothes she had intended. She also purchased a new outfit for the night.

Normally, she wore outfits that showed off her boobs, since they were the only thing that were descent about her body. But since she was still too bruised, she had to find something else to wear. With Molly's help, Jez found a tight white top and a corset to go over it. Paired with a pair of tight black jeans and knee high black heeled boots, Jez looked almost sexy. The outfit did accentuate her curves, even if they were a little too curvy. It would pass for tonight. The girls had just enough time to rush back to Molly's to get ready before heading out to Toro's.

Toro's Race Track was an old abandoned two miles straight away that was now only used for illegal street racing. There were few rules to the races that were held there, but you had to agree on them up front. And breaking them would cost you more than the money you were betting. Jez hadn't been there in four long months, and as Molly pulled to a stop just outside the gates, Jez's heart raced.

"It's going to be great." Molly wrapped her arm around Jez's. "I didn't tell anyone you were coming."

Jez didn't know if that was a comfort or not. But the two girls walked through the cut chain link fence and through the old pit entrance. The straight away separated two pits and both were humming with activity. Molly pulled Jez to the nearest one and waved at the one person Jez had prayed not to see tonight. "Hey Paulie."

The guy turned around and stopped in his tracks, stunned by what he saw. "Molly, Bel. Good to see you."

Jezebel didn't answer, but Molly was more than happy to. She let go of her friend's arm and ran over to hug the lean, squirrely guy. "Surprised?"

"Uh, yea, where you been, Bel?"

Paulie's older brother, Sean, stepped over and looked her up and down. "Heard you were in rehab and found God or some shit like that."

Jez couldn't help the smile that curved her lips. "Don't believe everything you hear."

"I cut her choke chain and set her free for the night." Molly laughed.

Paulie stepped over close to Jez though. "Come to check out the new kid in town? He's kicking everyone's ass."

"I hadn't heard. I've been out of it since …" she didn't need to finish the statement. Paulie had been there, they all had been there, the night that Jezebel had wrecked.

"Bet he could even take you." Sean chuckled. "He's that good."

"Nobody's that good." Paulie said. "Bel's the best."

Jez was about to say something when Paulie got that sparkle in his eye. She hated that look. It was the look that had gotten her into so much trouble over the years. "No Paulie."

"Come on, Bel. You gotta. I lost so much money on your last race. You gotta do this for me."

She took two steps back. "No. I haven't been behind the wheel since that night. I don't anymore."

"Bels, you not racing is like you not breathing." He purred stepping up to her. He wrapped an arm around her shoulder. "You know you want to."

"I don't have a car."

"You can use mine. It was gonna race tonight anyway, but I would feel a whole hell of a lot safer if you drove it instead of Sean."

"Sean was going to race?" She laughed outright, but then stopped herself. Shaking her head, she added, "If Jordy finds out, we're all dead, you know that."

"Jordy ain't gonna find out." Molly smirked. "He thinks you're at the movie with me."

During this whole time, the three of them had been moving Jez closer to the supped-up street racer. It was pretty, she had to admit. Blue with black accents, and she knew the engine would fly. Paulie only had the best when it came to cars. He couldn't drive it worth a crap in a race, but he always had a good one. "Come on Bel, I built her for you."

Jez mentally kicked herself, but asked, "Who's the new guy?"

Paulie smiled and Sean smacked him on the back. "He showed up here three or four weeks ago. He sits out two weeks and then jumps on a race. Comes outta nowhere. He's been winning them all ever since."

"What's he driving?"

"A 1970 black Barracuda. He's gotta it supped up and sweet. There ain't no way that thing came off the assembly line."

Jez allowed her eyes to drift across the track as her heart sank. Sure enough, she spotted Boone leaning against his car talking to some cheap slut. "I can't race him."

"What? Why not?" Paulie got the words out just seconds before Sean did.

"He knows me. He knows Jordy."

"Does he know you race?" Molly asked softly from just behind.

Jez shook her head no. "But if he sees me, he'll tell Jordy and I'm dead. Then he'll hunt you all down too."

"I ain't scared of your brother." Paulie said toughly, but Jez knew it was just as act. When Jordy was mad, everyone was scared of him.

"Well, if he doesn't know you race, he won't be expecting to see you here. And you don't exactly look like yourself right now." Molly said with a smile. "Let's find you a hat."

Jez watched as Molly wandered off, but Paulie pulled her attention to him. "Look, I know you've been out of the game for a while. But I also know you well enough to know you can do this. My car, your skills. We will make a killing tonight. Please Bels, I need this."

"I don't know…"

"Ok, so if you don't race for me tonight, I'm going to your brother first thing in the morning and telling him everything." Paulie's eyes grew nasty and dark.

"You wouldn't because he'd kill you right there on the spot."

"I ain't got nothing left to lose," he said with more honesty than she had ever heard come from his mouth.

Jez weighed the reality of it all. Paulie was as stupid as Jordy was temperamental. She didn't doubt that Paulie would go to Jordy just out of spite. And she couldn't have that, not when she was just getting back on her brother's good side. "Fine, but one race, and I mean, one race only."

"Just beat the shit outta him, Bels, and I'll consider you retired."

Molly came bouncing back not two seconds later with an over-sized beret style hat. It was horribly ugly but might do the trick. Molly situated it on her head and pulled it down low. After pulling Jez's hair forward a bit, she felt a little more hidden. "Just keep your head down." Molly suggested.

A whistle sounded, calling the racers to the middle mark to go over the rules. Paulie stood in front of Jez, partly blocking the view, and facing off with Boone. The mediator and bookie, Mel, was a man that Jez knew well, so she turned just a bit away from him as well.

"Three rules. One, stay in your own lane. This is a race not a derby. Two, first car to the end wins. And three, no cheating." Paulie nodded once, Boone did too. The mediator looked over at Jez. "Drivers got to agree."

Jez nodded once.

"OK, so who's driving tonight?" He asked.

"Boone." Boone said loudly as if it should mean something.

Paulie answered for their side. "Bels."

The stunned hush fell over those who had been able to hear. As Jez turned and moved back to the car, the rumors and talk started, spreading like spark in a firework factory. Jez tried to block it out as she got to the car. Sliding into the driver's seat, she looked up at Paulie. "This better be white lightning, Paulie."

"She's faster." He smiled.

Then Molly rushed over carrying a bottle. "Tradition." She said handing it over to Jez. Without a thought, Jez took a swig and felt the burn all the way down to her toes. "The rest will be at the finish line. Go get him, Bels."

As Molly scooted away, Paulie leaned in. Jez locked the seatbelt and scanned the dash. "It's all muscle, but you've got speed. Let him get off the block first, then kick it in."

Jezebel looked over at Paulie a little disgusted. "Shut up, Paulie." She put her hand to his face and shoved him away.

Turning over the engine, Jez took a moment to feel the purr. She put it into gear and stalled it. A chuckle could be heard outside but she pushed it away, and tried again. Suddenly, a hand thrust something through the open window. She smiled at the CD and looked over at Sean. "Tradition."

She took it and put it in the player, then drove the car around the pit crowd. She took some time to get the feel of her. She rode smooth and Jez could feel the power of her. "Hey kitty, I know we don't know each other, but I bet we could be friends." Jez pulled to the starting line and tilted the hat to help block Boone's view of her. Jez hit play on the CD, and then centered herself as the music started.

The first three beats of the music counted the beats of the count down. When the girl dropped the white pantie flag, they were off. Both cars left the line at the same time. They stayed equally paced halfway down the track. At the halfway point, Jez kicked it into fifth and shot off, her hat flying out the window as the loud music shattered the windows in the back of the car. Less than a minute later, the race was over. Jez spun the car around and pulled to a stop just as Boone was crossing the finish line. He got out of the car, and Jez grew fearful that he had recognized her, but the crowd swarmed her, cutting him off from getting through. Molly was suddenly there handing her the bottle of Moonshine, and Paulie was hugging her happily.

Jez took a sip from the bottle and moved away from Paulie, while he turned to talk to Sean. Jez's song still blared from the car as she shook the small glass shards from her hair, then made her way to the opposite side of the crowd and the track. It took twenty minutes for the crowd to calm and move away so the cars could be moved. A second race was set to run, but Jez didn't really care to watch it. Stepping over the concrete barriers, she walked slowly around the grandstands and out to the parking lot. Taking another swig from the bottle, Jez made her way to Molly's car, where she intended to wait for her friend. Although as she walked, she was seriously debating their friendship status.

Jez had almost made it when the familiar rumble of the muscle car came up behind her. Jez knew she was busted before she even turned around. "I wanted to congratulate the guy who had balls enough to beat me, but looks like I was wrong on several counts."

"When did you figure out it was me?"

"As soon as I heard the music." He smiled. "It's the same song you hum when you're thinking."

"Please don't say anything to Jordy." Tears filled her eyes just thinking about her brother.

Boone cut the engine and got out. Stepping over to her, he took the bottle from her hand. Taking a sip, he almost choked on it. "Wow. Um," he shook his head. "I'll make you a deal. I won't say anything about this to any of the three amigos, if you let me take you to get something to eat and then home."

Not seeing any way out of it, Jez nodded. He looked down at the bottle in his hand and chucked it across the parking lot. He opened his door and offered her in. She slid across the bench seat and fastened the seatbelt as he got in. Giving her a sideway looks, he shook his head.

"What?"

"Just reminding myself of rule three." He smiled and drove them away from the track. Jez wondered what no cheating had to do with anything.

Chapter 17

Boone found an all-night diner and pulled in. He took her hand and led her in, finding an empty booth about halfway down the side windows. A waitress came over and took their drink order, Jez got a soda and so did Boone. When she had walked away, Jez looked across the table. "Why are you doing this?"

"Because we're friends." He looked confused.

"What is it that you really want?" She narrowed her eyes, the alcohol still fueling her honesty.

He smiled. "I just want to be friends, Jez. Nothing more." He shrugged. "And I'm sure that Jordy would want me to make sure you get home alright."

Her eyes grew big. "You promised that you wouldn't tell him."

"Don't worry, I'm not." He smiled. The waitress brought their drinks and took their food order. Jez wasn't really hungry but she knew she needed to eat something to sober up, so she got chili cheese fries. Boone ordered a hamburger. "So, where'd you learn to drive like that?"

"Around." She answered vaguely.

He leaned into her. "Did Jordy teach you?"

"No." She was horrified at the thought. After taking a sip of her soda, she sighed. "Dad and Jordy taught me to drive when I was thirteen. They thought it would be good to know in case of emergencies. When I was a freshman in high school I met Paulie. His brother was big in the racing scene so Paulie would take me a couple of times a month. Paulie went every night with his brother, he held the money, but I could only go when dad was gone and Jordy was out on dates."

"They didn't know?"

She shook her head. "They'd have killed me."

"OK, so that's how you know about this, but when did you start driving?"

"One night, after the races, Paulie's brother tossed me his keys and asked me to move his car. I'd seen what he could do, and I tried to do the same thing." She paused while the waitress set the plates of food down in front of them. When she was gone, Jez continued. "Both Paulie and his brother were impressed. The next time I went, Paulie set me up against this other girl. It was supposed to be a joke. You know, watch the two little girlies play. They didn't even place bets. Sean gave me a few tips, and stood back."

"And you won."

"I was finishing before she even got it in gear." Jez smiled at the memory. She chewed slowly on a fry.

"Then what?"

"Sean took me out a few times after school and taught me a few more things. A couple weeks later, he put in a real race." She blinked back the memory.

Boone smiled as he set his burger back on the plate. "And you lost?"

"No, I won. And I kept winning. No matter who they put me up against, I just kept winning. Paulie and Sean kept teaching me little tricks, and building cars with me in mind. And I just kept on winning for them."

"So, you've never lost?" He was doubtful.

"I've lost." She nodded. "Twice."

"Twice?" He smirked.

"How many times have you lost?"

"More than I've won." He's chuckled. "But you're the first person I actually lost money on."

She cocked her head curiously. "And how do you do that?"

He laughed, "Later, I wanna know who in the hell could beat you. You drive like the Devil's on your ass."

She turned serious. "The first time it was because someone sabotaged my car, and the second was intentional."

"You intentionally lost?" His sense of humor gone. "Why would you do that?"

She shrugged. "It's a long story."

"We've got time." He pushed.

She leaned away from her plate, suddenly too sick to eat. She didn't really want to tell him, but the alcohol was keeping her walls down. "Paulie owed a debt to a guy. He made me throw it to pay the debt."

Boone put his burger down. "Must have been some debt."

"It was going to be his ass or mine. Guess he figured mine would be worth more." She swallowed the bile that was rising in her throat.

"Please tell me that isn't literal." Boone's face darkened.

"Sean and Paulie expected more than just money if I lost." She said softly. Tears were pressing on her eyes, but she was distracted when her cell phone went off. Grabbing it up, she checked the text that was coming through. "Shit."

"Who is it?"

"Jordy. Fuck, I'm late." She typed back that she was on her way, and looked up. "We've gotta go."

Boone nodded, and laid a couple of bills on the table as they stood. He placed a hand on her back as they moved back out to the car and got in. Boone had a lot more questions but could see that this wasn't the time to ask them. Jez was rattled. Whether it was the memories or the liquor, he didn't know, but she was more on edge than he had ever seen her.

They were almost home when she turned her head up to look at him with big eyes. "How are we going to explain you bringing me home?"

"Where were you supposed to be?"

"At a movie with Molly?"

"Is this Molly a …."

"She's the reason I was at the track tonight, and not at the movie like I had planned." It wasn't the total truth, but right now the little lie wasn't going to hurt.

He nodded and thought quickly. "What are the chances that Molly could have taken you to a party instead of the movie?"

"Very good." She smiled seeing where this was going. "Molly tends to meet guys and get us into situations."

"OK, then that's what we'll go with. Molly met a guy, you all went to a party, I happened to show with my date and saw you. I knew you shouldn't be there, so I brought you home."

Jez nodded. "OK. He might buy that."

Boone got off the freeway and drove down the main street that led past the store. As he turned onto her street, she reached over and placed a hand on his shoulder. "Thank you."

He looked over at her stunned, but then smiled. "What're friends for?"

As Boone pulled up in front of the house, Jordy was busting out the front door. Ty and OB were not far behind. "What the fuck, Jez?"

"I'm sorry. I'm sorry. I really tried to be home on time." She pleaded as she met him halfway across the yard.

"It's my fault she's late. I had to take my date home first, man." Boone called getting out of his car. "I didn't even think about having her call, I'm sorry man."

Jordy had grabbed Jez's arm but stopped and looked up at Boone shocked. "How're you …?"

"He gave me a ride." Jez said quietly.

Jordy glared down at her, eyes glowing the red fury that she hadn't seen in a long time. "Get your ass in the house." He shoved her to Ty. "Inside."

Ty nodded and moved Jez gently back toward the house.

"Hey man," Boone was stepping up to Jordy. "Look, I'm sorry. I found her at a party and knew you'd be pissed she was there. I gathered her up and brought her home."

"What party?"

Boone shrugged. "Some party on the north side. The girl I took out wanted to go. I didn't know anyone there."

As Ty pushed Jez into the doorway, she looked back and saw that OB had stepped up next to Jordy. He was prepped to jump in if needed. "How'd she get there?"

"Jordy man, I was trying to do you a favor. Just trying to look after your sister." Boone was trying to calm him down.

"And we thank you for that. Why don't you come in and have a beer and you can tell us all about it?" OB said, physically turning his best friend back to the house.

Jez looked up at Ty, who was glaring down at her. In an attempt to help, she whispered. "Molly took me. Don't let Jordy do anything stupid. It's my fault."

Ty sighed and nodded. "Get upstairs."

She turned and ran upstairs, but when she heard the front door close, she crept back down to listen in.

"She just told me it was Molly." Ty said smoothly.

"Fucking bitch. I knew it was a bad idea to let her go out." Jordy was pissed, and Jez could hear the hint of a slur. She glanced over and saw the beer bottles on the coffee table. With a sigh, she leaned against the thin, wood door and listened.

"Molly? Is that her friend?" Boone asked. "She said her friend met this guy and they came to the party with him. But then her friend vanished. Jez was sitting in a corner looking like she didn't know whether she was going to cry or kill someone when I saw her."

There was a chuckle as the guys pictured her. "And you brought her home?" OB asked.

"I figured Jordy would be pissed if he knew she was there, but I wasn't about to leave her either."

"And your date didn't mind?" Ty's light voice laughed.

Boone chuckled. "She was pissed. She didn't believe me when I said Jez was a friend's sister. She demanded I take her home, so I did. That's why we were late."

"And you didn't think to call me?" Jordy's voice was still upset but he was buying it.

"To be honest, I was kind of hoping I'd get her home before you'd find out." Boone said, his voice sounded guilty. "Look, I know I should have called, but I didn't want to get her into trouble either. She's a good kid, Jordy."

"But she gets herself into some real pickles." Jordy sighed. He sounded tired and Jez felt bad.

There was a sound like footsteps. "Really man, I was just trying…"

"I know." Jordy interrupted him. "And I appreciate it."

"So, we're good?"

There was a smack as two hands clasped together. "Yea, we're good."

Ty, OB, and Boone's voices faded. The first two were thanking him as they moved away from the house. Jez got up and rushed up the stairs. She heard the front door open as she pushed into her bedroom. Falling onto her bed, she sat up nervously as his footsteps pounded up the stairs. Jez had left the door open and wasn't surprised when he stepped into the doorway.

"I'm really sorry." She said.

"What happened to the movies?" He was still pissed, but she could tell he was softening.

Jez swallowed and tried to look remorseful. "Molly and I were at the mall and she met these guys. One of them invited us to a party, and you know Molly, she just can't say no."

"What are you wearing?" He eyed her.

She looked down at herself. "Do you like it? I got it for the party."

"You look like a hooker." He said bluntly.

She allowed tears to swell in her eyes.

"Where're the other things you bought at the mall?" He was beginning to question her story.

"In Molly's car. She was supposed to bring me home, but Boone showed up." She swallowed and looked away. "He grabbed my arm and dragged me out like I was … like he was you." She snarled. "It was embarrassing."

Jordy smiled. "Good."

Jez rolled her eyes. "Ass."

"You're grounded."

"You can't ground me. I'm nineteen." She stood suddenly.

"And when you act like it, I'll treat you like it." He snapped. "Until then, you're grounded. Work, school, home. That's it."

"What about treatments?" She replied a little too snotty.

Jordy narrowed his eyes. "And treatments. But Ty, OB, or myself will drive you."

"Why not just volunteer Boone while you're at it." She put her hands on her hips. "Since you're volunteering everyone else to chaperone me. He did a pretty good job of playing you tonight."

"Fine, Boone too, since he seems to be able to control you about as well as the rest of us." He growled. Then turning his back on her, he pulled the door closed with a slam.

Jez listened as his footsteps pounded down the hallway, and his bedroom door slammed shut too. She smiled and let out a breath. Digging out her cell phone which was still in her pocket, she texted Boone.

'Thanks for tonight. I hope Jordy wasn't too big of an ass. I owe you one.'

She went to use the bathroom and changed into her pajamas. By the time she got back to the bedroom, she had his reply.

'It was fine. You don't owe me anything. That's what friends do. Sleep well, Jez.'

She smiled and crawled under the covers. With a sigh of relief, she drifted off to sleep.

☐

Chapter 18

Jordy woke Jez early. She was hung over and felt like shit, which Jordy made sure to tell her she deserved. He drove her to class and said that he would be the one picking her up. She glared at him like a sister would, but smiled weakly in relief as she sank into her seat. Boone glided into class just seconds before the professor, as was usual. But instead of sitting with the mob of cute girls in the center rows, he took a seat next to her. She gave him an odd look, but couldn't comment as the professor called the class to order.

"Grades on your papers were posted yesterday, in case any of you care." The professor called loudly as the group packed up and headed out.

Boone walked close by Jez and she glanced up at him curiously. "You don't have to hover. I appreciate the help last night, but I don't want to cramp your style with the ladies."

He chuckled at her. "Friends sit next to each other in class, Jez. And you couldn't cramp my style."

His words stung as they hit her. She wanted to say something in return, but just couldn't bring herself to open her mouth. Instead, she hitched her bag higher on her shoulder, and headed for the door.

"Where're you going?" He asked dashing after her.

As they moved down the crowded hallway, she looked over his shoulder, surprised to see that he was keeping pace. "Jordy's waiting. If I take too long, he'll come looking for me."

"He's still pissed, huh?"

They broke out the building and Boone stepped up next to her as they took the steps. Seeing Jordy waiting at the curb, she looked at Boone. "Thanks again for last night. I really do owe you one."

She turned her attention back to her brother and smiled before Boone could comment.

"Get in the car, Jez." Jordy ordered, holding the truck door open for her.

Boone stepped up just as Jordy closed the door. With a bright smile, he said, "Made sure she was in class and no one talked to her."

"Thanks Boone." Jordy started to walk around the truck, but Boone spoke out.

"You know, I don't mind bringing her to and from school. I've gotta come anyway."

Jordy glanced over at Jez. "You have other classes though. I don't want her just sitting around."

"Naw, man. This humanities class is the only one I have this quarter. I dropped my other one." He gave a crooked smile. "No cute girls in it."

"Thanks for the offer. Maybe next week." Jordy replied as he moved to the driver's side. "Don't forget you have to work later."

Boone chuckled, but his eyes glanced to Jez. "Wouldn't forget."

Jordy slid behind the wheel and Boone walked off. As he started the engine, Jordy looked at his little sister. "What's up with you and him?"

"Who?" She asked surprised.

"Boone."

"Nothing. He's just trying to be nice. He says he wants to be my friend."

Jordy looked over at Boone who was leaning against his black car, talking to a pretty brunette. Boone reached out and played with the girl's hair making her giggle and blush. Jordy snorted. "You're right. You're not his type at all. Don't know why I was worried."

Reaching over, Jordy turned on the radio. Jez turned her head and watched the world go by outside the glass. Tears stung her eyes, but she refused to let them fall. She knew she wasn't pretty. She was fat and ugly, and sick. She hadn't ever thought she'd had a chance with anyone, especially not a good-looking guy like Boone. But did they really have to rub it in?

Jordy took Jez straight to the shop where OB and Ty were waiting. One of them had opened the shop, and the other one was waiting for Jordy to return. Jez dropped her bag in the back and returned to the main room. "We're going surfing. See you when you get home." Jordy said as he turned to the door.

The other two followed but it was Ty that turned back to her. "If you need us, call. OK?"

Jez nodded silently. She knew she was being punished. Jordy couldn't really ground her, but he could, and would, make it extremely difficult for her to do anything other than the necessaries. The shop was quiet and Jez restocked shelves and cleaned to kill the time. She straightened and did the paperwork that she could. Finally, she got out her textbook and started to read.

At three, Boone came striding in. He smiled at her and she smiled back weakly. "What's wrong?"

"Nothing, just ..." she held up the textbook as if it would explain her mood.

Boone gave her a narrow look but moved into the back room to clock in. When he came back out, he stepped up next to her and leaned on the counter. "So."

"So?" She asked glancing over at her from the corner of her eye.

"You were going to tell me more about how you got so good at racing." He smiled.

Jez thought that subject was closed, and allowed her eyes to drop to his tattooed arms. The swirls of black licked up his arms like flames. "Why do you race?"

"I'm an adrenaline junkie." He admitted. "I like living on the edge, and racing takes me right there. Why do you like it?"

"People looked at me differently when I drove. I wasn't just Jordy's ugly little sister. I was Bel, the girl no one could touch. Well, almost no one." She added softly, her head dropping a little as a memory haunted her.

Boone stood up straight. "Is that how you think people look at you?"

Suddenly feeling uncomfortable under the weight of his words and the look in his eye, Jez moved away. "I need to check on something." She moved quickly to the back room and grabbed up a clip board. She wasn't sure what she was looking for and it really didn't matter. All she really wanted to do was hide, but Boone followed her. He grabbed the clip board from her hand and put it back down.

"Answer me, Jez? Is that what you think? Do you really think that your just Jordy's ugly little sister?" He was staring into her eyes and she had to fight to keep her emotions in check.

"No." She lied. "But before I started racing that's how people looked at me. Once I started winning, that all changed."

She waited the few breaths it took for Boone to register what she had said. He had heard what she wanted him to, and only that. She had left out so much, and she was terrified that he would see it all in her eyes. But he didn't. He smiled crookedly, and was about to say something when the bell to the front door chimed. Without a second thought, Jez spun on her heels and headed out to see the customer.

Unfortunately, it wasn't a customer. It was Molly with Paulie right behind. "Hey Bels! You disappeared on me last night."

"Oh sorry, I, um, ..."

She held up the bags from yesterday's shopping trip. "I thought you might want these."

"Thanks Molly." Jez smiled and reached over the counter for them. Molly passed them over, and Jez set them on the floor.

Molly's smile turned from 'happy Molly' to 'sexy Molly' and Jez knew that Boone had just come out of the back room. Paulie was instantly by her side. "Hey, no wonder Jez has been so busy working." She reached her hand across the counter eagerly. "I'm Molly."

"Boone." He said briefly shaking her hand. Then turning to Paulie, Boone reached out to him. "Hi."

"Ironic, isn't it?" Paulie's smooth tone worried Jez.

"What?"

"That you work for the girl who kicked your ass last night." Paulie replied smugly, and Molly laughed.

Boone nodded, but didn't respond. Instead, Jez asked. "Why are you here, Paulie?"

"A couple of reasons." He moved his eyes from Boone to Jez slowly. Wrapping an arm around Molly's shoulders, he said, "Had to drive my girl here. And I also owe you a little money."

"I don't want your money." Jez tensed. "Last night was a mistake."

"But you earned it. And you could earn a hell of a lot more, if you'd come back. The buzz was huge. I've been filtering calls all day from people who want a shot at you."

Jez shook her head. "I can't. Jordy…"

"Jordy smordy." Paulie interrupted. "You use to get around him before. You can do it again, if you wanted to. And I've got some big bills that say you'll want to."

Paulie pulled a wade of bills from his pocket and set it in front of her. Jez's eyes widened. "That's all from last night?"

"That's your cut from last night." He smiled. "I took my percent and the car fee, just like we use to do it. That's your piece."

Jez looked at the stack of cash.

"We can run it just like we did before, baby girl. You drive my cars. You win, you win big. You lose, …." He shrugged his shoulders. He didn't need to finish. She knew the deal. Boone tensed beside her though.

"She loses, what?"

Paulie looked over at him with his greasy smile. "She knows the deal."

Jez reached out and took the money in her hand. She didn't need to count it to know it was a lot. Tucking it in her pants pocket, she shook her head. "I can't. I'm sorry."

Paulie's smiled faded a bit but then it grew. "You just give it some thought, baby girl. You know how to reach me when you change your mind."

The bell to the door chimed and Paulie was lifted from his feet and flung backwards. Shock and confusion registered on his face, but only anger filled Jordy's. "What the fuck are you doing here? You're not welcome."

Paulie, being the weasel he is, put his hands up in surrender. "I'm just driving Molly."

"Hey Jordy," Molly put on the sexy smile again. "Long time no see."

"What do you want?" Jordy's anger now turned on her. Ty and OB entered and stood looking at the group, unsure of what to do.

"I was just dropping off the stuff Jez bought when we went shopping. She forgot them in my car last night."

Jordy glanced up to Jez, who nodded. Reaching down, she lifted the bags so he could see them. "She just dropped them off. They were just leaving."

Paulie was getting to his feet. "Yup, just leaving, man."

Jordy turned to watch as Molly stepped over next to Paulie. Looking at both of them, he raised his finger. "You stay away from my sister. You are not welcome here. And if I find out that either one of you were within fifty feet of her, I'll ...."

"Jordy." Jez said interrupting his threat. "It's fine. They were just leaving."

Molly glanced over just in time to catch Jez's look. She reached out and took Paulie's wrist. "Come on, Paulie. Let's go. Bye Jez."

They backed out of the store, OB and Ty moving out of their way to give them space. Then as they stepped through the threshold, Paulie turned back over his shoulder, "Bye baby girl."

Jordy just about took off after him, but Ty and OB stopped him by grabbing his arms. "He's not worth it man."

"Yea Jordy, he's just a little shit who likes to piss you off. Let it go."

Jordy eyed the blue car as it tore from the parking lot, then spun on his sister. "What the fuck!"

"I didn't know they were going to come in. Molly just wanted to give me my stuff." Jez was shaking.

Jordy fumed. "And what was that little toad doing here?"

"I don't know. Guess he gave her a ride."

"He said they were a thing." Boone added.

Jordy was beyond angry. He started to pace, and it reminded Jez of a lion in a cage. She looked to Ty and OB for help. They looked to each other and nodded, as if they both had the same idea. Ty moved over and leaned on the counter. "Hey Boone. You ever go to the Match Box?"

"No." Boone eyed them curiously.

"Really? It's this great gym just over on Chase Street." OB added to Ty's question. "Hey, Jordy, let's take Boone over to the Match Box and show him around."

Jordy looked up darkly. "Sure. I think beating the hell out of something might be good right about now."

"But I have to work." Boone said, but Jez looked over at him with big eyes.

"Naw, Jez's got it covered." OB smiled. "Come on."

Boone turned and headed to the back room. "Let me go clock out then."

"I'll do that." Jez said as she followed him, dragging the bag with her.

When they were standing next to the time clock, he looked down at her. "Are you alright?"

"Yes. Just be careful. Jordy's …"

"I know." He didn't smile. "Trust me, I know."

He walked away from her and followed the guys out to the parking lot. They all piled into the two cars and tore off down the street, leaving Jez alone. She dropped her head onto the counter as soon as they were out of sight. She didn't know what was worse. Being tempted by Paulie's offer, or seeing how pissed her brother was. Part of her wanted to go back. To call Paulie and tell him that she was in. The money that formed a hard spot in her pocket was so delicious. And yet, going back was something she promised herself she wouldn't do. Not after she'd seen the look on her dad and brother's face when she woke in the hospital. The terror they had felt at the thought of almost losing her in the car accident was too much guilt to bare. Even though they didn't know the truth, even though she'd protected them from the worst of it, she didn't think she would ever be able to put them through that again.

But then she remembered the feeling. The rush of adrenaline. The ability to focus only on the one moment in time. The looks of those around her who suddenly wanted to be her, or wanted to be with her. Those were things she craved. When she was out there on the strip of asphalt she wasn't ugly or fat, she wasn't someone's little sister. Out there, she was Bel. Bel of the ball, someone had called her once. And she really liked being that girl.

☐

Chapter 19

Jez was perfect for the next month. She did everything her brother asked without argument. She went to school, work, and treatments. She never once complained about being watched over by one of the three guys. Boone was social when he was around, but he was only around when he worked. It was a Monday after her dad had left when the next medical bill came. They had been receiving them slowly over the past few months, ever since her hospitalization at the beginning of summer, but this one showed the latest addition of hospitalization. The bill, which had just started the signs of going down, was now almost doubled again. Even with the insurance, they still owed well into the five figures. She wanted to cry. She had cost her family so much, and while she had the money to help out, she was unable to do so without bring up questions she couldn't, or wouldn't, answer. As she stared at the bill, Jez decided she needed to do something about it. Rushing up to her room, Jez pulled out the small box she kept hidden in the back corner of the top shelf of her closest. Aside from putting last month's winnings in it, she hadn't touched it in months. Sitting on her bed, Jez opened the lid. She had forgotten how much money she had saved up, but it looked rather impressive as it was piled in the colorful hat box.

She began the process of pulling out the bills, straightening them, and sorting them. It was quite a mixture of bills ranging from singles to hundreds and everything in between. She knew she'd won a lot over the years and had intended on saving it for college or for when she moved out on her own, but since neither was going to happen now, this seemed like a good use for the money. Once it was all sorted, she began the process of counting them out. When she was done, she realized she was just a few thousand dollars short of paying off the entire medical bill. It was then that she made the decision. It was both the easiest, and hardest, decision to make.

Before she could change her mind, Jez grabbed up her cell and text Paulie. 'I'm in.'

His reply was faster than she anticipated. 'What changed your mind?'

'I need the money.'

'I'll arrange it. Get back to you soon.'

Jez took in a big breath. There was no getting out of it now.

Three days passed before she heard anything from him. She was sitting in her class, Boone next to her, when her phone vibrated. She pulled it from her pocket. 'Friday night. Eleven. Don't be late.'

'I'll be there.'

She shut the phone off and pushed it in her pocket, trying to refocus on the lecture. Boone was watching her closely though. "Everything alright?"

"Sure." She whispered, not glancing at him.

He stared at her for a few more minutes, then returned his eyes to the professor. When class was dismissed, Boone stopped Jez from leaving the room so they could talk. In hushed voices, he leaned down and looked into her eyes. "What's happening?"

"Nothing. Why?" She held her blank expression.

He tilted his head. "You know you can tell me anything."

She looked around the room. The students had cleared the room and the professor was leaving as they spoke. "I don't want to put you in the middle."

"I would rather be in the middle and help you, than to be on the outside and have something bad happen." He narrowed his eyes. "Are you racing this weekend?"

"What would make you say that?"

He gave her a knowing look, his dark blue eyes cutting into her.

She swallowed and nodded. "Friday night."

"How can I help?"

"I need an excuse and a ride."

He thought for a moment. "I might be able to come up with something. Give me a couple of hours."

"I've got treatments. Text or call me when you've got something." She smiled and turned away from him, but then looked back at him over her shoulder. "Thanks Boone."

"Anytime."

She walked out of the room and down the hallway, breaking out into the daylight. Jordy was waiting, as usual. As Jez stepped up to her brother, Boone came jogging up to them. "Hey, Jez. Are you interested in going to the movie the professor mention? I could really use the extra credit."

Jez turned and looked at Boone. "Um, I don't know." She glanced at Jordy.

"What's this about?" Jordy asked curiously.

Jez was thankful when Boone jumped in. "Oh, there's this horrible foreign film playing at the … shit, that little movie theater on the east side."

"The Loft." Jez offered.

"Yea, the Loft. But it's only playing late on Friday and Saturday night. It's on its way out, I guess." He shrugged. "We get extra credit if we go and write a paper on it."

Jordy turned to face his sister. "You need to go?"

"It can't hurt. Extra Credit doesn't come around often." She agreed.

"I was thinking that I could take her if she wanted to go. Unless you want to go, Jordy. I mean, I'm sure you would love to sit through a three-hour foreign film with subtitles."

"No, it's fine." Jordy waved. "Friday night?"

"And maybe Saturday, depending on how horrible this thing is." Boone rolled his eyes. "God knows I might fall asleep."

The guys laughed but Jez didn't understand. Jordy nodded. "I can trust you to a make sure she's safe, right?"

"Absolutely." Boone promised. "It's just the movies, man."

Jordy nodded again, "OK. What time you gonna pick her up?"

Boone looked over at Jez. "Movie starts at eleven, I wanna be there by ten-thirty. It's a forty-five-minute drive. I know I'm going to need some coffee. Would it be OK to get her around nine?"

Jez looked to Jordy. "As long as you promise to stick with him and don't do anything stupid. Don't you dare get yourself into another pickle." Then Jordy turned to Boone. "This better be exactly what you say it is."

"Why would I lie? You think I want to go see some dumb ass foreign movie?" Boone smiled, "and I promise to have her home no later than three."

"Three?" Jordy sounded suddenly doubtful.

"Sure, three-hour movie and then the forty-five-minute drive home."

Jordy looked from Boone to his sister, then back. He didn't seem happy but with a sigh he nodded. "Fine. Get in the car, Jez, you got treatment."

Jez turned and moved to get in the car, Jordy walked around it, and Boone tried not to smile as he watched them go. Jordy dropped Jez at the center, and said he'd come back to get her when it was over. As soon as Jez was set up and her fluids running through the thin, plastic tube, she pulled her cell phone out. 'Thanks Boone.'

She set the phone down and pulled out her textbook. Her phone rang then, but it wasn't a text. "Hello?"

"Hey baby girl. Can you talk?"

"Paulie." She sighed. "What's up?"

"Can you make it earlier?"

"How early?"

"Ten. I've got a race for you at ten. If you win, you'll race at eleven." He sounded excited.

Jez didn't like the sound of that. "Two?"

"We've got some out of towners coming in. They heard you were back and wanted a crack at you. They run bracket races though."

"How much are we talking?" Jez kept her voice low.

He hesitated. "Buy in is a grand and a half, at each level."

"Three grand times four. Winner takes home twelve?" She was impressed.

"Ten. Handler gets two off the top."

"And how much do you get, Paulie?"

"My usual. Ten percent of the win and ten percent for the car."

"So, I can take home eight." She calculated.

"If you win." Paulie's smirk was obvious.

"And if I don't?"

"You're out your grand, plus a grand for the car." He said. "And the bonus for me."

Jez swallowed. "I don't do that anymore, Paulie. You're with Molly."

"The rules are the same. You agreed." Paulie sounded pissed. "And you better not back out, I've got a lot riding on this."

Jez thought it through. "Eight plus side bets for a win, right?"

"If you win."

Jez was tensing. She heard the beep of an incoming text but ignored it for the moment. "That car better be perfect, Paulie, because I plan on winning this. See you at ten." She cut the line and looked at the incoming message. As expected it was from Boone.

'I've got us covered. You don't have anything to worry about. Air tight.'

'Thanks. Race got moved to ten, will that be a problem?'

'Not at all. See you at nine.'

Jez breathed a sigh of relief and let it go. She would trust that Boone meant what he said, until he proved untrustworthy.

Chapter 20

The following night just before nine, Jez came down the stairs. She was dressed in jeans and a big sweatshirt, flip flops on her feet. She grabbed a note pad and a pen, and slid them in her bag. Jordy watched her closely. "What's that for?"

"Notes." She said as if it was a stupid question.

"It's going to be dark in the theater. You can't take notes."

She rolled her eyes. "Maybe not in the movie, but right after, on the way home. How else will I write the paper?"

"I thought you were going to see it twice." Jordy said, taking a swig from his beer.

She stopped mid-packing. "You're going to let me go?"

"If you need to. School comes first." He said just as the rumble of the muscle car could be heard at the street. "You'd better go."

She dropped the note pad and gave him a quick kiss on the cheek. "Thanks bro."

"No later than three, or I'd better get a call." Jordy stood up and followed Jez out to where Boone was coming across the yard. Jordy gave her a little kiss on the head and then told her to get in the car. As she did, Jordy spoke to Boone in a low voice. Jez had to strain to hear, but she got most of it. "Keep an eye on her at all times. Protect her with your life, understand. And remember rule number three."

Boone was facing away from her so Jez couldn't hear what he replied but the look Jordy gave her over Boone's shoulder was dark. She shut the car door, and waited. It wasn't long before Boone jogged over and climbed in. He started the car and pulled them away from the house. When they were a few blocks away, she turned to Boone. "What did he say to you?"

"Just reminded me how much he loves you."

"And you said?"

"Nothing." He smiled and tossed her a weird look. "Why?"

She shook her head knowing better. She was annoyed and he saw it.

"Look, I told him what he wanted to hear. I'd watch out for you, etc. Don't worry, Jez." He smiled at her. He turned on to the freeway.

"Do you mind if I change?" Jez asked, changing the subject.

"No." He smiled, then watched from the corner of his eye as she slid into the backseat.

"Eyes on the road, Hot Shot." She giggled as she noticed his eyes flash in the rearview mirror. He smiled and chuckled a little.

Jez pulled off her sweatshirt and made sure the tiny, tight tank top was covering all her important parts. Digging into her bag, she pulled out a lacy shirt that covered her but was very see through. Her flip flops got changed for three-inch heels, and she darkened her make-up then fluffed her hair. She put on big earrings and then slid into the front seat, just as Boone pulled off the freeway. She gave him a curious look. "Where are we?"

"A quick stop, to cover our tracks. Don't worry."

Jez glanced down at her phone. "I'm supposed to be there in twenty minutes."

"I know, relax. You'll get there."

Jez was nervous, but so far he hadn't proven untrustworthy. He pulled into the Loft movie theater parking lot, and found a spot in the back. A girl waited next to a sweet, jet black racer. She stood up and came over to Boone. Standing a little too close to him, she spoke in a seductive voice that annoyed Jez. "It's all ready."

"Thanks." He smiled. "I appreciate it."

"So we're even?" She asked.

"When this is done." Boone said. Grabbing the keys from her hand, he tossed them over to Jez who caught them in mid-air.

The girl looked over at Jez and narrowed her eyes. Turning back to Boone she said, a little too loudly, "You're letting the cow drive her?"

Boone tensed, his jaw tightening visibly. "She's the best driver I know."

The girl rolled her eyes and turned away. "We meet at one. Don't be late." She stalked away, giving Jez a nasty look.

Boone locked his muscle car, and walked over to where Jez waited by the black car. She gave him a curious look then tossed a glance at the girl storming off. "Do I even want to know?"

"Probably not." He admitted.

"Tell me about the car." She said running a finger along the back hood as she rounded it.

Boone moved to the passenger seat. "She's fast, and well-tended. I want you to drive her and see what you think. If you like her, you can drive her tonight."

"Paulie's got a car." She said as they got in.

"But Paulie's comes with strings. And I don't like things that come with strings." He said. "And I don't trust Paulie."

Jez had readjusted everything and started the engine. It purred like a kitten. "I don't trust him either."

Boone looked over and narrowed his eyes. "Then why work with him?"

"He's the only one I've got." She backed out of the spot and drove focused. She was getting a feel for the car and the road. The gears felt odd, but she settled in to their rhythm. By the time they made the track ten minutes later, she had the feel of the car. They drove into the pit, people moving away looking at her. Paulie eyed the car and stepped over to it when she popped out of it. Boone moved quickly to be right next to her.

"What's this?" Paulie asked curiously.

"I've got wheels." Jez smiled.

"They aren't as good as mine." Paulie said trying to hide his displeasure.

Boone stepped closer to Jez. "Maybe, maybe not, but I'm driving this tonight."

"It's your loss, and you know what happens if you lose." Paulie narrowed his eyes, anger growing in him. She recognized it and had to swallow down the fear.

Boone wrapped an arm around her shoulder, pulling her close. "She's not going to lose."

Paulie stepped close to them, but his words were directed at Jez. "A new boy toy, Bels? And a loser no less, not your style."

"Fuck you, Paulie." She snapped. A whistle sounded, and she turned back to the car.

Boone walked close to her, but it was Paulie that followed and started talking. "The guy drives a Nissan."

Jez held up her hand. "You know that means nothing to me. Tell me something I can use."

"He's an ass."

Jez rolled her eyes and turned to Boone. "Can you get the car to the line?"

He wasn't happy but took the keys from her anyway. As he started the engine, she gave him a wink and then wrapped herself around Paulie as they neared the monitor. The closer they got, the more she giggled and twirled her hair. Paulie whispered, "Ease up, too much."

She giggled louder and shoved his shoulder. In a loud voice, she said in a silly, high girlie voice, "You're really going to let me drive, Paulie baby?"

"Absolutely Bels!" He kissed her ear and turned his attention to the monitor and her competition.

The other guy looked at her doubtfully. "This is Bel. The Bel?"

Jez looked up at him and blushed. "You've heard of me?"

He rolled his eyes. "You're really going to let her drive?"

The monitor took the buy in and went over the rules. They were supposed to shake hands, but he kissed hers instead. "I'm sorry, girl. You know, if you weren't such a whale, you'd be kind of cute."

Jez yanked her hand back, her smile souring. She spun away from him, and stalked over to the car. As she did she heard him tell someone that it was going to be taking candy from a baby. She was pissed. That was the last straw. Paulie moved away, climbing back over the concrete barrier. Jez didn't look at him; she didn't want to see his smirk. Boone was still standing next to the car door, holding it open for her.

"Are you alright?" He looked worried.

"Fine." She snapped. She got behind the wheel, but Boone knelt beside her, keeping her from closing the door.

"Let it go."

"I'm going to enjoy kicking his ass." She snarled.

Boone looked up at him through the window. "I know him, Jez. Be careful. He doesn't play fair."

Jez looked over at Boone, all business and serious. "I got this. As long as this car is as good as you claim she is, this is a piece of cake."

The monitor banged on the hood of both cars and motioned for them to get ready. Boone leaned in and kissed her cheek quickly. "Go get him, Ace."

He backed off and shut her door. She cranked over the engine and smiled as her song started. It was a heavy metal song that had absolutely nothing to do with racing but everything to do with take a risk. Lemmy's voice screamed the first lines and she looked down at steering wheel and focused. She smiled at the Spade with the A inside that was in middle of the steering wheel. Ace of Spades. It was her song.

The tall, thin girl stood out in front of the car and waved the white panties before holding them above her head. Jez took in a deep breath, and cleared her mind. The count was four and the panties dropped. The other car was off the mark before Jez, but she was on his heels. She smiled as she kept on him, moving slightly up on him as they raced down the track. At the halfway mark, she made her move. She slammed the car into fifth gear, and tore away from him. As the song broke into the solo, she crossed the finish line a half a car length in front of her competition.

She pulled to a stop and cut the engine as the guy followed in suite. He jumped from the car, and rushed at her. She had barely gotten the door open when he was dragging her out by her hair. "Fucking, cheating, bitch!"

He tossed her down to the ground and raised his hand to strike, but a large body stepped in the way. Boone grabbed the guy's hand to stop him. "Touch her and die."

Jez climbed to her feet and stepped over next to Boone. "I didn't cheat. You just suck."

The guy fought to pull his hand away from Boone, who still held his wrist. Jez took advantage of the guy's inability to move and lashed out. With a fisted hand, she clocked him across the jaw. His head only moved an inch or so, but it stunned him, and everyone else that had stepped up.

Paulie and the monitor stepped up, "Ok, let's clear the field and get ready for our next race. Let's see who's taking on Bel." They started to clear the area, as Boone grabbed Jez up and move her back to the car. He got behind the wheel and drove back to the pit.

"Are you alright?" He asked her, obviously concerned.

Jez cradled her hand and tried to open and close it, but it hurt. "I'm fine."

When he parked the car, he turned to her. Placing a hand on the side of her face, he smiled. "I didn't know you had it in you."

She glanced over at him. She opened her mouth to speak but wound up closing it again. She popped the door open, "I need to see the next race." She stood and moved out of the car, over to the concrete dividers. It took several more minutes before the race began. During that time, Boone came over and stood next to her. She kept her eyes focused on the car and the drivers while he glanced over at her. She was watching for their tells and their hints. She found several on both drivers. Boone moved a step closer to her as the girl with the panties stepped up to the line. Jez watched even more carefully as the race began to start. The car closest to her was a white road demon and jumped the line fast, and kept the lead the entire way. The driver could barely control her though and spun out at the end, almost wrecking both cars.

Paulie voice startled Jez as he spoke in her ear. "Did you see that?"

"Yep." She said. "He's reckless. I'm going to have to stay in front if I'm going to win."

Paulie smacked her on the ass and walked away. Boone spun, but didn't leave Jez's side. Jez looked up at him. "You need to step back. I need to focus on this one. I can't be worrying about you while I'm trying to stay out of his way."

"You've got him easy." Boone smiled.

"He can't control that beast. It's too much for him. I can beat the driver, but I'm not sure I can beat that monster." Jez watched as the white car was brought back and reset on the line.

Boone looked at her deeply. "I believe in you, Ace. You got this." He moved away from her, disappearing into the crowd. She turned and watched the crowd. There was a lot of money being passed around.

Paulie stepped up and handed her a bottle. "Where's your body guard?"

"Hopefully moving the car." She accepted the bottle and took a swig. It burned going down and fired her up.

"You need to win this one." Paulie said. "Don't get me wrong, I'm going to enjoy it if you lose, but I would rather have the money."

"I'm not going to lose." She stated and took another sip from the bottle. She handed it back as her car came to the line. Boone got out and looked around for her. She climbed over the wall and made her way to the car. Just as she reached it, she tossed her head upside down and pulled her hair into a ponytail, then pulling her head back up, she tied it into a knot. Looking at Boone, she asked, "Got a pen or stick?"

He gave her an odd look, but she waved him off.

"Don't worry about it." She moved to get into the car when Boone reached out and grabbed her arm. She looked back and he leaned down and placed a kiss on her cheek. It was light and gentle, hardly a kiss at all.

"Good luck."

"I don't need luck." She turned around and got in the car. She turned the engine over and rolled the windows down. The music had been turned low, and she heard a loud yell from the group gathered by the other car.

"Take that whale down, Mike."

Anger, fueled by the shots of moonshine, flared in her. She set her jaw, and turned up the music. Motorhead filled the space around her and spilled out into the night. She focused on the girl who was walking out in front of the cars, and let everything else fall away.

Boone heard the murmurs from the group around him, and the sneers from the group across the track. He watched as a peace came over Jez, and a look he had never seen filled her eyes. He didn't know if she could hear the nasty things being said about her. He hoped not. While he waited for the race to start, he identified the guy who she had beaten in the first round. He was calling her all sorts of horrible things, and Boone made the decision to beat the crap out of him as soon as she won. Music spilled out of her car, and the group of supporters started to chuckle. Paulie stepped up and stood next to Boone. Someone behind them, chuckled. "She's going to kick his ass."

"Does she stand a chance?" Boone hated to ask, but he was suddenly very nervous.

Paulie looked over at Boone, a sly smile crossed his face. "If anyone can, it's Bels."

The panties dropped and they were off.

Jez kept pace with him but he pulled a little ahead of her. He began to swerve and she had to back off as he cut into her lane. In an attempt to get around him, she jumped into his lane and shifted gears. It took several seconds and a few attempts but she finally got by him. She took the lead in the last seconds and just barely beat him over the finish line. The white beast swerved again and cut her off after the line as they were coming to a stop.

Jez cut her engine and jumped from her car. She stocked over to the driver of the other car as he was slamming the car door in disgust. He turned to face her, as she approached. He held out his hand in a gracious jester, but she decked him instead. "You stupid, son of a bitch. You could have gotten us both killed. Either learn how to drive or don't get behind the wheel."

He rubbed his jaw and looked at her stunned. "I can drive her just fine."

"So you meant to cut me off and almost run me off the road?" She yelled. She gripped her fist again and let it lose on the side of his stomach. He doubled over a bit and she clobbered him again in the jaw. "You fucking, dumb ...."

Strong hands wrapped around her waist and lifted her from the ground. As she fought to get free, Boone's voice spoke in her ear. "Settle down, Ace."

She fought to get free a minute longer, but then slumped in his arms. He set her back down on the ground, but didn't remove his arms. The monitor was racing over to them, followed by a large group of people. There was quite a commotion until the monitor climbed up on the hay bales that sat at the end of track and blew his whistle. The group quieted.

"A rule was broken tonight, but since it had no bearing on the winner, the point is mute. Tonight's bracket winner is Bel of the Ball."

There was a cheer, followed by a grumble. But one voice was talking a little too loudly. "Can't believe that fat cow won. Guess she doesn't have anything else to do but drive, no one in their right mind would give her the time of day, let alone fuck her."

Jez swallowed and looked over at the guy who was talking. He was the one she had beaten in the first round. A thousand nasty things came to her mind, but she decided not to say any of them. She knew he was stating the truth. She slumped weakly, and Boone released his grip. He moved away from her and approached the man who was speaking.

"You are one pathetic guy." Boone commented and the man looked up at him.

"What?"

"Which is bugging you more, that you lost, or that a girl beat you?" Boone stepped right up in his face.

The man stood a little taller. "Girl? I don't see a girl? I only see a heifer."

Boone moved so fast hardly anyone saw it. His fist connected with the man's jaw, sending him to the ground. As Boone stepped over the fallen man, he raised his fist and hit him twice more before he was pulled off. Paulie and the monitor both yanked on Boone's arms, but it wasn't until Jez stepped in between the two men that he calmed down.

"Boone, it's time to go." She said sadness overtaking the joy of winning.

He shook Paulie and the monitor off and wrapped an arm around Jez. He walked her back to the car, and helped her into the passenger seat. When he closed the door, he moved around to where Paulie was watching. "Are we racing tomorrow night?"

"Sure. I can set something up." Paulie watched him with wide eyes.

"Do it." Boone said as he turned and got behind the wheel. He started the engine, and Jez turned the radio off. They drove in silence all the way back to the movie theater's parking lot.

When he pulled in to a spot, he looked over at her. "Can you drive?"

She began to laugh and gave him a confuse look. "Um, yes."

"Good. I need you to follow me." He got out, and she moved over into the driver's seat. "When we get back to my place, I want you to pull into the garage. I'll park behind you."

She nodded and he closed her door. She waited until he had pulled out of the parking spot before pulling out to follow him. In the darkness and isolation of the car, the emotions of the night hit her. She began to tremble and tears filled her eyes. She allowed them to fall, knowing that there was no one there to see them. When they arrived at the quiet street, he pulled to a stop in front of building that looked oddly built. Boone raced up the driveway and opened the garage door so she could pull in. As she did, Jez saw that the garages were built underneath the apartments, which was why it looked so different. When she had pulled all the way in, Boone pull the door partly closed and then went to get his car, pulling it into the driveway behind the racer. While he did this, she brushed away the tears.

When he had parked the muscle car, she met him in the garage doorway. "Do you want to change upstairs? You don't have to be home for another hour."

Jez looked down at herself. With a little smile, she admitted, "It might be easier. If you don't mind."

"Not at all." He smiled and offered her his hand. She took it and allowed him to lead her up the stairs to his apartment.

It was what you would expect a bachelor place to be. Mixed matched and hand me down furniture, new electronics, and clutter filled the main living room. "Sorry about the mess," he said embarrassed as he flipped on a light. "I wasn't expecting company."

She looked at him doubtful. "You know who I live with."

He chuckled and nodded. Then stepping over to her, he looked down at her, really seeing her. "Why were you crying?"

"I wasn't." She said defensively.

He sighed, his shoulders falling. "Why do you always try to be so strong?" He reached out and brushed away a tear she had missed earlier.

"I'm fine. Really." She grabbed the bag that he was holding, the one with her clothes in it. She turned and looked for the bathroom.

"In the next room." He said.

She didn't look back at him, but walked steadily to the back room. It was a one-bedroom apartment with the only bathroom attached to his room. She tried not to look too closely. She didn't want to pry. She used the bathroom and changed her clothes, replacing the lacy top with her sweatshirt and heels with her flip flops. She washed off her make up, then brushed down her knotted hair. When she was finished, she returned to the main room, where Boone was waiting patiently.

He asked if she felt better, and she shrugged. But when he walked up to stand in front of her, she swallowed and looked away. "You look prettier like this."

She looked down confused. "I …"

"I know why you dress like that for the races. But I like you better like this." He reached up and brushed some hair behind her ear. "You look more like you."

"Me?"

He started to lean down, his eyes pulled hers to his, but just before their lips met he pulled away. "I'm sorry. It's wrong. I didn't bring you up here for this."

"It's OK, you know. I…"

"No," he interrupted. "No, it's not OK. You expect me to take advantage of you, but it's not right."

Jez sighed. She knew what he meant but didn't say. He wasn't into her like that, and it would be wrong to lead her on. While it hurt, she had to accept the goodness in his honestly. She nodded, and blinked back the hurt. She looked down, avoiding his eyes. She didn't want him to see her pain.

"How's your hand?" He asked out of the blue.

"It's fine." She said and looked at it. She had completely forgotten about the pain in it. "How's yours?"

He smiled crookedly. "It's good. That ass deserved it."

"Thanks for … stepping up for me tonight. You didn't have to."

"Yes, I did." He turned her chin so she was staring at him. "Yes, I did."

"Thanks." She smiled and looked away, not wanting to meet his eyes for too long. "Maybe you should take me home now."

He nodded. "I asked Paulie to set up another race for tomorrow."

She was stunned. "Why? I can't get out…"

"I already cleared it with Jordy. He thinks we are going to watch the movie again remember. If I bring you home early, he'll know we didn't finish it and we'll have to go back again. Oh," He pulled something from his pocket and handed it to her. It was a movie ticket stub. "Just in case."

"And what do I say when he asks how it was?"

Boone laughed. "Tell him it was boring. I have someone going for us tonight. Tomorrow I'll have a summary that you can share with him."

"You had someone actually go to the movie for us?"

He nodded. "She owed me a favor."

"You did all that for me?" She was confused and flattered.

He smiled. "I'd do anything for you."

Boone reached out and took her hand. Without a word he led her down to his car and drove her home. She entered the house, while he watched from the street. Jordy was asleep on the sofa. She kissed his cheek and headed up to bed, listening to the Barracuda rumble away. As she lay in bed, Jez thought about the night. She remembered how he'd surprised her with the car, and then kissed her cheeks for luck. She recalled how she had wanted him to kiss her but how he didn't. Was he really just being a nice guy, not wanting to lead her on or take advantage of her? Or was there something more there? Something that made him afraid. She sighed because she didn't have answers, and she wasn't sure she would ever really want to know the truth, because it might just break her heart.

Chapter 21

Jez had to open the store the next morning. She was exhausted and had to work at getting herself ready and there. Once inside the shop, she snacked on pickles and drank her hydration drinks to get through. She did a lot of sitting as well. She had mixed feelings when Boone came in to start his shift. Her heart fluttered when he pulled in the parking lot, but then she reminded herself that he didn't want to be any more than just friends. He smiled brightly seeing her behind the counter. "Hey Ace, how are you feeling today?"

"Fine." She smiled. "You?"

He slid behind the counter and went to check in. "Great. Looking forward to tonight."

She looked up at him as he came over to her. "Tonight?"

"We're going again tonight." He said, his smile fading a little. "Remember."

"Oh yeah, sorry. It must have slipped my mind."

He looked at her thoughtfully. "Are you up for it?"

She forced a smile. "Yep. Absolutely."

"Good, because you've got three and I'm running two."

"Five?" She couldn't hide her surprise. "We never run that much."

"Paulie's set it up. He said there's a lot of interest because you're back on the scene." He leaned on the counter, a little close to her so he could talk softer. "Your near loss last night teased a lot of them."

"That wasn't my fault. He cut me off."

Boone smiled and placed a hand on the side of her face. "I know that, and you know that, and Paulie knows that too. But other people don't but that's what builds this up."

She knew and nodded. Paulie's brother had always told her not to make it look too easy. She wanted to say something, but the front door chimed and he pulled his hand away from her face just as Ty and OB walked in.

Ty looked between them and lost his usual cheeriness. "What's going on?"

"Nothing," Boone said as he pulled away. "She had some dust on her cheek I was brushing away. Can't have our eye candy dirty." He chuckled.

The others chuckled too and moved to the back room to clock in. Everyone but Jordy had been scheduled to work that day. He was expecting a busier day since he had placed an ad in

~ 129 ~

the paper with a great coupon to help bring in business. And as expected, they were swamped. Jez manned the register while the others helped customers and answered questions. It was a long day, and when eight o'clock rolled around, they were glad to ring up the last few customers and lock the door. As they did the final closing chores, Jez overheard OB ask Boone if he wanted to go to a party with them.

"Sounds great man, but I've got plans."

"Another date? Boy, you're getting more pussy than an old maid." Ty laughed, obviously not realizing or caring that Jez could hear him.

There was a noise, and Boone replied in a carefree voice. "I wish. Naw, I'm taking Jez to a movie."

There was an awkward silence before OB spoke. "You and Jez?"

"It's for our Humanities class. We have to see it and write a paper."

"Isn't that what you did last night?" Ty asked and Jez could hear the curiosity in his voice.

"Yep, but she fell asleep through it." Boone laughed. "I was worried I'd be the one to sleep through it, but she was out like a light."

"And Jordy's OK with it?" Again, Ty spoke.

There was a shuffling of feet. "Sure. It's not a date. You guys are more than welcome to come too. It's a foreign movie with subtitles."

"No." The word was strong and clear from both of the guys. Boone just laughed. Ty laughed louder. "I don't know if you are a glutton for punishment or if you really do dig her, but I can see why Jordy is OK with it. No one in their right mind would suffer through that for a girl."

Jez had finished the reports and money. She slipped it into the safe and got to her feet. She glanced at the clock. It was already a little past nine. She wouldn't have time to go home and change. Stepping out of the office, she pulled her phone from her pocket. Paulie had text her three times. Each was a reminder to be on time.

She rolled her eyes and text Jordy. 'Hey bro. Going back to see that horrible movie with Boone again. Grabbing a bite to eat first. Love you and see you as soon as possible.'

Ty and OB were already slipping on their jackets. Ty chuckled. "Have fun at your movie."

"Fuck you." Jez said irritated as they walked across the store and vanished into the night outside. When they were gone, she turned to Boone. "I don't have time to change."

"Don't worry about it. I got you covered." He gave her a wink, and headed out to his car. He waited patiently while she set the alarm and locked the door. When she got into the passenger seat, he smiled and tossed his head to the back seat. "You might want to change."

"But I didn't bring ..." She stopped when he rolled his eyes and pointed to the back seat. She gave him a nervous look but slid into the backseat as he suggested. She pulled open the bags and looked at the clothes. They were not what she had expected, and she hesitated.

"Just put them on." He said glancing up in the mirror.

"But..."

"Trust me, Ace. Just put them on." He smiled and returned his eyes to the road. He pulled onto the freeway and she pulled off her shoes, socks, and jeans. The skirt looked short, too short for her big thighs, and too small to fit her waist but she pulled it on anyway. Surprisingly, it fit her. Jez could feel the cool vinyl under her upper thighs as she sat back on the seat. As she pulled off her t-shirt, she pulled on the cut up one that was in the next bag. "Do I even want to know how you knew my size?"

He chuckled. "I'm a good guesser."

She smiled as she saw the Ace of Spades decorating the front of it in sparkly stones. She found a pair of thigh-high fishnet stockings with a lacy top cuff in a third bag. A ridiculously high pair of heeled boots hid in a box on the seat. She shook her head and wondered how she looked as she dug into her bag for her make-up and hair brush.

"What are you thinking?" Boone asked breaking the silence that had rested in the car.

She was yanking the brush through her tangles. "I was wondering how much of a hooker I looked like."

He frowned. "You don't like it?"

"I didn't say that. I was just thinking of what Jordy would say." She smiled and shook her head. "He about had a fit with the outfit I wore a couple weeks ago."

"That was really tame for this group." Boone said thoughtfully. "You looked hot, but it was very tame."

"Is that why you got me this?" She asked. "It's not so tame?"

He glanced up and she thought she saw a blush on his cheeks, but it could have just been taillight reflections. "No, I just wanted to see you in it." He cleared his throat and then said, "Besides, you're drawing attention. You need to stand out."

Jez had finished and was sliding back up to the front seat, carefully keeping the skirt down, when she noticed they were almost to the track. "We're not going to get your car?"

"I've got a friend bringing it." He said.

She looked over at him. "The girl from last night?"

He showed her a crooked smile. "Jealous?"

Jez glances out the passenger window. "I don't have the right to be. We're just friends, right?"

She heard him chuckle. "No, I wouldn't trust her to drive any of my cars. You'll meet him tonight."

Jez looked over at Boone, but his attention was on the traffic before them. He drove them around the lot and found a place without too much trouble. He got out and came around to open her door. She hadn't meant for him to do it; she had just taken a minute to do one last make-up check before getting out. But Boone was there reaching out his hand and helping her to her feet.

"Thanks."

He smiled and stepped out of her way.

"No, I mean it. You didn't have to do all this for me." She closed the door but stood just before him.

His eyes slid down her body, making her feel exposed and uncomfortable. She ran a hand down to smooth the short skirt. "I wanted to Jez."

"I can't pay you back for all this."

"I never said I wanted you to." He was watching her closely. "I've got something else for you too."

"You've done enough, Boone."

He sighed, and leaned against his car. "Look, in about two minutes we're going to walk into that crowd and you're going to become someone completely different. I don't know if I like her or not, but I understand her. And I know that she has to take over in order for this to work. I'm just trying to help you find her. We all need this to work tonight." He reached in and pulled out a black velvet box. Slipping it into her hand, he continued. "This is for her, not you."

Jez swallowed and opened it. Inside sat two diamond encrusted hoops, with a spade set carefully inside each. She was speechless and looked up stunned. She dropped her eyes back down to the sparkling jewelry. "Holy ..."

"Do you like them, Ace?" Boone sounded a little nervous.

"Um, wow, … they're too much." Jez said. "I can't …"

"Yes, you can, Ace." He punctuated her name.

Looking back up to him, she blinked. "How did you afford all this?"

He smirked and looked away. "I bought it all with what I won off our first race."

"But you lost that race."

He smiled but didn't answer her. Jez quickly pulled out the stud earrings she had on, and put them in the velvet box as she put on the hoops. She was just finishing when a familiar whistle echoed though the lot. "Baby girl! You look fucking hot!"

Jez turned her head and saw Paulie and Molly walking towards them, hand in hand.

As they approached, Paulie stepped up behind her and ran a hand up her thigh. "Ooo … baby girl."

Boone took a step toward him, obviously pissed about what he was seeing, just as Molly punched him in the arm. "Knock it off, Paulie."

"I was just playing." He chuckled and stepped away. Wrapping an arm around Molly's waist, he said, "We should go."

Molly and Paulie led the way, as Jez turned and followed with Boone right behind her. With each step away from Boone's car, Jez felt herself slip away and someone else took her place. When they came through the gate, the girl that followed Paulie and led Boone, was someone completely new. Paulie turned his head and looked at Jez, but his eyes went questioning, as if he saw a completely different person.

"I wanna see the car." She said so Boone could hear her. Boone motioned in the direction that he thought it was, as Paulie stopped to talk to the monitor.

When they were cleared of Paulie, Boone leaned down and in her ear whispered, "Are you alright?"

She smiled with one side of her mouth. "Absolutely."

The crowd parted for her as she approached her car. It looked the same as it had the night before, jet black with blacked out tail lights and tinted windows. There was one new addition to it though, a white spade with a red A inside was painted on the hood. Jez looked up at Boone. "Ace of Spades?"

"You're winning card." He smirked.

She walked over and pulled open the door. Taking a seat behind the wheel, she looked over the controls and interior. It was just as it was the night before too. She ran a hand around the steering wheel, and smiled. Boone stepped into the open doorway. "You like her?"

"I think I'm in love." She smiled up at him.

He licked his lips but looked away for a second. "I've put a new version of your song in there too. It's still Lemmy but with Slash and Dave Gohl. It's a great version."

"Can't wait to hear it." She smiled up.

A figure moved up behind Boone and placed a hand on his shoulder. Boone looked over and his smile brightened. "Skye."

"Hey Buddy." The man wrapped his arms around Boone in a big hug that was more family than man-hug. "How you been?"

Jez stood up, leaning gently between the car door and the top. She watched as the two men talked briefly about random things, then Skye's eyes drifted over to her.

"So, this is her?"

"This is Ace. Ace, this is Skye." Boone introduced them. She nodded, and he smiled. "Wait until you see her, she's fucking incredible."

"I can see that." Skye's voice was lust filled and Jez allowed herself to smile at him seductively. Normally, she would have shied away but right now she was Ace, and Ace loved the attention.

Boone reached out and slapped the back of Skye's head. "She's off the market. We already talked about this."

Skye looked darkly at his friend, but then smiled. "Taken doesn't mean I can't look."

"Look, but don't drool." She said with soft eyes. As she moved between the two men, she reached out and wiped his chin with her thumb. Rolling her head around to look up at Boone, she said, "I've got to go touch base with Paulie."

She made sure she rubbed her ass against Boone's leg as she pushed past them, and then tossed her hips to make the skirt bounce as she walked away, hoping they were getting a good view of her big ass and black panties. As she moved through the crowded pit, Jez screamed to get herself into control, but Ace had taken over completely.

Paulie and Molly were sitting on the concrete barriers, speaking to a few others when Jez stepped up. Eyes turned to her and she smiled seductively. "Are we going to do this or just sit around?"

Molly handed Jez a cup. Without a thought, she took a small sip of the strong liquor. "We're just waiting for the whistle."

The guy who had been ogling Jez, his left hand around his girl's neck, reached out with his right. "I'm Chris."

Jez looked at his hand and back at the girl, who looked less like a hooker than Jez did in that moment. "Ace."

"You here to cheer on your boyfriend?" Chris' eyes flashed over to the black Barracuda that Boone was pulling into the pit area.

Jez watched for a moment, and then turned back, giving Paulie the 'keep your mouth shut' look. "Yep. Are you who he's racing?"

"Naw, I'm racing some little girl. Apparently, she thinks she's the shit."

"Oh, you must mean Bel." Jez allowed her eyes widen. "She's really good."

He laughed. "I've raced all over the state, and never lost. I'm not going to lose to some bitch."

His girlfriend shifted her weight, obviously uncomfortable with term. Jez glanced at Paulie who was whispering something to Molly. She turned and darted off across the track. Jez returned her attention back to Chris. "Well, I'd better go. Boone doesn't like for me to be gone long. Good Luck with your race."

Jez turned back and almost skipped back to where Boone and Skye were standing next to the car. She wrapped an arm around Boone's waist and snuggled in to him. He smiled, wrapping an arm around her, but continued to talk to Skye about some car thing that Jez didn't understand. When they were finished, Skye looked over and saw something that caught his eye. With a wink to Boone, he drifted off after a too tight pair of gold spandex pants. When he was gone, Boone turned and leaned against the hood of his car, his arms looping around Jez, keeping her close.

"What's this for?"

"Show." She smiled. His smile faltered slightly, but he put it back quickly. "So, I met my competition."

"Oh?"

"He's arrogant. Talked about Bel like she was some school girl who didn't know her stick shift from her steering wheel."

Boone laughed outright. "Does she?"

Jez frowned. "Maybe."

He smiled and leaned in to her ear. To anyone around him it might look like he was nuzzling her neck. "Bel may not, but Ace knows how to drive like a bat out of hell."

Jez giggled and pulled back slightly. "So, who are you racing tonight?"

"Have no idea." He replied. "Don't really care."

She turned serious. "You don't want to size up your competition?"

"Nope." He pulled her close. "The only thing I want to size up right now is you."

Jez tensed. "Please don't fuck with me before I race."

"Ace," he let go of her and brushed some of her hair behind her ear. "I'll never fuck with you."

Her heart started to pound in her chest, but a familiar whistle sounded and pulled her attention. She pulled away from Boone and turned to her car. She pushed everything that had just happened away, as she pulled her seatbelt on. She turned the engine over and moved the car to the start line. The monitor approached her window and smiled at her.

"So, you're going by Ace now, Bels?"

"I don't care what you call me, Mel. Just get this damn race started."

Mel the Monitor smiled and allowed a little laugh. "You don't want to face him?"

"Not until I kick his ass."

"You know the rules. Good luck, baby girl." Mel tapped on her door and walked away.

She watched as Mel approached the other guy's window and spoke to him. They talked for a few minutes longer than Mel had talked to Jez. When he was finished, he tapped both hoods and motioned for the panty girl to come forward. When the girl got into place, Jez reached over and tapped on the stereo. The familiar fast beat blared through the speakers and she smiled. The flag girl raised her hands and on the fourth beat dropped them.

☐

Chapter 22

Less than a minute later, Jez crossed the finish line, her opponent two seconds behind her. As she turned the car and pulled to a stop, the other car pulled alongside. The guy, his arrogance gone now, stood sheepishly and rubbed his head as he rounded the hood of his car. Jez cut the engine and climbed out. As she stood, the guy's face moved from embarrassed to shocked, and finally broke into a smile.

"Well, I'll be damned."

"So, you can add losing to some bitch to your resume." Jez smiled sweetly.

He shook his head. He held out his hand and this time she did shake it. "You can drive, girl."

"Thanks. You're not too bad yourself." She said. Mel came over and let them know they had to move the cars for the next race. He gave Jez a wink and let her know that she should line hers up. "You're racing third and fifth. Boone's got the next slot and fourth."

"Isn't anyone else racing?" She seemed surprised.

Mel smiled. "Not tonight."

Jez nodded and started her engine. She hit skip on the CD and moved slowly through the crowd to get her car around the track. She had hoped to see Boone race, but the song that came on next stopped her from getting out of the car when she lined it back up. It was rock song that was on the edge of being a ballad. She looked down and saw the song title and artist roll along the stereo's screen: 100 in a 55 by Pop Evil. The words crushed her chest and she had to turn them off before the song ended. She had to focus and not think. If she started thinking, she was doomed.

Molly knocked on her window and gave her an odd look. Jez stepped from the car and pushed it all down. Molly held out the cup and Jez took it. "What's with you?"

"What do you mean?" Jez said after taking a second sip and handing it back.

Molly's face wasn't happy or friendly. "You. Your name, the outfit, the attitude. What's going on?"

Jez shrugged. "Bel's got a reputation and it's hard to live down. Maybe I just wanted a fresh start."

"You're trying to distance yourself from Paulie?" Molly asked and Jez caught the hopefulness in her voice.

"I'd like to, yes."

Molly smiled. "You got a thing for Boone?"

Jez looked away not wanting to answer.

"He's a hottie. And he seems into you."

"He's a friend of Jordy's." Jez replied.

Molly leaned in and smiled. "But he still brought you here. That's saying something." A cheer came up from the crowd and both Jez and Molly looked over. "You're going to be up soon."

Jez moved back to the car and Molly walked away. Jez pulled the car to the starting line and waited. She focused on her movements. She mentally went through the race, picturing it over and over again. A bang on the car hood pulled her to the moment. Mel gave her a look and she smiled. Rolling down the windows, she hit the radio on and turned it back to the first song. The monitor pointed at her with a knowing look, and chuckled as he walked away. Three minutes later, the race was over. Jez was shaking hands with a green haired girl who was close to tears at the amount of money she had just lost.

Jez moved the car around to the starting line for the last time. Paulie hadn't spoken to her and she hadn't seen Boone or Skye since before that first race either. It wasn't typical but nothing about this night was typical. As she lined up, she watched the crowd storm the cars and drivers at the other end. She couldn't tell who won, and once again she hoped it was Boone. A knock on the window started Jez, and she jumped in the driver's seat.

"Jumpy much?" Mel's voice spoke from outside the window.

Shaking her head at her stupidness, Jez climbed out. "What's up?"

"The other driver wants to meet you." Mel said looking odd.

Jez narrowed her eyes. "Why?"

"I don't know, Bel, Ace. Fuck, you need to pick a name and stick to it." He said slightly annoyed.

"I have a name. But you all keep giving me different ones." Jez pointed out.

Mel rolled his eyes and walked away. He led her over where the flag girl stood flirting with Skye. He stopped and gave her a look that said for her to clear out, which she did quickly. Then turning back to the two drivers he spoke. "Ace, Skye, Skye, Ace."

Skye reached out and took her hand, giving it a kiss.

"You both know the rules. Right?"

"No cheating, stay in your own lane, first one to reach the end wins." Sky said with a smile.

~ 138 ~

Mel threw his hand in the air, and turned to walk away. "Why do I even bother?"

Ace looked at Skye curiously. "Why the met?"

"I wanted to apologize."

"For what?"

"For making you lose." He stepped close to her. "It's not my idea." Without another word, he turned and walked to his car. Jez watched, confused about what he had just said, then turned and got into her car. Flag girl returned with her panties and took her mark. Jez hit play on the radio. Skye looked over and gave her a sad smile. Jez turned up the radio and turned her eyes back on the white panties.

On the count of four, the white cotton fell and the two cars pulled off the line. Skye had quick reflexes and a fast car. Ace struggled to keep up with him. The music blared and fed her need for speed. She clutched and tossed it into fourth, but Skye was already pulling away. She pushed it more, almost catching him. She tossed it into fifth and then it all went horribly wrong. The car began to shake and rattle, and a horrible scream came from the engine. She fell behind by half a car length as they crossed the finish line.

Skye spun his car around and stopped. The crowd was loud and rushed him, forcing Jez to hit her breaks to keep from hitting some of them. She killed the music and rolled the windows up. It took her a few moments to calm down. Her anger was through the roof, but she knew she had to keep it in check. She closed her eyes and took some very deep breaths. She opened her door, and slid out. She shut the door and turned to walked towards Skye. She had planned on shaking his hand, then slapping his face. But a hand reached out and grabbed her arm. She spun on her heels and was face to face with Paulie.

"Tough loss, Baby Girl." He smiled. His eyes were narrowed and he weaved on his feet.

"How much have you had to drink, Paulie?" Jez's anger was quickly dissolving.

"Not enough to forget our deal. You lost, your ass is mine." He cornered her against the side of the car and ran a hand up her thigh. "I like this skirt. It'll make it easy."

"I thought you were with Molly now." She asked softly.

"Molly ain't got nothing on you, Baby Girl." His fingers brushed her panties, and Jez hit it away. He smiled with a sneer. "You know I like it when you fight me."

"I … I… can't." She tried to move away from him, but he grabbed her arm.

"You can and you will. It's a debt and you'll pay up." He held her arm so tight that she whimpered in pain as he pulled her through the crowd. He dragged her to the edge of the group and then across the track. She saw that his car was parked in the far corner, opposite to where most of the others were. It was half hidden in a dark shadow. It took a few moments for Jez to put it all together, but when he shoved her in the backseat, she tried to fight back.

"You fucker. How much? How much did you pay?" She kicked at him.

He chuckled. "I didn't pay. You lost."

"My car was sabotaged." She screamed.

He climbed in and held her down. Tears streamed down her face as he forced her legs apart. His hand yanked her panties, snapping the elastic. Jez screamed and tried to fight him off, but her head began to spin and her heart raced. One of his hands grabbed at her wrists, holding them tightly, while the other fought his zipper. She knew when he had freed his dick because his fingers shoved into her roughly, scratching her and bringing tears to her eyes. She screamed more from fear than from the pain. Her heart started to skip beats and her head became fuzzy. Her vision began to grey.

Suddenly the weight was lifted off her, she saw Paulie get pulled away by his feet, his face slamming down on the edge of the door jam. Jez heard the scuffle but was too far gone to do anything. She had the thought to smooth her skirt down and cover herself, but as she did, the darkness rolled through her head.

☐

Chapter 23

Jez came around slowly. She was being held in someone's arms, but she was cold. Her head felt heavy and a headache was just starting. Bright lights flashed across her face, and she whimpered.

"It's alright, Ace, I got you." Boone voice was soft and gentle. She felt his arms wrap a little tighter around her.

"Fuck man. She doesn't look good." Another voice said, and it took Jez a few minutes to remember it was Skye.

Jez fought back to consciousness. There was pain, but she set it aside and focused on the anger that was growing in her. She remembered Skye apologizing before the race. She remembered the car and how it failed. The movement slowed and Jez's feet lowered to the ground.

"Think you can stand for a minute, Ace?" Her feet hit the gravel, but her heels wobbled. "Skye, man, hold her."

Jez waited until Boone's hands were replaced by a different set. Then she balled her hand into a fist, and opened her eyes. Boone was moving to unlock the car door, and Skye's attention was on him. In a smooth turn, Jez slammed her fist into Skye's jaw. Between his distraction and her hit, he stumbled back, stunned, and fell on his ass.

Boone turned at the sound of the hit. She staggered and started to fall back. Boone grabbed her though just in time. After making sure, Jez was stable, Boone started to chuckle.

"Damn Ace," Skye said from his place sitting on the ground. Rubbing his jaw, he looked at her. "What was that for?"

Lashing out had used the last of her energy though, and Jez could only look up to Boone. "I'm tired."

He gathered her up and set her in the car. Skye was climbing to his feet and Boone spoke to him a moment after closing her door. Skye laughed and rubbed his jaw. He shook hands with Boone then wandered off. Boone settled in next to her behind the wheel. He started the engine and the music blared. Jez cowered and he reached out to turn it down. "How do you feel?"

"Not good." She admitted.

"What can I do?"

Jez let out a shaky breath. Tears filled her eyes. Her silence drew his attention.

"Baby girl, what can I do?"

"Don't call me that, please." She whispered.

He glanced over again. He could see her trembling. Pulling to the side of the road, he parked. Slowly, gently, he reached out to touch her shoulder. She shuttered. "Jezebel. You're safe now."

She nodded her head, tears still streaming down her face.

He scooted over just a bit and opened his arms to her. She hesitated for a moment, but then moved into his grasp. He didn't say anything, just held her while she sobbed and trembled. It felt like a long time before she finally stopped. But even when she quieted, he still continued to hold her.

"I'm sorry." She said pathetically.

Boone smoothed her hair, but refused to let her go. "For what?"

"For breaking down. For losing." Her voice was little more than a whisper.

He swallowed and there was a look in his eye that she couldn't identify. "Don't you ever apologize for crying in front of me."

She looked away, but he pulled her chin to him.

"I mean that, Jez. I don't ever want you to hide from me. I don't want you to hide from me, or lie to me. OK?"

She nodded, but bit her lip. She could see that there was something behind his eyes. "But then the same goes for you."

"I'm not going to promise that." He said. "I'll promise to keep you safe, and protect you. And I promise to always love you. But I can't promise to always be honest with you. You can always, and I mean always, trust that I will do right by you, Jezebel."

She looked down at his hands, wrapped all the way around her and gripping her shoulders. "Why are your knuckles scuffed?"

"Because I beat the shit out of Paulie."

She looked up into his eyes. "Because he broke your car?"

He looked down at her with furled eyebrows. "Because he broke you."

"But your car..."

"Stop worrying about my car, Jez."

"But he broke it so he could have me." She said, fighting down the emotions

"I broke my car." He said confused and irritated. "I broke my car so you'd lose."

She pulled away from him. "Why?" Her eyes grew wide. "You wanted me to lose. You wanted him to hurt me?" Her breathing grew rapid, and she got light headed.

"Hey, hey, Jez, no, no, that's not why." His eyes widened watching her grow pale. "Jez, listen to me. I needed you to lose. I can't explain why, but I did it for you. You have to trust me."

"But you knew, you knew, I told you, I ..."

"I didn't realize he ..." He took a breath trying to calm himself. "I didn't know he was going to take you so fast. I thought I could protect you. I tried. Skye and I got to you as soon as I could find you. I'm so sorry, Jez, you have to believe me, I ..."

"You pulled him off me?" She was confused.

He nodded. "I beat the crap out of him and told him if he ever laid a hand on you again, I'd kill him. And I mean that."

She was growing tired, her head felt fuzzy and her blood pressure was dropping. "Take me home, please."

"Jez?"

"It's got to be late. Jordy will be looking for me. Please take me home."

She moved away from him, and after a moment he turned back to the wheel. The drive was silent and cold. Boone would look over at her every once in a while, but she just looked at her hands resting in her lap. When they were pulling off the freeway, he suggested she change. Without a word, she crawled into the back seat and pulled on her jeans and t-shirt. She pulled her shoes on and pulled out the earrings, dropping them back in the box with the heels. She found make-up removers in her bag and wiped off most of what was left after her tears. She dragged a brush through her hair and hopped back into the front seat just as they pulled onto her street.

Jez had the door open and was jumping out of the car before Boone got it to a complete stop. He looked over and called to her, but she hiked her bag on her shoulder and rushed up the yard. She stumbled on the steps, and Jordy opened the door for her. Ty and OB were both sitting in the living room as well.

"You alright?" Jordy asked, his eyes flashing to Boone darkly.

"Yep, just tried." She started up the stairs. When she got to the top, she called back, "Good night."

Jez headed for the shower. Under the hot water old feelings surfaced. Paulie's hands on her, the fear, the voices telling her she deserved it. It took all her strength to try and fight off the urge to fall into other old habits as well. But in the end, those won out, and she allowed the sting of a blade to eat the emotional pain ripping her apart. With a heavy heart, and spinning head, Jez crawled into bed. She heard the front door close as Ty and OB left, then listened as her brother climbed the stairs. He knocked on her door and pushed it open. "Are you sure you're alright?"

She nodded and forced a smile that Jordy could see through easily. He walked into the room and took a seat on her bed. He was tense and his jaw worked hard. "What happened? Did he do something?"

"No." She shook her head. Tears glistened in her eyes. "He didn't do anything."

"Then why are you upset?"

"Sad movie." She lied and he gave her the look that said he knew she was lying. With a sigh, she looked away. "He didn't do anything."

It took a minute but then it sank in. "You like him. You thought he liked you too."

Jez nodded. She knew if she opened her mouth that he would see the lie, then she realized that it wasn't really a lie after all.

Jordy reached out and pulled his sister to him. He wrapped her up in a big hug. "I'm sorry, Jez. You're a special girl, but you're just not his style. He's too fast. Don't worry, the right one will come along."

His words stabbed into her heart. She allowed the tears to fall and allowed him to comfort her. She knew it was wrong to lie to him. She knew it was wrong to allow him to comfort her something he didn't understand. But she needed it. She just needed her big brother right then.

☐

Chapter 24

Jordy let Jez take Sunday off to rest. The dads came home Sunday night so Jez had an excuse to stay home. Her dad said that she looked tired and pushed for her to take most of the week off. He covered her shifts and the other guys helped out. Jordy had told Ty and OB that she had a crush on Boone, but told their father that she had been pushing too hard. Ty and OB knew that it was best to give her some space from him. None of them even asked if it was possible that Boone would like her too, they just assumed he wouldn't. Jordy took Jez to treatments but left to surf while she was infused. Boone text her three times on Monday. But she didn't reply. She didn't even read them.

Jez went right home after treatments and laid on the couch. Jordy took over for his dad at the shop, who came home and spent the time with her. They watched movies and ate popcorn, just like when she was little. It was nice. On Tuesday, Jez wasn't up to going to school. Jordy normally worked the morning shift, so Jez stayed home with her dad.

When the tenth text message that day came through, he looked over at her. She ignored it, cutting her phone completely off. With a deep breath, her dad came over and sat down on the sofa next to her. "Are you going to keep ignoring him?"

"Who?" Jez didn't take her eyes off the television, even though he had her full attention.

Dad smiled. "The guy who's been texting you for the last two days."

"How do you know it's a guy?"

Dad chuckled. "I'm not stupid, Jez. I remember what it was like to be in love, and hurt, and confused."

She looked over at him, then fell over into his arms. "I just don't understand."

"Some guys are just stupid. They think with their dicks and not their brains." Her dad held her close. "One day, you'll find the right guy. He'll see through your walls, and he'll love you at your best and at your worse. He'll fight for you, protect you, and probably even piss you off."

Tears filled her eyes. "What if I already found him? But I can't have him."

"And why couldn't you have him?"

"Because I'm not good enough. Because I'm not pretty enough. I'm not ...." Tears choked her.

Dad lifted her chin so he could look in her eyes. "If he's made you feel like that, then he's not the right one."

"It's not him. He … he makes me feel normal."

"Is there someone else?" Her dad was really trying to follow. "You don't know where you stand." He nodded.

She sighed and stood up. Nervously walking around the room, she debated how much she should say. "He told me he loved me."

"OK, I'm going to chalk this up to a girl thing. I really wish your mother was here." Her dad wiped a hand over his face. "But let me try. You like this guy and he likes you. So what's the problem?"

"I'm not good enough for him." She said weakly.

"Who says?" His eyes narrowed.

"Everyone." She came and fell down on the sofa. "Daddy, I'm sick and I'm fat. I'm ugly and I have nothing to offer anyone."

Her dad pushed her up and looked at her. "You are beautiful. You have some challenges, yes, but you have the biggest heart of anyone I know. You work hard and fight harder. There is not a man alive who is good enough for you."

She wanted to argue, but she knew it was pointless. Her dad loved her and he only saw the good in her. "So, what do I do?"

"You talk to him. Tell him that you're scared. You explain about your condition. If he's a good man, he'll take you in his arms and promise to do his best to protect you and help you."

"And if he's not a good man?"

"Then he wasn't the right one, and it's his loss." Her father pulled her close and kissed her head.

The conversation helped Jez feel better even if it didn't give her any answers. Boone had done exactly what her father had said a good man would. He had promised to protect her and love her. And she had walked away, terrified.

They sat quiet on the couch watching television for several long minutes before, she ventured to ask. "Daddy, what happens if I screw this up?"

"If it's meant to be, you can't." He smiled and pulled her close. "And if you're worried about your brother, remember he just wants what's best for you. He'll come around."

Later that night, when Jez was tucked into bed, she pulled out her phone. She debated looking at the messages, but elected not to in the end. Instead, she left it off and cried herself to sleep.

Chapter 25

Jez was set to open the store on Wednesday so all the dads and boys could go surfing. She was still tired but wanted the guys to have a good time. She had been monopolizing the time and she was beginning to feel guilty. Jordy dropped her off at the store and asked if she was going to be alright.

"Of course." She smiled. "Go and have fun. I'll see you all tonight."

She got out of the truck but Jordy called to her. "That's not what I meant. He's supposed to come in for the afternoon shift. Will you be OK? If not, I can come back."

"I'm going to have to face him sooner or later. I might as well just get over myself." She smiled.

"Did you tell him? That night you came home so upset, did you tell him you liked him?"

Jez signed and turned back, just before shutting the truck door. "No. I didn't tell him."

She slammed the door and walked away. She felt a stab in her chest where the thorn of honesty pricked her. She hadn't told Boone that she loved him. He had spoken everything to her, but she hadn't said a word. And that was what she regretted most.

She unlocked the store and got it ready to open. She spent the morning cleaning, organizing, restocking, and straightening. She worked on the paperwork and then the schedule. She tried hard to work opposite shifts from Boone. She was sure he wouldn't want to see her again. But with the dads leaving again and their class schedule, Jez knew she'd have to work with him sooner or later. She did her best though. When it was finished, she sat and stared out at the cars that drove past. She fought back the memories and her tears. Not one single customer came in.

At three o'clock the door chimed for the first time all day. She looked up with her customer service smile, but it quickly faded as Skye walked toward her. His smile was bright and he looked almost relieved. "So you aren't dead?"

"No. Why?" She asked suspiciously.

He leaned against the counter, eyeing her. "No one's seen or heard from you for a few days. We were beginning to worry."

"We?"

"Boone, myself, Mel, Molly, and even Paulie was getting a little concerned."

"Liar." She stood up straight. "Now do you need something?"

"I need a lot of things." He searched his pockets until he pulled out a list. "Here."

She opened the folded paper and looked at it. As she glanced down, she nodded. "Most of this stuff we have, but there are a few things I'm going to have to order. They won't be in for a week or so." Then her eyes fell on the last thing on the list.

'Talk to him.'

Jez looked up at Skye. "What?"

"Boone spilled his heart to you, and you ripped it out. That's not a very nice thing to do." Skye said honestly.

Jez looked down, tears filled her eyes. "I know. I didn't mean to. I just didn't know what to say."

"You didn't know what to say?" He repeated in disbelief. "You say. I love you too. Or you're crazy. Or …"

"Or I'm not good enough for you." She said softly, knowing that's what she should have said.

Skye had been about to say something, but he just looked at her dumbfounded. After a moment of recovery, he said, "Good enough? What are you talking about?"

She shook her head and waved him off. Jez put the paper back down in front of him. "Write your name and number on the paper and I'll place the order. Someone will call you when it all comes in."

Skye narrowed his eyes. "Give me your cell."

"What?"

"Give me your cell. I'll put my number in your phone. You can call when it's all here." He was playing the cool guy again and she sighed.

"I left it at home. Just write your number on the paper please." She sighed.

He picked up the pen and then leaned across the counter. "I will if you promise to put it in your phone."

Jez rolled her eyes. "Fine."

Skye smiled and wrote the information down on the paper. Sliding it back to her, he stood and smiled. "I look forward to hearing from you, Ace."

Giving her a wink, he turned and walked out the door. She watched him carefully. He was almost to his car when he pulled out his cell phone and made a call. She couldn't tell what he was saying but he did turn back and look at her with a sly smile before sliding behind the wheel of the emerald green street racer. She recognized it as the one he had driven the night of their race.

When he was gone, Jez took the time to start looking for the things on the list. She found a crate and began pulling some of the items from the shelves. The things they didn't have in stock, she worked on ordering. It took a little over an hour for her to do it, but she was thankful for the distraction. She was just finishing when a battered blue hatch back pulled into the parking spot in front of the door. She watched as the familiar looking, dark skinned man pulled open the front door making the chime sound. He was dressed in a pair of nice slacks and a button-down shirt and tie. His normally wild hair, pulled back into a tamed ponytail. It wasn't until he removed his sunglasses that Jez could even begin to identify him. But he was already smiling at her.

"Mel? What are you doing here?" She breathed, as if someone else was there to hear.

He looked shocked, and almost hurt, by her tone. "Delivery." He pulled out a large manila envelope and set it on the counter before her. "From Paulie."

"Why didn't he bring it himself?"

"Because he's more terrified of your boyfriend than your brother, but he doesn't want to piss either one of them off anymore."

"Boyfriend? I don't have …" she realized who he meant. "Boone."

Mel raised his hands. "Hey, I'm just a monitor. I don't get involved in the disputes. I just try to solve them. Paulie asked for my help. He needed this delivered to you, so here it is."

"Thanks Mel." She said grabbing it off the counter.

He nodded and turned to leave, but then stopped and looked back at her. "Hey Ace, are you coming to the big desert run in a few weeks?"

She shook her head no. "I don't have car."

"Too bad." He frowned. "I've got a lot of people who want you there. Looks like it could be big money."

She hated the thrill she felt inside. "If I had a car, I'd be there."

"Well, find one, Ace." He smiled and left her to her own misery.

After counting the money in the envelope, then mentally adding it to cash she had at home. Jez realized she was still three thousand short of paying off the medical bills. She knew she could make it up in a few local races, no problem. Or maybe in the one day of races at the desert run. But she didn't have a car. For a half a second she debated calling Paulie, but that wasn't going to work. If he was too scared to deliver her winnings when she was alone, he'd never allow her back on his team. Frustrated and growing tired, Jez tucked the money in her bag and looked at the clock.

Almost five. Boone should have been in two hours before. Had it been anyone else, she would have just called them, but she couldn't call Boone. She couldn't even think his name without tears choking her. Calling him wasn't going to happen. So, she let it just slide.

She closed and locked up at eight, just like any other weeknight, then walked the two blocks home. The street was filled with cars, as was typical, but one of them stood out to her. A jet black, Barracuda sat across the street from her house. Jez was silent as she made her way across the yard. She could hear the voices talking as she approached, and decided to eavesdrop a little before going in. Jez slid under the porch railing and sat on the hard wood under the open window.

"This is stupid." Her brother said.

"What is? That I love her? Why is that stupid? She's amazing, beautiful, talented, smart." Boone.

"She likes you too." Ty added. "She's been a mess ever since last weekend."

"Shut it, Ty." Jordy snapped. "You don't even know her. You can't possibly love someone you don't even know."

"What?" Boone asked, he seemed shocked.

"She told me that she wasn't good enough for the guy she liked." Her dad's voice was calm, too calm. "But I'm not sure she had that right."

"I'm not asking to marry her. I just want to be able to ask her out on a date." Boone was losing his cool.

There was a moment of silence before her dad said, "Why would you need to ask us? She's a big girl."

Again another moment, and Jez could picture them looking at each other. "Because it was made very clear when I got hired, that she was off limits."

"We're just trying to protect her. Jez isn't very smart when it comes to picking boyfriends." OB said.

"Paulie." Boone said a little angrily. "I've already taken care of him."

There was a moment of silence.

"You were the one who beat Paulie?" Jordy asked, a little surprised.

Jez worried that he was going to tell them everything but instead, he lied. "Saturday night when I took her to get something to eat before the movie, he showed up. He'd had too much to drink and got grabby with her. I put him in his place."

There was a collective sigh, and then Ty offered. "I don't know whether to thank you or kick your ass myself."

Obviously confused, Boone spoke, "That little shit deserved it and more. Had she not been there, …"

"Jez was upset when she came home. We assumed you had led her on or hit on someone else, or somehow hurt her." Jordy explained.

"I told her I loved her. I told her I'd never let anyone else hurt her ever again."

Tears formed in Jez's eyes. It felt so wrong to be listening in, but she couldn't stop. She wanted to hear it all.

"And what did she say in return?" Dad asked.

"Nothing. She didn't say anything." Boone sounded different, hurt maybe? "I didn't know what to think. I tried to text her and call. I just wanted to let her know it was alright if she just wanted to be friends. It'd suck, but I'd rather be her friend than nothing."

There were a few moments of silence, someone walked around the living room. Then Ty asked, "So if you thought she wasn't into you, why'd you come here tonight?"

She heard Boone sigh. "A friend of mine went into the shop to order some parts for a project we're working on. He talked to her for a little bit. He told me that she seemed off. And she had said something that didn't sit right with him. He said that she looked rough, and with her comment to him, he knew that she was hiding something. I wanted to make sure she was alright." He sighed, "I guess I thought if I came here, and spoke to you all, that maybe she'd give me a chance."

"You don't need our permission." Dad said.

"I may not, but I think she does." Boone said. "Have you ever seen her when she's not surrounded by you all? She's a totally different person. She's brave and feisty. Gorgeous and confident."

"Are you talking about at school?" Ty again.

"No, I mean out, like at a party or shopping, or anywhere. If she thinks she's alone, she's a completely different person. I'm not saying she's better but she's different. It's like when she's with you all, she has to be this prim and proper little girl. She can't like guys or take risks, or be herself."

"I don't want her to get hurt. Last time …" Jordy's temper flared.

"I don't know what happened last time. But I know that she's so much stronger than you give her credit for. And I do see that she needs protection sometimes, absolutely. Does she push too hard to be too strong? Sure. But it's because she's trying to keep up with all of you." Boone stopped and she heard footsteps. "Do you know that she asked me why I wanted to be her friend? And what I wanted from her? She had this idea that everyone wants something from her, or wants her to be a certain way. It's a big weight on her shoulders, and it's making her tired. Look, I'm not trying to tell you things you don't know. And I'm not claiming to know her better than any of you. All I want is a chance to get to know her. I want to take her out. To try to show her how special I think she is."

Tears spilled down Jez's cheeks. She didn't know what she should feel. Part of her wanted to be angry, since all this was supposed to be taking place without her knowledge. But part of her wanted to rush in and throw her arms around Boone. She had never, ever heard someone say all those things about her. And either he was one hell of a good liar, or he really meant what he said. Then the words that he said to her that night in the car came back to her. "I can't promise to always be honest with you." And it hit her. He wasn't being honest. He was out right lying to her dad and brother and friends. She didn't know why, and she wasn't sure she cared. All those amazing words, about her being pretty and strong, and brave, they had all been lies. Did he even care about her? Or was that a lie to?

The pain was like a vise grip on her heart. She couldn't take it anymore. Sliding back under the rail, Jez debated going into the house to confront him. She could call him out in front of everyone. Jordy would kick his ass for sure. That thought stopped her. Even though he lied, she still wanted to believe him. She wanted to see the best in him. Like she had with Paulie.

Jez took off walking. And with each step, she compared Paulie and Boone. They were all too similar now that she could see it. But there was one massive difference, she liked Boone. And she really wanted to believe that he liked her too. But what was truth and what was lies?

One step in front of the other. One tear drop after another. Jez didn't know where she was headed, nor did she care. She just kept walking.

She reached the beach and set her feet in the soft sand. Sinking down to remove her shoes, she saw the bruise on her leg where Paulie had grabbed her. It was almost gone, but she could still see it. It was then that it hit her. She knew now why Boone had come to the house, and why he had said all those things. He wanted her to race. He needed her to race. If he got her family's approval to take her out, then he could take her to the races without having to make up excuses. Just like Paulie had.

But as much as Boone and Paulie were the same, they were different too. She didn't think Boone would hurt her like Paulie did. If he had only wanted sex, he could have taken that on so many occasions. He hadn't. He hadn't hurt her in anyway, aside from the most painful way. Nothing he could do to her body would ever hurt as much as shattering her heart.

Jez walked to the water and put her toes in it. It was freezing, and she realized she couldn't think about Boone and racing here. This was where her peace was, not where her brain was. She needed to be at the track. She could think clearly about racing at the track. Things were in perspective there. On the water things were fluid, changing and peaceful. But at the track, she had tunnel vision. She could focus on what lay ahead. That's where she needed to be right now. She'd be able to see clearly there, without the saltwater in her eyes.

Checking her bag, Jez made sure she had enough money for the taxi. She found the money Mel had dropped off and knew she had enough to get her there and back several time over. Without a second thought, she returned to the street. Five blocks later, she got to a busy street where she was able to use an app to catch a ride.

☐

Chapter 26

The driver seemed nervous about leaving her at the deserted drag strip, but she gave him a big tip to make him go. Jez had to crawl under the loose chain link fence, before she could cross the parking lot and into the grand stands. It felt odd to be here when it was empty. It was dark and quiet. Usually it was filled with people and cars, music drifting from various speakers. But tonight, she was the only one there. The pits were empty, the stands silent. She jumped over the concrete barriers and walked out into the center of the asphalt strip. Standing there, she looked at one end, then turned and looked at the other. Three and a half miles of asphalt in a straight line. Two miles of race strip with a half mile at one end for start-up and a half mile at the end to slow with the center mile for racing. Jez walked slowly back to the starting line, thinking about how her life was so messed up. She lived at opposite ends of the spectrum.

On one end, her family. Beach city people. Hard working, family oriented. They built their entire life in safety. Working jobs that had been handed down from one generation to the next just like the homes they lived in. They took pleasure in the simple things in life. Working hard, free time spent with family and friends at home or at the beach. It's a simple life, and she did love it. There was comfort in simple.

But she also loved the fast lane. She loved the focus and the adrenaline. The speed and the danger and the edge put everything into focus. Things seemed clearer when taken two miles and just seconds at a time. She needed this to be able to go back and live the other. She had to have both. If she didn't, she realized sitting there on the white start line, neither one mattered.

Lights flashed across her, and Jez turned to look. Her immediate response was that it was security or the police. Her family would be pissed, but at least she'd have a ride home. She stood and took in one last look at the track. She knew what she had to do. Her feelings for Boone set aside, she needed to race just as much as she needed to surf. She needed him as much as she needed her family also. Friend, or something more, she'd take him in any way she could. He understood her better than anyone.

"Ace?" A voice called making her turn around. A thin beam of light crossed her face, making her look away until it lowered. "Ace, is that you?"

Sighing, she moved to the approaching figure, meeting him at the concrete barrier.

"What are you doing out here?" Skye looked around at the vacant arena.

"Thinking. What are you doing here?"

His eyes fell back on her. "Looking for you."

She looked down as she climbed over the barrier. "Why?"

"Why? Because your family is going out of their minds right now." He spoke with such surprise, as if he didn't understand how she could not know this. "They're walking up and down the beach and driving to every place they could think of looking for you."

"How'd you know I'd be here?" She walked next to him as they crossed back to the fence, where his car was parked just on the other side.

"I didn't. Boone text and asked me to drive out here. He said that he thought you'd be here." Tears stung her eyes as he held up the fence allowing her to slide under. When she was clear, she held it for him as he did the same, and as they brushed off the dirt, he added. "He would have come himself, but he ..."

She looked over at him as he moved to the driver's side. "He what?" Her tone was icy, and Skye looked across the car at her. "He didn't want to give me the wrong idea?"

"He didn't want your family to know." He replied confused.

Jez opened the door and slid into the darkness. After a moment, Skye dropped in also. He started the car and turned down the radio. Before pulling away, he pulled out his phone and made a call.

"Got her. Yep, right where you said she'd be. Sure." Cutting the line, Skye pulled off the dirt shoulder and drove them back to the west side. They didn't speak until Skye pulled into the parking lot of the auto parts store.

"Thanks for the ride. Sorry I put you out." She popped the door open and put a foot out.

"Hey Ace." Skye said before she could stand. Turning back to look at him, Jez saw an expression she didn't expect: honesty. "I don't know what's going on with you and Boone, but it's been a long time since I've seen him like this. Be careful, OK?"

Jez got out of the car and shut the door. Be careful. The words echoed in her head as she crossed the parking lot and started down her street. What should she be careful of? She kicked herself for not asking. But then, she never did know the right things to say or the right questions to ask in the moment. She turned herself inside out as she got closer to the house. The lights were on and there was a group of men on the porch. As she cut across the neighbor's yard, Jordy saw her first.

Jumping over the porch rail, he dashed at her and wrapped his arms around her. "Where the fuck have you been?" His angry tone was contradictory to the warmth of his hug, but she knew it all came out of his love for her.

"What's wrong?" She tried to act innocent. "I was hungry after work, so I went to get some food."

A second set of arms engulfed her, and her dad's musky scent filled her. "It's been four hours since you closed the store, Jez. We've been worried sick."

"I'm sorry." She said honestly. "I didn't mean to worry you."

They released her from their embrace, but each man took hold of her arms, walking on each side of her as if to make sure she didn't bolt. Ty and OB smiled to her from the porch. The other dads were moving across the living room as the three moved up onto the porch. Boone leaned against the farthest beam, his eyes shadowed, and Jez tried not to look at him. Ty pulled her in for a hug. "Where've you been, Pickle?"

"I was hungry after work, so I walked down to that new place over on Spruce. I didn't realize how far it was though." She smiled weakly.

"Why didn't you just call? One of us would have taken you." OB asked.

She shrugged. "Guess I just needed some time to think." She allowed her eyes to glance over at Boone, but they didn't stay there long. She was wrapped in hugs by the other two dads and then everyone backed into the house to call off the search, leaving her and Boone alone on the porch.

He stood up and made to move away, but as he passed her, she reached up and touched his arm stopping him. "Thanks."

"For what?" He didn't smile. His eyes didn't move to her.

"For not giving my secret up." She said so softly he almost didn't hear her. "You could have just told them, but you didn't."

He looked down at her, eyes filled with conflicted emotions. "We're friends, Ace. Friends don't rat each other out. Friends help each other."

"Then help me race." He looked away from her eyes, looking out at the dark night. Jez turned her head down, glad he didn't see the tears in her eyes. She hadn't meant to say that, but it had just come out.

He sighed. "OK."

Taking the three steps in one, he crossed the yard and got into his car. Jez didn't turn to watch him drive off. She was too busy trying to stop the tears that were falling down her cheeks.

☐

Chapter 27

It took a while before everyone calmed down and went home, each giving her a big hug before leaving. When the house was quiet again, Dad sent Jordy up to bed reminding him that he had to open the store tomorrow. He seemed reluctant to go, but they all knew that Jez was about to get the talk. When Jez was alone with her dad, he motioned for her to come sit at the dining table with him. He had pulled a beer from the fridge and rolling the bottle between his hands nervously. She sat silent and waited.

"It's hard for me to see you as the young woman you've grown into. I still see you as the little girl who kept trying to do everything her big brother did." He smiled. "And getting yourself into some real pickles in the process."

"I know, Daddy, it's OK. Jordy and the others still see me that way too." She smiled.

"But that's my point. We treat you like a child, but you're not. You're a beautiful young lady. And it wasn't until that boy, that man, pointed it out to me that I understood." He took a swig from his beer. Jez stayed quiet, unsure of what to say. "When you got in that car accident, I thought …"

He stopped choked on the memory, and Jez reached out and took his hand. "I know, Daddy."

He shook his head. "No, that's the thing. Keeping you safe was the only thing that Jordy and I could think about from that phone call until now. We just wanted to keep you from getting hurt again. But in doing that, we've hurt you. For some reason, our good intentions backfired. Instead of protecting you, we haven't allowed you to live. We've kept you from …"

"Daddy, please, stop." She begged. "This isn't just your fault. I'm scared too. After everything that happened, with mom and Paulie and the accident. I didn't want to put myself out there. I didn't want to get hurt again either. This isn't your fault. It's mine."

"But if we didn't shelter you …"

"I don't know who to trust, Daddy." Tears brimmed in her eyes. "My head and my heart are a mess. And I don't know which one to listen to."

"And I think that might be my fault. I was so angry after your mother left that I wasn't a good role model for what love is. And I can't say I've given you a lot of wonderful role models to look to either." He finished his beer and tossed it into the trash can. "The only thing I can say is that if you follow your heart, it might get broken. But then again, it might not. But if you follow your head, you'll regret never knowing that might have been."

"Do you regret any of it? You and mom?" She asked. They had never spoken like this before. Her father was a prideful and private man. He had never once opened up about how he felt about her mother, or just how much it had hurt when she had left, even though his children could see it plainly on his face every day.

He shook his head, but didn't look her in the eyes. "I only regret that I couldn't make her happy. You know, you remind me of her. She had this light in her eyes when …" He stopped and smiled at a memory he didn't share. "She loved the high."

She gave him a minute with his memories, then quietly asked, "Daddy, what do I do?"

"About what baby?" He pulled from his thoughts and smiled softly at her.

"Everything."

He sighed. "I want to tell you to stay here. Stay in this house, work at the store, listen to your brother. But I know that's not fair. You need to do what you want. You need to live your life the way you want to live it, not how we want you to." He reached out and took her hand again. "I love you, baby, and I will always be here for you. And I promise …. I'll try … not to tell you I told you so."

He smiled and so did she. She reached out and hugged her father. She could see the tears in his eyes and knew this was one of those once-in-a-lifetime conversations. He was being honest with her, even if it killed him to do so. "I love you, Daddy."

"I love you too, Pickle."

Chapter 28

The next morning, her father drove her to school. He smiled as he said he'd pick her up, unless she called to tell him she had a ride. "And who's going to give me ride?" She asked doubtfully as she jumped out of the truck. He chuckled as if he knew something she didn't, but she slammed the door before he could say anything. She sipped on the bottle of grape flavored hydration drink as she walked through the halls and into the classroom.

The professor was already in the front of the room, and smiled at her as she made her way to her usual spot. She stopped short as she saw Boone sitting in her seat though. He offered her a crooked smile and slid over one chair as she moved slowly toward him. "I wasn't sure you'd make it today. You were out awful late last night."

"So were you." She mentioned as she sat down. On the desk in front of her sat a black velvet box. Jez swallowed as she looked at it.

He chuckled and leaned in to whisper in her ear. "You left it in my car the other night, Ace. Don't look so scared."

She glanced over at him as he leaned back in his chair. Picking up the box, Jez opened it and saw the hoops he'd given her the other night. "I thought you'd want them back."

"Why? I bought them for you." He asked his eyes searching her curiously and he smiled. "Besides, they're not really my style."

The professor called the class to order, ending their conversation. But about halfway through the class, Boone wrote a note on a piece of blue lined paper and slid it over between them. 'What are you doing after class?'

'I have an appointment.'

'Need a ride?'

'Dad's dropping me off.'

'Let me take you.'

'No.'

'Why?'

'I don't want', Jez stopped and crossed off the words. She didn't want him to see her get her treatments. But she didn't want to tell him that. He looked at her darkly, and she could feel his gaze even though she was staring at the teacher. As if the professor could see that Boone wanted to talk to Jez, he told the class it was time for a break. As soon as the words were out of his mouth, Boone grabbed Jez's arm and lifted her from her seat. Half dragging her, half walking her out of the room, he pushed her into the hallway.

"You don't want what?" He was controlled but angry. Jez didn't answer but dropped her eyes to the ground. "Don't want me to take you? Don't want me? What don't you want, Jez?"

"I …" She started but she stopped, biting her lip to try and stop the tears that were forming.

"You promised to be honest with me, Ace." He lifted her chin after he had spoken and was taken aback by the tears he saw.

"I don't want you to see me like that." She whispered.

"Like what?"

"Getting treatments. I don't want you to see me get treatments." She allowed a tear to fall. Embarrassed, she turned her head away.

He deflated, and fell against the wall. "What if I told you that I wanted to? I want to know. I want to know everything about you."

"No, you don't." She said, her eyes falling to the ground.

He lifted her chin. "Why is it so hard for you to let me in?"

When she didn't answer, he pulled his cell phone from his pocket. He scrolled through his contacts and found who he was looking for. Placing the phone to his ear, he smiled at her, then leaned down so she could listen in.

"Hello?"

"It's Boone."

"Hey, I thought I might hear from you." Her father's voice chuckled.

"If it's OK with you, sir, I'd like to take Jez to her appointment today."

There was a moment of silence, then he said. "OK, and maybe you could take her to get something to eat after."

"Well, I have to work. I blew off last night so I'd better be there tonight. I'd hate to get fired."

"I got you covered, Boone. Don't worry about it." Her dad sounded odd. "Just be careful with my baby."

"Kid gloves, sir."

Jez heard her father hang up and leaned back away from him. "Why'd you do that?"

"Because I wanted to." He took her hand and led her back into the classroom.

When class was over, he carried her bag and took her hand. Leading her out to his car, he smiled as he held the passenger door open for her. As she got in, she noticed the looks she was getting from the girls around them. Jez covered her face with her hand and leaned her elbow on the door.

"Are you alright?"

Dropping her hand, she smiled tightly and nodded. "Fine."

He touched her arm and she looked over at his face. "What's wrong?"

"They're looking." She said with a toss of her head.

He looked out the windows and saw the people standing around the parking lot. With a chuckle he started the car.

"What's so funny?" She asked irritably.

He backed out of the parking spot. "On the track, you don't notice that everyone's looking at you, but here, you notice the one girl."

"On the track, they aren't seeing me." She said softly, playing with her nails.

Boone reached over and placed a hand on hers. He looked over at her with a thousand different thoughts spinning in his head. In the end, he didn't say any of them. "So, where're we going?"

"Do you know where the cancer center is on Campbell?"

"Um..."

"Campbell and Tenth. The big blue building."

"Yeah, sure." He nodded making a right turn. Jez reached down and turned up the radio. The song was a heavy one, a new release from a popular band. She liked it, and tapped her finger to the beat. Boone just smiled.

He parked in the closest spot he could find, and held her hand as they entered. Jez checked in with the front desk and got her pager. She smiled at the receptionist, who glanced at Boone and winked at Jez. Boone's attention was elsewhere though, taking in everything around him. He noticed the pleasantly painted walls and the pretty art. He saw the various ages of the people who sat and wandered the halls. Some looked healthy, others not. Many of them wore scarfs or hats over their bald heads. He was suddenly very conscious of his bald head.

Jez led him down the hallway and into a corner doorway. "I need to use the bathroom. Would you mind getting me an ice coffee?"

He looked down at her. "Sure. Any particular flavor?"

She smiled and looked down for a second before meeting his eyes. "Just tell Joe it's for Jezebel. He'll know."

As she turned and walked into the ladies' room, she thought she saw a flash of jealousy erupted in Boone. She wasn't sure about that though and rushed for the safety of the bathroom. After doing her business, she stood at the sink and washed her hands. She looked at herself in the mirror and took a deep breath fighting off the nerves. This was the first time she'd let someone see this. Even her dad and Jordy hadn't been with her when she got treatments. It wasn't that it was horrible or anything, but it hurt some, and she hated that it made her feel so very weak. She had also wanted to keep her family from this because it was a reminder of all that she had gone through and all that she still battled daily. And now, she was letting someone in. And not just anyone, but Boone. She wondered why he wanted to do this, and why was she allowing it? She began to tremble, and pushed the thoughts aside, not wanting to give it anymore of her energy right now.

The older man with greying hair finished making her drink and asked about something for Boone when Jez met up with Boone. She heard him ask for a soda, then he paid. Jez stepped up and smiled at the man behind the counter. "Hey Joe."

"Hello Jezebel." His eyes flashed to Boone for a second. "You have a good day."

"You too." She smiled and took the drink that Boone handed over. She left the small room, giving Joe a blush filled smile.

As they entered the elevator, Boone looked over at her with a crooked smile. He opened his mouth to speak but the pager in her hand vibrated. She looked down at it and pressed a button. The doors opened and she led him out into a sterile white hall. It was lined with pretty pictures of landscapes that looked generic. They walked by a waiting room that was empty and continued down to where a nurse in pink scrubs waited with a clip board.

"Sorry, I needed a fix." Jez smiled and held up her plastic cup.

"No problem, Jezebel." The lady was middle aged with salt and pepper hair and bags under her eyes. "I see you brought a friend today. That's good." Then turning to look at Boone, she said, "Jezebel never brings anyone. It's nice that she has some support."

Boone smiled but didn't say anything. The nurse led them down the hallway, but at a crossroads of halls, Jez stopped and placed a hand on his chest. "Stay here a minute."

He gave her a dark look, but did as she asked. He could see her follow the nurse down to the end of the hall where she put her drink on a small window ledge. She stepped on a large platform, and Boone's concern faded. He smiled realizing that she was being weighed. The nurse said something to her and Jez looked over her shoulder with a smile. They returned to where Boone waited and the nurse led them down one of the corridors. They past two rooms that held hospital beds, and then two more room that each held four recliners that were pushed into each of the corners. She finally stopped at the end of the hall and pointed at the room on the left. Boone reached out to put his hand on Jez's back as they moved into the room. There was only one recliner open out of the four, and Jez made her way to it. A chair sat beside her chair and Boone sat in it. The nurse smiled and stepped from the room.

Jez glanced around the room. She didn't know anyone here. There was an older man sleeping in the chair next to her. A woman who had earplugs in watching a movie, wrapped in a blanket, across from her, and in the last chair sat a teenager, ear plugs in, eyes closed as she focused on something besides the pain. Jez swallowed and offered Boone a smile as his eyes returned to hers. They only stayed there briefly as he continued to take in their surroundings. She didn't even see the monitors and IV stands anymore. The red haz-mat bins and cabinets full of medical equipment were just as much a part of the background as were the landscape pictures on the wall. But to Boone this was all new, and while his face didn't register any emotion, she knew it must be bothering him.

Reaching out she wrapped her hand around his. "You are alright?"

He looked back at her and then smiled. "That's my line."

She giggled and then turned her attention to the nurse who approached. "Hi Margie."

"Jez," she smiled, turning her attention to Boone, "and friend."

"Margie, this is Boone. Boone, Nurse Margie."

They shook hands briefly, then Margie stepped over to the sink. "It's nice to see Jez bring someone around. You two been friends long?" There was a way about that Margie said friends that made Jez squirm in her chair.

"Long enough." Boone said, but he didn't say long enough for what. Jez gave him a curious look.

Margie snapped on her gloves and came back to Jez, who was pulling off her t-shirt, revealing the tank top she had on underneath. Margie put some cream on the small bump that was just under the inch-long pink scar on her chest. Boone watched closely, as if interested. Margie noticed and smiled. "It's just a numbing agent. It helps when we put the needle in."

Boone watched as Margie put a clear plastic patch over the cream, and then walked away. "Does it help?"

"A little." She smiled. His eyes were locked on her chest, and she knew he was looking at white blob under the clear patch, but she couldn't resist. Pointing to her eyes, she smirked. "Hey, up here, Mister."

Boone looked up suddenly, but then chuckled. "But the view is nice."

His comeback made her blush and look away for a minute. When she looked back, she was more serious. "Why did you want to come?"

"I told you I want to know."

"Why?"

"Why what?"

She was growing frustrated. "Why? Why do you want to know? What do you want to know?"

He reached out and placed a hand on her cheek. Looking her right in the eye, he said with all seriousness, "I want to know everything about you."

"Why?" She whispered.

"Because I love you."

She was about to call him a liar, tears brimming in her eyes, when Margie came back and distracted her. It stung when Margie ripped the plastic patch off and Jez hissed and looked down. Margie looked up apologetically, "Sorry."

Boone watched closely, but Jez took in a deep breath, laid her head back, and closed her eyes. She hated this part the most. She felt Margie clean the area, and then felt the nurse hold the sides of the quarter size PORT. Jez focused on her breathing and clinched her fist. The needle prick was painful and brought tears to her eyes. When Margie laid another plastic patch over the needle to hold it in place, Jez felt a finger brush her cheek. Jez opened her eyes and saw the worried look on Boone's face. The single tear balanced on his index finger. She smiled at him and relaxed. Margie hooked the IV tube up to the needle in her chest and stepped away for a moment.

"Are you alright?"

Jez nodded and smiled as brightly as she could. "Yep."

Margie returned with a syringe. She inserted the needle into one of the splits in the tube and patted Jez on the shoulder. "OK. Do you need anything?"

"Nope, I'm good. Thanks."

Boone looked at the IV bag and the tube that was now attached to Jez's chest. He looked at the pump that controlled the flow of the fluid, and the fist that Jez's hand was still held tightly in. Margie walked away and stopped to check on the other patients in the room. Boone scooted closer to Jez, and wrapped his hands around her fists. "Please tell me what's happening."

She took in a deep breath and relaxed. Her hands loosening enough for him to push his fingers into them. "I'm OK. The medication is rough."

"What's the medication for?"

"It helps keep the infections away. They started it in the hospital. I only have a few more days of it."

"And why the bags?" Boone looked up at the clear fluid pumping into her.

Jez glanced up at it. She sighed and looked back at him. "Did they tell you anything?"

He watched her but didn't answer.

"You know how I got started in racing and why I kept doing it." She swallowed. "But no one told you why I stopped?"

He brushed some hair back from her face. "Someone said there was an accident."

She nodded. "Last June, I was racing this guy. He drove a Jag. I don't remember much except it was a sweet Jag painted bright yellow with black racing strips. He looked like a bee. I was in the lead at the half."

Boone's eyes narrowed.

"I got her across the line before him, but as soon as I braked, there was nothing there. Someone had cut the lines...I don't remember anything else." She physically had to shake off the chill.

"Yes, you do. Tell me."

"I came to in the car, upside down. I couldn't see anything but darkness and random lights. But ..." She stopped and he watched as she processed her words. "Everyone was leaving. Not one person stayed."

Boone's jaw tightened, the muscles in his cheek went hard as stone. "Paulie? Molly? Mel?"

"They all just split. I don't know how long I was there. They tell me that I called 911, but I don't remember. Everything is blurry until I woke up in the hospital."

Boone was silent for several long moments.

"What are you thinking?"

"I wish I hadn't just beaten him into a bloody pulp the other night. I wish I had killed him." His voice had taken on a tone that she had never heard before, dark and almost evil sounding.

Jez rubbed his arm. "It's gone and done. I've put it past me. I don't want you doing something stupid over this."

"He left you to die in that car." Boone's voice was dark.

"Please Boone. Please just let it go." She begged. She moved her shoulder as she sat up in the chair and it pulled on the needle in her chest. She flinched.

"What's wrong?" He was suddenly on edge.

She held up her hand indicating she needed a minute. When she could, she sighed. "I'm OK. It just hurts when the needle moves."

"So how does that lead to this?" He asked, obviously not seeing the connection.

She took a sip from her coffee and sat back in the chair. "Most of my injuries healed quickly. But there was damage, trauma, done to my nervous system. It doesn't heal as well as bone apparently."

He narrowed his eyes. "I don't understand."

"There is part of your nervous system that controls things you don't think of, like your heart rate, blood pressure, digestion, that stuff. Mine is out of whack. It doesn't work properly. That's why I get so tired, and pass out, fall down."

"And this helps?"

"It adds volume to my blood so it flows easier." She explained.

"And all this happened because of the accident?"

Jez nodded. She could see the questions forming behind his eyes. "Don't. I've already asked them all. It doesn't do any good."

"Will you have to do this forever?"

"Have no idea. We are just taking everything one step at a time right now."

Margie came over and checked the bag stopping their conversation. "How're you doing?"

"Good." Jez smiled.

"Cold yet?"

"Not yet." Jez chuckled.

Margie nodded. "Just let me know when you want a blanket."

Jez and Boone watched her walk away. When she was far enough away, he said, "I'm surprised you got behind the wheel again."

"I wasn't going to. I hadn't been back to the track since that night, but Paulie had been reaching out and I really needed the money. None of this is cheap."

"Doesn't your dad have insurance?"

"Sure, but it only covers about half."

Boone let out a breath in surprised understanding. "Won't they wonder where you got the money? I assume they aren't going to understanding when they find out you're racing again."

"They never knew. As far as I know, they don't even know exactly where the accident happened. No one ever asked me about it, and I never said. And yes, if they ever found out where I got the money…" She rolled her eyes just thinking about the reaction she'd get.

"So how do you plan on explaining the money?"

She shrugged. "I hadn't gotten there. I figured I'd worry about getting the money first."

"How much do you need?"

"No." Jez shook her head. "No, this is my problem. You're already going to be in enough trouble if they ever find out you were involved in this."

Boone was quiet for a long time. He sat back in the chair thinking. She could tell because his thumb tapped on the arm of the chair. She watched him, while she drank her coffee, a smile slowly growing on her face. After about fifteen minutes, she couldn't take it anymore. "What are you thinking?"

He looked over at her. Seeing the smile on her face brought one to his too. "A lot."

"I've been honest with you. You've got to be honest with me."

It was his turn to shake his head. "I told you, there are going to be things that I can't be honest about."

"Well at least give me something." Her smiled faded a little.

"I was trying to figure out how we could get you out to that desert race. Mel was talking to Skye about it last weekend."

"He mentioned it when he was in the shop yesterday." She nodded. "Getting me there is only half the battle. I don't have a car remember."

Boone smiled. "You have a car, Ace. Don't worry about that."

"You broke that car." She pointed at him. She was still pissed over that issue, so she didn't want to dwell on it.

Seeing her anger, he leaned in to her. "If I had known, I never would have done that to you. I'm sorry."

"Will you tell me why you did it?"

He bit his lip and then wiped a hand down his face. "I needed … you're going to hate me."

"Not knowing is worse. I know why Paulie wanted me to lose. He made it clear. But why would you?"

He closed his eyes and then looked at his hands. He refused to look at her. "Skye needed the win. I figured it would also help you in the long run. If people think you're invincible they don't want to race against you. I figured I could help both of you out at the same time."

"So you didn't do it for Paulie?"

He looked up shocked that she would even suggest it. "I would have never done it if I thought Paulie would have tried that."

Jez nodded, unsure about her feelings. She didn't totally believe he was telling her the truth.

"I swear, if I had known. I never would have done it." He said as if he saw her doubt.

"How do I know you're being honest with me?"

"I'll never lie to you, Ace. Ever. There may be things that I can't tell you, but I swear I will never outright lie to you."

"Swear on your car."

While she was serious, he smiled at her. "I swear on my car, my sweet baby, that if I ever outright, knowingly lie to you, I'll give her to you."

"I don't want her." She said. "Swear that if you outright, knowingly lie to me you'll beat her to death."

He looked horrified but after he saw she was serious, he agreed. "If I ever knowingly, willing, outright lie to you; I'll let you beat her to death. But I want you to agree that if I say I can't explain, you'll let it go."

"OK." She agreed.

He got a devious smile on his face. "So how do we seal this deal."

She stuck out her hand to him, but he shook his head. Raising one finger, he scooted to the end of his chair, and motioned for her to come close to him. When she was close enough, he leaned in and put his lips to hers in a gentle kiss. Jez leaned in for more, but the IV tube pulled and she was forced back, grabbing at her chest.

Seeing her pain, Boone's eyes widened. "Are you alright?"

She smiled weakly. "Would you take it the wrong way if I said your kiss is painful?" She couldn't help but giggle as she leaned back in the chair.

He smiled and gave a weak chuckle too, but reached out to take her hand. Worry painted his face. Jez began to tremble a little. "Wow, I've never done that to a girl with just a look before."

"I'm cold from the fluids." She smiled.

"Sure you are." He winked.

They caught Margie's attention and she brought Jez some warm blankets. Boone helped wrap Jez up, even though she told him she didn't need help. Then he took the seat next to her and held her hand until the bag was drained dry.

Margie came over and changed the bag, giving her another shot. As the pain gripped her, Jez asked Boone to tell her something.

"Like what?"

"I don't care. Just something about you. You know everything about me, but I don't know anything about you." She said through clinched teeth.

He sighed and thought, feeling her death grip on his hand. "I don't like the water."

"Really?"

"Yep."

She relaxed as the pain subsided. "Interesting." He chuckled, and she looked down at his arm. The black tattoos that laced their way up his arms were beautiful. "I love your arms."

Again he chuckled. "Really?"

She blushed. "Sorry."

"Don't be." He brushed the back of her hand with his thumb.

"Are you close with your parents?"

He shook his head. "Depends. My mom died when I was young and I only talk to my dad when I have to."

"That's sad. I can't imagine … well, I can." She said softly, her eyes dropping.

"Everything still OK?" Margie said coming over to check Jez's bag.

"Yep." Jez said with a smile.

Boone looked closely at her and narrowed his eyes. When Margie had left them, he asked, "Why do you do that?"

"What?"

"Lie."

"I don't lie." She said defensively.

He tilted his head. "I can see it in your eyes when you do. And that fake smile doesn't help."

Jez glanced at the others in the room. The sleeping man had woken and was now reading a book. The others continued to be wrapped up in their own distractions, only looking over at them occasionally with sly smiles. "Compared to them, I'm fine."

Boone glanced around and nodded once. He seemed to understand, but he wasn't happy about it. As if wanting to distract her, he started talking about the car he was fixing for her. He went into detail and she didn't really care about any of it. When he saw the glazed look in her eye, he laughed and stopped. "You don't really care do you?"

She smiled easily. "I care that it runs, and runs fast."

"She will. I promise." He leaned back in his chair, but still held her hand. In the silence of the room, Jez traced his tattoos with her eyes. Over and over, in silence, until the second bag was dry.

Margie came over and unhooked the bag. She cleared the PORT line with a saline flush and a Heparin syringe that made Jez cringe. Boone watched closely as all this happened and then as Margie pulled the needle free of Jez's chest. It hurt and Jez gritted her teeth. His eyes held their worried expression as Jez stay still while the nurse cleaned the area with alcohol that stung, and placed a bandage over the new hole.

"OK, that's it." Margie smiled as she rolled her chair back.

"Will it always hurt like that?" Boone asked her out of the blue.

Margie smiled softly. "No. After a few months it gets better. The area is very tender since she just had surgery. As the wound becomes older, it toughens up."

Jez had to remove her hand from Boone's so she could unwrap herself from the blankets. She tried to stand, but grew dizzy and sat back down quickly, making Boone reach out to help her. Margie watched carefully with concern.

"You do that every time, Jez. You know better."

"I know." Jez sighed. She took another minute then stood slower, Boone's hand on her arm and back just in case. They said good bye to Margie and then he walked her back to the elevator. He stood protectively close even though she was more stable. When they were out by his car, he walked her around and opened her door, but she hesitated before getting in.

"Are you alright?" He asked concerned.

She nodded, and gave him a nervous half smile. "We never did seal that deal."

A bright smile graced his lips. He reached up and placed a hand on the back of her neck, leaned in, and brushed his lips across hers. She instantly melted and pushed against him.

Feeling her desire for more, he wrapped her in his other arm and pulled her closer. Their lips grabbing at each other's hungrily. He slipped his tongue between her lips and she grew needy in places she didn't know about. He pressed her against the car as she wrapped her arms around his neck. As he traced her lips and then bit on them gently, her knees grew weak. Feeling her weaken in his arm, he pulled away.

"Are you alright?' He asked quickly, troubled eyes looking into hers.

She smiled with a blush, and looked down. "Oh yes. I'm great." She bit her lip and looked up at him from under her dark lashes.

"Don't look at me like that." He growled.

It was her turn to be troubled. "Why?"

"Because it makes me want to do things to you that your dad and brother would kill me for."

She smiled and giggled. She turned and slid into the passenger seat to keep herself from saying that his kiss had already made her want those things. It was too early to go there though, and while her mind and heart knew it, her body had other ideas.

Chapter 29

Boone took her to get an early dinner at a favorite local restaurant. While she expected him to sit across from her, he slid into the booth next to her. As he wrapped his arm around her shoulders, she gave him an inquisitive look.

With a devilish grin, he asked, "What?"

"Nothing." She blushed at his attention.

"Tell me."

"I just, … I'm not use to this." She admitted.

"Use to what?" He wasn't teasing or trying to be mean, but seemed honestly curious about what she was thinking.

She played with the utensils in front of her. "This. This closeness. The openness."

"Does it make you uncomfortable? To have me want you near?"

"No, yes, … no." She didn't know how it made her feel. "No one's ever treated me like this."

He gave her an odd look. "You and Paulie dated."

"Sure, but he never held my hand or sat next to me. He never wanted people to know." She admitted softly, her chin lowered and eyes on the white paper napkin before her.

Boone reached over and turned her chin to look into her eyes. "I want everyone to know. I don't want another person to look at you without thinking about me."

"Are you sure? You could have any girl. There are over a dozen in this place right now who would go home with you right now." Tears pressed on the back of her eyes.

"I don't see anyone but you."

"Why? I'm nothing special."

He sighed, the light smile left his face and he ran a finger down her cheek. "You are so much more than special." He leaned in and gently kissed her lips, but pulled back before she could lean in for more. "You're gorgeous, sexy, smart, funny, fast, and a thousand other things that I haven't even begun to understand yet. "

She gave him a doubtful look. "Me? Fast behind the wheel maybe, and funny looking … but …" She shook her head.

"You're …" He stopped and placed a gentle kiss on her lips. The waitress showed up and interrupted their conversation. She was young, skinny, cute and flirted pathetically with Boone. He smiled his amazing smile at her, but didn't give her any more attention than was needed to place his order. Jez ordered a salad, suddenly very aware of her size. When the waitress walked away, Boone gave her a narrow look. "Just a salad?"

She smiled. "I'm not very hungry."

"Don't you go and do that girl thing on me?"

"Girl thing?" She laughed.

"Yeah, you know where you start all these stupid diets because you think you're too fat or some stupid thing like that."

"I am fat." She said turning serious.

His eyes narrowed unhappily. "You're not fat. You're healthy." She gave him a doubtful look and he rolled his eyes, "OK, not the best word, but you are not fat. You've got curves, and I like that."

She opened her mouth to say something but he put his fingers to her lips. In a completely unpredictable move, she took his finger in her mouth and gave it a little suck. His eyes grew wide, and he pulled his finger back from her. Wiping a hand over his face, he shook his head slowly, "Fuck Ace, you're going to be the death of me."

She smiled and gave a little giggle. With innocent eyes, she looked at him and apologized. "I'm sorry."

He shifted in his seat and took in a deep breath. With a gentle growl he leaned into her. Resting his head against hers, he whispered, "You're not as innocent as you pretend to be, are you?"

"I'm as innocent as you want me to be." She hushed, rolling her head to look into his eyes.

He groaned and she smiled crookedly. "God, I can't wait to get you alone."

The waitress practically dropped his plate of food on the table as she overheard his comment. He looked up startled but then laughed outright, as Jez turned bright red. The pretty red head looked from Boone to Jez with a nasty look. Jez could almost hear her thoughts. 'What's she got? She must be a slut.' Then before leaving the waitress gave Jez the 'fat bitch' glare and stalked off.

Jez's breath caught in her chest and her head fell for a moment. She picked up her fork as Boone removed his arm from around her and lifted his giant hamburger. As she poked around her salad a little, he looked over at her. "If you want something else, just order it, Ace."

"No, this is fine. I'm not very hungry." She said hoping the sadness was covered.

She knew she hadn't hidden it well when he put his burger down and turned to look at her. "What's wrong?"

"Nothing." She smiled up at him and he gave her the knowing look. She allowed her eyes to flash to the waitress. "She likes you. She doesn't understand why you're with me. I'm not good enough for you. She's right, you know."

He didn't take his eyes off Jez to see who she was referring to, but instead leaned closer to Jez. "Do you think that I would be with anyone I didn't want to be with?"

Jez shrugged.

"Ace, I only hang out with people that I like. And I really like you." He was looking her in the eye. "I want you. You're better than I deserve."

She wanted to call him a liar, or at the very least argue with him, but his look didn't leave room for argument at that moment.

He pointed to her salad. "Either eat or order something else, Ace. If I take you home hungry, your dad will wonder what we've been up to." His smile was intoxicating.

He picked up his burger and watched as she speared a piece of lettuce. They both took a bite and chewed, watching each other as if they would only eat if the other did. They ate in silence until Jez put her fork down and claimed she was full. Boone finished his burger and fries though and then paid the bill. He pulled her close and kissed the top of her head as they walked through the restaurant. Jez felt all the eyes on them as they pushed through the glass door.

He put her in the car and then climbed in behind the wheel. As he drove her towards home, she asked, "What are you doing tonight?"

He smiled as he looked at her. "Why?"

"I'm just curious. I don't know what you do when you're not with me."

"I'm going to stop and see Skye, then go to the gym, and maybe work on your car, if there's time."

She looked out the window at the city passing by. "I can't remember if I thanked you for sending Skye to come get me."

"I'm just glad you're safe. We were all really worried." His jaw tensed at the thought. "Why'd you take off like that?"

"I guess I just needed some time to think." She admitted.

"Were you there the whole time?"

"No, I started at the beach, but I couldn't think there."

He glanced over at her. "How were you planning on getting back?"

She shrugged. "I hadn't thought about that."

He shook his head and chuckled at little.

"What?" She looked at him a little annoyed.

"Just something your dad said that night." She stared at him until he continued. "He said you get yourself into these pickles, where you find yourself in the middle of something you can't get out of."

"That's why they call me Pickle." She said softly.

He reached over and grabbed her hand. "Not with me around. I'll always get you out, no matter what."

"You'll run at some point and I'll be in a pickle then." She whispered, more to herself than to him, but he overheard her.

Yanking his hand away, he pulled onto a side street and pulled to a stop. Before she realized it, he had both seatbelts unlatched and was pulling her to him in the center of the bench seat. Startled, Jez looked at him. "I'm not running, ever. If this doesn't work out, it's because we both make that decision. But I won't leave you. I don't give my heart lightly, Ace. You can even ask Skye. He'll tell you the truth if you don't believe me."

Jez didn't know what to say, so she just sat there quietly, her lips rolled between her teeth.

"What are you thinking?"

"That I don't know what to say. I want to call you a liar. But I don't want you to be lying."

"I told you Ace, I may not tell you everything, but I'm not going to lie to you."

Jez bit her lip and her heart skipped a beat.

"Did you love Paulie?"

"No." Her answer was fast and true. "I wanted to. I tried to." She whispered, "But I couldn't. I didn't even like Paulie."

"Then why were you with him for so long?"

"Because I needed him."

"To race."

"He said he loved me."

"But you didn't love him."

She shook her head but her eyes never left his. "Jordy says you can't love someone who hurts you."

"Love shouldn't hurt, Ace."

Tears brimmed in her eyes, "Then why does this?"

Boone looked at her deeply. Motioning between them with his fingers, he asked, "This hurts?"

She didn't want to be honest, but she couldn't help herself. Nodding her head, she said, "Yes."

"Why?"

"I don't know." She swallowed, a tear escaping her eye.

He pulled her closer and wrapped his hand around the back of her neck. "Does this hurt?"

He felt the shutter run through her as he touched her. Her voice was barely a whisper. "No."

He leaned in and kissed her cheek. "Does this?"

"No."

He moved to her lips, placing three light kisses across them. "And this?"

"No." Her voice getting weaker.

"So what hurts about this? Because it feels really right to me, Ace." His voice was as hushed as hers.

Jez's brain was foggy, and all she could think about was how she needed to be closer to him. She climbed onto his lap, straddling him, and pressed her lips to his. He wrapped his arms around her and ran his hand up her back. Their lips danced and their hands grabbed. And when it got to a point where she was digging at her clothes, he stopped her.

"Ace, no. Not like this." He had to grab her wrists and held them to his chest. "Ace, no honey."

She looked back at him, huffing with need. It took her several long minutes to register what he was saying, but then she pulled away. He saw the hurt in her eyes. "Ace?"

She crawled back to her side of the car, fighting down the emotions that were conflicted and confusion.

"Ace? Talk to me."

"This. This hurts." She said softly.

Boone sighed and slid over next to her. He wrapped his arms around her and dragged her back onto his lap. "Now?"

She looked up at him and shook her head. She couldn't say it but this stopped the hurting.

"Ace, when I stopped you, it wasn't because I wanted to. It's because I didn't want to." He looked deep into her eyes. "I made a promise to a lot of people, Ace. But mostly I promised myself I wasn't going to fuck this up. We're going to take this slow."

"I don't do well with slow." She responded.

"Then I'll be the brakes. You steer and I'll break."

"I don't know how ..."

"Yes, Ace. You drive and I'll make sure that we don't crash."

Tears swelled in her eyes again. "And what happens when we do?"

"We won't."

"But …"

He took her chin in his hand. "We're not going to crash. But if, and that's a big if, we do, I'll be right there pulling you out. I'm not running."

She opened her mouth to say something but he put his thumb over her mouth.

"Do you trust me?"

She nodded.

"Then trust me, Ace. I'm not going to hurt you."

Tears brimmed in her eyes and he pulled her to him in a big hug. He held her for a long time. They kissed a little but they basically just held each other. Jez didn't cry much but he held her tight anyway. He held her until she yawned.

"Are you tired, baby?"

"Please don't call me that. He calls me that."

"I'm going to kill him for hurting you." His tone was dark and it scared her, but Jez just snuggled in to him more. She felt him smile. "I need to take you home. Your dad's going to be on my ass."

He kissed her head and moved her off his lap. Sliding back behind the wheel, Boone started the engine. She slid over as close as she could get and he wrapped his arm around her. Boone drove her home, and walked her to the door. The night was growing dark but the lights from the house were warm. As he stood on the porch in front of her door, she looked up at him. "You wanna come in?"

"Naw, I gotta go see Skye and hit the gym."

She nodded, the knot forming in her throat. "OK."

"But I'll see you tomorrow." He leaned down and kissed her gently. She reached up for more, but he stopped her. "Brakes Ace. Tomorrow's another day."

She sighed and nodded. Boone opened the door and held the screen as she slipped inside. He waited until she started to close the door and then walked back to his car. Jez's heart fluttered a bit as he walked away, but she breathed through it. Jez closed the door and fell against it with a sigh. As she rolled around to place her back on the wood, she heard the chuckles.

"Pickle's got a boyfriend." She heard the teasing, kid-like sing-gong voice of her brother.

"Shut up, Jordy." She said.

"Leave your sister alone, boy. She looks happy." Her dad said, shuffling the cards on the table. "Did you have a good time?"

Jez had to think but eventually she decided she did. "Yes, Daddy, I think I did."

"Good. You look tired. Why don't you just head on up to bed?"

Jez went over and gave her dad kiss on the cheek. "Thank you, Daddy."

"We'll talk more tomorrow." He patted her back. "Sweet dreams."

Jez went upstairs and showered. She kept thinking of Boone and the way he kissed, and the things he said. Fear grew inside her as she realized that she was putting herself on the line again. She had done it once before. Paulie had said some pretty things to her too. He'd promised her the world. But then he'd hurt her time and again, then left her to die. She wanted to believe that Boone wasn't the same, she needed to believe it. But there was a part of her that hurt and questioned, and wondered why her.

She had been in bed an hour, tears now rolling down her cheeks, when Jordy knocked softly on her door and pushed in. Hearing her sniffle, Jordy came to his sister's side and curled up next to her on the bed. He wrapped his arms around her. "Did he hurt you?"

"No."

"Then what's wrong?"

"Nothing." She said.

He breathed out and it ruffled her hair. "You're scared he's going to hurt you."

She nodded.

He held her just a little tighter. "I don't think he's like Paulie, Jez. I think he honestly cares about you."

"He claims to. But why me?"

Jordy was silent for a long time. "How about if I promise to kick his ass if he hurts you?"

She giggled. "You and what army? Have you seen the size of his arms?"

She felt him nod. "I think Ty, OB, and myself … with the dads, we could take him."

She giggled again at the thought. He laughed too. "I love you, Jordy."

"I love you too sis."

Jez drifted off to sleep in her brother's arms, wrapped in her dad's old t-shirt, dreaming of the guy she was falling in love with.

☐

Chapter 30

The next morning, Jez woke up alone as she usually did. She dressed and met her family downstairs for breakfast. While there was coffee already made, they hadn't started the bacon and eggs she had expected. Jordy sat at the table eating a bowl of cereal and smiled as Jez moved in to the room. "Morning, sis."

"Hey." She smiled. She made her way over to get some coffee but her father stopped her.

"How about you and me go get some breakfast, Pickle." He smiled gently at her.

Jez's eyes looked to her brother, who was avoiding her by reading the back of the cereal box with great interest. She gave him a frown but then smiled at her dad. "Sure, Daddy."

He grabbed up her jacket from the back of the chair and handed it to her. As she wrapped it around her shoulders, she glanced at Jordy for a little enlightenment, but again he avoided her eyes. Jez followed her dad out to the truck and climbed in. She felt pretty good considering her emotional hangover. Her emotions were still very conflicted and raw. She'd think of Boone and smile, but then question herself and his intentions. It was an exhausting roller coaster.

As they pulled into a locally owned Mom and Pop diner, her dad looked over at Jez. "What are you thinking about?"

"Nothing." She smiled back at him brightly.

He sighed and shook his head. "Come on, Jez. I've been watching that brain smoke the entire trip."

When she didn't answer, they both got out of the truck and headed inside. He walked her over to the only empty booth and sat across from her. In silence, they both pulled menus out from the holder at the end of the table. In unison, they glanced over the laminated paper menu and then put them back. With a chuckle from her dad, and a smile from Jez, they made eye contact.

"Same thing, different day." She said. Her smiled faded as she realized that was true for so many things in her life.

"Is it the guy?"

Jez nodded.

"You said you had a good time yesterday."

"I did." She sighed. "He's incredible, but …"

"You're wondering if he's too good to be true." Her dad finished for her. "Or are you wondering if he's too good for you?"

Jez's eyes looked up into his and her mouth hung open until she snapped it shut. Unable to answer, she grabbed up her water glass and took a drink.

"I'm sorry." He dropped his eyes. "I'm sorry if we did that to you."

Jez looked at her father surprised.

"We don't think about what we say and how it might affect you. We're guys." He said as if it was an excuse. "But we do love you, and we want to see you happy. And last night was the happiest I've seen you in a long, long time."

The waitress came towards them, but then turned and walked away seeing the look on Dad's face.

"Daddy, I want so badly …" she stopped, "He makes me feel … good."

"And that's all I could ask for." Her father reached out and took her hand. He smirked.

"What?" She asked curiously.

"All I've ever wanted is someone who would love you and make you happy. A good man, who loves cars and surfing. Two out of three ain't bad." He chuckled.

Jez rolled her eyes, and smiled.

Her father waved the waitress over and they ordered their usual. She teased them about not wanting to assume anything and then wandered off to put in the food order. Jez and her dad sat silent until someone they knew came over. Her dad held a long discussion with the man about some local business, and then their food was up. They ate in silence, then he drove her to the store. Giving him a quick kiss before jumping out of the truck, Jez ran to open the store and get the day started.

She was alone at the store until a little after twelve, when Boone came in. Seeing her behind the cash register, ringing up a customer, he smiled. "Hey Ace."

"Boone." She smiled, and blushed as she glanced up at the customer. The older man glanced at Jez and then over to Boone. He smiled and waved good-bye as he walked out that door.

Boone slid behind the counter and walked back to clock in. She watched as he disappeared around the corner, but a second later, he leaned back into view and wiggled his finger at her. She glanced around the store and made sure no one else was there, before heading into the back room. As she rounded the doorway, he pulled her into his arms. She was stunned for a moment, but then relaxed when her eyes met his. He pulled her in for a kiss as she wrapped her arms around him.

"How's the pain today, Ace?" He said not letting her go.

"Much better now." She sighed. "Did you have a good night?"

He twisted his lips and looked up deep in thought. "The first part was incredible, the second part was just alright. How about yours?"

"Fine." She smiled and he saw right through it.

"What'd you do?" He watched her carefully.

She looked down and tried to avoid his eye. "Went to bed."

He moved his hand to her cheek and caressed it. "Something happen?"

"No, I just … I'm …"

He sighed and lifted her chin. After placing a gently kiss on her lips, he moved to look into her eyes. "You were over-thinking things, weren't you?"

"I don't over-think …" She said defensively. His laughter cut her off. "What's so funny?"

"You." He smiled and kissed her again. "You don't think I see it. I didn't need your family to tell me how you over-think, and how you don't think you're worth it, or even how amazing you are."

"They said those things?" She was horrified.

"Don't get upset, Ace. They just wanted to make sure I knew what I was getting into. They were hoping I'd run." He smiled. "They don't want you hurt again. They see more than you know, Ace. They may not know what Paulie was into or what he did to you, but they know he hurt you. They're just trying to protect you."

She was pissed. She knew she shouldn't be. She knew they were doing it all out of love for her. But the fact that there had been more to the conversation she had overheard just made her madder. She dropped her arms from around his neck.

Boone watched the dark cloud form. "Ace, don't do this. Don't get mad because we all love you."

"You were fucking talking to my family about me. And they were talking back." She moved under his arm and away from him. "I don't know which pisses me off more right now."

"It was just a harmless conversation, Jez. Mostly in passing. It's nothing to get so upset over." He turned to face her.

She glared at him. "Mostly in passing? How long were you at my house the other night?"

He deflated as he let a breath out. "How'd you know?"

"I went home after work." She shook her head in disbelief. "I saw you in the house and then I sat outside and listened. I heard you talk to my brother and my dad."

She watched as he thought back to what they could have said that would have upset her so. "It was just a conversation."

"About me. Without me." She pointed out.

"Is that why you took off?"

"I needed to think. I needed to decide if I could handle this. I'm not use to the overlap." She admitted.

He moved over next to her and placed a hand on her shoulder. "I know, and I get it. I wasn't …" He stopped and then restarted. "I want to be on your dad and brother's good side, Ace. I wasn't trying to hide my visit from you. I just wanted their permission."

She looked away annoyed and he grabbed her chin.

"When I got hired, they told me the rules. They made it clear you were off limits, and I tried." He dropped his head and his hand. "I wasn't looking for this. I didn't want this. But I see something in you, Ace, something I can't stay away from."

"I don't … if you just want sex, say so." She snapped. He looked like she had slapped him, but the front bell rang, giving her an escape. She turned and stomped off.

Boone gave her a minute, while he recovered. He heard her speak to the customer in a pleasant voice, and stepped out to see if he could help. They seemed to have an endless string of customers after that. If one of them had a free moment, the other didn't. And it was that way until OB came in to relieve her. As soon as she had finished with her customer, Jez walked back and grabbed her bag from the office. She walked out of the store without a word to either man.

She didn't get far though before Boone was grabbing her arm. "Ace, please."

"I'm tired." She said spinning on him.

"You can't leave mad. We need to talk about this."

With a sigh, she looked at the busy store behind him. "You have to work, and I need to go home."

"Can I stop by later?"

"I don't know." She turned and walked away. Halfway down the first block, she pulled her cell phone from her pocket and found the contact she was looking for. As the ringtone ended, a familiar cheerful voice answered.

"What's up?"

"Skye? It's Ace."

There was an awkward pause on the other end. "Hey, everything OK?"

"Sure. I was just … I was wondering if you know if there was a race tonight?"

Again an awkward pause. "Um, yeah, I think there is. Why?"

"I want in, but I need a car."

"Oh, um, didn't Boone tell you, yours isn't ready yet." He seemed nervous.

"Mine?" She stopped walking and leaned against the nearest tree. "I don't have one. That's why I was hoping you could help me out. Loan me one or let me borrow yours."

"How does Boone feel about this?"

It was her turn for the awkward silence. "Boone, um, …"

"He doesn't know, does he?"

"No. He's working and this is kind of a spur of the moment thing." She shuffled her feet and waited, but when Skye didn't say anything she said. "Look, I get it. If you don't feel right about this, I'll call Mel. Thanks anyway."

"Wait, Ace. That's not what … I'll take you." He finally gave in. "Where should I pick you up?"

"You know the pier?"

"Sure. I'll meet you there at ten."

She smiled. "Thanks Skye."

"Don't thank me, Ace. Just promise me, you'll win." He didn't wait for her to make the promise, but cut the line quickly.

Jez had a block to decide how she was going to get out of the house. By the time she walked in the front door, she had a plan.

☐

Chapter 31

Over dinner an hour later, Jez broke into the conversation to ask, "Dad would you mind if I went out for a little while tonight?"

He smiled and looked at Jordy. "Not as long as you promise to be home with me tomorrow night. Jordy's going out tonight too, so it'd be nice to have some peace and quiet."

"You're not going to a party, are you?" Jordy asked pointedly.

She giggled. "No. Just out. Maybe a walk on the beach or a movie."

"Just don't be home too late. You have to open the store tomorrow." Her dad warned before returning to his dinner.

After they had eaten, Jez cleaned the kitchen and Jordy vanished upstairs to get dressed. He was dressed fairly nicely when he came back down thirty minutes later. She whistled at him as he crossed the room, and he smacked her arm. "Shut it." Laughing, she headed upstairs to shower and change too.

Jordy was gone when she returned and started for the door. Her father's voice stopped her when she pulled the door open. "You're not dressed as fancy as I thought you'd be."

"I'm going for warmth and comfort, not sexy." She said glancing down at her jeans and sweatshirt, wiggling her toes in the tennis shoes that wrapped her feet. "I thought you'd be happy about that. If you want, I can go put on something a little sexier. I've got this great mini skirt I bought for my Halloween custom, if you think that would be better."

"No, no, I like this outfit just fine." He nodded, obviously not pleased with the mental imagine he got. As she pushed further out the door, he called, "In my day, the guy picked the girl up at the door."

"Well, you're the one who asked him to close the store. I just thought I'd meet him there. Oh and in your day, they also drove horse and buggies." She turned and looked at him over her shoulder. He tossed a pillow in her direction as she hopped out the door laughing. "Love you, Daddy."

"Be careful, Pickle."

Jez cut across the yard, heading towards the store, but a block down made a left and the backtracked toward the pier. She figured she'd have to wait quite a while for Skye, since she was early. Taking a seat on the bench at the base of the pier, she pulled out her make-up case. Under the dim glow of the street light, she darkened her eye shadow and added more mascara.

When she was pleased with the darker look, she pushed the case into the bottom of her bag. Pulling free her brush, she ripped the ponytail holder from hair and yanked all the tangles free. She was just disposing of the shed hair in the trash can when Skye pulled up.

Surprised, she got up and headed for the car. As she slid in, he gave her a curious look. "Have you been waiting long?"

"Not as long as I expected." She admitted.

He raised his eyebrows. "I didn't want you to have to sit in the cold. I was trying to beat you."

"I had to leave early." She smiled. "Thanks for thinking about me though. I was just getting ready."

"Um, forgive my stupid question," he said pulling away from the curb, "but weren't you suppose to do that before you left the house?"

"My dad's home and I couldn't leave the house dressed like, well, like Ace." She shrugged. "He'd kill me."

He gave her an odd look, but she didn't see it. She was pulling off the sweatshirt to reveal a black tank top with a silver design on the front. She pulled silver heels and the hoop earring Boone had given her from her bag before kicking off her tennis shoes and shoving them in, then pushed the sweatshirt in on top of it all. She looked over when she heard Skye laughing as she put in the earrings. "What?"

"I always wondered why girls carried such big purses."

"I can't speak for every girl, but I have to carry a spare set of clothes with me on nights like this." She shrugged.

"What about other nights?"

"I have to carry the same bag all the time or it will look obvious."

He glanced over as she reached down to slip her feet into the heels. "So your folks really don't know."

"No, my dad would kill me and my brother would … well, he'd do worse." She said with a shake of her head.

"And your mom?"

"She took off years ago."

"Sorry." He replied softly. They were silent for a long while and eventually he reached over and turned up the radio. It was a hip hop song, and she looked at him. "What?"

"Just didn't take you for a dance hall guy."

"I thought you'd like it." He smirked.

"Do you mind?" She asked and motioned to the radio. When he shook his head, she reached over and spun the nob. She found the station she liked best and smiled. Heavy metal poured from the speakers and he looked over at her with questioning eye.

"You really listen to this?"

"Yes, haven't you heard what my song is?"

"I thought it was just a front. Like the look and the attitude."

She lifted her chin. "A front?"

"Sure. The tough girl act. It's great for the races, but it's not who you are."

"And how do you know?" She said a little sharply.

"Don't get defensive, Ace. I don't mean anything bad by it." He said gently. But when he saw her stare, he explained further. "Look, I may not know you, but I know Boone. I know that Boone ain't going to fall for some hot rod hussy."

"What kind of hussy does he fall for?"

Skye twisted his lips, and decided what to tell her. "Don't tell him I said this, but he doesn't fall."

"Liar."

"He might have taken some home, before, but he doesn't fall." Skye said and for some reason she believed him.

She looked at him. She wanted to ask so much more, but she knew she shouldn't. It wasn't Skye's place to tell her.

"Ace, look, I don't mean to step in the middle of your business, …"

"Then don't."

"But…" he continued like he hadn't heard her, "I see the way he looks at you. And I don't want to see him get hurt. If you're not in this, don't fuck around with him."

She turned her head and looked out at the night passing by. "He's the one you need to warn. He shouldn't be getting involved with me. He can't fall for me."

"It's too late, Ace."

"I'm too much for a mess for a guy like him. I'm too much for anyone." Tears filled her eyes, and she blinked them away.

"Huh." He replied and she turned her head to look at him.

"What?" She asked annoyed.

"Who knew you'd fall too?" He was honestly stunned and smiled at her.

He turned his attention back to the road and turned off the freeway. She watched him for a long time, echoing those words over and over again in her head. Finally, the lights of the track came into view and her attention was draw outside the car. The group was growing and Skye drove them around to the opposite side of the track than she was used to being on. It was the side that was considered the visitor's side. Ace took in a deep breath.

"Don't worry Ace, I got your back. No one will touch you on this side."

"It's not this side I'm worried about." She said. She reached down and pulled out a tube of bright red lipstick. As Skye pulled the car to a stop, she grabbed the rearview mirror and turned it so she could apply the first of two crimson coats. He watched, and was amazed at what he saw. In the matter of seconds, she went from the girl he saw in the auto parts store, scared and young and innocent, to the woman who he had first met. Ace was suddenly there. Jezebel was nowhere to be seen.

Chapter 32

They got out of the car, and he stepped around to stand near her. She glanced around the area. "So, where's my car?"

"It'll be here." He said as he smiled at a half-dressed tramp that walked by.

She rolled her head to him. "I need to get the feel of it before I race, you know."

He rolled his head to her. "Yeah, I know."

They stood side by side for several long moments, eyeing the other drivers and Skye flirting with whatever girl's attention he could catch. Suddenly the sound of two engines pulled their heads around. One was the deep rumble of a muscle car, and the other the smooth murmur of a street legal cheetah. The rumble cut off on the driver's side of Skye's car while the purr pulled up in front of Ace. She eyed it without emotion. The driver's door popped open and a gaunt kid popped out. He didn't look much older than Ace herself, and was so scrawny he could have passed for someone not old enough to drive at all.

"Skye!" He laughed and stepped over to them. They shook hands in a complicated fisted way, then the kid looked over his shoulder at the car. "So, will this do?"

Skye looked at Ace. "I don't know, will it?"

Ace looked from the shiny yellow beauty with black tinted windows to Skye. She tried to look cool but he saw the excitement in her eyes. "What is it?"

"What is it? What is it?" The kid gasped like he couldn't believe what he was hearing. "It's only one of the top ten fastest cars in the world."

Ace stepped over and traced a finger along her smooth, rolled lines. She looked more like a naked woman than a car. Curves and cuts that would make even a straight woman wet with desire. When she had walked the entire exterior, she pulled open the driver's door and sank into the soft leather seat. The kid stepped over and began rattling off facts about her.

"She's a SRT Viper. Top Speed is estimated at two hundred six mph. She's got a 640 HP 8.4L V 10 engine."

Ace ran a finger over the interior only catching the most important piece of information: top speed 206. After a moment, she got out and stepped over to Skye. Standing toe to toe with him, she leaned over and whispered into his ear. "Yes, I think she'll do." She placed a gently kiss on his cheek before pulling away.

"Now if I was a jealous man, I'd be pretty pissed right now." Boone's deep voice said. He didn't seem very pleased, with a dark tone to his voice and a tense stance.

Ace looked over to him, weighing her emotions. "I thought you'd be hanging out with my dad or my brother tonight."

"Thought about it, but my best friend called and said my girl was racing. Thought I'd better be here for her."

Ace turned her eyes to Skye, but didn't move her head. Skye's face was turned down, eyes on the black pavement beneath his boots. He looked uncomfortable. "If you hadn't brought me such a sweet present, I'd slap the crap out of you."

"Then it's a good thing I know the right people." Skye's said softly as Boone stepped up to them.

It was an awkward triangle. One that Skye was slowly sliding out of, as Ace faced Boone down. She didn't know what to say. She was glad he'd come, but she was still annoyed. He looked pissed about her being here, but also looked like he was ready to take her in his arms. Ace knew that if he did, she'd melt. Finally, feeling herself about to give in, she called over her shoulder. "You got the keys, kid?"

"No keys needed." He chuckled from somewhere behind her. "Just press the start button."

Ace felt the smile grow across her face. As it did, Boone's face grew darker. "Where'd you get it, Bandit?"

"Oh, you know, around." The kid laughed.

"No." Boone said looking directly at Ace. "It's hot. You don't want to be anywhere near it. Wait until next week. Your car will be ready and we'll take it to the desert."

"I promised Skye a win." She replied coldly. "And Bandit went through all the trouble."

There was another silent stand-off, until Skye stepped up behind Ace. "Bandit's taking it across the border in two hours. She's got one, maybe two races, Boone."

"Well, then we'd better get started." Ace turned her head with a crooked smile. Skye moved a step back and Ace turned to the car. She slid into the seat and glanced back at the kid. "Anything I need to know?"

"I didn't know you were driving it." The kid turned serious, and looked to Skye. "You didn't say a chick was driving it."

"Don't worry, she's got it." Skye replied with a little smile.

Bandit sighed and shook his head in disbelief. "She's fast. Be careful."

Ace nodded and pulled the door closed. As she adjusted the seat and the mirrors, a tap came at the window. After pressing the start button and feeling the purr begin beneath her feet, she rolled it down and looked up into Boone's eyes. He handed her a CD. "Don't forget this, Ace. It's your lucky charm."

She took the CD with her two fingers as if it was a cigarette. "Go set it up." With only a quick glance, she pulled away from the three guys and scattered a group of race car groupies.

She drove carefully around the parking lot, and then over to the circular track that sat to the east of the drag strip. They didn't use this track for anything, and it was deserted. She pulled into the concrete path that wrapped around the oval circle of grass. She drove the first lap rather slow, getting a feel for how she handled, then made three more laps increasing speed. As she took the last lap, slowing down, she couldn't help but smile. "Oh, I think I'm in love."

She pulled into the parking space next to Skye's car and parked. As she popped the door, he approached. "Well, Ace, what'd you think?"

"I think I'm in love."

Skye laughed as Boone came up next to them. "Do I even want to know?"

"No brother, I don't think you do." Skye patted Boone's shoulder and walked away.

Boone knelt down next to Ace, resting his hand on the doorframe. "I've got you set up. You win the first one, you get another. They don't know it's you though."

"Why?"

"You're racing Paulie." Boone tried to hide his smile.

Ace bit the inside of her cheek. "I haven't raced Paulie since they were teaching me."

"You wanna back out?"

"No. I wanna kick his ass."

Boone smiled, but it wasn't a friendly smile. "So do I."

"You already did from what I understand."

He stood up and looked across the parking lot as if he heard something. When his eyes returned to hers, he said, "You're up."

He closed the door and she reached for the CD case she had set on the seat beside her. It was a freshly burned disk and she inserted it into the player, as she pulled out and drove over the start line. From inside the tinted windows, she could see everything clearly but knew no one could see her. She hadn't been able to see Bandit when he drove up so she felt comfortable with her obscurity. It wasn't until the flag girl raised the white panties, that Ace hit play and the music blared out of the speakers. The familiar chords vibrated through her body and she hit the gas as the panties dropped.

She hadn't even gotten a chance to blink before she was crossing the finish line. She was already stopped when Paulie pulled his piece of junk across. As soon as he was parked, he jumped out of the car and raced at her. Ace sat silently behind the wheel enjoying the chorus of her song. He yanked open the door and grabbed her arm, dragging her from the vehicle. She had been so lost in the song and in the win that she hadn't seen him coming, so when Ace was hauled from the seat, she fell on her ass on the asphalt.

"You fucking bitch!" He screamed. "Ungrateful slut!"

He raised his hand to strike her, but another hand caught his. Boone was instantly there. But it was Skye who was stopping the blow from coming. Boone's voice trembled with fury. "Lay one finger on her, and I'll kill you."

Skye released Paulie's arm, but it lashed out and struck Ace's face. She fell the rest of the way to the ground, her hair falling around her face as it turned down. She didn't see what happened next, but the sound of the scuffle was all around. Ace waited until the pain had subsided to a dull throb and the tears had cleared slightly before looking to see what was happening, and by then Mel was in the middle stopping the action.

"Get him off my track, Mel. I never want them allowed here again." Paulie said, blood pouring from his broken nose and mouth. Jez couldn't tell which injuries were new and which ones were old, all the red, black, and blue melted together into a barely recognizable figure of Paulie.

Mel looked to Boone, who was being held back by Skye. "He hit Ace, Mel. I was only protecting my girl."

"Baby girl is mine." Paulie snarled, and Boone lunged at him, but Skye held him firm.

Mel looked down at Ace who was picking herself up from the ground. "You OK?"

She looked up with an odd expression at Mel. She didn't answer, but brushed her hair back away from her face and showing the red mark across her cheek. Once she was stable on her feet, the crowd hushed. Jez walked over to stand just before Paulie, who spit blood near her foot. She fisted her hand and hauled back and slugged him in the crotch. It was hard enough to double him over, and made him fall on his knees.

She spun and walked over to Boone. Skye had dropped his hand, watching in shock. Boone didn't know if he should smile or be nervous as she stepped in front of him. In a smooth motion, she rose up on her toes and kissed him, wrapping her arms around his neck. He responded, pulling her closer and gripping her head in his hands.

After a moment, he pulled away from her. He looked up at Paulie who was trying to stand, eyes glowing red, as red as his battered face. "Fuck you, bitch."

As he hobbled away, Mel turned to them. "You've got another race, Ace. You'd better get ready."

She didn't answer but turned and climbed back in the car.

Chapter 33

She won the second one easily as well, and soon, they were back in the parking lot. Skye had stepped away to see Mel, and they returned the car to Bandit. He seemed relieved to have her. "I'm impressed."

"She sure was fun. Kind of hate to let her go." Ace admitted as she swung from the driver's seat.

Boone pulled her to him, wrapping his arms around her. Ace had the thought that she wasn't sure if it was to keep her close to him or far from the car. "Be careful, Bandit, and get it across the border. I don't want this coming back on her."

Bandit nodded. "No worries, Boone."

They watched him drive away and Ace felt sad. "That was … amazing."

"How amazing?" Boone whispered in her ear. "Better than kissing me?"

"Definitely."

"Better than sex?"

She smiled and thought. "Probably."

"You've never had sex with me, Ace." He nuzzled her.

"And whose fault it that?" She turned her head to look up at him.

He didn't answer but kissed her deeply. As she melted into him, he pulled back. "Look, we need to talk before we let this go much further."

She sighed. Stupidly, she thought they might be able to move forward without a hassle, but the look in his eyes told her differently. "OK."

"Not here." He took her hand and led her back to his car, but she stopped him just short.

"My bag's in Skye's car."

He looked at her with raised eyebrows. "Your bag?"

"Yea, you know my gigantic purse that has my change of clothes and shoes in it." When his eyes darkened, she rolled her eyes. "You didn't think my dad let me out of the house looking like this, did you?"

His eyes glanced down at her outfit. She felt the heat in her body rise. "Now that you mention it, that's something else we need to discuss." He twisted the corner of his lip down slightly and pulled her to his car. "I'll get your bag. You stay here, in the car."

"Really?" She asked surprised, a little confused by his protectiveness.

"Yes, really. I'm not in the mood to fight anymore tonight." He helped her in and hit the lock button as he slammed the door shut.

She crossed her arms across her chest and leaned back irritated. When he had walked far enough through the crowd that she didn't see him anymore, she kicked off her heels and pulled her feet up under her. Pushing any real thought from her mind, Jez began to unwind. As she did, her hand began to throb. She rubbed at it, and it wasn't long before she saw Skye and Boone walking toward the car. They chatted easily as Skye grabbed her bag from the passenger floor. They laughed as the bag was passed from one set of hands to the other. Boone looked down at it and then over at her, saying something that made Skye chuckle. They shook hands in a friendly street way, then Boone came over to his car.

He pushed the bag into the car first, and she pulled it to her as he slid in. "Are you carrying a body in that thing?"

"Wouldn't you like to know?" She smiled.

He started up the car and the song that came through the speakers made her stop and look at the radio. Frankie Laine's voice floated out of the speakers and called her name. Jez's heart pounded in her chest as she listened to the last half of the song. Boone's eyes were focused on the road before him so he didn't notice her reaction. Nor did he see how the tears came to her eyes when the next song poured from the mesh near her feet. Iron and Wine sang out her name and called that they would love her while she fought down the mixture of emotions. It wasn't until she reached over and cut off the radio that Boone even noticed she was in the car with him.

"Oh sorry, I …" He shook the thought from his head.

"Where did you find those songs?" She whispered.

He looked over and saw how upset she was for the first time. He reached out and grabbed her hand. With an embarrassed smile, he answered, "YouTube."

"Why?"

He turned his attention back to the road before them. They were well down the freeway and by how far they had gotten in such a short time, she figured he had to be going well over the speed limit. "You might want to put on something warmer if you've got it, Jez."

"Why?"

"Because it might be cool where we're going."

She didn't ask any more questions. Instead, she filled the time changing back into what she had left the house in. She removed her earrings and a good portion of the make-up, then pulled on her sweatshirt and tennies. By the time he pulled up near the pier, she was back to being plain old Jez. She pulled out the ponytail holder and pulled her hair up into a messy do as he got out of the car and walked to her side.

Taking her hand, he walked her out to the far end of the pier. It was windy and cold, but he pulled her close to keep her warm. "You looked hot tonight, but I like you like this better. I know why you put on the show and the costume, but you really don't need to."

"It helps me separate from her."

He looked down into Jez's eyes. "You are her."

"No, no." She shook her head. "She's ... strong."

"And so are you. Ace is just one side of you, Jez. You're one and the same. I wish you'd show as much strength and confidence when you looked like this as you do when you're painted up."

She glanced out at the black water. "It's all an image. I'm so scared out there."

"Scared of what?" He looked honestly shocked.

She debated quickly if she should let it go, but she knew it was too late. "Of failing. Of crashing. Of ... what happens when someone else is better. And until tonight I was scared of Paulie."

"You don't ever have to be scared of him again." Boone's voice was still tense with the thought of him. "If he even looks at you the wrong way, I'll kill him."

She leaned into him, completely believing every word. "I know. Thanks."

After a moment, Boone lifted her chin so he could see her eyes in what little light was shining down from the moon. "You don't ever have to be scared, Jez. I've got you. Win, lose, draw, or anything else that comes our way, I've got you."

"For how long?"

"Forever or for as long as you want me."

"I don't believe you." Her voice cracked.

His eyes softened. "What don't you believe? You think I'm going to leave?"

She looked away and shook her head and the knowledge came from her heart.

"You think I'm going to hurt you?"

She couldn't answer. Just the thought was too painful to bear. After a moment, she asked, her eyes still case away from him. "Who was she?"

"Who?" Boone asked lightly but by how he tensed she knew he knew exactly what she was talking about.

"Tonight, Skye said that you were falling in love with me. He also said that you don't fall."

"And why would he tell you that?" Boone asked darkly.

She glanced up at him, but his eyes were on the dark horizon. "He was warning me not to fuck with you. He just doesn't want to see you hurt."

A tight, slightly annoyed grin crossed his lips. "And what did you say?"

"I told him that he should be warning you not to get involved with me. I told him that I would hurt you." She watched the annoyed grin turn to one of amusement. "Tell me what happened with her."

"It's ancient history, Ace. You don't need to worry about her, or me, or us." He looked down into her eyes. "You're nothing like her. You aren't going to …." He stopped and didn't finish this thought. Instead he leaned down and kissed her. She clung to him, wanting nothing more than his lips on hers forever, but he did pull away. "Ace, I gotta ask you something. Why'd you call Skye tonight?"

"I needed a race, and I didn't know who else to call."

He closed his eyes for a moment and then opened them. "Why'd you want to race?"

"I was pissed. I needed to blow off some steam."

"And there was no one else you could have called?" His eyes were locked on hers searching for the truth.

"Normally, before you, I would have called Molly or Paulie. But … I didn't know anyone else that could get me a car that I thought you'd trust."

"That I'd trust?" He repeated in disbelief. "But I was the one you were pissed at."

"Just because I was pissed doesn't mean I'd do something to hurt you. I just needed some space, to think. I'm not used to … I've kept my two lives separate for a long time. It's hard to see someone cross over. I was scared you'd tell them."

"But they know Paulie and Molly." Boone said trying to see the puzzle pieces.

She nodded. "They've met them, but Paulie and Molly never hung out at my house. They never said more than five words to my family. I couldn't risk one of them saying something stupid and getting me caught."

"You thought I wouldn't keep your secret."

"I wasn't sure." She admitted. "I … when Skye pulled up at the track, I thought it would be my dad or the cops. I never dreamed it would be Skye. That's why I called him tonight. I figured if you trusted him enough to send him to come get me when you couldn't, I might be able to trust him too."

Boone pulled her to him and rested his head on her head. "Why didn't you just call me?"

"I was pissed at you. I didn't want to see you. I wanted to race you away for a little while."

"You were racing from something, not to something?"

She nodded and a thought came to her. "When you came to the track, what were you thinking?"

"I was thinking that I needed to find you."

"And when you did." She prompted.

He took in a breath. "When I saw you pressed against Skye, I thought the worst. I thought that you …." He couldn't finish but he didn't need to.

"I was thanking him."

"Don't ever thank anyone like that again." His tone was dark.

She smiled. "I just whispered into his ear that the car was amazing, and I gave him a kiss on the cheek. It was nothing."

"But it didn't look like nothing, Jez."

She bit her lip and looked to her feet.

"Were you trying to make me jealous?" He suddenly asked as if it just dawned on him.

"I hadn't purposefully thought about it. And to be honest, I didn't even know you were there. But maybe I was. Maybe I was trying to see what you'd do if you found out."

"What did you expect me to do?"

She shrugged, thinking about all the things Paulie had done when he was jealous. She knew Boone wouldn't do those things, or she hoped he wouldn't.

"What did Paulie do when he was jealous?" Boone seemed to understand. He gave her a couple of minutes, but when she didn't answer, he pulled her face up to meet his. "Did he hurt you?"

She didn't need to answer. Tears filled her eyes and he pulled her into a tight embrace. Still holding her, but after a moment to compose himself, he promised, "I would never hurt you like that. Ever."

"I guess, without realizing it, I needed to make sure." She whispered.

He held her tight for several minutes, then spoke. "Did Skye …"

"No." She interrupted his thoughts. "No, he was amazing. He called you after all. I told him not to, but he did anyway." Then as the thought occurred to her, she pulled back and looked up at Boone. "I should be pissed at him for that."

Boone chuckled. "Naw, Ace. Don't be mad. He didn't actually call to tell me. We were going to get together tonight but he called to cancel and I asked what he was doing. When he said he was going to the races, I said I'd come along, but he got weird. He's not a good liar. Eventually he told me that you were racing and he was getting you a car. He told me not to show, but he knew I would anyway."

She couldn't have been mad at Sky. "You know he promised to watch my back, between hitting on other girls." She smiled.

"He's a good friend." Boone nodded. "But can I ask you to do something for me?"

He waited until she nodded, but she was doing it uncertainly slow.

"Next time, just call me. I'll take you wherever you want to go, no matter what." He rubbed the side of her face with a finger.

"But if you aren't around, or we're fighting like tonight, …"

"Still call me. Or, I guess, if you can't get me, Skye. But don't trust anyone else, OK?"

"On the racing front, alright." She agreed.

"On all fronts, Ace. I don't trust anyone else." He was being so serious, it was scary.

"OK, you, Skye, and the three amigos." She smiled.

"I'm still not sure about them." He offered her a small smile.

"Well, they're just as much family as Jordy, so get use to them." She said. Her phone vibrated and she pulled it from her jeans. It was a message from Jordy.

'You better get home in twenty minutes or I'm waking dad.'

She typed back a quick message and put it back in her pocket.

"Who was that?"

"Jordy. He beat me home. He's threatening to wake dad." She replied taking a step away from Boone.

He allowed her too, but took her hand in his as they moved back toward his car. When he parked in front of her house, she leaned over and kissed him. But he didn't let her go with just a gently brush of her mouth. He pulled her in and she melted as his tongue traced her lips.

He walked her to the door and they stood under the dim porch light kissing more and making her light headed. When she stumbled in his arms, he pulled back. "I …"

"You?" She asked trying to get him to finish that thought.

Boone just shook his head though. "You'd better go in."

"I'm not going to get much sleep." She admitted.

"I'll see you tomorrow." He kissed her again, then tucked something into her sweatshirt pocket.

"What's that?"

"You're cut." He stepped away from her.

"I didn't race for money tonight. It's all Skye's."

"Skye got his cut, and the rest is yours."

"But what about you?"

"I won tonight too, Ace, don't you worry."

"Boone, come on," She put her hand in her pocket. "Then put it toward the…"

Boone ignored her and walked down the steps. As he got into his car, she pulled the money from her pocket. She looked wide eyed at the wad and then looked up to the car as it drove away.

☐

Chapter 34

Jez only got three hours of sleep before she had to get back up and open the store. She was barely on time, and was surprised to see a delivery truck waiting at the back door. She signed for the items and opened the door, allowing the driver to carry the boxes inside. He wished her a good day as she checked the manifest. Most of it was the typical things they usually ordered, but there were a few specialty items. It took her a moment to remember why they were ordered, but eventually she did, with a deep breath. She waited another hour before calling Skye's number.

"You know Boone's going to be pissed if you keep this up." Skye said before he even greeted her.

"I'm not calling to ask about a race, Skye. Those parts you ordered came in this morning."

"I'll come by later and get them." A high-pitched giggle could be heard in the background. There was a metal groan and a woman moaned. "Oh, and Ace, thanks for last night."

"Why are you thanking her?" The female asked. "I'm the one doing all the work."

"Shut up, slut." Skye replied.

"Hey." Jez said into the phone.

"Not you, Ace. I'll stop by later." He said into the phone. Jez heard the woman ask who the bitch was on the other end as Skye cut the line.

Jez couldn't help but laugh as she turned her attention on other duties.

Jez worked until four. OB came in at eleven to help her out and took lunch at three, which was when Skye came in to pick up the parts. She offered to pay for half of them since they were to replace what had been damaged on the car she was driving, but he rolled his eyes at her. "No. We were the ones who sabotaged the car, we'll repair it."

"But the money from last night's race..."

"You earned." He shut her down.

She looked at him curiously. "I didn't want to race for the money. I shouldn't have got any of that. And I should pay you a percent for the use of the car anyway."

"Ok, I'm going to say this one more time, so listen up." He leaned on the counter and got dangerously close to her. His eyes sparkled and she swallowed nervously. "First, you won me twice what you got last night so don't even worry about the winnings. Second, I don't charge friends for favors. That car wasn't exactly what I wanted but it did in the pinch."

"It was sweet." She said softly, thinking about the speed and smoothness of the ride.

"Third," He continued. "That was your one free-be. I will help out and do favors, but don't you ever think that I'll hide something from Boone."

"You didn't hide anything from him. You told him about the race." She said stunned.

"But I hadn't planned to. The only reason I did was because he backed me into a corner." He leaned closer, nose to nose with her. "You make him happy. He's my best friend. So in turn, you make me happy. If you want to stay in that place, don't ever ask me to keep anything from him again."

Jez swallowed and nodded slowly. "Bros before hoes. Got it."

His lips broke into a smile and he chuckled. "You are a curious one, Ace."

The bell over the door rang and Skye leaned away from her as she peeked around him to see Ty watching them closely as he came in. "Everything OK, Jez?"

She took half a step back and smiled. "Yep. Skye was just here picking up his order."

Ty stepped around the counter and looked at the order form that lay between Skye and Jez. "You got some nice stuff here. You're building something fast."

"I like them fast." Skye smiled and glanced at Jez. "So how much do I owe you?"

She moved over to the register and began to ring the order. Ty moved back to gather the items, which Jez had already pulled together on one of the work benches in the back. Skye paid and winked at Jez as he lifted one of the five large boxes that he was picking up. Ty followed Skye out and Jez gathered a third box. She placed it in the back of a truck as the two guys got the last ones. When it was all loaded, Skye turned to Jez. "See you soon, Ace."

She shifted uncomfortably under his gaze, just as Ty called from the open doorway. "Jez."

"Bye Skye." She turned and headed inside, Ty walking close to her.

"So ... Skye?" He asked interested.

"He's a friend of Boone's."

"And very interested in you." Ty said. "If you like Boone like we all think you do, be careful. This guy's trouble."

She turned and looked at him. "You say that about all the guys who take an interest in me."

"And it's true." He leaned against a shelf.

"So, you think Boone's trouble?"

Ty thought for a moment. "I don't know about Boone. I think he could be trouble, but not when it comes to you."

Jez looked at him. "Why?"

"He seems to really care about you. He ... I probably shouldn't tell you this, but he's done things that most guys wouldn't."

"Like what?"

"Like ..." Ty sighed, not wanting to tell her but unable to stop himself. "Like he came and spoke to Jordy and your dad one night. He wanted to make sure it was OK to take you out. Most guys wouldn't have done that. They'd have just asked you out or left you alone. But he cares enough about you to do the right thing."

"The right thing." She repeated to herself. She thought about all those times that he had pulled away from her.

"Look, Jez, I know you have to go, but I just think that between Boone and another guy, a guy like Skye there, Boone's a better choice."

She looked up at Ty, confusion and shock rolling through her. "Between Boone and Skye? What are you talking about?"

"I saw the way he was looking at you when I came in. He was really ... close."

"Skye is Boone's best friend. He was warning me not to hurt Boone. He's not interested in me, at all, not like that."

Ty chuckled darkly. "Sure Pickle. You keep telling yourself that."

Jez turned away from Ty and moved into the back room. The bell over the door rang and she heard OB come in. She grabbed up her bag and moved back into the main room. The two guys stopped talking when she came in. "What?"

They both grinned like monkeys. "Have fun tonight."

"It's just family dinner, just like every Saturday." She said moving across the room. But before she got to the door, she stopped and turned back to them. "What do you know?"

"We don't know anything," OB said with faked innocence that wouldn't have fooled a five-year-old. Ty turned his eyes every place but on her.

Suddenly annoyed, she moved back to them. Dropping her bag on the counter, she jumped up on it and spun over it on her butt. Coming to her feet right in front of them, she grabbed their shirt collars. "You had better tell me what you know, or I could make your lives incredibly miserable."

Ty laughed at her threat, still casting his eyes on anything but her. But OB was more interested in her face. She had left her hair down and had worked hard to keep her cheek hidden, but standing just in front of him now, he could easily see the dark mark from the bruise. "Jez, what happened to your cheek?"

Ty's eyes jumped down to her instantly. He grabbed her chin, and although she fought him, he turned her just enough to see the mark. "Please God tell me…"

"I fell." She lied. "Now tell me what you know."

Both guys were serious instantly. They glanced at each other and then back at her, but it was Ty that spoke. "You tell your secret, we'll tell ours."

She narrowed her eyes. Dropping her hands from their shirts, she replied. "I'm not playing games."

"Did Boone do it?" OB asked quickly as she turned from them. When she spun around to face them again, he explained. "Look Jez, we know that you fall. We can tell the difference between bruised knees and elbows and a bruise from being hit. You just tell who it was and we'll take care of it."

She had about two seconds to debate what to do. Stepping up to them again she said in a hushed voice. "It wasn't Boone. I'm fine, and he took care of it. Please don't say anything about it to anyone."

"You honestly think you can keep it hidden from your dad and Jordy?" Ty asked.

She swallowed knowing they might be right. "I don't know but I'm going to try. Promise me that you won't say anything."

"Ok, we won't say anything. But if we even get a hint that he laid a hand on you …" Ty started.

"I swear. It wasn't him." She agreed. "He wouldn't."

She grabbed up her bag and headed out the door, too worried about her friends to remember that they knew something she didn't.

Chapter 35

It wasn't until she was two houses away from her own and saw the Barracuda sitting in front of her house that she remembered. She cursed herself for forgetting and then worried what Boone was doing there. She pushed into the front door and heard the men's laughter outback. Setting her bag on the sidebar table, Jez went to investigate. Boone, Jordy, and her dad were all standing around the bar-be-cue talking, each had a beer in his hand. As if sensing her presence, Boone looked up with a bright smile.

"Hey gorgeous." He crossed the yard as she moved out back. Leaning down, he gave her a gentle kiss. He tasted like beer. Jez had to fight not to push for more.

"What are you doing here?" She asked him.

"Your dad invited me." Boone answered wrapping an arm around her shoulders.

Her dad smiled at her. "I thought we should hang out and get to know him better. After all, he's the first guy you've allowed us to meet more than in passing."

"Not by choice." She mumbled under her breath.

"Why don't you go get cleaned up and come hang with us? Dinner should be done soon."

Jez nodded and went back inside. She heard them laugh about something as she started up the stairs. She headed for the bathroom and washed her face, then changed clothes. She was standing at the sink brushing out her hair, the door open, when Jordy rounded the corner. "Hey sis. Dinner's almost ready."

"Thanks. I'll be right down." She smiled and pulled the brush across the side of her head. She realized her mistake when her brother's eyes grew wide.

"What the fuck happened to your face?"

"Oh, I fell." She tried the same lie again, and just like before, it failed.

"No you didn't. I know better. Did he do this?" Jordy was growing angry, and he grabbed for her arm as he drug her down the stairs. She told him over and over it wasn't Boone, but Jordy was too mad to hear. He pushed her into the yard and then directly in front of her dad and Boone. Gripping her chin, he turned her head so the mark was visible. "Did you do this?"

Jez saw her dad bristle. "I told you, it wasn't him."

Boone remained calm though. "No, I didn't."

"Then who did?" Jordy was almost beyond hearing because of his rage.

Boone looked at Jez calmly. "You tell them or I will."

Tear blurred Jez's eyes. She puckered her lips but then gave in. "It was Paulie."

Jordy dropped his hands from his sister, as Boone explained. "We ran into him last night. Jez had gone to the bathroom and he cornered her. I saw him raise is hand but by the time I got there it was too late."

The group was silent for a moment as they processed the information. Jez didn't look up at Boone, too scared that her startled reaction would let them on to the untruth. Finally, her dad ordered, "Go on."

"He's pissed I'm seeing Boone." She added to the story.

"He won't be laying a hand on her again." Boone said.

"Did you kill him?" Jordy's voice was as dark as Jez had ever heard it.

"No, but I wanted to." Boone admitted. Jez knew that wasn't a lie. "I broke his nose, a few ribs, and hopefully his jaw though." Then as a smile crossed his face, he added. "And Jez punched him in the balls."

Jordy and her dad looked at her in surprise. "You did what?"

"Good girl." Her dad smiled.

Another moment of silence settled over them. Boone looked Jez in the eyes as she blinked back the tears. Her dad took a few swigs of his beer, and Jordy just shook his head processing the information. Finally, he looked at his sister. "Really? You punched him in the balls? You could have just kicked him."

She looked at her brother and shook her head. "If I had kicked him, I might have fallen over."

They all looked at her and then started to laugh. Jordy wrapped an arm around her and gave her a hug. "You're something else."

Her dad was next, putting a kiss on her head. "Oh my Pickle, I guess I don't need to worry about you as much as I do."

When he let her go so he could remove the steaks from the grill, Boone wrapped her up in his arms and held her tight. "I love you so much, Ace."

They ate dinner around the dining room table and the boys talked about everything from cars to sports. Jez didn't understand most of what they were discussing, but they were having so much fun, she didn't mind. When dinner was over, Jordy and Jez cleaned the kitchen while Boone and their dad went outside to talk. Standing over the kitchen sink, Jez looked out at her dad and Boone laughing.

"You like him?" Jordy asked drying a plate and looking over her shoulder.

Jez nodded. "Yea, I do." When he didn't say anything, she looked over at him. "He says he loves me. Do you think it's possible?"

Jordy turned to her as if she had just told him the world was going to end. "Possible? Possible to what, love you or love you so quickly?"

"Either or both." She said softly turning to face her brother. A tear swelled in her eye.

He put the plate down and grabbed her by the shoulders. "Jezebel. It is completely possible for someone to fall in love with you. Do I think he could have fallen so fast? I don't know. I know that I did. I fell in love my little sister in about ten seconds."

"Liar." She smirked and then flicked soapy water from her hands onto him.

He got a wide eyed look and smiled brightly. He reached in and grabbed up a handful of suds. She started to laugh as he blew the large mass at his sister. It landed on her face and she looked stunned that he would do that, but then she reached her hand in and grabbed for more. In a fit of laughter, soap suds, and wrestling; the siblings had an all-out war right there in the kitchen. When Boone and their dad came into the kitchen, they found the two of them wet from head to toe, half the floor covered in suds and water, laughing so hard they couldn't even stand.

"Well, I haven't seen this in a long time." Her dad chuckled.

Jez sat in a pool of water giggling. "I'll clean it up, Dad."

"You bet, you will." He tried to sound stern but couldn't quite manage it. "Right after you walk Boone out. Jordy can start without you."

They watched as he grabbed a beer from the fridge and headed into the living room. Boone stepped over and offered Jez a hand up. She took it and practically flew into his arms when he pulled her up. He caught her and wrapped his arms around to steady her. He smiled and gave her a look she didn't understand. Without a word, they turned and headed out the back door. They walked around the house and out to where his car waited patiently. At the curb, he pulled her close. But before kissing her, he glanced down with the same curious look.

"What?"

"I've been wondering what you looked like wet." He smiled and she knew he didn't mean covered in water. "Guess I've got a little bit of an idea."

She blushed. "You want to make me wet?" It was as much as she could say, telling him that just his presence had the same effect seemed more than she could openly admit to right now.

His eyes rolled back in his head, and offered her a small moan. "More than you will ever know."

"How about I make you wet?" She said and then jumped into his arms, rubbing her wet clothes against him.

He laughed and held her close to him. His eyes turned from fun to sultry. He grabbed the back of her head and leaned in to brush his lips against hers. Her breath quickened and her blood pressure rose. The longer he kissed her the more light-headed she got. But she didn't stop kissing him. She couldn't get enough. When the darkness threatened, she pulled her head back, and he trailed kisses down her throat. He didn't stop until her knees gave out.

"Ace? Jez?" Boone's voice was near but she had a hard time seeing him through the black. After a moment, she came to.

She was seated on the curb. "Sorry."

"For what?" He smiled. "I should be the one apologizing."

It took her a minute but she looked over at him with a sly smile. "Don't ever apologize for doing that."

The screen door slammed. "Jez? Jez, you OK?"

"I'm fine." She smiled at Boone as her brother and dad came up behind them. "You might want to leave now."

He shook his head with a small smile, but he still held concern in his eyes. "Not until I know you're alright."

Jordy and her dad were standing over her then, looking down with worry. She smiled up at them. "I got light-headed but I'm fine."

She tried to get up. Boone, Jordy, and her dad all were quick to reach out to her. "OK little pickle, time for bed."

She weaved a little and Boone scooped her up. She giggled as he turned and carried her back inside the house. He started up the stairs but then stopped and turned to look at her dad. "I hope I'm allowed upstairs."

Her father chuckled. "Absolutely not." Jez watched as he turned his back on them and walked into the kitchen.

Boone looked down at her and winked. He headed up anyway. Jez heard the second set of footsteps and knew that Jordy was right behind. "Second door on the left." She said.

Jordy stepped around them and pushed open her door. Boone stepped in and Jez hit the light switch with her foot. She was suddenly very thankful that she had cleaned her room recently.

"So this is where you sleep."

Boone took it in, still holding Jez in his arms, and she looked around her as if seeing it for the first time too. Her walls were sea foam green, the same color that her mother had painted it when she was five. There were posters on the wall. One of the ocean, another of a famous surfer, the third of a band she liked. There were shelves along one wall that held books, music, and a couple of trophies she had won in competitions through the years. Her stuffed animals sat along the top shelf. She had a double bed and a dresser. A single nightstand sat beside the bed with her clock radio and a single light. There was a ceiling fan with light that illuminated the room as well. Boone stepped over and placed her gently on the quilt that her grandmother had handmade.

"Not what I expected." Boone murmured. Jez looked up at him, wanting to ask but knew she couldn't with Jordy hovering in the doorway. Boone leaned down and kissed her gently, and she leaned up for more. He pulled away with a smile. "Rest, Ace. I'll see you tomorrow."

She watched him leave the room and heard his footsteps pound down the stairs. Jordy stepped into the room as she gasped for breath and gripped her chest. "You alright?"

"Yep." She smiled. "I'm fine."

He climbed onto the bed. "No, you're not."

She looked up at him, trying to hide the pain in her chest. "It's worth it."

"Are you sure?" He didn't sound as certain.

She looked over and nodded. "He's worth everything, Jordy."

He twisted his lip and poked her in the ribs. "Who'd have thunk, my kid sis fell in love."

She smiled and settled back into her pillow.

☐

Chapter 36

When the alarm went off on Sunday morning, Jez was in the middle of an amazing dream. Saddened that it was over, she swallowed the lump in her throat as she pushed out of bed. She seemed more tired and emotionally heavier than usual. It wasn't until she stumbled into the bathroom and remember what day it was that she knew why. Sunday. Her least favorite day of the week. She was ready for work thirty minutes later and headed downstairs. She got halfway down the stairs when she heard her dad and Jordy talking. She lightened her steps and listened in curiously.

"Next weekend, your sister's going away with Boone. Work it out so they have the time off."

"What!" Jordy voice was high pitched with shock. "You can't be serious."

"Shh, I am completely serious. He asked yesterday. Apparently that band she likes, Stone … whatever, is playing at some festival out in the desert. He asked if she could go. He already had planned on going with a group of his friends, and thought she might like to go also. I told him it was fine."

"Dad, you know that's not a good idea. He thinks he loves her, and she's falling for him."

Her dad laughed. "I know. But I think we need to trust them." There was a banging sound. "Look, this is the first boyfriend she's ever brought around."

"Not by choice." Jordy mentioned.

"Maybe not, but he seems like a stand-up guy. Besides, she's nineteen. She's not a kid. Almost everyone she went to high school with is gone. All off at college doing hell knows what. We have a chance to show her we trust her, so she doesn't have to sneak around. I really don't want to have a repeat of high school. Remember what that was like?" Her dad sighed.

Jordy sighed too. "The rumors, the secrets, never knowing what was true." Jez could hear the heaviness in his voice. "But a weekend away?"

"I know, but if she wants to go, let her."

Sensing a pause in the conversation, Jez pounded down the rest of the stairs. "Morning Daddy, Jordy."

"Hey baby, how did you sleep?"

"Good." She smiled at him and poured herself some coffee.

While she sat and drank it, her father went over the usual things he did with them before he left. At one point, Jordy even mimicked him because the speech was used so often. This made Jez snicker and her father frown. "It's only because I love you both so much. "

"We love you too, Dad, but we got this." Jez smiled and dumped her coffee mug into the hot soapy water.

She waved at Jordy and gave her dad a quick kiss good-bye. But he followed her out the back door, "Jez?"

She turned to face him. "What dad? I'm going to be late."

"I think your boss will understand." He smiled at their running joke. "Look, I just want you to be careful."

"Dad." she started to argue but he held up his hand.

"I'm serious. Boone is a nice guy, but he's a few years older than you, and way more experienced. I want you to … protect yourself. Make sure that …" He stopped and swallowed. Jez saw the pain in his face as he started again, "If you're going to have …."

"Dad." She stopped him right there knowing where this was going. "I'm not sleeping with him."

With a grimace, he said, "yet."

"And if I do, I'll be careful. I promise." She smiled. "Daddy, I love you and I know you're scared. This thing between Boone and I came out of nowhere. I know."

"You both seem to be moving very fast." He nodded.

"I know, and if I knew how to slow it down, I would. But it just feels right." She knew those words would have a high impact on him. Whenever her or her brother would ask about falling in love, he would always say it would feel right. And whenever Jordy wasn't sure about a girl, their dad would ask if it felt right. It usually didn't. Paulie had never felt right. But this, with Boone, it just did.

Her dad slowly nodded understanding. "Then I'm going to trust you."

She gave him a quick kiss on the cheek and a big hug. "I love you, Daddy." With a smile, she turned and bounced down the drive.

She had only gotten two houses when her smiled began to fade though. The conversation she had overheard played over and over again in her head. She wasn't upset that her brother and father were talking about her, what seemed to eat at her was that Boone had spoken to her father about going away first. She wasn't sure she had even wanted to go, but it seemed she was already on the road. She had to admit that Boone's cover story was good, but she didn't like that he had spoken to her dad before talking it over with her. The closer she got to work, the more pissed she got about it. She realized it was because it was just the thing that Paulie would have done. He never asked what she wanted. He just made the plans. And that's what this felt like, plans being made without her, like she was just one of the cars. She was in quite a mood when she pushed into the front door of the shop.

An hour later, her mood hadn't improved. She had tried, turning up the radio and doing as much physical labor as she could manage. When OB came to work, the shelves were stocked, the place was dusted, and the floors swept. The radio was still a little loud, and he gave her a curious look, but she just smiled tightly and turned back to the schedule she was working on for the coming week. "Everything OK, Jez?"

"Just fine." She replied as he rounded the counter and moved to drop his jacket in the office.

He stayed out of her way most of the morning, helping customers and watching her closely. At a little after one, sunlight sparkled off the metallic flakes in a bright green paint job caught Jez's eye. She watched as the car pulled into the spot directly in front of the store, stopped for a moment, then pulled out again. Jez sighed recognizing the signal. She waited until OB was done helping his customer and then called that she was going to get something to drink. He waved her off dismissively as she headed for the door.

There was a Circle Go on the opposite corner from the shop, and Jez made the short walk easily. As she crossed the street, she spotted the neon green Mazda sitting in the parking lot. By the time she was crossing the parking lot to it, Mel was leaning against the side with a smile. "Hey. "

"Mel? What's up?"

"I got a call from Boone. He said you wanted in on the Desert Run this weekend." He watched her face carefully, judging her reaction. "Is this true?"

"If he says so." She replied trying to keep the venom out of her voice.

Mel's eyes narrowed. "They don't play games out there, Bels."

"You don't think I can handle it?"

"You've got the balls, but I'm worried about your nerve." He replied. "Ability is only part of the equation out there. Equipment and presence play into it too."

She waited as he looked her over.

"I'm not sure you're got all three, kid."

"Really?" She was getting annoyed at all these men, and it started to show. "You don't think I can play with the big boys?"

He smiled. "Oh, I know you can. The question is will you."

She felt her shoulders and back tense.

Mel sighed. Standing up and taking a step toward her, he looked her in the eye. "Look. Between us, you've got this. I'd put big money on you. But if you go, you can't show them any weakness. They thrive on eating people up out there. It's the best of the best. I know you can dominate, but you've got to be like you were before."

She nodded in understanding. "You get me in, and I'll be there."

He rolled his lips as he leaned back against his car again. "You should know that Sean's going too. There's a chance, not a big one but a chance none-the-less, that you'd have to race him."

She shrugged. "I've beaten him before; I can do it again."

"Do you have a car?"

"Not your problem, Mel."

"It is if I'm placing money on you." He was dead serious, and she couldn't hide her surprise. Mel was notorious for not betting, and the few times he did it was only on a sure thing. He loved money way too much to waste it on anything less than the best.

"You're betting on me?"

"Every time. So don't blow it." He winked at her, and pushed off the side of his car. "See you Friday."

She watched him get back into his car, and she stepped back onto the sidewalk. Pushing away the shock, she headed inside the Circle Go to get that drink she said she wanted.

Jez and OB worked until close. He tried to talk to her several times, but she always ended the conversation quickly. She still wasn't in the best of moods and as they locked the door. As he gave her one last glance, he said, "Are you sure you don't want to tell me what's wrong?"

"Nothing's wrong." She snapped, but then twisted her lips with a release of her breath. "Sorry, I guess I'm just tired."

"Well then, let me give you a ride." He pointed to his car, and while she would have rather walked, she knew she couldn't decline the ride. She walked over and climbed into the passenger side and slumped down in the seat. The ride was sort and silent, and she wasn't surprised when he pulled into the driveway and parked. He followed her inside, where she smiled at her brother before climbing the stairs.

"What's up with her?"

"Says she's tired, but she's been in a mood all day." OB replied to Jordy's question.

Jez was at the top of the stairs and listened as the two guys talked. She heard the bottle pop open and wished she'd taken one up with her.

"She was in a good mood when she left this morning." Jordy said absently mindedly.

"She's probably just got the curse." OB said dismissively.

Jez rolled her eyes and headed into her room and then into a shower. She was tired, she realized: tired of all the crap, tired of men who didn't get her, tired of men who wanted to run her life for her. As she stood under the hot water, Jez reached for the razor. It was an old-fashioned kind with a metal blade that was held in by a small screw. Carefully, she freed the sharp blade and held it in her fingers. While she knew she shouldn't, she knew in the long run it wouldn't help, something inside her just wanted a release. She pressed it to her ribs and held it steady. It had been a long time since she had been here. She tried to talk herself out of it. She thought of how Jordy would freak if he found out. How embarrassed she'd be if the others knew. She allowed her mind to think of what Boone would say if he knew. She pictured him being angry, of him being disgusted by her dirty little secret. He would leave and never return. He wouldn't want her. That would be better, wouldn't it?

It didn't take much pressure to slice through the first few layers of skin. It wasn't a deep gash, practically a scratch. Just enough to draw little beads of blood and release the pressure that had built up. Just enough to remind her she was in control of something in her life. She felt like a deflating balloon. Her anger and frustration slowly leaked out, like the blood that now tracked down her stomach. Replacing the blade in her razor, Jez placed her hands flat against the shower wall and dropped her head allowing the water to run down her back. Tears swelled in her and she allowed them to fall down her cheeks. She stayed like that until her feet turned red with the blood that pooled in them making her head spin. She finished getting ready for bed and then crawled under the covers. She felt weak and exhausted in more ways than she could count. She was spent.

It wasn't much longer before her brother came in and curled up on her bed. She didn't turn to him. She couldn't face him on this night. Not after what she had just done in the shower. "Are you alright, Pickle?"

"Yes."

"OB said you seemed upset today."

"Just tired."

He was silent for a moment. Jez wondered if that would be all, but then he asked. "Did you talk to Boone today?"

"Nope."

"I'm sure he was just busy."

The room grew silent again. It was in that stillness that she realized that Jordy was thinking her mood was because she hadn't spoken to Boone. She thought about it and knew it wasn't true. She had been avoiding Boone most of the day. He had text and called her several times, but she had purposefully tucked her phone into the depths of her bag. She wasn't ready to face him yet. She was still too mad. She adjusted herself and felt the soreness of her new cut. Shame filled her.

Jordy leaned over and put a kiss on her head. "Good night, Jez. I love you."

"I love you too." She replied weakly. She forced her eyes to close and it wasn't long before she was in a happier place.

Chapter 37

She woke alone as usual. Her alarm buzzed and pulled her from her dreams. As she sat up and took in a deep breath, the weight of everything settled on her. Her mind pulled back the events from yesterday. She remembered learning that Boone had gone behind her back and spoken to her father, Mel's conversation about going to the races, and then her moment in the shower. Jez got up and went to the bathroom. She looked at her cut. It was red and angry as they often were the day after. She cleaned it, and then prepared for her day. Once she was dressed, she took a moment to give herself a pep talk before going downstairs. Jordy was sitting at the kitchen table eating breakfast while OB and Ty gave Boone heavy looks.

"What's going on?"

Jordy looked up at his sister as she entered the room. "Boone here was just going to ask you something."

Boone got up and smiled at her brightly. "You look pretty." He wrapped his arms around her stomach as he pulled her close. She tried not to flinch as his fingers pressed her shirt into the thin scratch.

"Thanks." She glanced over to the three guys who were eyeing them darkly. "Why do they look pissed?"

Of course, Jez already knew what this was about, but she didn't want them to know she knew. So with big, curious eyes, she looked up at Boone. He was smiling down at her. With a quick wink, he said. "I have a surprise for you. You know that band you like?"

"Stone Cold?"

"Yeah, them. They're playing this rock fest out in the desert this weekend. I got us tickets."

"Really!" She smiled brightly, then allowed her smiled to fade. "You're just teasing me."

"I wouldn't do that to you." He smiled, then chuckled as she jumped into his arms and squealed. "We leave Friday and will be back on Sunday."

She forced herself to fall away from him. "But I have to work."

"Taken care of Jez." Jordy said over a mouthful of food. "You just go and have fun."

She moved around Boone and walked over to stand next to the table. "You're OK with this?"

The tension could have been cut with a knife, but each of the three guys nodded their heads. OB spoke on everyone behalf. "You deserve to have some fun, Pickle. You work too hard. Go and enjoy."

She forced an excited smile. As she walked around the table, she gave each guy a peck on the cheek and a big thank you. She stopped at Jordy a second time and wrapped her arms around him. "Thank you."

"Don't Jez." He patted her hands and then pulled them away. She knew he wasn't happy about this. Just as she knew he wasn't doing it for her, or for Boone. He was allowing her to go because of what their dad had said yesterday.

"Hey Ace, we've got to go if we're going to get you to treatments on time." Boone said from the other room.

"Don't forget you're closing every night this week." Ty called to Boone as he led Jez to the front door.

"Don't worry, I won't be late." Boone smiled, wrapping a hand around Jez's and pulling her out the front door. When they were safely in his car, she turned her body to glare at him. He pulled away from the curb before noticing her dark look. "What?"

"You spoke to everyone about this before me." She was more annoyed that she realized.

"It was supposed to be a surprise." He replied confused. "Besides, you knew about this."

"I hadn't made a decision about going. I thought we were going to talk about it more. Then I would be the one to tell everyone a story."

"I'm sorry. I didn't do it to upset you." He was being honest she could tell by his expression. "It just kind of happened."

"How? How did you making up this elaborate lie just happen? How did it happen that you talked with my dad, and Mel, and the three amigos before talking to me?" She snapped.

He kept glancing over at her with the same worried look, before having to dart his eyes back to the road before them. He was truly oblivious to why she was so upset. "I had planned on talking to you and coming up with something, but Saturday night when I saw the poster in your room, I just knew what to do."

"You just knew?"

"Yes," his eyes darted to her. "That band is playing at the race. They have these concerts each night of the races, and they're playing. Skye and I are going no matter if you decided to go or not, Ace."

"And you just decided to speak to my dad?"

He took in a deep breath as a light turned red and he pulled to a stop. "I mentioned to him how I didn't know you liked Stone Cold, and how I was going to see them this weekend. The words just slipped out as I asked if he thought you'd like to go with me. At first he seemed pissed but then I said that it was a big group that was going to the festival together and that I could probably get an extra ticket."

"And he just said yes?" She asked doubtfully.

"He didn't say no. He was just quiet and thoughtful for a bit. Then he asked me a few questions."

She interrupted, "Like what?"

"Like how we were getting there and where we were sleeping, and who was going. Normal stuff." He shrugged.

"And then he just said, hey sure, take my daughter."

Boone smiled. "Not in those words, but ...yes."

"What were his words exactly?"

"He said that he thought you would enjoy it. He told me that I had to be very careful though, because of your condition. And he was very clear about how you and I were not to sleep together."

"And you promised that?" She gave him a narrow look.

Boone looked away as they continued up the busy street. "Not really. I promised I would keep you as safe as I possibly could. I told him I'd watch you every second of each day, and I'd make sure that you were taken care of and protected."

Jez turned her head and looked out the side window. "And when were you going to discuss all this with me?"

"I had planned on talking to you yesterday, but you wouldn't answer any of my calls." He said pointedly.

"I was busy. I had to work." She snapped.

"And that's why I'm here now, taking you to treatments and talking about it." He reached out and took her hand in his. "If you don't want to go, just say so."

"I already told Mel I would." She replied darkly. Her mood was not improving.

"I didn't mean to piss you off, Ace. I swear. I guess I just thought it would be easier for you if this all came from me. Then you wouldn't have to be put on the spot with your family if they shot us down."

"I'm surprised they didn't."

"Well, if Jordy had any say, they would have. He's pissed. I'm not sure I'm going to be able to get back on his good side for quite a while." Boone said with a smile.

"He's so protective. He's been through a lot, and I just keep putting him through more and more." Her memories pulled back images of him holding her as she cried, cleaning her cuts, holding her as she drifted off to sleep, screaming at her about Paulie, staying by her bedside in the hospital and then again at home after the accident. He was always right there, by her side.

"It's harder for him to admit your growing up than it is for your dad." Boone agreed. They were silent for a little while. Boone reached their destination and pulled into a parking spot. "Are you going to forgive me? I honestly thought it would be easier this way. I didn't mean to hurt you."

She swallowed and looked at him. "You've got to include me."

"If you don't want to go, just say so."

Jez shook her head. "I already told Mel I'd go. I have to now, so you better have a fucking fast car for me." She pointed her finger at him.

He smiled. "Don't worry about that, Ace. I've got you covered all the way around."

They popped the doors open and he pulled her to him as they walked into the center. They checked in and Boone went to buy them coffee while Jez used the bathroom, before they headed upstairs. They had to wait a few minutes before being called back, but when she was finally settled and hooked up, she turned back to the conversation. "So, what's the plan?"

"Well, I want you to drive the car a couple of times before we head out. Then Friday we'll come get you and bring you home Sunday." Boone said.

"It better be a fast car, Boone." She threatened. Her mood was only a tiny bit lighter than it had been on the ride over, and he knew he was in trouble with her.

"It is." He smiled and took her hand in his. His cell phone chirped and he pulled it from his pocket. His face frowned as he read the text. He glanced up for a second, then pulled his hand back from where it was wrapped around Jez's.

"What is it?"

"Nothing, Ace." He smiled, but it was forced.

"You don't have to sit here with me, you know." She said as he typed his reply.

"It's fine. I want to be here. I don't like thinking of you doing this alone." He said hitting send.

She watched him. He seemed tense now. Something in the message had upset him. "Who was it?"

"No one important."

She grew annoyed. "Look, if you want this to work you can't make plans for me. Don't treat me like I'm property. And don't lie to me or keep secrets from me. I get that you won't tell me everything, but be upfront about that. Just say so if you don't want to tell me something."

"Is that what Paulie did? Keep secrets? Lie? Treat you like property?" Boone watched her face carefully.

"It's what they all do, and if this is going to work, you need to be different from them." Jez wasn't sure where all this honesty was coming from. She hadn't felt particularly strong this morning, and the spot on her stomach rubbed against the shirt reminding her of her own secrets and lies. But maybe that was why she was saying all these things. She knew she held enough pain and deceit for both of them.

His phone chirped again and he looked to it. She could tell whatever it said didn't make him happy. His jaw tightened, but when he looked up to her again he forced another smile.

"It's fine." She said, "Go."

"Nope."

Anger grew in her. "I don't want you here. I don't want you, or anyone else, to see this."

"I'm not leaving you." He shook his head and spoke softly as if that would calm her. His phone chirped again, he fought against looking at it, but eventually he did. He typed back a response then brought his attention to her. She was staring at him with such intensity, he seemed to shrink. "It's nothing that you need to worry about, Ace. It's nothing important. And definitely not as important as you are."

It chirped again.

"I don't want you here anymore. Leave." She snapped.

A nurse appeared in the doorway and it was only then that Jez remembered they weren't alone. Everyone in the room, three other patients and two visitors plus the nurse, were all watching them. The nurse stepped over and placed a hand on Boone's shoulder. "Maybe you should go."

His head snapped up and he glared at her. But then he turned back to Jez. "Is that really what you want, Ace?"

"Yes. How many times do I have to say it? Go away, Boone." Jez said, pushing as much intensity as she could into the words.

He looked closely at her, trying to see if she was being honest with him, but she was putting up such a front he couldn't tell. All he could see was the pain. But he didn't know where the pain was coming from. "Fine. I'll go. Text me when you're done and I'll take you home."

She watched him stand. She could tell he was pissed. She also knew it was half because of her dismissing him, but the other part was because of whatever was going on the other end of the phone. He leaned over to give her a kiss, but she turned her head and he placed it on her cheek instead of her lips. He narrowed his eyes at her, and then turned from her. "Call me."

She didn't watch him directly as he walked away. Instead she saw him type on the phone from the corner of her eye as he headed from the room. Tears formed in her eyes and the minute he was far enough down the hall to not see her, she pulled herself into as tight of a ball as she could. Dropping her forehead onto her knees, the tears spilled out. She hated crying in front of a room full of strangers. Especially a room full of strangers who just watched their first fight. But she just couldn't be strong anymore. She felt weak and spent again. Much like she had last night. Shame and fear mixed with the physical pain of the needle in her chest, and she just couldn't be strong anymore.

No one spoke as she cried silently in the chair. They gave her space for a long time. She heard their soft conversations pick back up and listened as the nurses came and went from the room. But she kept her head down, tears streaming from her eyes to her cheeks and then falling onto her jeans. She would sniffle every so often but that was the extent of the noise she made.

She felt the body come and sit down in the chair next to her, but Jez didn't look up until a tissue was shoved under her nose. "Sniffling is gross and could make you sick."

Jez raised her head a little and saw the nurse sitting next to her. She was a newer nurse with pretty blonde hair that was cut into a bob and big brown eyes. She held out a box of tissues and a weak, sad smile. Jez took two of the tissues and blew her nose. She tossed them in the trash can that sat beside her chair and then repeated the action twice more. When her nose was clear, and her tears were dried, she turned her attention to the nurse who was still sitting in the chair. "Thanks."

"You should let him be here. You need the support, you know."

Jez rolled her eyes. "I don't need someone sitting here looking at me like he does."

"You mean like he cares?" Her voice was kind but still cut.

Jez was silent for a few moments, then sighed. "You wouldn't understand. There's more to it that what you see."

"I'm sure there is. But I also know that he's the first person you've ever allowed in here, so you obviously like him. And you need to allow people to help you."

"I don't have cancer." Jez said with a little more snap than she intended.

The nurse's eyes were heavy on Jez. "No, but you are sick. You're fighting, and you don't need to fight this battle alone. Let someone, anyone, in to help."

"I'm fine." Jez said softer.

The nurse stood and put her hands on her hips. "Sure you are." With a shake of her head, the petite nurse walked away, leaving Jez to stew in her own thoughts.

When the rest of the treatments were done, all a little more painful than usual, Jez was weak and tired as she emerged from the center. The sun was warm but the air was crisp and cool. Jez glanced around looking for her ride, only to remember that the guys thought Boone had her, and Boone expected her to call. Too tired and emotional to face any of them, Jez walked to the nearest bus stop. She caught the next bus and took it as close to home as she could. She walked slowly, her feet growing heavier with every step, into her house and up the stairs. She barely made it to her bed, where she fell onto the covers and drifted off to sleep.

Jez woke to pounding feet and shouts. Her brother sounded frantic as he burst into her room. It took a breath for him to see her on the bed, curled into a ball, just lifting her head. She was groggy and confused. The darkness in the room didn't help. Jordy flipped on the light and rushed at her. "Fucking, Jesus Christ, Jez."

He wrapped his arms around her, pulling her into a tight hug as she fought to remember what was going on. "What's wrong?"

"You scared the fucking shit out of us. Don't you ever pull that shit again!" He threatened. He pulled back and looked her over.

"What did I do?" She remembered going to treatments and then coming home. She must have fallen asleep, but didn't actually remember.

He pulled out his phone from his pocket and sent out a text before returning his attention to her. "You were supposed to call for a ride home. Everyone thought you got a ride from someone else, until we all wound up at the shop together."

"I took the bus." She replied still not seeing why he was so upset. Feet pounded up the stairs and three other faces appeared in the doorway, then more feet pounded on the stairs. Jez looked up to see Ty and OB smile in relief, Boone looked pissed. In the hallway, she heard Skye ask is she was alright and another voice too. It sounded like Mel's, but why would he be here?

"She's fine, I think." Jordy called before asking Jez. "Why the fuck would you take the bus? Anyone of us would have come to get you?"

She shrugged. She didn't have an answer that would please them at the moment. Anything she could say would only piss them off and she was still too tired to fight.

"Come on, let's go downstairs." Ty said, pushing at OB, and then at Boone. "Give them a few minutes."

Jez listened to the sounds of the footsteps on the stairs as Jordy watched her. "What happened?"

"Nothing." She answered.

"Boone said you got upset at treatment and made him leave."

She shrugged. "I don't need him sitting there watching me get fluids."

"Come on Jez, you gotta let me in. What's going on?" The fear in his eyes was as clear as the tears that were forming.

Tears came easily for her too. As one traced her cheek, she debated on what to tell him.

"Is it this weekend? If you don't want to go, just say so. You don't have to go if you don't want." He was quick to jump to a conclusion.

She shook her head. "No, I want to go." It wasn't completely accurate it, but close enough. She felt obligated to go, and she would.

"Then what is it?"

"I'm scared." She whispered, tears dripping onto her shirt.

Jordy sighed and climbed onto the bed. He crawled behind her and pulled her onto his lap. Wrapping his arms around her like he used to when she was a child, he held her tight. "What are you scared of, Pickle?"

She had to take a minute to think about it. She really didn't know. Everything, all of it was overwhelming, but she didn't know how to say it. She shrugged to give her more time.

"Is it Boone?"

That seemed as close to the truth as anything.

"Are you scared of him?"

"I'm scared of being hurt again." She admitted, knowing that it was true. She felt his lips press against her head.

"If he hurts you, I'll kill him."

"You and what army? Have you seen his arms?" She smiled and felt him laugh.

"We can take him." He said softly. He paused, and then asked. "Why didn't you just call me? I would have come and got you?"

"I don't know. I just … I just wanted some time, I guess."

"Well you scared the fuck out of us. When Boone came in and asked if any of us had seen or heard from you, I just about went out of my mind." She felt him shutter. "And then you didn't answer your phone."

"I was asleep."

"Look, I know that you aren't going to like this, but for my piece of mind, would you please be with someone at all times, or at least let me know where you are?" She tensed, but he continued. "I know, you're not a child, but when you vanish I have these horrible images of you passing out somewhere, or … and …."

She heard him swallow and realized that, like herself, he always expected the worse. Guilt weighed on her shoulders because she knew this was all because of her. Her condition, her past, her secrets, and her lies had put her in the position. She had made her brother so scared for her safety that he couldn't breathe unless he knew she was safe. Jez nodded. "OK, Jordy. OK. I'll be with someone at all times, or you'll know exactly where I am and why I'm alone."

He sagged against her, pulling her tighter in his arms. "I just can't lose you, Jez."

She hadn't realized he was crying until this moment. Jordy was strong. He was one of the strongest people she knew. He didn't cry easily. He didn't cry when their mom left, or when he broke his arm. He didn't cry when dad left. The only times he cried was when it came to her. "I love you, Jordy."

"I love you too, Pickle."

Footsteps came to the doorway and a head peeked into the room. "You guys hungry?"

Jez looked up to see Ty smiling around the doorframe. She smiled weakly. Jordy answered though. "Hell yes, I'm starved."

"Good, because Skye and Mel just went to get some food and beer." Ty stepped into the room. "Why don't you cry babies clean up and come down?"

Jordy let go of Jez and she scooted away from him. She was slow to stand and Ty reached out to give her a stable hand while Jordy bounced off the bed and walked out of the room. As his footfalls vanished down the hall, Ty looked at Jez with knowing eyes. "I'm sorry. I didn't mean to scare you all."

"Are you OK?"

She nodded and swallowed down the emotions that threatened.

Reaching out, he brushed the half-dried tears away. "It's only because we love you."

"I know."

He hugged her and then let her go. She moved to the bathroom while he left her room. Her first thought was to just wash her face, but then elected to take a shower. She wasn't ready to go downstairs and face them all yet. A shower bought her more time. Under the hot water, she talked herself stronger. She built up the wall and leaned against it for support. As she pulled on knee length sweatpants and a collarless sweatshirt that hung off one shoulder, Jez knew she could face whatever waited below. She braided her hair and left her face make up free. She knew Skye, Mel, and Boone were downstairs probably sitting with Ty, OB, and Jordy. They would be talking and eating. Her two worlds, the two worlds she had worked so hard to keep apart, were colliding. Closing her eyes, Jez took in a breath and mentally placed her hands against her wall for support. She felt Ace there beneath the surface giving her strength. Ace wouldn't be allowed out tonight, but she could stay in the shadows giving her support. Jez told herself she could do this as she walked down the stairs.

The guys, as she expected, were all sitting around the living room eating pizza and drinking beer. Their conversation, no surprise to her, was about cars. She rolled her eyes and smiled as she crossed the room to the kitchen. There was a half a pizza left, but it didn't look appealing to her. She grabbed a cup from the cabinet and pulled a ginger ale from the fridge. As she poured the soda, she felt a change in the room's energy. Looking up, she saw Boone watching her closely. She gave him a little smile and turned back to the foaming liquid.

"Are you alright?"

"Sure." She smiled over her shoulder.

He stepped over and put a hand on her. "Do you want to talk about what happened?"

"Nope." She bit the inside of her cheek to ward off the emotions. She turned and looked up at him. "Did you get your problem solved?"

"Yep." He answered dismissively, and she could tell he wasn't going to say anymore on that subject, just as she wasn't going to about the events of the day. He placed a hand on her cheek and brushed his thumb across her lips. "I'm not going anywhere, Ace."

"Ok."

"No matter how hard you push."

"Fine."

His eyes narrowed. "I'll make you believe it."

She opened her mouth to reply but OB laughed into the room. He stepped over to the fridge and pulled it open. Grabbing a beer, he wrapped an arm around Jez, who stood right next to the white box, stepping between Boone and herself. In a smooth motion, OB pulled Jez back to the living room and away from Boone. He tossed her onto the sofa, next to Ty, who pulled her in for a half hug. Boone appeared next to her a moment later, setting her soda down on the table. Jez allowed her eyes to take in the scene before her and tried to hide the cringe. To her right sat her brother, OB, and Ty; to her left, Boone, Skye and Mel. She was the center, the balance point of the two groups. They were so different and yet so similar too. She sat and listened as they debated engines and cars for another hour. Then their conversation turned to surfing. Mel laughed as Skye talked about his adventures surfing in Australia, which impressed the rest of the group. When Jez finished her cup, Jordy sensed it. He brought her a fresh drink, one he knew she needed. It was light purple and grape flavored. Boone was quiet but observant the entire time. He looked into her cup and glanced at her. She smiled but didn't offer any explanation.

When the hour grew late, Skye and Mel said their good nights. They shook hands with the guys, and gave Jez an easy hug. When Skye had her pulled to him, he whispered in her ear. "Glad you're OK, Ace."

Mel, on the other hand, asked, "Are we still on for this weekend?"

She nodded and watched them walk out to their cars. When they shook hands at the curb, she closed the front door. As she turned, all four of the remaining guys were watching her. She took in a breath and moved across the room. Gathering up the empty bottles and cups, she began cleaning up to avoid the heavy looks. She took the first load to the kitchen and tossed it away, the air silent and hefty. When she returned to get another handful, Ty pulled her back onto the sofa between himself and Boone.

"So, Pickle. How was your day?" He asked trying to sound light, but not making it.

"Fine." She said hesitantly. "And yours?"

"Compared to some it was better. We only one hour of terror today instead of three." He referenced the last time she had vanished on them.

"I'm sorry. I didn't mean to worry you all."

"Mean to or not, you did." OB snapped.

"Leave her be." Jordy said taking a swig from his bottle. "She's promised to keep someone with her at all times or let me know where she is. This won't happen again."

"For a while." OB added. Jez caught the nasty look he tossed at Boone.

It was then that she realized what was going on. She hadn't see it before. OB, and the others, thought Boone had done something to upset her. They thought she was avoiding them because of Boone. Rubbing a hand across her forehead, she sighed. "I'm sorry. I'm sorry I didn't call any of you for a ride. I'm sorry I just wanted some time to myself. I'm sorry I came home and fell asleep. I'm sorry I'm not a good enough sister, or friend, or girlfriend, or whatever the hell I am to you." She was practically shouting now.

Boone reached out and grabbed her chin, turning her face to look at him. "No one said you're not good enough, Ace." He looked concerned. "We were just worried."

"I'm sorry." She said exasperated. "I didn't mean to make you all worry. It won't happen again."

Boone's eyes boor into hers. She could tell he wanted to know something but wasn't going to ask in front of the others. It was Ty who broke the silence, and pulled her attention away. "It's only because we love you so much, Pick."

"I know."

"But that's the thing, I don't think you do." Ty said softly, keeping her attention. "I don't think you even have a clue how much we really love you. You aren't just a sister or a friend to us. You're part of us, a piece of us. When you hurt, so do we. When you're not happy, we aren't either. When OB gets pissed, we blow him off, but when you cry, our hearts break."

Tears formed in her eyes, as Jez listened to Ty say things that she didn't understand.

"You don't know what we go through because of you."

"Remember when we all got in that fight when she was in the hospital?" OB chuckled.

Jordy rubbed his jaw in memory. "You've got a left hook from hell, Ty."

"You guys don't fight." She said confused.

"We did that night."

"What night?"

Ty took her hand in his. "It was after the accident. You were fighting for your life, and we … we were lost. We didn't know what to do. We couldn't make this better. We didn't know what had happened or who to blame. We lashed out at each other because we didn't know who to lash out at as a group."

"I didn't know." She said, panic filling her.

Jordy gave Ty a dark look. "We didn't tell you for a reason."

"That's the kind of power you have over us. We may not be in love with you, Jez, but we love you none the less." Ty admitted squeezing her hand.

OB looked up at Boone. "Given a choice though, we would have rather beat the shit out of the one who let that happen, than each other." His eyes flashed to Jez. "Don't suppose you'd like to tell us now?"

She shook her head. "It was an accident. No one's fault."

"No one's fault you were behind the wheel of a car that does over 150 easy on a drag track?" OB spoke darkly.

Jez swallowed. They knew more about her accident that she wanted them to, and she had a horrible feeling they had put the pieces together to form a picture that was closer to the truth than she wanted. That's why they were being so overly protective. Why they wanted to know where she was every second of every day.

"We aren't saying that you crashed on purpose, Jez, we just don't think you knew what you were doing. And Paulie should never have let you behind the wheel of something so powerful." Ty said softly.

Jez looked to Jordy, who sat stiffly taking large swings from his beer. "It was an accident." She repeated softly.

Boone reached out and grasped her hand. "They know, Ace. I think their point is that if you get hurt, it's not just you who suffers." Jez looked back to him, her eyes wide with fear. But his eyes didn't meet hers, they worked through the room. "Message received. She isn't going to get hurt."

"She better not." Jordy said, jumping from his seat. He moved across the room and into the kitchen. She heard the empty bottle hit the others in the trash can. She waited for the fridge to open but instead heard the cabinet. She swallowed and closed her eyes.

"It think it's time to call it a night, boys." She said softly. Ty and OB were already standing. One of the benefits of being such close friends was they already knew. Jez walked the three to the front door as Jordy vanished out the back. She hugged OB first.

"Call me if you need me." He whispered.

She nodded and let him walk out the door.

Ty grabbed her up. "You sure?"

"Yes, I need to deal with him alone."

"OK. Call if you need me."

She smiled and pushed him out the door, leaving Boone for last. He wrapped a hand around her neck. "I don't want to go."

"I know. But you need to."

"Will you call me later?" He asked.

She sighed. "If I can. I'm not exactly sure how long this is going to take. I didn't realize they had put the pieces together to get that picture."

"What other picture would they get?" He said softly. "The truth would scare them even more."

She nodded and raised up to give him a little kiss, but he pressed into her and she began to melt. As he wrapped his arms around her waist, he pulled her close. They kissed for several long minutes, and then he let her go. "I've wanted to do that all day."

She smiled. "I'll call you later if I can. If not, I'll see you tomorrow in class."

He nodded and walked out the door. She watched him climb into his car before closing the door. As it latched, she leaned heavily against it. Her heart was still fluttering even minutes after his lips had left hers.

"What scares you more, how much he loves you or how much you love him?" Jordy's voice was soft but it still made her jump.

"Geez Jordy. Give me a heart attack." She said shaking her head.

"Sorry." He mumbled falling onto the sofa. She came over and fell next to him.

They sat silently for several long minutes. Jez didn't know how to begin, or what to say. She wanted to tell her brother not to worry. She wanted to easy his pain and worry, but she just didn't know how. "Jordy?"

"What?"

"I'm sorry."

"You keep saying that."

"I know. I mean it though. I never wanted to hurt you or make you worry." She heard him pull from the bottle as her eyes were on her hands.

"I don't worry as much when you're with Boone as I did when you were with Paulie. Boone may have some qualities I don't like, but at least he's honest about his intentions."

She didn't know what to say so she stayed silent for a while.

"Do you feel safe with him?" Jordy finally asked.

She nodded. "As safe as I do with you."

"Then why do you think he's going to hurt you?"

She shrugged. "Don't guys always hurt girls?"

He looked at his sister. She could feel the weight of his eyes. "If they love you, they try not to."

"Try, but not always succeed." She said.

Jordy wrapped an arm around her and pulled her to his side. She heard the bottle slosh. "What scares you more, the falling in love or the pain that could come later?"

She shrugged.

"I'm more scared of the falling. The pain would be worth it if you knew the love was real. Like dad says, at least you have the good memories to cling to. But I'm not willing to risk the fall."

"I don't want to fall either." She said.

She felt him chuckled. "I think it's too late for that."

"Is that why this hurts so much?"

"Maybe. Falls always hurt, and they tend to hurt more when you try to stop it from happening."

"How do you stop falling?"

"You can't. It just happens. You know that better than anyone." The bottle made a noise again.

"So how do I stop the pain?"

"Give in to the fall. Roll with it. Just like they taught you in gymnastics." She looked up at him, his eyes were growing heavy and there was a slight slur to his words.

"How did you get so smart, big brother?"

He smiled, but it was weak and drunk. "By having a little sister who's taught me so much."

She smiled and moved so she could kiss his cheek as his eyes closed. She pulled the bottle from his grip and when he didn't fight her, she knew he was asleep. She smiled and got up. Upstairs she found her phone and text Boone.

'Everything's fine. Are you home?'

'At Skye's. Is he pissed?'

'No. He may not want to trust you, but he respects you enough to give you a chance.'

'How about you?'

She sat and looked at the words. She didn't know how to answer.

'Ace?'

'I'm scared.' She replied back.

'I know.'

She cut the phone off and plugged it in. She grabbed up a blanket from her bed and headed back to Jordy. He was still sitting on the sofa, head drooped onto his chest and he was snoring. Jez curled up next to him and wrapped the blanket around them as best she could. She drifted off to sleep as she did most nights, to the sound of Jordy's breathing in her ear.

Chapter 38

They woke to the sound of the front door slamming open. Jez sat up and stretched, she was stiff and sore from sleeping on the couch. Her brother roused and groaned as he too moved stiff muscles. "Damn, Jez. What the hell?"

"Don't blame me, you were the one who drank yourself to sleep."

"Well, aren't you two cute." OB chuckled.

"You better hurry Jez, or you'll be late for class." Ty said moving into the kitchen.

She stood and stretched. "Make some coffee, please." She headed upstairs to get dressed.

Twenty minutes later, she returned. She was dressed in jeans and a t-shirt, her make-up done, and hair hanging in waves down her back. Ty grabbed up the two travel coffee mugs and headed for the door. Jez glanced at Jordy as she pulled her bag onto her back. "You OK, Jordy?"

"Yep," He waved, then held his head to keep it from exploding.

She smiled and shook her head. Ty honked for her and she raced out. As he drove over to the school, Ty grew more uncomfortable. Jez noticed him squirming. "Just say it."

"I don't like you going this weekend."

"Neither does Jordy."

"Then why are you?"

"Because I want to. Because I need to." She glanced out the window and then back to him. "Haven't you ever had to do something just to prove a point?"

"You think going away with Boone for the weekend will prove something?" He sounded doubtful.

"It's going to prove a lot of things."

"Like what?"

"Like that I can survive without my brother. That you guys can trust Boone. That I can trust Boone." She answered without realizing how true it was. As she heard the words come out, she knew they were true. "All of us are waiting for him to pull a Paulie. This weekend is his chance to either do it, or prove us wrong."

"You don't have to go so far away for that to happen." He said with so much concern that it was almost physically painful.

"Yes I do." She said. "He's on his best behavior when you guys are around. He's so worried about fucking this up, he isn't himself."

"Is he different when you two are alone?"

"A little." She smiled. "He's even better."

Ty gave her an odd look.

"That's why I need to get him away from here. I need him to be around his friends, without the pressure of this place and all the eyes. I need to know what he's really like. If he can get me there and back safely, and we have a good time, then we all know that he's for real."

"And if not?"

"Then he's too good to be true, just like I suspect." She swallowed.

"But you're going to get hurt. And like I tried to tell you last night, we can't …"

"If I get hurt, you all can have at him. At least you'll have someone to blame." She smiled as he pulled to the curb.

"You're sure about this?"

She nodded. "Besides, if nothing else, I get to see Stone Cold for free."

"The cost is too high if you get hurt." He was serious.

She leaned over, placing a kiss on his cheek. "I love you too."

She hopped out and walked up the path. She felt lighter, as if the weight wasn't all on her shoulders now. Maybe it was just that she knew she wasn't carrying it alone now. She shrugged and pushing into her classroom to find an anxious Boone standing in the isle. "Are you alright?"

She smiled. "Fine. Why?"

"You didn't text me back." He looked her over and then pulled her into his arms.

"I went to sleep."

"I sent you like a dozen messages and then called a half dozen times." He moved her into a chair.

"I guess it cut off." She reached into her bag and pulled out her phone. It was dark. Jez pressed the power button and heard the familiar ping as it came to life.

"You have no idea what horrible images were going through my mind. Another five minutes and I was going over to your house."

She looked over at him. "What are you talking about?"

"Your brother was getting drunk when I left." He said as if that was an explanation.

"And I told you everything was fine."

He shook his head. "Drunk brothers are never fine."

She saw something in his eyes that she hadn't seen. A dark memory haunted him. "My brother doesn't hurt me, Boone."

"If he ever …" Boone's voice darkened as the threat hung in the air.

"He wouldn't. What would ever make you think he would?"

Boone swallowed and looked to the door that had just opened. The professor came in and set his things down. Their conversation was cut short by the start of class. She checked her phone when the lecture got boring. There were six voicemail messages from Boone and a dozen texts. She scrolled through them.

'I'm scared.' She had written.

'I know.'

'Do you want me to come over?'

'Ace? I'll come over right now if you want me to.'

'He better not hurt you.'

'How much has he had to drink? Ace?'

'Ace get back to me. I'm getting worried.'

'Ace? Skye says I need to stay out of it, but one word from you and I'm on the road.'

'Are you OK?'

'What's happening?'

'Ace?'

'ACE PLEASE!'

'Ok, I'm calling. You'd better pick up.'

Jez looked at Boone. He was watching her scroll through his messages. She gave him a curious look. Dropping the phone back in her bag, she reached out and took up her pen. On a clean sheet of notebook paper, she wrote, 'why were you so worried?'

Underneath what she had written, he scribbled. 'I have experience with drunk brothers.'

Her heart sank. She made a mental note to ask about his family the next time they were alone. But for the moment, she contented herself with leaning her head against his shoulder. Her eyes were on the professor so she didn't see him look down at her and smile. He placed a soft kiss on her head, then returned his attention to the lecture.

Boone took her hand and led Jez out to his car. They were both scheduled to work that afternoon, so he figured on giving her a ride. When they got to the car, he opened her door for her but she stopped in front of him. "Will you tell me about it?"

"What?"

"Why you're so freaked about my brother? What your brother did?"

He brushed the hair from her shoulders as she leaned against his car. "I left it all behind me when I came here, Ace. There's nothing to talk about."

"There is if you think my brother would do the same."

He kept his hands on her, as if touching her made everything just a little better. "You said you were scared and I didn't know why. I took a guess."

"I meant I was scared of this." She placed a hand on his chest, right above his heart. "This is so intense, so fast, I … I'm scared."

"I'm not trying to pressure you, Ace. We can take it as fast or as slow as you want. Just don't lock me out."

She wrapped her arms around his neck and pulled close to him. "I'm not use to having a co-pilot. The closest thing I've ever had is a backseat driver or a tow truck."

"A co-pilot's job is to help guide the craft. The pilot actually gets them there. I'll help guide you, if you let me. But you can't lock me from the cabin, Ace. I've got to know what we're dealing with." He brushed his nose against hers. But that wasn't enough for her. She leaned up on her toes and placed her lips against his. As he felt her lips move on his, he mimicked her moves. When hers opened, his did too. He waited until she reached in with her tongue before going in to taste her. When she pulled back, he did too. He was letting her steer and while she knew he was doing it to prove his point, she also knew at some point he was going to have to take control. There were just some things that she wanted but didn't know how to get.

As she moved into the passenger seat, she pushed that thought away. When they got there, she'd let him know.

"Are you hungry?" He asked as they drove across town.

"No." She said.

"When was the last time you ate?"

She thought back. She didn't eat last night, and had skipped lunch and breakfast. She couldn't remember eating Sunday night, but she might have. The longer she was quiet the more his thoughts were confirmed.

"We're getting you some food. Anything sound good?"

She bit her bottom lip and looked down. "Whatever."

"Ace, guide me."

"Senior Pedro's?"

He looked over at her quickly. "Really?"

She nodded. "It's my favorite."

"That tiny little place on Beach Street?"

"Have you ever eaten there?" She asked, although she already knew he hadn't. If he had, he wouldn't have asked about it.

"It looks like the kind of place that would give you food poisoning."

She smiled. "Do you trust me?"

"Absolutely." He made the next right and drove down a mile or so. The place was packed as she knew it would be at this time of day. They had a drive thru and Boone took his place in line. As they finally approached the order box, he looked at her. "So what are we having?"

"Bean and Cheese burritos would be a good place to start. If you're more daring later, I would recommend the fish tacos or the shrimp burritos."

"What's your favorite thing on the menu?"

"It's all good."

"I didn't ask that, Ace." He said giving her a look.

"The fish tacos." She bit her lip.

He pulled up to the order speaker and order two fish tacos, two bean and cheese burritos, an order of chips and salsa, nachos, two steak tacos, and two pink lemon-aides. Wide eyed, Jez just stared at him. When he had pulled forward and begun digging in his pocket for his wallet, he noticed her look. "What?"

"You just ordered a ton of food."

"I'm hungry." He said with a shrugged. She smiled and looked out the window at the crowded parking lot. She recognized several people and waved to them when they waved or tossed her peace signs. They moved up another car and her attention was on her hands again, when a bang came on her window. She jumped and then heard the laugh from outside her window. She rolled down her window and felt Boone's hand reach out to find its new home on her knee. "Hey Jez! Long time no see."

The surfer was grinning like a Cheshire cat. His hair still wet, and his wet suite pull half down to reveal a deeply tanned and firm torso. She couldn't help but smile. "Hey Herb. How you doing?"

"Getting by and hanging loose. Where you been? We missed you."

"Sorry, I'm been working and taking classes. Jordy's got me on a tight leash these days." She smiled.

His brown eyes glanced from her over to Boone. "Not tight enough I see. Hey man."

"Oh Boone, this is Herb. Herb, Boone." Boone nodded but didn't say anything, his fingers gripping her knee just a little more tightly.

"I'm going to have to stop by and hang out with you if you don't get your ass to the waves soon." He chuckled.

"I'll try. I'm going away this weekend but maybe my next day off after I get back." She said.

"Don't make me hunt you down, Gidget." Herb said as the car behind them honked. Herb waved at them and wandered off as Boone pulled up more.

"You can let go of my knee now." Jez said with a smiled. Boone looked down and pulled his hand away quickly. "He got the message."

"He was high." Boone growled.

"Herb's always high." She laughed. "That's where he got the name."

Boone didn't laugh. His eyes were dark and his jaw tight.

"Boone, seriously, relax. Don't blow a fuse."

"Is he an ex?"

"Herb? No." She giggled, then quieted. "He was my first kiss though."

Boone's eyes darted to her. He pulled up one car from the pick-up window.

"We were five, Boone. He stole a kiss from me behind the lifeguard tower." She smiled. "He's harmless."

"Not with the way you were looking at him. You don't smile like that for many people, Ace."

She looked back at the group that was gathered around Herb. She knew most of them. "It's just one piece of my life, Boone."

"He doesn't approve of me." Boone smiled, but it was a dark and dangerous smile. He was looking in the rearview mirror at Herb and the other surfers.

"He doesn't know you. You're different. That group is leery of outsiders." She said as Boone pulled up to the window. He handed the lady the money and took the drinks she offered. She returned his change, then started hand over the bags. He seemed surprised when she handed over three full bags. Jez took them from him and laughed at his wide eyes. "I told you that you ordered a lot."

"Shit," he chuckled as he pulled away. "I didn't think I ordered that much."

He drove them back to the shop, and grew quiet. She watched him from the corner of her eye. He seemed to be thinking about something. Finally, she got the nerve up to say something. "What's eating you?"

He glanced over at her and then smiled. "Just thinking about you."

"Me? What about me?"

"Have you always kept your lives separate?"

"Yes."

"So your surfer friends don't know about your racing side. And your racing friends don't know you surf? How have you managed that?" He seemed honestly curious.

"It was harder in high school, when we all went to school together. But if anyone asked I just said I knew them from classes. No one questioned it really."

"Didn't Paulie overlap?"

"Not really. I only saw him at school, or at night. I never had him over to the house, and he never came to the beach."

"Jordy knows about him though."

"From the store. Paulie use to come in and buy parts. Jordy knew I went to school with him. He put two and two together when he caught us kissing at a party."

Boone's grip on the steering wheel tightened. "I would have killed him."

"Jordy wanted too." She smiled remembering. "Now I wish I had let him."

"Me too." Boone said softly.

Jez reached over and placed a hand on his shoulder. "You need to let it go, Boone. He isn't worth it."

"You are."

"And you've managed to break every promise I made myself, so please, don't fuck this up. Let it go." She said sternly.

"What promises?" He turned to look at her when he stopped at a red light.

"I swore I would never date another racer. I swore I would never let my worlds collide. And I swore that I'd never fall in love."

He smiled, "And not only have you fallen for a racer, but one you let into your worlds. You've let me behind the curtain."

"And you brought your friends." She said sourly.

"I didn't know I wasn't supposed to." He said as he crossed the railroad tracks. "You never said not to."

She shrugged. "I didn't think I needed to."

"You're steering this, Ace, you got to tell me what I need to know." He reminded her.

"Sorry. Paulie was just as secretive as I am. He just knew. I forget that everyone doesn't live that way." She replied, her eyes falling on her hands. "You just have to make sure they don't say anything. If any of the three amigos finds out about me racing, it's going to get ugly."

"Don't worry. They know." Boone pulled into a parking spot in front of the shop. He turned to face Jez. "Ace, don't worry. It's easier to keep the trust if they know who they're trusting."

She nodded.

"Hey Ace, I'm not going to let anything bad happen, alright?"

"Promise?"

He leaned over and placed a gentle kiss on her lips. "Promise. Now, let's go eat, because I'm starving."

They took the bags in and made their way to the back room. They had no sooner got the food laid out then the guys followed their noses in. "I see someone is making brownie points."

"Shut it OB." She sighed. "He's never eaten at Pedro's."

"What?" Both Ty and Jordy said in unison.

Boone smiled. "Heard I was missing out."

"Shit yeah you are." The trio started nibbling on the nachos, while Boone began on the larger than a fist sized burrito. Jez ate her fish taco and smiled as she listened to the banter.

"Holy crap. This isn't a burrito, this is heaven." Boone said with a nod. The others smiled and agreed, then they began making comments that made her giggle. She heard the door chime, and left to go help the customer.

When the food was gone, the boys left too. Boone and Jez worked until it was time to close, using the quieter moments to complete the homework they had been assigned. When they locked the doors, he drove her home. As he parked in the driveway, he looked at her. "Tomorrow night I want to take you out after we close."

"Why?"

He chuckled. "Do I need a reason to take my girl out?"

She narrowed her eyes. "Where are we going?"

"Dinner, and maybe a drive?"

"A drive? Like up the coast?"

"Like around the track." He smiled.

"The car? You're going to let me drive the car?" She smiled excitedly.

"I'm going to let you test drive your car, yes." He smiled. "You said you needed to drive it before the race, so how about it?"

She smiled and nodded eagerly. When he smiled too, she leaned over and kissed him. He allowed her to take the wheel, and followed her lead. When she pulled away, he dropped his head back on the seat. "You're killing me, Ace."

"I'll see you tomorrow." She said sweetly. He watched her bounce into the house.

"You're in a good mood." Jordy said she pushing into the house. He had been watching from the window.

"It's been a good day." She smiled. "Hey do you mind if I go out with Boone tomorrow night after work?"

"Where you're going?"

"Dinner and a drive." She answered pulling a bottle of water from the fridge.

"Think you can be home by one?"

"I can try." She smiled. She kissed his cheek and headed up to bed. After a quick shower, Jez crawled into bed. She sent Boone a quick text.

'Headed for bed. We're good for tomorrow.'

His response was quick. 'I'll make the arrangements. See you tomorrow, Ace. Sweet dreams. I love you.'

She smiled and settled in. She drifted off to sleep, alone and content, for the moment.

Chapter 39

Jez got up and got ready for work. She heard Jordy snoring from down the hall, and smiled. Her brother didn't sleep much or well these days. She knew it was because of her. She was glad he was sleeping now though. She wrote a note and left it on the table for him and then scooted out of the house quietly. She stopped by the Circle Go and got a coffee on her way to the shop. She opened up and checked to make sure the shelves were stocked. She did a little work around the place and then sat down to do her homework. She hated working Tuesdays and Wednesdays because they were so slow.

She had just about finished her reading when the bell rang signaling a customer. Jez marked her spot and then looked up, and right into Paulie's older brother's unhappy face. "Hey, Baby Girl."

"What do you want, Sean?"

"I, um, heard a rumor." He looked around and softened his voice.

"We're alone. Speak."

He smiled but it wasn't friendly. "Don't go to the desert this weekend."

"Too late." She told him.

"It's too much for you, Sweetheart. You're going to get hurt."

Jez bristled. "I'm going to be fine, but you and your brother might not. Are you ready to get your ass handed to you?"

He smirked but as he spoke his face contorted into something ugly. "I taught you everything you know. I know all your tricks and all your secrets. You better hope that you don't come up against me because I will bury you."

"I'd love to see you try."

He raised his hand and smacked her. She took it, not wanting him to see any weakness. Mel's words came back to her. They feed on weakness.

"Get out."

Sean smirked and turned back to the door. He was just pulling out of the parking lot as Boone pulled in. Boone didn't waste any time rushing in to check on Jez after seeing Sean leaving. She had dropped her head and focused back on her reading. She couldn't see the words anymore, but she needed to swallow the emotions before facing Boone or she knew he'd flip.

"Ace? Who was that?" Boone asked as if he didn't already know.

"Sean." She replied not looking up. "Paulie's brother."

"What'd he want?"

"To warn me away from racing this weekend." She said still not look up at him.

He rounded the counter and grabbed her shoulders. Spinning her around to face him, he lifted her chin to meet his eyes. "Are you alright?"

She couldn't hide the red mark, and once she saw his face, she couldn't hide her tears either.

"Fuck." He dropped her and made to leave, but she chased after him.

"Please don't. Please Boone. Just..."

"Just what? Let him get away with hurting you, intimidating you? No, Ace, it ends. They've done it long enough."

"Just hold me." She said, falling to her knees in tears.

Three steps was all it took. Three steps and he had her scooped up in his arms. He put her on the stool and held her tightly. They didn't speak. He just held her tightly and let her cry. When she had quieted, he pulled her chin up and looked at the red mark on her cheek. "We'd better get some ice on that."

"I'm fine."

"I know. But I'm still going to run over and get some ice." He turned and walked out of the store. She couldn't say anything. She stepped back into the back room and washed her face off in the bathroom. Her eyes were bloodshot, and her cheek was red and swollen again. She sighed and splashed some water on her face. It didn't help but at least she felt like she tried. The bell rang on the door and she forced a smile as she rounded the corner and just about ran into her brother, who was followed closely by Ty and OB.

"What the fuck happened?" Jordy was beyond angry.

"Nothing." She replied wide eyed. "Nothing happened, why? What are you doing here?"

He grabbed her chin and turned her head, eyeing the red hand print on her cheek. "Nothing happened? Then how do you explain that?"

"Shit Jez. Did Boone do that?" OB said stunned.

Her eyes flashed to him. "What? No. Boone? No."

"Then who did?" Jordy snapped.

Jez's eyes returned to him and she swallowed. The bell sounded again and Boone came in. He stopped but they all turned to look at him.

"You called them?" Jez asked heart broken.

"I called to ask them to help cover the store tonight so I could go do something."

"I'm coming with you." Jordy said.

"No. Neither one of you are going to do anything." Jez said. She walked over and took a seat on the stool. Boone came to her on the other side of the counter and handed her the ice. She took it and placed it against her face. All four men stood around her. They all looked at her, tense and angry, waiting for her to say something. "What?"

"Who did it, Jez?" Ty said in the darkest voice she had ever heard from him.

She swallowed and glanced to Boone, who answered. "It was Paulie's brother."

Jordy turned without another word and headed for the door. Boone took off after him, chasing him into the parking lot and then finally catching him. They spoke for a moment, and Jez thought they were going to come back in, but then they turned and headed directly for Boone's car. Fear gripped Jez's heart and she lunged over the counter. She stumbled and almost fell into the plate glass window but Ty's arms caught her. She slammed her hands into the glass and cried as the black muscle car pulled from the lot. Panic filled her. She yanked her cell phone from her pocket and found Skye's number.

"Hey Ace, what's happening?" His voice was light and happy.

"Skye, you gotta find Boone. You gotta stop him."

"Woah, slow down, kiddo. What's going on?" He turned serious.

"Boone is going after Paulie and his brother. Please Skye, you've got to stop him."

Skye didn't speak, and the phone line went dead. Jez looked at it and then slid her cell in her pocket and Ty tightened his grip on her. "Come on Pickle, let's get some ice on that."

She allowed Ty to walk her back to the stool, and held the ice pack to her face. Ty and OB took turns looking at her and talking. They helped the customers and checked on her frequently. She sat silent and numb well after her ice pack had melted. Ty went and got them lunch, but she didn't eat. Jez couldn't do anything but look at her phone and wait.

Two hours past and two cars pulled in to the lot. Boone's black muscle car and another car she didn't recognize. She jumped off the stool and rushed to the door. She was just pushing out when the car doors started to open. She saw Jordy first and raced to him. She was in his arms in second.

"It's OK, Jez." He soothed. After a big hug, he released her.

She turned to the figure coming around the car. His jaw showed a dark shadow. "Boone."

"I'm OK." He walked to her and she threw her arms around him. Tears swelling in her eyes, she pulled away and looked at his jaw. "It's nothing, Ace."

"Too bad Sean can't say the same." Skye spoke and pulled Jez's attention.

"I asked you to stop them." She said, spinning around to face him.

"We didn't touch him." Boone said grabbing her shoulders and turning her back to him. Looking deep in her eyes, Boone repeated himself. "We didn't touch him."

"But ..." She started but Boone placed a finger on her lips.

"Let's go inside and I'll tell you everything." He said. Taking her hand, he led her back into the shop and then into the back room. He lifted her up and sat her on the workbench. Jordy and Skye moved into the area, and Ty and OB stepped into the doorway.

"We left with every intention of beating the hell out of him, Ace. But when we got there, he ..." Boone stopped.

"He came at us, Jez. Paulie's crazy and his brother's worse. He was talking crazy shit. He said horrible, horrible lies. We just stood there, stunned. He got in one hit on Boone, when he went to strike again, Boone moved and Sean slammed his hand into the brick wall behind him." Jordy finished. He stepped up and placed a hand on his sister's arm. "Boone didn't lay a finger on him."

"Did you?" She asked.

Skye smirked.

"He deserved it for the shit he was saying about you." Jordy said softly.

Boone took his turn. "He only got one punch in, Ace, and then Skye stopped him."

Jez flashed her eyes to Skye. "Thank you."

"It was a hell of a punch." Skye smiled.

They hung out the rest of the night together. At dinner time, someone ran off and got them a pizza. They talked cars and engines, and Jez just tried to feel at peace in the presence of the men she cared most about. When they locked up, there was an awkward moment where Jez didn't know what to do. Part of her still wanted to be with Boone, but after the day's events she thought she might need to go home with Jordy. As they stood in front of the store, he pulled her in for a big hug.

"Not too late tonight. You have class tomorrow."

She smiled. "Thanks Jordy."

"Love you, sis."

"Love you." When he released her, she jogged over to Boone, who helped her into his car.

The drive across town was fairly quiet, Jez had slid over next to Boone and he had his arm around her shoulders. She could tell he was thinking about something but elected not to ask. When he was ready he'd say something. She wasn't all that hungry but elected to get a soda and some fries when he stopped at a local diner. She watched him finish off a hamburger, fries, and a large soda. When they were safely tucked back in the car, headed to the track, he finally spoke what had been eating him. "Hey Ace. Why didn't you want me to hurt that prick?"

"Paulie and Sean are the kind of guys who would run to the cops and file charges. They're not worth going to jail for." She said softly.

"They may not be, but you are."

She looked up at him, and then out the window. In a whispered breath, she said. "No, I'm not."

He glanced down at her. He didn't comment back and she was grateful. She didn't want to get into a fight over this. "How's your cheek feel?"

"It's fine." She said honestly. She hadn't given it much thought since the guys had returned to the store. Sean hadn't hit her very hard, just enough to make it red and a little tender. He, and his brother, had done so much worse to her over the years, this felt more like a love tap.

"What did he want?"

"He didn't want me going to the Desert Run. He heard I was registered and came to warn me away."

"He's scared you're going to beat him." A devious smile came across his face. "Or worse, actually win."

She shrugged. "Makes me want to do it even more."

"And you will. Wait until you see your car."

She gazed up at him and his pleased smile. "Why are you doing this?"

"Because you deserve it and you're worth it."

She shook her head. "All I do it cause trouble." Her eyes drifted out to the dark night. She thought about all the problems she'd caused for those she loved. All the fights Jordy had gotten into over the years and the fight that Boone almost had today. She remembered the pained look in her father's and brother's eyes as they watched her in the hospital. The way the guys were always readjusting their schedules to accommodate her. She was more trouble than she was worth, Paulie use to say. She hated to agree with him, but it was true.

Boone pulled to a stop. He reached over and grabbed the belt loops on her jeans and pulled her over closer to him. Reaching down, he turned her face so he could see the sadness in her eyes. "You're no trouble. And if there ever was any trouble because of you, it's worth it."

Tears glistened in her eyes as she listened to what she knew were lies. She tried to blink them back but they wouldn't fade. A single tear fell from her eye. Reaching up, Boone brushed it away. "Don't lie to me. You promised." She whispered.

"I'm not lying. I would take on a hundred Paulies and two hundred Jordys to spend a day with you." He leaned down and kissed her lips. As if he knew she needed him to lead, he pulled her to him and gripped her head with his hand. He worked his mouth on hers and she relaxed into him. The more heated the kiss became the more she wanted it, the more she needed him to take the next step. But he didn't. Instead, he pulled away and dropped his forehead onto hers and closed his eyes.

"You're killing me, Ace." He whispered.

"You're the one who keeps pulling away." She said sadly.

His eyes flashed open and looked directly into her. "Not because I want to. This just isn't the right time or place."

"Promise?"

A sly smile crossed his lips. "Promise. I'm not fucking you in the backseat like a cheap date, Ace. I want time and space to enjoy you."

Something inside her gripped with need and she let out an uncontrolled whimper.

His smile spread as he saw the reaction. "Soon Ace, I promise."

She made a move to kiss him again, but a hand banged on the window beside them. "Stop fogging up the windows, love birds. I got shit to do."

Boone looked over and popped the door open. Skye and Mel stood outside giving them curious looks. Bandit sulked just behind them. "Damn, it was just getting hot."

Boone stepped out of the car and took a playful swing at Bandit who stepped back hooting with laughter. Jez slid out behind him and closed the door. As the five of them walked over to the track, Boone wrapped an arm around Jez and pulled her close. She looked over at Mel curiously. "Hi Mel."

"Hey Ace." He winked.

Mel smiled and she noticed how easily he had switched from calling her Paulie's nickname to Boone's. She vaguely wondered if he even knew her real name. "What'cha doing here?"

"I'm checking out my investment." He said pulling a pack of cigarettes from his pocket and placed one in his mouth. Bandit yanked it from his hand though and took off running. Mel made a show of starting to chase, but then gave up and pulled another from the pack.

Bandit was already over by the sleek, ruby red and black car when the others came around the end of the stands. Jez tried not to look too excited as they approached but she couldn't help the broad smile that spread across her lips. The body was low and smooth, with lines that would make a woman jealous. The sparkling paint was just the shade of red that Jez loved and the black accents made her look fast. There were tiny details that came clear the closer they got. Black spades decorated key points on the entire car, from the headlights to the taillights. Most were so small that the eye may not have caught them, but Jez was drinking in every detail.

Boone pressed her forward as he stopped a few feet away with Mel and Skye. Bandit swept his hand along the side, and spoke. "The Ace's chariot."

Jez glanced back at Boone. "Really?"

He nodded with a pleased smile.

"And just like our Ace, she's not just a beauty to look at, she's got balls." Bandit smirked.

Jez only caught part of what Bandit said after that. She walked the outside and noticed all the details, from the spade shaped lights to the invisible door handles. The blacked out windows added a mysterious quality to her, and Jez hoped it would add to the effect. As she rounded to the driver's side, Bandit popped the door open.

"Inside it's top of the line luxury as well. Leather seats, red display, top of the line stereo, and ..."

Jez stopped him with a wave of her hand as she slid behind the wheel. "Is she as fast as she looks?"

Bandit deflated like a popped balloon. "Really? I just told you all that and …"

"Is she fast?" Jez repeated.

"She's as fast as they come, Ace." Skye answered stepping up to them. He handed her the key, which wasn't really a key, but a circular device that unlocked the ignition and allowed the push button start to work. "Take her for a spin."

"Easy at first, Ace, until you get the feel." Mel offered, and Jez gave him an attitude filled look.

Bandit slid the door closed and took a step back. As the group of men moved back to the other side of concrete barriers, Jez settled in. She checked the mirrors and her seat placement, both of which had to be reset. She checked to make sure the guys were clear before she started the beauty up. It purred like a kitten, so soft that had it not been for the vibrations in her ass, Jez might have thought the car hadn't turned over. This was no man's muscle car; it was a sleek huntress. As Jez shifted into first, an image of a jaguar came into her mind. She smiled and pressed on the gas.

Jez giggled like a little girl as she took the turns and accelerated. Even that stolen SRT Viper didn't match this. While the Viper was just as fast, this seemed to have a strength that kicking in when she hit one hundred mph, and where the Viper had felt just as much as show piece as a racer, this put her beauty aside for the run. The image of the big African cat came back into Jez's mind. She made four laps, gaining speed each time until the guys began to flag her down. She took one last lap and slowed the beast down, then pulled up in front of them. The engine cut off as Boone popped the door.

"Well?" His smile matched hers.

She jumped out and into his arms, wrapping her arms and legs around him. "Is she really mine?"

"One hundred percent, Ace." He laughed as she kissed his cheek over and over again.

She felt the others join them. But it was Bandit's voice that broke her actions. "Hey now, I did most the work."

Jez dropped off Bonne and he let her go. She walked over and placed a big kiss on Bandit's cheek also, making the boy blush. "Thank you. She's amazing."

"I did the body work." Skye commented and opened his arms. She laughed and shook her head, but moved to give him a hug and a quick peck on the cheek also.

When she was done, she noticed Mel leaning back against the concrete barrier, his face holding a quirky smile. "And what about you, Mel? Do you need a thank you kiss too?"

He chuckled, and pulled the cigarette from his lips. "Nope kiddo, I just help fund it. I'll get my thanks when you kick ass at Desert Run this weekend."

"I'll take another one." Boone said as he stepped up behind her. She looked up at him and he smiled at the twinkle in her eye. "You like her?"

"Like her? I love her. I'm glad you got rid of the ugly old Viper."

"Hey, that Viper was not ugly." Bandit defended his selection. Jez turned to look at the black cat behind her. Boone laughed as she pulled away and moved back to her. She barely registered the conversation that was happening behind her.

"Boone, I think she's found a new love." Skye said.

"Looks like you out did yourself, and in the process ousted yourself." Mel chuckled.

Boone said something under his breath but Jez didn't catch it. She was still walking the outside of the car.

"It's got a stick too." Bandit said laughing at his friend's discomfort.

Jez looked up just in time to see Boone take another swing at Bandit and for the kid to duck out of range. The others laughed but Jez saw the look in Boone's eye. She returned to him and wrapped her arms around his waist. He looked down at her and smiled tightly. "So I take it you like her."

"Ever girl likes a shiny new sparkly bobble." She giggled.

"I haven't bought you one of those yet." Boone said softly as he leaned down so only she could hear.

Jez looked up into his eyes and saw that he was serious. Nerves racked her and she had to fight not to lose her smile. The word 'yet' echoed in her brain.

He placed a gently kiss on her lips, then looked back at his friends. "I need to get her back."

"We got this." Skye nodded. He moved toward the car and a Jez had to push away a variety of emotions. "See you later, Ace."

"Bye Skye." She said. Then deciding that wasn't enough, she left Boone's side and stepped up to the car as Skye sank behind the wheel. He looked up at her a little surprised. "Hey Skye, thanks for everything."

He smiled. "No problem, Ace."

"No really. You've been really nice to me. You've come every time I've called. I'm sorry if I've been a hassle."

He looked a little taken back. "You're no hassle, Ace." He pulled the door closed, cutting her off. As the engine came to life, she stepped back to Boone.

"What was that about?" Boone looked down, green jealousy coloring his eyes.

She smirked and replied. "I asked him to be careful. I don't want any scratches on my new baby."

Boone closed his eyes, shook his head, and scoffed. "Only you, Ace. Only you."

"Only me what?" She asked, snuggling into his side.

"Only you could tell him that and not get hit." Boone winked and pulled her away.

Chapter 40

The drive back was as quiet as the drive there, but this time it was Jez who was nibbling on her lip in thought. Boone let her think for a long time. He was just pulling onto her street when he finally asked what was wrong.

"Nothing." She said distracted. Her teeth still worried her lower lip as she faced the night beyond the glass.

Boone reached out and placed a hand on her leg. "If you keep eating your lip there won't be anything left for me."

She barely heard him thought the voices in her head. Turning to look at him, "What?"

"What's wrong, Ace?"

"Nothing." She smiled. "Just tired, I guess."

He pulled to a stop at the curb in front of her house. Once he cut the engine, he unfastened both their seatbelts and pulled her to his side. "Ace?"

"It's nothing." She smiled up at him. His look told her he wasn't accepting that answer though. With a sigh, she gave him a little more, but looked down at her hands nervously. "I was just wondering why, I guess."

"Why what?"

"Why all of it?" She looked up into his eyes. "Why are you doing this?"

He still didn't understand. "Because I love you."

"You don't build someone a car because you love them. And you can't love me." She said fighting down her irritation.

"I can and I do." He smiled, and she couldn't help but smile too. He leaned over and kissed her gently. When he pulled back, he nudged his nose against hers. "You'd better go get some sleep. We have a busy day tomorrow."

She groaned and dropped her head onto his shoulder. "I don't want to go to school tomorrow."

"Good because I thought we could go shopping instead." He said.

"Why?"

"You need some new outfits for Desert Run."

Jez turned her head to look up at him. "I have …"

"No, I want you sexy and intimidating not looking like a hooker."

Jez didn't want to get offended but she couldn't help it. Sitting up and away from him, she spun to face him. "Well, tell me what you really think."

"I didn't mean it like that." He sighed. "It's going to be hard enough to know everyone's watching you, but I don't want them getting the wrong idea. You're my girl."

"Your girl?" Two little words that made her feel less like a person and more like a piece of property. "Well then, I'd better get in. Don't want to look like trash for you."

Jez spun and jumped from the car. She was halfway across the yard when she heard the car door slam closed.

"Ace, wait." She moved quicker up the steps but didn't quite make the door before Boone's hand grabbed her arm. "Wait. What's wrong now?"

"Nothing." She forced a smile as she turned to look at him. "Just need my beauty sleep."

"Stop it." He turned irritated. "What the fuck, Ace? Why the attitude all of a sudden?"

"I told you I'm tired." She sighed. Even if she knew how to explain, she didn't think he would understand. "Please Boone. I'll see you tomorrow."

He leaned down and placed a kiss on her lips, but she didn't lean in for more like she usually did. He didn't look happy as he moved away. "Call me if you need me."

"Good night." Jez said softly just before she headed inside. She was fighting back tears as she came eye to eye with Jordy. He stood on the bottom of the stairs, clad only in his pajama bottoms, a beer in his hand. She didn't say a word, but took the bottle from his hand and finished it.

"Date didn't go well?" He asked curiously.

She pushed by him and ran up the stairs. Five minutes later she was standing under the hot water, rethinking the entire night. She tried to tell herself that she wasn't worth the car and all the attention. She tried to convenience herself that Boone was just using it to control her, like Paulie had. She reworked the words she had said and replayed them in her head. But no matter how she justified it, she still felt bad for the way she had behaved. A tiny little voice told her that Boone did it all because he really did love her, but the louder, angrier voice reminded her that no one loved her. They used her and controlled her, and even dominated her. But they didn't love her because she was unlovable. As the hot water filled the room with steam, she reached for the razor blade. With a dizzy head, she silenced the voice by drowning them in bright red blood.

Chapter 41

The bang on the door woke Jez and Jordy. Jez opened her eyes and groaned as she stumbled down the stairs. Yanking the door open she cringed against the bright light outside. "Good Morning, Ace."

She groaned and stepped back as Boone stepped into the room. "Is it?"

He smiled at her. "Yes, it is." She watched as his eyes wandered down her body. As usual, she was wearing sweatpants and an oversized sweatshirt that had the collar cut off.

"What?"

"Not the sexiest of looks, but it does spark my curiosity." He offered her a devilish grin and moved towards her.

She stopped him with a hand. "Morning breath." She started to push the door closed but it was stopped by Ty and OB pushing in behind Boone.

"Morning Pickle."

"Where's Jordy?"

She gave up closing the door and walked towards the kitchen to start the coffee. "My room."

Boone had been following her, his heavy boots stomping on the floor behind her, but they stopped short. Likewise, the slap of flip-flops stopped on the stairs. Ty leaned over and asked in a worried voice, "Rough night, Pickle?"

She didn't look up, just nodded as she made her way to kitchen. When she didn't hear Boone following, she looked over her shoulder to him. He was stone still, fury burning in his eyes, his fists clinched. She walked back to him. Standing directly in front of him, Jez placed a hand on his chest. "What's wrong?"

"What did he do?" His voice was so scary quiet it took Jez a moment to figure out what he had asked. "Ace, if he laid one finger on you…"

"Nightmares. Boone, I have nightmares. Relax. Jordy doesn't hurt me. I told you that." She grabbed his face and standing on tip-toes, she pulled his face down to look at her. "He didn't do anything but comfort me. Nightmares, Boone."

It wasn't the whole truth, but it wasn't a lie either. Boone took in a deep breath and forced himself to relax. "Would you tell me if it was more?"

"Wouldn't you be able to see it?" She answered the question with a question. It was always a good way of avoiding the truth.

One day, if they made it through, she would have to tell him the truth. One day, he would see the scars and ask the right questions and she wouldn't be able to avoid him. But for now, it was as close to the truth as she could bring herself to share with him.

He swallowed and relaxed a bit more. There was a bang upstairs and the sounds of the boys messing around. Jez cringed and hoped they didn't break anything. She smiled at Boone and then turned to make some coffee. She was just finishing as the trio pounded back downstairs. Boone watched Jordy as he came up behind Jez and kissed the top of her head.

"Everything's better in the morning light." He smiled.

"Everything's better with coffee." She elbowed him. She noticed Boone watching Jordy closely and caught Ty's eye. "I'm going to go get dressed."

She moved from the kitchen and Ty followed. Boone didn't notice. His focus was still on Jordy. Once at the base of the stairs, Ty stepped closed to Jez. "What's up?"

"Boone took what you said wrong. He thinks Jordy ... well, just ... he thinks Jordy's hurting me. Could you help me out?"

Ty twisted his lips. "Sure." She turned and started up the stairs slowly. Ty moved back into the kitchen and she heard him ask her brother, "So was Jez's nightmare a bad one?"

"Same one as always." Jordy replied as if it was true. She smiled suddenly very thankful that her brother understood. The nightmare story had been what they had told her father when he questioned why Jordy had started sleeping with his sister on a regular basis. He bought it too, probably because he didn't really want to know the whole truth. Jez wasn't completely lying, she did have nightmares, horrible ones that woke her with migraines. And while this wasn't the whole reason Jordy had slept with her almost every night, it was a good enough excuse to keep most from questioning things deeper. Jordy was the only one who know the dark secret she carried. He was the only one she trusted with it, and that was only because she didn't have a choice. He had found her on a bad night, in tears, bleeding on the bathroom floor with the razor still in her hand. He'd picked her up, cleaned her up, and held her tight vowing to always keep her close to him. He might not be able to fight her demons, but he was going to make sure she was as protected from them as possible.

Jez's heart fluttered in her chest and her head began to swim. She caught herself on the railing and decided it was time to go sit down and get dressed.

Chapter 42

After taking a lot longer to dress than she expected, having found herself on the floor of her room with her jeans half up, Jez finally headed back downstairs. The guys were still in the kitchen, their voices slightly muffled. Jez could smell that they had cooked breakfast, and she realized that's why they hadn't noticed she had been gone so long. Silently, she said a thank-you prayer whoever was listening. It would have been embarrassing enough to be found passed out in her room, but being half-dressed would have made it worse. Not to mention the questions that would have followed when they saw her new cuts. She shuttered at the thought.

"Don't forget Jez has treatments today." Jordy said. "Who's picking her up? We are not repeating Monday."

"I've got her." Boone replied. She noticed he didn't sound pissed anymore.

"You sure? One of us could …"

"I said I've got her." Boone replied sternly. "I'm not letting her kick me out today like she did on Monday." There was a pause. "Damn, your sister can be stubborn sometimes."

There was a collective chuckle and agreement. Jez decided she wasn't going to let that conversation continue. She finished bouncing down the stairs and into the room, stumbling a bit but catching herself before she fell. "We're going to be late for class, Boone."

"I told you we're going shopping today, Ace." He turned and smiled. "I'm not letting Skye and Mel buy food for the trip. We'd wind up with beer, corn nuts, and more beer."

Jez smiled and rolled her eyes as if she understood. He got up and she turned to get her shoes on. When she sat on the sofa, with the pretense of sliding her sandals on but really just needing a minute to rest, she heard Jordy say, "Remember what we talked about Boone."

"Don't worry. That's why we're doing the shopping. I've got her covered, Jordy. Really." Boone's voice was light but serious.

When Jez felt like she could stand, she moved into the kitchen to give her brother a kiss. He looked at her and saw what she had hoped to hide. "Are you OK?"

"Yep." She smiled and nodded. "Glad it's Thursday though."

He nodded hearing what she wasn't saying. "Call me if you need me."

"I've got her, Jordy. Stop worrying." Boone wrapped a hand around her waist and pulled her towards the door. "See you all later."

When they were out the door, Jez looked up at Boone. "What did you and Jordy talk about?"

"He's not happy about his little sister going on a trip with her boyfriend." He smiled down at her.

"How would you feel about your sister going off for a weekend with her boyfriend, who you've only known for a few weeks?"

A dark shadow crossed his face. As he pulled open her door, he said distantly, "I see your point."

He closed the door and she vaguely wondered if he even had a sister, so when he got in behind the wheel, she asked. "Do you have any siblings?"

His response stunned her. "A sister who's a couple years younger than me and a brother who's three years older."

His eyes were distant and she could see the flashes as memories played in his mind, like the lights under a movie theater door. "You remind me of her sometimes. You get the same dark look in your eye when you are hiding something from me, and when you're pushing me away." He blinked and the shadow was gone. "Guess that's why I can tell when you're fucking with me, Ace." He forced a smile and turned his attention to getting them on the road.

Jez swallowed and wondered about Boone's sister. Then her mind brought up how angry he was about Jordy's drinking and him in her room. She didn't want to put the puzzle pieces together that way, but it was an ugly picture that came to her. She knew she'd have to ask one day, but if he told her his scary stores, he'd want to know hers. She couldn't share hers yet, especially not now. He wouldn't understand.

Neither had much to say on the way to the mall, both seemed preoccupied with their own issues. But when Boone pulled into a parking spot and cut the engine, he leaned over and kissed her deeply. "Hey, let's leave the black and whites in the trunk, OK?"

"Black and whites?" She smiled never having heard that term before.

"Sure you know, the pictures that haunt us. We'll bring them out and share another day, but right now, let's leave them here and go have some fun." He smiled, and she agreed.

Their first stop was the coffee house. She hadn't gotten any before they left since she had taken so long to dress, so he offered to buy her one at the mall. Then they started the long, and surprisingly difficult, shopping excursion. It took a lot of compromising to find outfits that she thought would be appropriate and that he approved of. Most of the things she wanted he deemed too short or too tight.

"It's not that you don't look good in them, Ace. It's that you look too good in them." He whispered in her ear at one store. He could see that she was taking his disagreements hard. "If you get some of these things I'm not going to be able to let you out of my sight, even for a second."

"Have you ever considered that maybe that's my plan?" She smiled. In the end, they found five outfits that were edgy enough for her to think of herself as Ace in, and yet Boone could agree too also. One of the outfits though, he said she could only wear if he was going to be right next to her. She agreed because it was the one she liked the best.

Before leaving the mall, Jez ran into an accessory shop and picked up a couple of last minute things, while Boone stepped next door and picked up something that had caught his eye.

They made a stop on the way to treatment to get some lunch and then after they were on their way back to the shop. Boone and Jez were both scheduled to work the closing shift since the others would be working all weekend. Jordy was already gone when they entered the parts store. Ty and OB seemed anxious to get out. Laughing about some joke, they both gave Jez a kiss on the cheek and waved to a slightly jealous Boone, who made sure he came over to hold her tight as they drove away.

"You need to let it go." She smiled up at him.

"Let what go, Ace?" He asked as if he didn't understand what she meant.

She smiled and shook her head before laying it on his chest. "They've known me a long time. I'm like their sister."

"Doesn't mean I have to like watching them kiss you." He growled.

She lifted her head and looked up into his eyes. "The more you show you hate it, the more they'll do it. The only time they ever get touchy feely is when someone else is interested."

"They get too touchy feely and I'll cut those hands off." He was serious and she wasn't sure how to take it. But then he smiled and she smacked his arm.

"I'm sure Jordy is feeling just about the same way right now."

"He knows I won't be touching you if you don't want me to."

"Maybe that's what's got him worried." She bit her bottom lip trying not to smile.

He groaned and leaned in to kiss her. "God you're killing me, Ace."

He lifted her easily and set her on the counter in front of him. She opened her legs so he could get as close as possible and wrapped her arms around him. With one hand on the back of her neck and the other on her back, he allowed her to lead their kisses from gentle and innocent to deep and needy. They were so into each other, they barely heard the bell on the door as it rang.

"Oh young love." The older voice sighed, and Jez jumped. She turned and saw Mr. Morlick smiling at them.

Boone stepped back and Jez slide off the counter. "Hey Mr. Morlick. Sorry about that."

"Don't apologize." He waved his hand. "I'm sorry to interrupt. I just need some oil and a filter."

He turned away and Jez blushed. Boone smiled and moved to help the old man with what he was looking for. Jez tried to occupy herself with random things, but eventually pulled her phone out and texted Jordy.

'Hey, will you be around when I get home? I might need a ride to the store.'

It didn't take him long to respond. 'Sure. I'll be home no later than ten. What do you need?'

'Just a few things I don't want to ask Boone to buy. See you then.'

Boone was ringing Mr. Morlick up and giving her curious looks at the same time. When they were done, Mr. Morlick said good night and they waved in return. When he was gone, Boone leaned on the counter. "What was that about?"

"What?" She asked with a pleased smile.

He gave her a look that she could only interpret as displeasure. "The texting."

"Jealous?" She teased but he wasn't playing. With a sigh, she gave in. "It was Jordy. I was just asking if he was going to be home tonight."

"And?"

"He said he'd be home around ten."

"And this is good news?" He wasn't happy.

Jez stepped up and wrapped her arms around him. "I can count on one hand just how many times I've spent the night away from him. This is going to be hard on both of us, Boone."

"Who's it going to be harder on? You or him?" Boone's voice was dark.

"I don't know. I guess that depends."

"Depends?" His eyebrows raised curiously.

"Depends on where I'll be sleeping." She smiled. She didn't have a doubt in her mind that she would be sleeping right next to Boone the next two nights, but she thought she'd better play it safe and not assume.

He smiled a devilish grin. "Don't you worry about those nightmares, Ace. I'll protect you from them and anything else that threatens to hurt you."

She forced a happy smile, but in her head she wondered what he would say if he knew she was the biggest threat to herself.

At dinner time, he went and got them food. The store stayed fairly quiet most of the night and they were ready to leave as soon as they closed and she counted out the register. He took her home and reminded her that they'd be by to get her around eight. She allowed her excitement to show and pushed away any anxiety she felt. When they kissed good bye, he wished her sweet dreams.

Jordy wasn't home just yet, which was fine. Jez made a short list of the things she needed to get at the store. More hydrations drinks, a new travel cup, preferably one that wasn't clear, and some of her favorite pickles. She was just about to text him, when Jordy came in the back door. He seemed in an odd mood, but Jez didn't mention it until they were on their way to the store.

"You alright?"

He glanced at her. "Yup."

"Jordy?"

"I'm fine." He reached over and took her hand. "Just don't know what I'm going to do to without you for three days."

She laughed. "Oh think of the possibilities. You could work, or clean the house, or go out with your friends, or go out on a date." She allowed her eyes to get big and she covered her mouth. "Or you could bring a girl home."

He gave her a horrified look and then broke out into laughter just as she did. "Bite your tongue, missy. You know I'm trying to get into the priesthood."

She giggled and swatted at his arm. "I'm serious. Come on Jordy. Go out and have some fun. You don't have to worry about me. Dad's gone. Have a party. Get drunk. Get laid. Act like a 23-year-old for once."

"You've been hanging out with the guys too much." He snapped. "Listen to that mouth."

She rolled her eyes but smiled. He did too, eventually.

Once at the store, she gathered the things she needed and he seemed to understand why she wanted him to take her. He seemed to know that she hadn't told Boone everything just yet, and he was happy about that. She didn't tease him when they walked down the liquor aisle and he picked up a few of his favorites. She knew that was how he was going to get through this weekend without going crazy.

When they got back to the house, he headed off to shower and fell into bed, claiming to be tired. She packed her bag, which was mostly the drinks and her bathroom items. She tossed in a few pieces of clothing just for show, just in case. She charged her phone and climbed into bed, only to have Jordy join her a few minutes after she had shut her lights off.

Lying in the dark, he whispered. "Jez, promise me you'll be careful."

"I will." She rolled over to face him, even though he was hidden in the shadows. "You too."

"I'm not stupid enough to think you won't sleep with him but please Jez, really think about it. Make sure it's what you want and not what you think you need to do." Emotion was thick in his voice.

"Jordy, if I tell you something, will you keep it between us?"

"Always."

"He's been the one stopping us." She felt her brother move and wasn't sure if it was in surprise or nervousness. "Whatever is going to happen out there, will happen. Don't worry, OK? I love you but we both need to have a fun weekend."

"Just don't come back married or pregnant, alright?"

She couldn't tell if he was joking or not. "I promise."

They were silent for a few minutes, and then she whispered, "Hey Jordy?"

"Yeah, Jez?"

"I'm going to miss you."

"I'm going to miss you too."

Chapter 43

Morning came quickly and Jez woke to her brother's snoring and the sound of banging. It took several minutes before she realized the banging was coming from downstairs and she stumbled down to see what was going on. OB and Ty were attempting to break into the house, using the way that they use to when they were children, by taking a screwdriver to the large screen on the front window. With a curious and amused look, Jez stepped in front of the window, scaring both guys and making them jump back. As she started laughing, she moved to the door.

"What the hell?" She shook her head as they came in.

"We've been knocking forever. Shit, where were you?" OB commented coming into the house and crossing to the kitchen.

"Asleep." She said as if it was obvious. Ty smiled at her, but Jez rolled her eyes and turned to go back upstairs. "I'm going to shower. Make some coffee."

She heard them start talking but she didn't stop to listen. Instead, she headed into her bedroom and then to the bathroom, glancing at the clock. She had just under an hour before Boone was supposed to be there to pick her up. She spent a little longer in the bathroom than normal, deciding to do a lot of personal grooming, just in case. She made sure her make-up and hair were done before she pushed into her bedroom, wrapped only in a towel. Jordy was still snoring in her bed, bare upper torso uncovered. She smiled and rolled her eyes. When he was tired enough he could sleep through just about anything. She grabbed up her underwear, a pair of jeans, and a clean sweatshirt. Keeping the towel around her, she pulled on her underwear and her jeans. Jordy rolled over and she turned to keep her back to the door as she dropped the towel. She had just gotten her bra on when a small noise came from behind her.

Jez looked over her shoulder to see Boone standing in the doorway watching her. His eyes were on her and a crooked smile graced his lips. She smiled over her shoulder, but pulled on her sweatshirt, without turning to him. As her hand pulled down the hem of the top, her fingers ran across the scabs on her stomach. Her smile fell, she was glad she hadn't turned around to face him.

Jordy moved in the bed again as he began to wake. Boone's attention was draw to the movement, only then seeing him half naked in her bed. Boone's eyes flashed to Jez, and seeing her sad face, Boone bristled. It took less than a second for her to put it all together and she dashed across the room before Boone could move. Putting her hands up to stop any movement, she rushed to him. "It's not what you think."

"This doesn't look good, Ace." He said as she pushed him into the hallway.

"He's wearing pajama bottoms, I swear."

"What's he doing in your bed?" Boone was flushing with anger.

She sighed and backed him into the far wall. "We were talking and fell asleep."

He looked down into her eyes. He saw that she wasn't lying but he still wasn't happy. "I still don't like it."

Wrapping her arms around his neck, she pulled herself close to him. "Well, tonight it will be you next to me." She smiled and pressed into him.

"Now I don't like it." Jordy's groggy voice said from behind her.

Jez sighed and closed her eyes, dropping her head so her forehead rested for a moment on Boone's chest. A second later, she lifted it and spun away from both guys. She couldn't win for losing. Walking down the stairs, Jez focused on the coffee she wanted. She could hear Boone and Jordy talking above and behind her, but she didn't really care what they were discussing. With her luck, they were planning her future for her.

Ty and OB had made coffee and were busy making breakfast when she came into the kitchen. They glanced at her but didn't stop their conversation. She filled a mug and started to drink it while she looked around for her flip-flops. She heard Boone's heavy footsteps come down the stairs and looked up.

"What the hell you got in this thing, Ace? Rocks?"

She smiled at him. "Just the things I couldn't live without."

He got to the door and yanked it open just as Skye and Mel were about to knock. "Perfect timing." Boone chuckled. "Here, take this."

"Jesus." Skye commented as he grabbed the bag from Boone. "What the hell's in here?"

Jordy didn't say anything as he passed the guys but leaned down to her. "And that bag better be lighter when you come home."

She looked up at him and smiled weakly. "It will, I promise." She said very thankful that Jordy understood that she didn't want to announce what was hidden in the bottom of the duffle. She'd have to work hard to keep her secret over the next few days, but she'd find a way.

"Hate to say it, Ace, but we need to get on the road." Boone called waving at something that was going on in the front yard.

Jez nodded and move to the kitchen to dispose of her coffee mug. She gave OB a hug and then one to Ty. When she had Ty close, she whispered into his ear. "Keep an eye on him for me. Make sure he has some fun."

Ty pulled back and smiled. "Already planned."

He gave her a quick kiss on the cheek and she moved into the living room to say good-bye to Jordy. He looked miserable. Wrapping her arms around him, she smiled brightly. "It's only three days. I'll be back before you know it and you'll be wishing I was gone again."

He held her tightly. "That's never going to happen. Please be careful."

"I will."

A honk sounded from out front. She pulled away and smiled at him, fighting down the tears. He smiled at her too, but seemed tense. As she moved to the door, Boone stepped over to shake Jordy's hand. "Don't worry man, I've got her. I'm not going to let anything bad happen."

"Better not." Jordy warned. "One more bruise and I'm coming after you."

Boone smiled and nodded, but he knew Jordy was completely serious also. The three of them walked out to the large travel bus that was parked on the street.

"Shit, at least you're going in style." Jordy comments obviously impressed with the transportation. "I thought dad said you were camping."

"Normally we camp, but not with Jez going. Top of the line all the way. Nothing's too good for her."

Jez fought down the overwhelming concern that rose in her as she stepped over and gave her brother one last kiss on the cheek. "See you on Sunday."

"Be careful."

Boone took her hand and walked her the rest of the way across the yard to the side door that flew open. "It was only partly because of you, Ace."

"And the other part?"

"Mel don't camp." Boone smiled as they got to the door and he helped her step inside.

Skye sat behind the wheel of the large bus and smiled back to her. "Hey Ace."

"Morning Skye, Mel."

The engine started and Jez took a seat on the small sofa next to Boone. She turned and looked out at the three amigos, who all now stood on the porch watching. She waved but knew they couldn't see her. As Skye pulled away from the curb, they waved anyway. She fought down the emotions.

Mel moved to sit in a chair that was angled across from Boone. "One more stop and we are on the road."

Jez looked up at Boone who was watching her closely. "You OK, Ace?"

"Sure. Just odd. I'm not the one who gets to leave." He nodded in understanding, and then she asked. "One more stop?"

"We have to get the cars."

"Oh." She said. She hadn't thought about them.

"We thought it would be better not to bring the trailer here. Might raise too many questions."

It was her turn to nod. "But you brought the bus?"

Skye laughed. "Boone thought it'd make brownie points with your brother if you were being treated with style."

"I think it worked." She smiled back. "He seemed impressed."

"Good." Boone said and leaned into her. When she didn't turn her chin fast enough, he turned it for her. He placed a gently kiss on her lips and smiled when she did. "I want to stay on your family's good side."

"Well, treating her like a princess is a good way." Mel said. "Paulie treated her like shit, and they didn't like that very much."

Jez looked down at the mention of Paulie. She didn't want to think about him right now.

"Hey." Boone said softly seeing the change in her.

"Sorry Ace. But it's true." Mel shrugged.

She smiled weakly and nodded. They were just getting on the freeway and Jez needed to leave the past here. "How long will it take us to get out there?"

"Four, maybe five, hours." Boone said. "You look tired. Want to go lay down for a little bit?"

Jez thought about it, but he didn't give her a chance to answer. He stood up and grabbed on to the roof to keep his balance. Reaching over, he grabbed her hand and lifted it so she'd stand up too. Walking carefully, he led her to the back of the bus and into a closed off section at the very back. As they walked, he pointed out where the kitchen, bathroom, and bunks were. She expected him to give her one of the bunks to sleep in, but he pushed open the door and showed her the full-sized bedroom at the back. "This is your room."

"My room?" She said doubtfully.

"Your room. Can't have our star too tired for her races." He smiled.

She looked around. It was almost as big as her room at home. She took it in and looked back up at him. "Where will you be, if this is my room?"

He smiled and stepped closer to her. "That depends. If you would prefer, I can take one of the bunks like Skye and Mel."

"Or you could sleep here with me?" She asked softly.

"I would never assume that." He said, but then his devilish smile appeared. "But I'm not going to deny any of your wishes either."

She smiled and reached up to wrap her arms around his neck. Pushing up on her toes, she pressed her lips to his. Following her lead, Boone parted his lips and allowed her to explore his mouth. Then explored hers. When she side stepped to the bed, he moved with her and helped her lay down. They wrapped around each other on top the soft comforter. He laced one of his hands into her hair and allowed the other to trace her arm. Jez's breathing was growing more ragged as her desire and need grew. Sensing this, Boone pulled back.

"Easy Ace, we've got all weekend." He smiled at her and they felt the bus slow and then make a turn. Skye said something from the front and Boone sighed. "You get some rest, Ace."

She put out a pouty lip and Boone chuckled. "You're killing me, Ace."

The bus slowed even more and Boone moved off the bed. As it made a sharp turn, he held the roof and moved back through the doorway. He pulled the door closed, leaving Jez alone. Frustrated and needy, Jez wanted to cry. She was hungry with desire and was being teased with a piece of prime rib. Allowing herself a deep breath, Jez rolled over and grabbed the pillow next to her. Pulling it into her arms, where she would have much rather have had Boone, she cuddled into it. The soft billows rubbed her sweatshirt into her abdomen, grating them against her cuts. She hissed in discomfort, and then her desire fizzled out. Suddenly she was very aware as to why it was a good thing they hadn't gone any further. She swallowed back more tears as she wondered how she was going to lie her way out of these injuries.

The tears were even closer now, and Jez closed her eyes against them. She took in a few deep breaths and tried to relax. She allowed her thoughts to flow freely and before long, she was riding the waves next to her brother and dad, and the rest of her friends.

☐

Chapter 44

"Ace. Ace." A hand touched her arm and Jez's eyes popped open. She sat upright, almost hitting her head against Skye's. "Woah, Ace. It's ok."

She looked around wide eyed, and swallowed down the fear that had gripped her. She recalled that she was in the bus, riding to the Desert Run races. She took in a deep breath to calm her racing heart and then gripped her chest as the pain shot across it. Her breath stopped and she cringed.

"Ace? Are you alright?" Skye's voice hushed as he reached out to place a hand on her shoulder.

It took a second, but Jez nodded and then took in a weak breath. The pain began to subside and she took in slow breaths. After several long moments, she smiled up at Skye, who looked like he didn't know what to do. "Sorry. I'm fine."

"You don't look fine. What happened?"

She smiled a little brighter. "What's up, Skye?"

"We're almost there." He said slowly, watching as Jez's color started to return. Her breathing was easier and she was relaxing with every passing second. "Boone thought we should wake you so you could get dressed."

She nodded and smiled. "Thank you."

"Are you sure you're OK? You didn't look good."

"I'm fine. You just scared me, that's all." She said and forced herself to relax even more. "Hey could we keep this between us? I don't want Boone to get all over protective. I'm fine, see."

He nodded but still seemed leery. "OK."

"How long do I have?"

"About ten minutes." He got up and moved to the door. He looked back at her and then she saw him relax. He shook off his concern and moved out into the main part of the bus, pulling the door closed behind him.

Jez took another moment to make sure she was indeed alright. Her chest pains were gone and her pulse was returning to normal. She wasn't sure what that was all about but she hadn't liked it. She scooted over to the side of the bed and put her feet down. She moved slowly, not wanting to fall or pass out. That would not be a good way to start the weekend.

Boone, or Skye, had brought her bag in and placed it on the floor near the closet. Curious, she moved the bag and pulled the closet door open; inside hung the new outfits that they had purchased the day before. She selected a tight pair of jeans and a tank top. After changing, she took up her make up bag and brush, then moved to bathroom. She darkened her shadow and thickened her lashes. She brushed out her hair and pulled it into a ponytail that she teased a little fuller. She put in her hoop earrings and then applied her crimson lipstick. All but the last hints of Jez were gone when she stepped from the bathroom. With her head held high, she moved back into the bedroom. She dropped her things into her bag, slid on her high heels, grabbed a bottle of hydration drink that was hidden in the bottom of the bag and her new travel cup. She took a private moment to empty the plastic bottle into the cup and put the empty bottle back into her bag. As she moved out of the room and back to where the guys were chatting in the front of the bus, she stopped and added ice to the cup. She screwed the lid on tight and closed her eyes. She took in a deep breath and opened her eyes, releasing Jez and allowing Ace to come out completely.

The bus pulled to a stop and Ace moved to the sitting area in the front. Boone was driving now, Mel sat in the same chair he'd been in earlier, and Skye was on the sofa. Ace took a seat next to Skye but smiled up at Boone when he glanced at her around his shoulder. "Hey sleepy, have a nice nap?"

"Guess so. Could have been better though." She smiled a sly, knowing grin that made the guys all chuckle.

"Slow down, Ace, it's going to be a long weekend." Boone smiled and returned his attention to the line in front of them.

She took a sip from her cup and Skye looked over to her. He shook his head and allowed himself another small laugh. "What?"

He cocked his head. "Nothing, not a thing." He smiled and turned his attention to Boone as they moved to what appeared to be the front of the line.

Boone opened the window next to him and leaned his head out. He spoke to someone for several minutes and then leaned back in. He seemed pleased as he hit the gas and moved them forward. Jez tried to watch out the windows, but there was so much to see that she didn't know where to allow her eyes to wander to first. There were hundreds of people spread out over a large open area. Some had campers and some tents. It looked like a small refugee camp. As they passed this area by, Mel chuckled at her wide eyes.

"Incredible that so many people would come just to watch some street racers do their thing, huh?"

Jez turned her head and looked at him. "Those people are just spectators?"

He nodded with a smile, then leaned forward and turned serious. "Don't you start getting a case of the jitters now, Ace. We need you at the top of your game."

She nodded attempting to get a grip on the butterflies that were forming in her stomach. She turned and looked back as the flash of sunlight from a car hood caught her eye. The refugee camp was well behind them, and Boone was now driving them past an equally large group of campers, tents, and trailers. Unlike the last group though, Ace didn't see many people, just vehicles of different sizes and shapes. Racing cars sat between trailers and campers and tents. They glistened in the afternoon sun and sparkled like gems in all colors of the spectrum. Boone turned and moved them down a row then pulled to a stop at the end, parking the large bus next to a small fabric tent and bright orange race car. A thin guy stepped out of the tent and looked up at the bus and gave a thumb up to Boone.

After Boone cut the engine, he spun around and looked at the others. "So, Mel, how about going to find out the race schedule? Skye, you and me get the cars out and ready."

"What do I do?" Jez asked softly.

"You can go with me." Mel suggested. "Might give you a chance to check out some of the competition without them knowing."

Boone didn't look pleased, but he gave in. "Keep a close eye on her."

Mel gave a weak salute and stood up. While he moved to the door, Skye followed. Boone stepped over and helped Jez to her feet. He wrapped his arms around her and she did the same. "Stay with Mel. I doubt anyone will cause trouble today, but ..."

She pressed her lips to his cutting off his warning. When she pulled back, she smiled. "Got it co-pilot. I'll be careful."

He sighed and shook his head. Mel banged on the outside of the bus. "Come on, Ace. Let's go."

Boone smiled as she pulled away and shook his head. Being careful in her high heels, she took the steps and landed next to Mel. Without a word, he started off and as she followed, she heard Boone jump from the stairs as well. He whistled as she sauntered after Mel, and she wiggled her hips a little more for his benefit.

Mel walked faster than Jez did normally, but with the added distractions she found herself slipping further and further behind.

Her eyes wandered over the guys and the cars that surrounded her. Most of the cars look impressive, the guys not so much, a few caught her eye though and she smiled back at them if they smiled to her. As she made the walk down the long, dirt path, she was also able to size up the competition, or those she thought were competition. There were a few she could tell were too confident, and others that had a slyness about them that made her nervous. She was carefully eyeing one car, a sleek European sports car with purple strips on an orange frame as she walked past when she heard Mel call to her.

"Bels! Hurry up!"

Jez's head popped up and she glared at him. He was several camp sites ahead but stood waiting for her. She sighed and walked straight at him with an annoyed gate. When she was near him, she looked up at him. "Why'd you call me that?"

He smiled. "One to get your attention. Two because I wasn't thinking, and three, it's better to not let the cat out of the bag too early. The more these guys don't see you as a threat, the more of chance you have of taking them off guard."

"No one is going to know me here." She said, cocking her hip to one side and putting her hand on it.

"You'd be surprised." He said, his smile fading. "Keep your mouth shut and listen as we walk over to that tent."

He had tossed his head and she glanced over. Just a few camp sites away was a large white tent with big black letters. She couldn't exactly read them from her vantage point. He grabbed her hand and led her over to one of the three tables that were lined up under the shade. Several men stood around talking as they approached and one smiled as he saw Mel. His gold front tooth glinted in the bright sun.

"Mel!"

"Hey Grey." Mel replied. While he sounded friendly enough, Jez could hear something just under the words that made her listen a little closer.

"I've got two racers this year."

Grey laughed. "What's their names?"

"Skye Bolton and Ace McIntosh."

Grey nodded and looked through a paper on a clip board. He checked off their names. "The cars and drivers need to be in the large hanger in two hours."

"Why?" Jez asked before she could stop herself. Then as an afterthought, she giggled and twirled her hair around her finger.

Both guys looked at her a little shocked. Mel spoke her name as a warning, "Bels."

"It's OK. We check the cars to make sure they are within the rules. We also like to give the drivers a chance to check each other out." Grey said leaning against the table and smiled. He was checking her out and she played the girl, leaning in and giving him a flirty look. He winked and introduced himself. "I'm Grey Loacher by the way."

She smiled. "I'm..."

"This is Boone's girlfriend," Mel interrupted.

"Boone? Boone Kingston?" Grey had obviously heard of him. "I didn't know he was here."

"He came to hang with Skye and Ace." Mel replied.

Grey nodded. He had seemed a little nervous at first, but now relaxed. "Cool."

"Well, I'd better get back." Mel reached out and tugged on Jez's arm.

Grey's eyes returned to Jez. "It was good to meet you."

She smiled and giggled as she took a step back. Mel gripped her arm and pulled her along as he turned and walked out of the tent. When they were a couple camp sites down, he turned to her. "Watch out for Grey."

"Why?"

"He's a player. I don't know all the details but him and Boone had issues a few months back."

Jez nodded, remembering the look Grey had when he found out she was with him. "How's he going to take it when he finds out I'm Ace?"

Mel turned and shrugged. "Not sure. I'd recommend you play the girl card again before you race. The less these guys take you seriously the better."

She gave him a curious look. "But ..."

"You'll have enough time to prove them wrong and be taken seriously later. Make them think you're just a dumb girl, and then kick their ass." He said softly and bumped her arm with his.

"Sneak attack?"

He winked as they approached the camper. Skye and Boone had the cars out and sitting next to the camper and trailer. They were leaning up against the camper. Boone had a beer in his hand and Skye had a soda. Boone smiled and wrapped an arm around her as she stepped up to him. "So how'd it go?"

"Well, she made quite an impression on Grey." Mel said. He handed one paper to Skye, who instantly looked at it.

"Oh?" Boone bristled.

Jez leaned in and kissed his cheek. Whispering into his ear, she said, "You're going to have to fill me in later."

"She played the girl thing up well. He doesn't have a clue." Mel smiled.

"OK, I have to play up this girl thing a little more. Can someone explain what happens now?" Jez asked feeling self-conscious.

She staggered a little on her feet and Boone looked down at her. "Why don't we go sit down and go over this?"

She smiled up at him, seeing that while he made a suggestion, it wasn't really a request. They moved into the rig and she took a moment to refill her cup with ice and then vanished into the bedroom to grab a bottle of hydration drink. She wasn't purposely hiding what she was drinking from Boone, but she wasn't being overly obvious about it either. As she tucked the plastic bottle back in her bag, Boone stepped into the doorway.

"What'cha doing Ace?"

"Nothing," she smiled up at him and screwed the lid back on. She stood, as slow as she could so she wouldn't get dizzy.

He gave her a curious look, but took her hand and led her back to the sofa. Jez took a seat and Boone plopped down next to her. She leaned against him and he pulled her close. "So, what's going on with you and Grey?"

"Ancient history, Ace. You don't need to worry about it."

She looked up at him but didn't speak.

"So, in a little while, you're going to take your car over to the hanger. You'll go in and park next to Skye. A couple of guys will come and look her over, and probably check you out too."

"Mel said I should play the dumb girl card."

Boone twisted his lips and nodded. "Not a bad idea."

"But the other day he said I had couldn't show any weakness." She was confused.

"Playing the girl card doesn't mean you're weak. It's exploiting their misconceptions. You play the dumb girl card today, and maybe even tonight, but then tomorrow you go for the kill." Boone explained. "It's like poker. You play into their hands for the first few rounds and then level them."

She nodded understanding. "Will they buy it?"

"If anyone can pull this off, it's you." He smiled. "You've got them all fooled."

"Mel introduced me as Bels." She admitted.

Boone's eyes darkened but he pushed it aside. "So they don't know, you're Ace?"

"Nope."

Boone smiled then. "This is going to be better than I would have hoped. No one is going to see you coming."

She took a big sip of her drink and sighed.

"I'm not going to be able to come with you for the inspection, Ace." He added even though she had already figured that out.

"But Skye will be there, right?"

"Yup, just follow his lead. He's already agreed to keep an eye out for you."

She nodded, and took another sip, wishing it was something stronger than just the grape drink. She mentally kicked herself for not bringing a bottle of Moonshine.

"After the inspection, they'll line you up and take you out to the track. You'll race twice tonight. Winners progress on tomorrow."

"And how many races tomorrow?"

"Fifty drops to twenty-five tonight. Second race drops it again to twelve."

"But half of twenty-five is twelve and a half."

"Not only are the losers cut, but the slowest car is dropped too." She nodded and he continued. "The twelve race mid-day, dropping to six. Six drops to three, with the slowest car being cut again. Last race is Saturday evening. Winner taking all."

"So, this isn't just about beating someone, it's also about fastest times." She said getting a better feeling about why people said she shouldn't come.

Boone pushed her chin up and turned her shoulders so she was looking at him. "Don't you even think about that. Matter of fact, I don't want you to think about any of it. Just go out there and do what you do. There's no pressure."

"But Mel will be pissed if I …"

"Mel can deal with me if he has any problems. I just want you to go out there and have fun." Boone smiled and wrapped a hand around her head.

She nodded but she still felt the weight of it on her. He seemed to see it in her eyes and leaned in. After several long minutes of kissing, he pulled away and smiled. "Better?"

Again, she nodded. She took a sip of her drink and breathed in a deep breath to calm her racing heart. Skye and Mel came into the bus then. "If you want to change, Ace, now's your chance."

Jez looked at Boone and he nodded to her. She got up and moved back to the bedroom. She looked through the clothes that they had brought and selected a just above the knee length, full skirt that was more girly than Jez would have normally chosen. Pairing it with a lacey tank top, Jez changed and pulled on thigh high stockings and strappy, wedge heels. She freshened up her make-up and curled her hair. She finished her drink and when she was dressed and ready, she took her cup to the kitchen and rinsed it out. Placing it on the counter to dry, Jez looked up to see the guys were all watching her.

"What?"

Mel dropped his head and headed out of the bus, looking uncomfortable. Skye smiled and gave Jez a wink before following Mel, leaving her alone with Boone. He was watching her as she moved from the kitchen area over to him.

"What? Do I look OK?" She asked getting nervous. Jez glanced down at herself and tried to see if something was wrong.

It took Boone a few moments to compose his thoughts, as he did he looked her over and worried his bottom lip between his fingers. "Ok doesn't begin to describe how you look, Ace."

Taking his answer wrong, she glanced down at herself again. "I guess I could go change."

He moved up to her and wrapped his hands about her waist. "As much as I want to tell you to go change since I won't be next to you tonight, I just …."

"So… I look …?" She asked

"Fucking gorgeous." Boone pulled her close and wrapped his arms around her. "I hate that I can't be with you though."

She smiled up at him. "I'll be fine. Skye will be close and I'll be as careful as I can."

He leaned in and kissed her deeply. Flooded with need, Jez lifted on her toes and pressed into him. She felt his hands work their way up under her shirt. The feel of his hands on her bare skin brought tingles to her, deep inside. Wanting more, needing more, Jez tightened her grip on his neck. He groaned in desire or in her response to his touch. Her breath quickened and she arched into him, but as his hands moved down her back, and over her skirt and ass, a bang sounded against the side of the bus.

"Let go of her, Boone. She's got to focus."

Boone pulled back and groaned. Jez whimpered and looked up at him with sad eyes. "Sometimes I wonder if Jordy didn't pay them to do this."

Boone chuckled. "After you race, there's not going to be anything to stop me from getting near you."

"After I win." She corrected.

"After you win," He agreed.

Another bang and Skye called, "We gotta go, Ace."

She sighed as Boone moved away from her. He took her hand and led her out to where the others waited. As they walked over to the cars, Boone spoke to Jez. "Follow Skye into the hanger. Park as close to him as you can. Follow his lead." She nodded. "When the inspection's over, you'll be told what number race you're in. You'll line up in number order, then progress out to the track."

Jez fought down the nerves. "No practice run, huh?"

He smiled. "Nope, but don't worry. You've got this."

"After the race?"

"After the race, you'll be directed back to the hangar if you win, and then you come back here. I'll meet you right here, OK?" She swallowed and nodded. Seeing her nerves, he pulled her close and kissed her. "You've got this, Ace. Don't worry."

"I've never raced like this."

"I know. But there's nothing major about this. It's just a regular race, just like on the track at home."

"Except for the process, the number of racers, the amount of spectators, the sun being out." She added.

He kissed her again but stopped when Mel stepped up. Smacking Boone out of the way, Mel tugged on Jez's arm and freed her from his grip. He turned her shoulders until she was looking directly at him. He had to lean down just a bit to look into her eyes, but when he had her undivided attention, he spoke. "Do you remember that night you raced that demon that came down from Torrance?"

She thought back and nodded.

"Do you remember what I told you?"

"You asked me if I knew how to get to heaven. When I said I didn't know, you told me all I had to do was out run the devil." She replied, feeling the change begin inside her.

"There isn't any difference today. Just picture yourself on that night. Outrun the devil, Ace."

Her mind flashed back to why she had been so scared that night; the night before she had lost her first race. Paulie and Sean had both raped her in the parking lot. She was terrified and shaken. She hadn't wanted to get behind the wheel again, but Paulie had forced her. It was only Mel's words and her own fear that had gotten her through it. Jez closed her eyes and took in a deep breath. "God, I wish I had thought to bring a little courage."

Mel slapped his head and rushed away. Jez gave a confused look to Boone, who was watching curiously at everything that had been happening. When he shrugged, Mel reappeared, the familiar glass mason jar in his hand. "Can't believe I almost forgot." He laughed and handed it to her.

She took a swig and felt the burn down into her toes. A smile spread across her face and she turned to get into her car. Skye was already behind the wheel, waiting for her. She started the car and pulled it around to follow behind Skye. She glanced back in her review mirror and saw Mel talking to Boone. She briefly wondered what they were discussing, but when Boone made a fist and took a swing at the side of the trailer, she knew. Pushing the vision aside, Jez turned on the radio and sank back into the darkness, giving herself over to Ace.

☐

Chapter 45

Skye fell in line with Ace right behind as they entered the old airplane hangar. It was a massive metal building with two huge sliding doors at either end. Ace couldn't see what lay beyond the other door because of all the people and cars that were between her and it. A guy in a bright yellow vest waved the line of cars to one side of the building, where another directed Skye to back into a parking spot and motioned for Ace to wait. When Skye was stopped, Ace followed his lead and backed into her spot. It was a little tricky for her since she had never gone in reverse before, but she got parked without too many issues and only slight embarrassment. To her relief, a few others had difficulty backing in also, and no one seemed to notice her struggle, except for Skye. He popped his hood and then stepped over to where Ace was moving around the front of her car.

"We need to teach you how to drive in reverse." He chuckled.

"I never go backward." She commented, annoyed by the fact he was finding humor in her.

He chuckled more. As she leaned onto the side of her car, he did too and bumped her arm with his. "What did Mel say to you?"

"He just reminded me how to do this."

Skye was silent for a moment. "Whatever he said pissed Boone off."

"I know." She sighed. "But I can't think about that right now."

Skye nodded and looked over at her carefully. She felt the weight of his eyes but she was looking over the others that were hanging out around them. Many were chatting with those around them, some shook hands or hugged, but others just stood by their cars and glared at their competition. Every race and color was represented, but everywhere Ace looked she noticed it was all guys. She looked more and more, but it was all muscles and balls. Turning her head, she saw that Skye was staring at her still.

"What?"

"Nothing." He blinked and looked away.

She wanted to push the issue. She had seen something in his eyes, but wasn't sure it was accurate. But she knew this wasn't the time or the place. "Hey Skye, do you notice anything about the group?"

He looked around them and nodded his head at a few of the guys who waved to him. "No, what about them?"

"I don't see any girls." She said.

"Mm, really?" He asked as if he hadn't noticed it before she pointed it out.

"Are we breaking some kind of unwritten rule?"

He smiled. "Naw Ace. There are a few girl racers here. They must be on the other side though. Don't worry. This ain't a boys' club."

"But?" She inquired, sensing that he wasn't telling her everything.

He allowed his eyes to return to her. "But nothing, Ace. You just go out there and do what we all know you can."

She forced her eyes from his, and glanced around again. "So who's the one to beat?" While she waited for his reply, she tucked her bottom lip between her teeth.

He laughed. "It's me, of course."

She spun her head to him, and gave him a raised eyebrow look. "I don't think so. I would have kicked your ass had you not cheated."

"I'm sorry about that by the way." His amusement faded. "I felt bad, especially after Boone told me about … well, the other times you'd lost."

She shrugged. "Just don't do it again, or I'll take a crow bar to your car."

"Ouch." He winced.

"Hey Skye, girlfriends aren't allowed in the hangar." A voice called to them from two cars down.

Skye and Ace both turned and look at who was shouting. A group of four guys stood together, laughing and commenting. They were all clean cut and well developed physically. They reminded Ace of the jocks she went to high school with. Too big for their britches and needing to be taken down a notch. One of them pointed to Ace, but a different one spoke loudly enough for them to hear. "You ain't going to get laid if you lose."

A different one said, "Or if she loses."

There was a collective chuckle as the fourth called, "Poor Skye, he ain't got a chance."

Ace rolled her eyes and looked at Skye. He watched for her reaction, a little tense. While she looked at him, the first voice called, "Hey Baby, why don't you come over here and hang with someone who's got a chance of winning."

"I'm going to enjoy kicking his ass." She whispered. She leaned a little closer to Skye and smiled. "If it wouldn't piss Boone off, I'd make a show that'd put that him in his place."

"Well, then looks like we'll just have to settle for you kicking his ass." Skye smirked.

An idea came to Ace, and she smiled crookedly.

"Shit, Ace, no. Whatever it is that you are thinking about, don't please." Skye shook his head, begging her. Unfortunately for him, the judges came upon his car just then, and he had to step over to talk to them.

While he was occupied, Ace slid away and walked over to where the group was still standing and talking. She moved up to stand in front of the guy who had started the comments and looked up into his eyes. They were shit brown and she could see right into him. Putting on her best innocent face, she twirled a piece of hair around her finger. "So, which car is yours?"

He smiled, and pointed to a bright yellow Honda Civic another car over. It was ridiculously bright and screamed for attention. Ace looked over at it and smiled. "She's fast, just like you, baby."

"I doubt it." She said in a high-pitched voice.

He seemed a little taken back. "She's got it where it counts. Ditch Skye and I'll show you."

"Ace!" Skye shouted for her.

She turned and started to walk back to her car. But after a few steps, she stopped and turned back to look at the group over her shoulder. "See you on the track boys."

She swung her hips and felt their eyes flaring her skirt a little more. She reached her car just as the judges were stepping up to it. She smiled sweetly. "Hi, I'm Ace."

The trio looked down at their paperwork and then back at her. "Ace MacIntosh?" One of them asked.

"Yep."

"Pop the hood please." Another one requested.

Knowing that the guys were watching, Ace leaned in through the open window, her ass lifting into the air, her skirt rising. She found the latch and popped the hood open for the trio of judges to take a look. When she stood back upright, she looked across the roof to an unhappy Skye.

"Don't play with fire, Ace. You promised to be careful."

She put on her big, innocent eyes. "I just wanted to know which car to look for."

A judge looked around the hood and motioned for her to join them. She gave Skye a worried look, but move up next to them. "Is everything alright?"

"It looks amazing." One of them said. He looked up at her with soft hazel eyes, and smiled kindly. "It's a lot of car. Are you sure you can do this? I would hate to see anything bad happen out there."

Ace giggled, and it wasn't all for show. "I can handle her."

The other two judges looked up as Ace twirled a piece of hair around her finger. An older man with the beginnings of crow's feet gave her a doubtful look. "You're a cute kid, but I'm not sure you're ready for this big of a step."

"What's the worst that can happen?" Skye jumped in. "She runs one and loses. No harm, no fowl."

The judges looked at each other in silent deliberation.

"Please, just let me do the first round. If I lose, I'm out. If I win, then you know I can do it."

One guy nodded to the others and then they sighed. Mr. Hazel-Eyes looked over to her. "Just be careful, Sweetheart. We don't like cleaning up crashes."

As if to reinforce her girlie side, Ace jumped up and down and clapped her hands. "Oh, thank you! I would hug you, but I doubt that's allowed."

Smiling brightly, she watched them move on to the next car. When they were occupied, Skye stepped over and helped her close the engine hood. "You almost over did it."

"Sorry." She rolled her eyes and allowed the girly voice and smile to fade. "Mel and Boone said to make it look good."

"Well that was damn near believable, even for me."

"So now what?"

"We wait until all the cars have been checked. Someone will come around and give us numbers. Then we just wait for our turn."

"What are they looking for?" Ace asked as she watched the trio point to something under the hood of a car two down. It was one of the cars for the group that had been assholes a few minutes ago. They seemed to be discussing something important.

Skye was watching carefully too. "A lot of the races out here don't have a lot of rules. They run like the street races at home. But this one is really structured. No NOS or other enhancements like that. We all pay to try, but the winner is the only one who wins a prize."

"So why the draw?"

"Almost everyone has side bets going on. It's not against the rules, but it's not exactly supported either. Most of the racers are here to make a name. The winner of this not only takes home a cash prize, but bragging rights for a lifetime. Even the ones who are new to it, who know they're going to lose, will come out and try because they get experience and then they can bet and network."

"Is that why Boone came and isn't racing?" She asked, watching the other drivers.

"Boone use to race, but he knows he isn't very good. And he knows he can't beat you. So, he's running side bets with Mel."

She turned her head to look at him. "But you're racing me. Aren't you worried about beating me, or me beating you?"

"Why? You aren't going to fuck me no matter what." He said honestly, without thinking about his words.

She dropped her head and gave him a disappointed look. "So, does that mean that if you thought I'd fuck you, you wouldn't race?"

"Is that an option?" He asked, a smirk forming on his lips.

She realized he was calling her bluff. She made a show of thinking about it, then shook her head. "No, I wanna kick your ass."

He laughed outright and several people turned to look at him. She smiled and giggled too.

They stood together for a long time and chatted. At one point, the standing became too much in the warm afternoon, and she popped open the door and took a seat inside her car. She wasn't paying attention to the time, but eventually she was aware of the crowd becoming thinner and thinner, as was the noise. When the cars ahead of them started to leave, Ace looked up to Skye.

"So what happens on the track?"

"You race." He said with a smirk.

"Smart ass." She sighed and smacked at his leg. "I mean; do they go over rules. Do I shake hands? What's the etiquette?"

"You just drive to the line, wait for the signal, and fly like a bat outta hell."

"And that's it?" It sounded too easy.

He shrugged. "It's alright to congratulate the winner. But if I were you, I wouldn't expect it."

"Do any of them get nasty when they lose?"

Skye nodded. "Oh sure, but you don't have to worry about that. Grey knows who needs to be watched when they lose. He tends to have extra security around. Besides you've got us."

She smiled up at Skye and a pretty girl came over. She was dressed in Daisy Duke shorts and a bikini top, that showed off her very thin body. She looked at Skye's car and down at a clip board in her hand. "Skye Bolton?" She called.

Skye took the five steps over to his car and she nodded. Handing him a magnetic number, she spoke softly to him. Curious, Ace got up and moved closer so she could hear. The girl saw her move and looked at Ace. "Girlfriends aren't allowed in the Hangar."

"I'm not his girlfriend." Ace replied.

"Groupies aren't allowed either." The girl's snotty attitude took Ace off guard and she tensed.

But before Ace could let the girl have it, Skye stepped in. "This is Ace MacIntosh. She's racing too."

The girl looked back down at her clipboard and seemed annoyed that Ace's name was indeed there. She handed Ace her number. "Here, it goes on the back of your car, on your plate. You're up right after Skye."

Ace nodded and watched as the girl turned and stalked off. She had to bite the inside of her lip to keep from laughing. Skye took the number from her hand and headed for the back of the cars. She followed and watched as he put the numbers on over the place where the license plate would have been, if either car had one. As Skye moved back he stepped close to her.

"OK Ace. We're up. Follow me to the doors but when I go out, stop and wait for the signal."

She nodded once as the nerve grew inside. "Then what?"

"After you're done, we'll meet you at the bus." He could see her nerves starting. Offering her a smile, he added, "You don't have anything to worry about, Ace. You've got this."

He stepped up and gave her a quick hug. She pushed up on her tip toes and placed a kiss on his cheek. "For luck."

"Don't need it, but thanks." He winked at her and moved to slide behind the wheel of his car.

Ace followed his lead and then drove behind him to the far doors. When he drove out to take his place at the starting line, Ace moved forward. Just outside the doors the smooth concrete widened and then smoothed out into a very long runway. A white line was painted a few yards away and she watched as Skye lined up on it. Next to him, on a parallel runway, was a deep purple car. As they sat waiting for the signal, Ace took in the area. Both sides of the runways were lined with stands, like one would see at a football stadium. They were packed with people as far down as Ace could see. She fought down nerves as she watched the flag girl wave a green flag and then saw Skye tear off just seconds before the car next to him. She cheered him on silently until a young man tapped on her hood and waved her forward.

Once situated on the white line, Ace took in a deep breath and hit play on the stereo. The flag girl raised her flag signaling to get ready. Ace hadn't even bothered looking at the car next to her. She didn't have time. She prepared herself and the familiar beats of her song started. Ace watched the flag girl bounce, once, twice, and then she dropped the flag. Ace's foot pressed the gas pedal.

Ace didn't even have time to think. It was all instinct. She saw a checked flag and knew she had reached the finish line. Pulling her foot from the accelerator, Ace began to allow the car to slow. She pressed the brake and looked around. Grey was waving at her and motioning for her to go in that direction. The concrete began to narrow and she pulled to a stop next to him. She rolled down her window and then turned down the music. He was smiling.

"Congrat ...." He stopped as he looked at her. He blinked twice and started again, obviously surprised. "You're ..."

She smiled. "Ace MacIntosh."

"Boone's girlfriend." He shook his head and smiled. "Figures."

"Did I win?" She asked still feeling a little confused.

"Um, you could say that." He laughed at her. She squealed in delight and clapped her hands, which made him laugh harder. "You need to go back to the hangar and wait for the next race."

She pulled away and turned to follow the smaller path back to the hangar. On her way, she turned up the stereo and allowed her song to spill out into the fading day. Once inside the hangar, she followed the painted lines back to where the other cars were parked. She turned her song up and listened to the last few bars before cutting the engine. She couldn't help but smile as she popped the door open.

Jez got up and stretched, feeling pleased with herself. As she glanced around to see who else had won, hands wrapped around her waist. She turned her head in surprised, and smiled when Skye lifted her off her feet. She giggled as he set her back down.

"I won."

"Of course you did." Skye chuckled. "Never doubted."

"The car felt faster." She whispered stepping closer to him.

He smiled and winked, but didn't say anything.

Someone approached from behind Jez and she turned around, stepping closer to Skye. Protectively, he put a hand on her back. The guy who walked to them, stopped a few feet away. He was only a few inches taller than Jez with jet black hair and deep brown eyes. He appeared to be of Hispanic decent and wore a white tank top and gold chains. His arms were decorated with black tattoos that caught Jez's eye but she forced herself not to stair. "Nice run."

"Thanks." Skye said.

The guy chuckled. "I wasn't talking to you."

"Thank you." Jez said nervously.

"Talk is you're a newborn. But I don't buy it." His eyes looked her over, and she grew uncomfortable. "What's your name?"

"Ace." She replied.

He offered her his hand, which she shook to be friendly. "Hector. So you run these races before?"

She shook her head. "No. It's my first time here."

"But you ain't no virgin." He smiled.

She glanced up to Skye who was stiff but silent.

"This your man?" Hector smiled.

"No." She replied. "Skye's just a friend."

"He ain't going to last long, but you just might." Hector nodded, his eyes locked on hers. "I hope I don't come up against you."

"If I beat you, I'm sorry."

He laughed. "Sorry. Well, that's a first. I like you, Ace. Good luck."

He waved and wandered off in the direction he'd come. Jez looked up at Skye, who looked down at her. "What was that?"

"Hector runs a gang up in the central valley." Skye said softly in her ear. "I didn't know he was going to be here."

"So is it a good thing that he likes me or not?" She asked nervously.

He chuckled and leaned over to put a kiss on the top of her head. "How could anyone not like you, Ace?"

She looked up at him doubtfully. "There are a lot of people who don't like me."

He shook his head. "So, tell me about your race."

"Not much to tell. I drove out like you said to and waited. As soon as the flag dropped I hit the gas and then I was over the line. I didn't even know I had won until that guy Grey said I had."

"Who'd you beat?"

"I don't know. I didn't even look at the car next to me." She shrugged.

He looked at her wide eyed. "Are you kidding?"

"No, I wasn't even thinking about the race. I was just watching the flag fall and my song was on."

Skye reached up and drug a hand down his face in disbelief and amazement. "Really? Ace, are you serious?"

She nodded. "Why?"

He let out a breath and just shook his head. He opened his mouth but a loud whistle cut through the hangar. Everyone turned to the big guy who was standing on a table working to get their attention. "Second round. Pull 'em up, two lines. Let's make this quick, I wanna get drunk."

There was a collective chuckled from the group of drivers. When he dropped down off the table, the group started back to their cars. Skye pulled Jez close. "Try and get in the same line as me. If I get kicked out, I'll have to go back to the bus. Meet us there as soon as they let you free."

"What do you mean?" She asked nervously.

"When you win, you'll be directed back in here for instructions on tomorrow's race." He said giving her a little nudge towards her car.

She didn't like the idea of being alone but she wanted to win too. Sucking up her nerves, Jez climbed behind the wheel. Because of their conversation, Jez and Skye were the last two on one side of the line. A jet-black car pulled up next to Ace and the passenger window rolled down. Hector smiled and nodded. "Good Luck, Ace."

"Good Luck, Hector. I'm sorry if I beat you." She called back making him smile. As he rolled up his window, she prayed that he would find it just as amusing when she did beat him.

While she waited in line, Jez tried to push away the thoughts that concerned her. She turned up the radio and focused on the songs. She allowed her mind to drift to thoughts of Boone. She wondered where he was and what he was doing. She imagined him sitting in the stands with Mel, drinking beer and laughing. It helped calm her. As the lines continued to move up, she listened to the heavy beats of the music. Her thoughts refocused on

Boone and she imagined him kissing her. Her breath quickened as she wondered what his touch would feel like on her skin. She flushed with desire as Skye drove out onto the track. Jez pulled forward and watched as Skye vanished into the falling night.

As she was waved forward, Jez pressed the button to change the song to Ace of Spades. The familiar beat started and Jez focused on it as she pulled to a stop on the start line. She started singing along while she waited for the flag to drop. It felt like forever, but it wasn't a full minute later when the flag girl bounced and then dropped the flag. Without a thought, Ace hit the gas. Seconds later, she flew past the finish line. As she pulled her foot from the accelerator, she glanced over and realized she was a half a car ahead of Hector. She hadn't thought about him in a while, and her heart sank.

Grey waved her over and smiled as she pulled up. "You're on fire, girl."

She didn't know how to answer so she just smiled.

"Head back to the hangar for a few minutes. And congratulations, Ace."

"Thanks." She restarted her song and cranked it up as she drove off. She was the last one to drive into the hangar and everyone turned to look at her. Her song was about half over and she refused to turn it down. She did allow her smile to fall though. She didn't see Skye and her heart sank a little. She pulled to a stop at the end of the line, cut the engine and opened her door. As she moved to take a seat on the hood of her car, like the others had done, she took note of the twelve other drivers. They were all quiet, eyeing each other, judging. Ace was the only girl.

It wasn't long before the big guy from earlier whistled and waved them all over. "Congratulations. You've made it through the first two rounds. First race is tomorrow at ten. Be here, in this hangar, by nine thirty. We'll pair you up based on the times you showed today. Be prepared, competition will be stiff." His eyes fell on Ace and he smiled. "Rest up, see you in the morning."

He jumped off the table and the group began to disband. They were quiet and serious, eyeing each other up. Jez knew that they should be happy and celebrating their wins, but there was still too much stress in the air. As Jez walked back to her car, she felt the weight of the men's eyes on her. She knew she should take it all as seriously as they were, but she just couldn't help herself. As more and more eyes fell on her, she smiled and gave a little skip. As she reached her car, she saw the small groups of men standing around talking. A few had gone back to their cars but many hadn't. She had no doubt that they were talking about her. She restarted her song and cranked it loud as she headed out of the hangar and off to find the guys.

Chapter 46

It took her a few minutes to get back to the bus and trailer. Boone, Skye, and Mel all stood around talking as she pulled up. Boone visibly relaxed when he saw the car. She pulled to a stop and cut the engine. Boone had the door opened before she had the seatbelt off, and he was reaching for her. She fought the buckle, and when she finally got it off, he lifted her into his arms. Wrapping his arms around her waist, he pulled her up, her feet leaving the ground. Jez wrapped her arms around his neck and they buried their faced in each other's necks. After a moment, she pulled back and looked at him. But he wasn't letting go.

"Did I do OK?" She asked with a smile spreading across her face.

He chuckled and moved to press his lips to hers. She began to melt into him. Sensing that Mel and Skye were waiting, Boone pulled back and put her back on the ground. But he didn't let go entirely. Keeping her close, with an arm wrapped around her shoulders, they turned to the others. Skye and Mel leaned against the bus, smiling brightly. Skye already had a beer in his hand and Mel was smoking his cigarette.

"Did I do good?" She asked them.

Mel shook his head. "You did fucking great, Ace."

Skye looked pleased too, but was a little more solemn. "Can't believe you beat Hector."

"Sorry you got bumped out." She said, looking directly at him.

"I didn't think I'd make it past the first round." He shrugged and took another pull from his bottle. He may not have expected to, but she could see he was disappointed.

They stood silent for a few moments, and the excitement and adrenaline of the day suddenly faded. Dizziness washed over her and her knees gave out. Boone tightened his grip on her arm just as Skye and Mel jumped to reach for her. "Easy Ace."

"I'm fine." She said, but she knew she wasn't fooling anyone.

Boone scooped her up just before she reached the ground. Mel pulled the door to the bus open and Boone carried her inside. As he placed her on the sofa, he pulled the unlocking devise from her fisted hand and tossed it down the stairs to where Skye grabbed them from the air. Boone looked at Jez closely. "Are you OK?"

"Yes." She smiled. "Guess it's just been a long day."

"Will you be OK if I leave you here alone for a little bit? I want to go get you some dinner. I think you need to eat."

She nodded. "If you all want to go do something, feel free. You don't have to babysit me, Boone."

"Babysit?" He sat back as if she had slapped him. "Is that how you feel when we're together? Like I'm babysitting you?"

"No, not usually." She smiled. "But when you look at me like that, and ask me if I can be left alone, it makes me feel like you see me as a child."

"I see you as anything but a child, Ace." His concerned look turned to a crooked smile. He leaned in close and whispered into her ear. "And as soon as I get you alone, I'll show you."

She flushed and blushed. Her heart sped up and she turned her head into his. Without a thought, she pressed her lips to his. Pressing into him, she reached up to put her hand on the side of his face. After a few moments, he pulled away with a groan. "You're killing me, Ace."

"Then stop pulling away." She whispered.

"I need to get you some food." He said.

"I don't need any food." She replied.

He moaned and pushed to his feet. "I promised I'd take care of you. I need to get you something to eat. You rest while I'm gone. I'll be back as soon as I can."

"Don't take too long." She said softly.

He looked back at her as he moved to the door. His demeanor changed as he looked back. "Don't take this the wrong way, Ace, but I'd really love to have Jez here when I get back."

Ace smiled and nodded her head. She knew exactly what he was saying and it filled her with more joy than she could express. She watched Boone walk down the stairs and off the bus. She heard the lock turn as he locked her in. Unable to hide her smile, Jez crawled off the couch and moved into the bathroom. She flipped on the lights and stared at Ace in the mirror. Her heavy make-up and curled hair looked fake to Jez. Feeling giddy, Jez looked at her alter ego. "He wants me." She had to fight down the tears of joy. "He wants me, and not you."

There were a lot of guys who wanted Ace. She was the one who got all the attention. But no one ever wanted Jez, herself. But Boone did. He saw her. He even saw her under and in Ace. She had never before felt so … loved, wanted, desired, … she didn't even know the right word. It was just a feeling that was indescribable to anyone who has never felt it before.

Realizing that she may not have very long, Jez rushed to the bedroom. She grabbed up her bathroom bag from her suitcase. Instead of pulling out the pair of pajamas she had brought, she stole a t-shirt from Boone's duffle bag. In her hands, it felt soft and smelled like him. Something deep inside couldn't wait for him to come back. She raced back to the bathroom and jumped into the shower. She washed Ace away and cleaned herself up, only pausing a moment when her fingers brushed against the scabs that were almost gone from the cuts on her stomach. She hoped she could keep him from noticing them.

When she stepped from the shower, she used the lotion she liked and then washed the last of the make-up from her face. Using a towel to dry her hair, she combed it out and let it fall loose in the natural waves. She pulled on the shirt and noticed just how big it was on her. It hung almost down to her knees and covered all her bulges. Checking to make sure she hadn't left a mess in the bathroom, Jez gathered her things and took them back to the bedroom. She tucked the dirty clothes into her suitcase and tossed the bathroom bag on top. The bus was still quiet, so she grabbed out several plastic bottles from the bottle of her suitcase and, using her secret razor, cut off the wrappers. If the races were going to start early and last most of the day, she would have to bring her drinks with her. The day was supposed to be warmer and she didn't want to get sick. She also didn't want people knowing what she was drinking, so clear plastic bottles with purple liquid wasn't going to let anyone know she was sick. And if she was correct, they might even get the wrong idea. After she had tucked the plastic trash in the bottom corner of her case, she tucked all but one of the bottles under her clothes. The one that she left out, she grabbed up and took out to the kitchen. Filling her cup with ice, Jez dumped the bottle into it. She had just tossed the bottle into the trash can and screwed the cap on the cup when she heard the keys unlock the bus door.

"Hey ... Jez? Ace?" He seemed nervous about what to call her as he came up the stairs.

"I'm here." Jez called as she moved back to the sofa. She took a seat, pulling her legs up under her, and smiled.

Boone stopped when he saw her and smiled. "There's my girl."

She smiled and brought her cup to her lips to take a sip. Her heart fluttered as he came toward her, looking her over slowly.

"Is that my shirt?"

"You can take it back, if you want." She bit her lip and looked up at him under heavy eye lashes.

He moaned and rolled his eyes back into his head. When his eyes closed, he muttered to himself. "She needs to eat."

Jez saw the twitch in his pants and knew she was about to break him. Standing up, she set her cup down on the nearest table. His eyes were still closed as she stepped up directly in front of him. Lifting up on tip toes, she got as close as she could without touching him. In a heavily breathed voice, she whispered, "But I'm not hungry."

His eyes popped open when he felt her breath on his neck. His movements became so smooth and fast she almost didn't register them. He placed the food down on the table to his left, the one that sat next to the single chair. When they were free, his hands grabbed onto her, one behind her head and the other on her back. He pulled her to him, pressing her against him. His lips met hers as all the desire that had been building up over the past few weeks became too much to bear. She wrapped her arms around his neck and pulled herself up as much as she could. As his tongue traced her bottom lip, she shuttered and whimpered. Her knees were getting weak and her legs were becoming Jell-O. He slid his hand down from her back, over her ass, and grabbed her thigh. She lifted it and he moved his other hand from her head to the other thigh. In a smooth jump, he grabbed her as she wrapped her legs around his waist. His hand slid up just a little and his fingers ran up under the shirt to her ass. He moaned when he didn't feel any underwear. She took his lower lip in her teeth as his hands moved up to her lower back, still under the shirt, looking for the straps of a G-string. She smiled knowing he wasn't going to find those either.

He pulled back a little and looked into her eyes. "Jez, seriously, you're making me crazy."

"Stop hitting the breaks." She said.

"Are you sure? I …" He swallowed, fighting his body. "I don't want to push you into anything."

"It's a green light. I'm handing over the wheel. Please, Boone, take over." She almost pleaded. He hesitated another moment and she loosened her grip, letting herself slide down a little bit. She felt his erection hard and growing in his jeans. It pressed against the tender areas of her body, and she tilted her hips just a bit. "If you don't, I will."

He rolled his eyes to the ceiling. "That isn't as much of a threat as you want it to be."

"OK," She sighed. She dropped her legs to the floor and let go of his neck. As she slid down his body onto her knees, Jez closed her eyes and stepped back, allowing Ace to come forward. When Ace opened her eyes, she was almost at eye level with his crotch. She reached for the belt and started to unbuckle it. Inside, Jez started to cry. It took several long moments, during which Ace had unfastened the belt, undone the zipper, and unbuttoned the silver rivet, before Boone realized that it wasn't Jez on her knees. Ace was just reaching into his underwear, gripping and stroking his massive cock as she freed it from the soft cotton, when he looked down and saw the change in her.

"Jez?" His voice was thick with concern. "Jez, look at me."

Jez wasn't there though, and Ace wasn't about to look up. Her sights were set on the soft skin before her. As she opened her mouth and licked her lips, Boone reached down and grabbed her chin. Lifting it so he could look into her eyes, Boone suddenly understood. With a heavy sigh, his shoulders slumped. "I'm sorry."

Ace didn't know what to do. After looking around unsettled, Jez pushed up a little and returned her eyes to Boone's. "What?"

"I'm sorry. I wasn't thinking. I didn't realize. I'm sorry." He let go of her chin and tucked himself back into his pants, then knelt in front of her. "I want to spend the night with my girl, Jez. Not with Ace."

A single tear fell from the corner of Jez's eye, and he reached up to wipe it away. "But Ace is better at this."

"I don't want better. I want you. I love you." He said softly.

Her breath caught. No one had ever said that, not like that. Jez closed her eyes and in her mind, Ace stormed off, slamming some imaginary door in her head. Boone's lips brushed hers, and she melted into him. Jez lost track of everything but the feel of him against her. She was barely aware of him lifting her off the floor and taking her to the bedroom. His lips caressed her and then moved down to her neck.

He pushed off his clothes before he laid down beside her. He kissed her and nuzzled her for a long, long time before sliding his hands down her sides to the hem of the shirt. Slowly, he raised the shirt and looked into her eyes, watching for any sign that she wanted to him to stop. When he didn't see it, he lifted the shirt off her body. His eyes looked her over, and his dick throbbed with need against her leg. She was nervous, laying there exposed before him, but the lighting was dark, so she knew he wasn't really seeing much.

"God you're beautiful." He said softly. With a finger, he traced her body from chin to breast, over her stomach, down her hip to her thigh. As he started back up, he moved to the inner thigh and up to her soft parts. Her eyes rolled back as he felt how wet and ready she was. He moaned. Leaning his lips to hers, he whispered. "I'm sorry I've kept you waiting so long."

Jez opened her eyes and looking into the dark blue pools. She swallowed and bit her lip.

He smiled, his finger tracing the outside of her as she opened her legs for him. "What are you thinking?" He whispered softly, his eyes watching every reaction she had to his touch.

"That I don't want to wait another second." She said before she realized she probably shouldn't have said that. Her eyes grew wide with embarrassment, and she closed them tight scrunching up her face as it turned red.

He chuckled at her reaction, then pushed a finger into her. She relaxed instantly, and had to hold her breath to keep from falling over the edge in that moment. His smile faded and something else crossed his face. "Let go, Jez. Let me see you. Let me watch how you feel."

He moved his finger in her and her body tightened in a good way. Her breath picked up and her heart started to race. She lost track of what he was doing in the pleasure of it all. She tried to keep her eyes open but the pleasure became too much and they rolled back in her head. He leaned down and took her breast in his mouth and that was all it took. She was flying high and soaring like a bird. When she was about to come down, he moved and pressed himself against her. Jez opened her eyes slowly.

"Am I hurting you?" He asked softly. Words couldn't form in her mind and she leaned up to kiss him as he pushed into her. He moaned as he filled her. "Oh God, Jez. I love you so much."

He held tight inside her for a few moments, then began to move. Pleasure filled her, and Jez arched in response. He continued to move slowly, aware of how she responded to him. When she indicated, with her body language, she needed more, he gave it to her. He kissed her and touched her gently. At some point, she reached up and grabbed his shoulders. Her fingers dug into him and he made a noise that she wasn't sure was all pleasure, but he didn't stop what he was doing. She began to climb again, desire and need building in her. She moved under him, and he smiled. He leaned down and wrapped his arms around her and rolled them over so she was on top. Wide eyed she looked down at him. Confusion and fear stopped her movements.

"It's OK, Jez. Go ahead." He said before leaning up to kiss her. He had to kiss her for several minutes before she relaxed into her desire again. But when she had, she moved tentatively at first, watching his eyes for signs that she wasn't pleasing him. Her fears were subsided though when he closed his eyes and bit his own lip.

With a little smile, she leaned down and took his lip in her teeth. Moving herself against him, he groaned and she felt him twitch inside her. It pushed her a little more and she had to sit up to move in a way that made it better. His hands gripped her hips for a moment and then traveled up to her breasts. Cupping them, and then tracing her nipples making them erect, she climbed even higher. At some point she was so close to the edge but just couldn't seem to get herself over. He seemed to understand and rolled her onto her back. With him taking control again, she fell almost instantly. As her thighs gripped his hips, he joined her.

Chapter 47

He held her as she dozed off and on for almost an hour. She woke when he had to get up to use the bathroom, although she tried not to let him know she was awake. When he had left the room, she pulled on his shirt and wandered out to find her drink. She found her cup where she had left it and grabbed it up. She downed half of it, before returning to the bedroom. She was weak and tired, but so very happy. The fuzziness in her head was well worth it. She crawled under the covers and set the drink on the window ledge above her. She relaxed and rolled onto her side as Boone returned to the bedroom. He slid up next to her and slid his hand under the t-shirt, ribbing it across her stomach and touching the marks. She swallowed back her tears, praying he wouldn't ask.

Unfortunately, he did. In a soft voice right next to her ear, he questioned. "What are those?"

She fought to keep her voice light and airy. "Nothing."

He was silent and ran his finger along them. She knew he was counting them. Five long, three short, six more that were so faint they could barely be felt. And so many more that he didn't know about. He pushed up onto his elbow, rolled her over onto her back, and looked down into her eyes. "They're not nothing, Jez."

She shrugged. "Cardboard cuts from the boxes at work?"

He looked deeply into her eyes. "You promised not to lie to me. Please tell me. Are they from your accident? Did Paulie do this? Jordy?"

She watched as he made it all worse than it was. Or maybe it would be easier to blame someone else. She wished she could. With a heavy sigh, she shook her head. In a last-ditch effort, she made one last attempt to change the subject. "This is the first time that sex hasn't hurt."

His eyes darkened. "It should never hurt."

"I didn't know that until you. I didn't know that love didn't hurt until you." She admitted.

He reached out and brushed a hand across her cheek. "If I thought it would help, I'd kill him. But it wouldn't take away the pain he inflicted."

"He taught me about pain." She sighed. She didn't know if it was connection that was growing between them, or if she was just too raw and open, but she suddenly didn't want to hide anything from Boone.

"What did he teach you?" His jaw was tensing.

"That pain isn't all bad. Sometimes it can also help." His teeth ground together. He wasn't understanding what she was saying. "There are times, when the voices in my head are really loud. They say things that I know aren't true, but sometimes it's hard not to listen. Sometimes, when nothing else makes them stop, pain does."

"Physical pain?" He asked gently.

She nodded.

"When did these voices start?"

"A few months after my mom left." She had never told anyone that. Not even Jordy.

"And what do they say?"

She took in a deep breath. "They say that I'm not good enough. That if I was better, things would be different. That I don't deserve things."

He brought his lips to her head, placing a gently kiss on her forehead. "Did being with Paulie make it better?"

"No. At first they got quiet, but then they got worse. They … it got really bad for a long time."

"Did it ever get better?"

She nodded. "It was good for the past few months."

"What was different?"

"I had the accident. I wasn't racing. Paulie wasn't around." She said.

He was watching her closely, but she couldn't look at him. His fingers traced the marks. She could feel his questions swirling in the air around them. But he didn't ask. Instead, he pulled her closer. He held her as tightly as he could. They didn't talk. And while she knew he was lost in his own thoughts and worries, she found peace in his embrace. His presence was soothing. She felt protected and loved. Her body was calm and tired. Her mind was placid. It was a new and wonderful state for her. She'd never been in this place. She allowed a smile to grace her lips as she drifted off to sleep.

Chapter 48

Jez woke with a start. It was still dark but she was alone. She wasn't in her room, and it took several minutes to remember where she was. When she did, it all came flooding back to her. She remembered making love to Boone and how loved she'd felt in his arms. How he had focused on her pleasure, and found his in her. She remembered how it hadn't hurt, and although she was a little sore at the moment, it made her smiled. But the smile faded as she remembered the conversation after. She sat up and grabbed for her drink as she replayed it in her head. Now she was alone.

The voices in her head started to laugh. You stupid girl. You showed him how crazy you really are. He's never going to want you now. No one wants someone who's bat shit crazy. No one could possibly want you. Tears stung her eyes. She shook her head trying to get them out of her head, but they only got louder.

She took the last sip from her cup. Tears spilled over her eye lids. She crawled out of bed, focusing on the one thing that she could: refilling her cup. She fell to her knees by her suitcase and dug for another bottle. In the process, she felt the pile of plastic wrappings and then the hard metal blade. Yanking her hand off it, she told herself it wasn't the answer. She wasn't going to give in. Fighting down the urge, she pulled out a plastic bottle. Gripping it tightly in one hand, she climbed to her feet. She grabbed up the cup and pushed into the main cabin of the bus. She had half hoped to find Boone watching television or talking with Skye, but the bus was empty. None of the guys were there.

See, they don't want to deal with your crazy. They left you all alone. And as soon as they get you home, you'll never see them again. If they even take you home.

Jez closed her eyes tight and pushed them away again. As she brought her hands to her head, she felt the cup and bottle clutched in them, and focused on what she was doing. She stepped over to the fridge and put ice in the cup, then filled it with the purple liquid. She dumped the plastic jug in the trash and screwed the lid on the cup. She focused all her attention on what she was doing. If she could just focus on each step, she could push away the voices.

The blade is just in the other room. It doesn't take much to shut us up. You know you want to. It makes it all so much easier to handle.

Too scared to go near the blade, Jez curled up in a ball on the sofa. She pulled Boone's t-shirt over her knees and wrapped her arms around her legs. The cup held in a death grip in one hand, she took random sips from it. She wasn't sure how much time had passed. She didn't look at the clock and didn't want to move for fear that the voices would be stronger. Tears traced her cheeks, but she saw no reason to stop them yet. Outside the bus, people milled around. Most of them were in small groups or couples. All moving in directions toward their camps, Jez imagined. She watched one couple as they came into view. He was tall and bald and reminded Jez of Boone. The woman was a taller blonde, with big hair and long legs. She was thin and dressed in short shorts and a halter top. They walked closer and seemed to be comfortable with each other. He pulled a bottle to his lips, and she laughed at something that was said. They stopped in the wide aisle outside the bus. She was standing just a little too close to him. When she put a hand on his chest, the voices in Jez's head started to laugh. He wrapped his arms around her and pulled her in for a big hug. His head turned and a light from somewhere illuminated Boone's face.

That was all it took. Jez's heart broke. She knew the voices were right. He didn't want her. She was too much for him. Too crazy for him to handle. Two personalities, voices in her head, cutting, her illness, of course she was too much for him. She was too much for anyone.

She put the cup down on the counter and raced for the suit case. She found the blade and dashed to the bathroom as she heard him come in the door. She sat on the toilet and yanked up the shirt as his footsteps got closer. She pressed the blade against her skin as the pounding stopped. Dragging the blade across her ribs, she heard the soft knock on the door.

"Jez? You alright?"

She gritted her teeth as the sting bubbled along with the blood. "Fine."

"What's wrong?"

"Nothing. I'll be out in a minute." She called with her eyes shut tight. She focused on the pain and she pictured the voices drowning on the red liquid. Her head began to spin and she fought to stay conscious.

She wasn't aware of Boone opening the door or stepping in until she heard him curse. "What the hell? Fuck!"

He took the two steps over to her and yanked the blade from her fingers. He grabbed a towel from the rack to his left and pressed it to her side. She was willing to give in to the darkness but it was pushing her back now.

"Jez? Jez? What the fuck?" Boone was calling her back and she blinked focusing on his angry face. "Why would you do this?"

The spinning was coming to a stop and she was suddenly exhausted. "They told me too."

"Who?" He was so confused. He pulled the towel back from her side and looked at the long, thin cut.

"The voices. They … you don't want me. I'm too crazy. I'm too much. Just leave me alone." She said, tears running down her cheeks.

Still holding the towel on her side with one hand, he rubbed his face with the other hand. Then grabbing her chin, he pulled her head up and looked into her eyes. "I love you. I don't know what this is all about, but I'm not leaving you. Not now, not ever."

She wanted to believe him so much. But the images of the blond came back to her. New tears surfaced. Boone turned his attention back to the cut. Jez watched as the emotions and thoughts washed over his face. Concern turned to anger, then back to worry, frustration followed. "Jez, I need to get the first aid kit. Can you hold the towel for me?"

She nodded and moved her hand under his. He stood up and rushed out of the tiny bathroom. He was gone for a while, but he did return. Jez was more coherent now, but the embarrassment of being caught was sinking in. As Boone knelt before her, she turned her face away from him. She refused to look at him the entire time he cleaned her cut, put butterfly bandages on it, and then taped gauze over it. When he was done, he tried to get her to look at him, but she refused. "Jez, please."

"I'm sorry. I understand if you won't want to see me after this is all over."

She missed the look that passed over his face because her eyes were locked on the floor. "I love you."

Tears came into her eyes again and a tiny voice called him a liar. She still didn't look at him.

"Come on, let's go back to bed."

He tossed the trash away and helped her back to the bed. When they were under the covers, he slipped his arms around her and pulled her close to him. He felt so good, and Jez allowed herself to pretend this was going to last.

"Jez. Can I ask you something?"

She nodded.

"Do the voices always talk to you at night?"

"No, sometimes during the day too, but they're easier to ignore when I'm around people. It's hard when I'm alone."

She felt him deflate a little. "Is this why Jordy sleeps with you sometimes? You don't really have nightmares, do you?"

She shook her head. "I do have nightmares, but not very often."

"Do the three amigos know?"

She shook her head no.

"Does anyone else know?"

"Just Jordy, and you now." She replied sadly.

"Did Paulie?"

"No, he never looked that close." Her eyes were growing heavy, and she closed them.

He leaned over and rested his head against hers. "Is it because I hurt you?"

"Hurt me?" She asked opening her eyes. She knew it was a lie, but just a little one. "You didn't hurt me."

"Then why did you do it?"

She shrugged. "I don't know."

She closed her eyes again, hoping that he wouldn't ask her anymore questions. She was too far gone to lie again. She didn't want to be honest either. She knew he would leave her as soon as they got home. She told herself that she would make sure she enjoyed tomorrow as much as she could. She would end this on a good note, no matter how much it hurt.

☐

Chapter 49

Jez woke alone again, but this time the sun was shining in on her face. As she laid there, she heard Boone and Skye talking in the other room. Skye was telling Boone about some girl he had been with last night. She heard Boone laugh. It made her smile. Her cell phone chirped and she rolled over to reach for it. In the process, her new cut pressed against the mattress and she whimpered. Her phone chirped again and she pushed through the pain to grab it from the nightstand. She pressed the button to wake it and saw a message from her brother.

'How are things? Are you OK? I woke up last night with this horrible feeling.'

'I'm fine,' she text back. 'This place is incredible.'

'Fine?'

'Yes. We'll talk when I get home. But all is good. I love you. Gotta go have breakfast.'

It was a lie, she had no intention of eating today, but it was a good excuse to get him to leave her alone. She wasn't sure what she would tell him when she got home, but she had another day to worry about that. Today she had to focus on the race. She needed to wake Ace and get to work.

She was just trying to sit up when Boone opened the bedroom door. "Morning."

"Hey." She smiled.

"How do you feel?"

She shrugged. "Great."

He narrowed his eyes, but didn't say anything. He watched her get up and walk over to the closet.

"What should I wear today?" She asked looking at the outfits.

"Anything but that one. You can wear that tonight for the concert." He said, knowing that she would understand which outfit he meant.

She smiled over at him. She pulled out a pair of jeans and a strapless top that was tight across her boobs but loose over her stomach. She pulled on a clean pair of underwear and then the jeans while he watched. Before she pulled off the t-shirt, she looked at him. "Are you just going to stand there?"

A devilish grin crossed his face. "I would help, but I thought you were trying to dress."

She giggled and rolled her eyes. "What time is it?"

"Almost nine."

She sighed. "I have to be at the hangar at nine-thirty."

He nodded, and took the three steps across the room. He wrapped an arm around her waist and threaded the other hand into her hair. He turned more serious as he looked down into her eyes. "Are you alright?"

A knot formed in her stomach. "I'm sorry. I didn't want you to …"

"I don't care about me," he interrupted. "I'm only worried about you."

"I'm fine." She smiled. "But I do need to find Ace."

He seemed to understand and let her go. He didn't kiss her, which she took as just one more sign that he would be leaving her when this was over. She pushed away the hurt as she grabbed up her make-up bag and headed into the bathroom. Twenty minutes later, she was gathering up four of her hydration drinks and headed out to where her car was waiting for her. The guys weren't visible, which she was glad for. She was able to drop the bottles in the back seat covertly and then get back on the bus to refill her cup. At nine twenty-five, she exited the bus and found the three guys waiting for her by the car. Mel gave her a smile and wished her luck. Skye gave her a gentle hug and told her to kick ass. Boone though hesitated before taking her in his arms.

"Will I see you at all?"

"Not until the end." He said. "But we'll be there watching. When you're done, just come back here."

There was something about how he spoke that she didn't understand. "You don't think I'm going to win this, do you?"

"I think you can win if you want to. I've never met anyone who's as strong as you, Ace." He laced his fingers into her hair and pulled her in for a deep kiss that made her knees weak.

It was Skye who interrupted them by reminding her that it was time to go. She nodded and looked at Boone as she climbed into the car. As she drove off, she glanced into the review mirror. Boone had covered his face with his hand and Skye had a hand on his shoulder. It was a painful sight. Once again, it let her know that he was done with her as soon as they got home. As she pulled into the hangar and parked, Ace made the decision that she was going to win this. If not for herself, then for all of them, and most specifically for Boone.

A crowd was gathering at the far end of the hangar, where the guy from last night had stood on the table and given them directions. Ace wandered over, taking sips from her cup, to see what was going on. As she approached, she saw a few guys with white papers in their hands. One guy, who had his back to her, shouted, "Fuck, really? Why do I have to race the bitch?"

"Someone has to." Another guy laughed.

"Sure, maybe you'll get lucky and she'll start her period and you'll actually win." A third guy said.

Ace tilted her head and thought about that comment. She didn't see how starting her period would allow someone else to win. As she stepped up to them, she said in a nice voice. "No, if I start my period, I'd only be bitchier because I wouldn't be able to get laid tonight. You better hope I don't."

The three guys, and a few others, turned and looked at her stunned. She winked and grabbed up the white paper. Playing with the straw in her mouth, she looked over the white paper as she returned to her car. She was slated to race second. It didn't really matter to her when she raced or who she raced. It only matter that she would win.

While she waited for time to pass, she watched the men around her. Not one of them came over to speak to her. A few of them glanced at her, and others spoke to some of the other racers. But not one of them came to talk to her. Ace realized that was fine with her. She wasn't here to make friends. She was only here to win. If she won, she could pay off her medical bills. If she won, the others would win too. And then no matter what happened tomorrow, they'd all have a good memory to share.

The skinny flag girl made a lap around the building and let them all know the racers would start soon. She recommended they line up and prepare. As she stepped over to let Ace know, she smiled. "Good luck out there."

"Thanks. Think I might need it." Ace replied.

The girl shrugged. "There are a lot of people who don't think you'll pull this off, but there are a lot who think you will."

"How about you?"

"I think that you're the fastest thing to come out here in years. As long as you don't let these bastards get under your skin, you'll be fine." She offered Ace a wink and then walked back across the hangar.

Ace moved behind the wheel and started the engine. The first two racers were lining up and she knew she had to get behind them. As she took her place in line, she turned on the stereo. Ace of Spades was already half over and she listened to it finish. It started a fire in her somewhere and she smiled. As the first two racers moved out to take the line, Ace forced herself not to look at the car next to her. At the track at home, she loved to play games with the guy in the car next to her. But this was not home. The stakes were too high here, and any games she tried to play could backfire. So she stayed focused on her song. When the song ended, she was waved to the start line. They had to wait for a while. Jez started her song over and it was well into the second verse when the flag dropped. In a blink of an eye, she was crossing the finish line a half a car ahead of the guy next to her.

They slowed and made the turn. Grey gave the other guy a wave good-bye and then waved for her to stop. "Good Morning."

"Hi." She smiled.

"That's a nice way to start the day."

"Yes, it is."

He smiled a little brighter. "You'll have about an hour until the next race. It's only going to get more challenging from here, so I suggest you do whatever it is that you do to prepare."

"Thanks."

"Good luck." He winked and tapped on the door. She pulled away and drove back to the hangar.

As she entered and parked, she saw the looks on those still waiting to race. Most had expressions of disbelief or exasperation, but one guy laughed happily. Knowing she had an hour or so, Ace cut the engine and grabbed up her cup. She needed to find some ice and a bathroom, both of which she found at one end of the hangar. When she returned to her car, she looked it over carefully. She held no doubts that someone would try to mess with it while she was gone. A big black guy dressed in all black walked over and gave her a curious look.

"Everything OK?"

She smiled up. "Yep, I was just making sure no one messed with my car while I used the bathroom."

He chuckled. "That's why I'm here. It's my job to keep an eye on the cars when they're in here. Some of these guys don't have any scruples."

"I kind of figured." She agreed. "Thanks for watching out for us though."

She popped the door open and grabbed a bottle from the back floor board. He watched as she cracked the top and poured it into the cup. "Nice car."

"Thanks. My boyfriend gave it to me." She replied. A twinge flashed in her heart, but she cut it off. Boone was still her boyfriend, at least until they got home.

"That's a good guy. Most guys would keep it for themselves."

She shrugged. "He's more a muscle car guy. Besides, he was the one who wanted me to come out here. He knew I'd need a car."

The man got a curious look on his face. "So it's your first race? But your man's been out here before?"

"We just met a few weeks ago." She said not really understanding.

His eyes narrowed. "I only know one guy who finds pretty young girls who can race and brings them here. Please tell me your man isn't Boone Kingston."

"You know Boone?"

He nodded his head. "Sure do. He comes out here every year with some hot new girl. He gets them to race and he makes bank on the side bets."

"Um, really?"

"You didn't know. I'm sorry." He looked uncomfortable.

"It's OK. I kind of figured I was the flavor of the day." She pushed off the hurt. "I just really need to win."

"It's good money, if you can do it. And the bragging rights are great too." He smiled.

"I just need the money for my family. I'm not racing again after this." She admitted.

"First and last. Wow, it's been that bad of an experience?"

She laughed. "No, I just …. It's just time I quite." She took a sip from her cup and leaned against the car.

"Well, I guess if you're going out, go out on top."

"I hope to." She smiled brightly.

He wished her good luck and wandered off to keep an eye on things. He seemed nice, but as he stepped over to speak to another driver, she wondered how much of what he said was true. Mind games were as much a part of racing as a fast car. While she pushed away his words, she knew she needed to focus on something else for a while. Sliding into the car, she lifted her cell phone and text Jordy.

'How's it going?'

It took a few minutes but his response came through. 'Things are good. I miss you though.'

'I miss you too.'

'How's the show?'

'Good. It's kind of a circus here. So much to tell you.'

'Can't wait to hear. Gotta go. Love you. Be careful.'

She made the decision then that she would tell Jordy everything, when she got home. It wasn't going to be pretty, and he wasn't going to be happy. But if she really was done with racing, she would need his support. It was just like with her other bad habit. The only way to get through the hard times was with her brother's help. And this bad habit would be hard to break, especially if it involved losing Boone in the process.

The thought stung, and she had to fight down the tears. But she was quickly distracted from her thoughts as a loud whistled called for the drivers' attention.

"Twelve is now six." The guy spoke. "Now it gets rough. Three of you will be eliminated because you lose. A fourth will be cut because of the slowest speed. That will leave two. Good luck out there."

He moved from the table and someone else stepped up. She called out the match ups, and Ace found she was racing last. As the drivers moved back to their cars, she realized she had not a clue who she was racing. Of course, she really didn't care. It wasn't about who she raced. From now on, it was about the clock.

As Ace returned to her car, she picked up her phone and saw she had a text message from Boone.

'I love you, Ace. Kick ass.'

She thought about what to respond with. She could tell him that she loved him, but that would be leading him on. She did love him, but she knew as of tomorrow it would be over. In the end, she shut the phone off and tossed it in the backseat. She didn't want to think about Boone, or Jordy, or anything else. She just wanted to drive.

As the cars lined up, she turned the engine over and changed the song. She needed something besides the Ace of Spades for right now. Three songs past her song on the disk was a Stone Cold song. It was her second favorite by them and she turned it up as loud as she could stand it. When everyone else was in line, she pulled out and got in line too. She sang along with the angry lyrics and allowed it to fuel her. She was still waiting when the next song came on. It too was by her favorite band, and she knew this one well. She moved out to the start line as it ended and she spun the track back to number one. As Ace of Spades came on, the flag girl tapped to the beat and dropped the flag with the music. Ace took off like a bat out of hell. She knew the car next to her was close on her, she could see his color in the corner of her eye, but she wasn't going to give in. He inched up on her and she gave it more. When they crossed the finish line, Ace had only beat him by two feet. It was the closest race she'd run in a long time.

As they pulled around to where Grey stood, the guy in the car next to her was screaming every cuss word he knew and she was pretty sure he was making some up as well. Grey waved them on and gave Ace a wink as she passed by. She cut off her song as she made another turn and came into the hangar. Fast forwarding, she found her favorite Stone Cold song at the end of the disk. It was a haunting piece, filled with anger and pain. Ace related to the entire thing, from the harsh beat to the lyrics that spoke of sharp edges that opened wounds and released tears stained red. As she pulled to a stop in the hangar, she sat and listened to the words. Her side twitched and she put her hand on the bandage. A knock on her window pulled her from her thoughts. The guy with the directions was waving her over.

She popped the door open and the music spilled out into the echo chamber. The two other racers and three workers turned to look at her as she cut off the music. She got out and walked over to where they had gathered. When she had joined them, the guy looked at each racer. "Jacob, your time was 18.5 seconds. Randy, 18.3 seconds. Ace." He paused for dramatic effect and they all looked at her. Ace felt numb though. "Ace, you ran it in 18 flat."

He waited for the news to sink in. Jacob cursed. He picked up the nearest thing, which happened to be a clipboard and tossed it across the hangar. The big black guy stepped up next to him and spoke softly. It took several minutes to calm him down, but eventually, Jacob got in his car and drove off, leaving rubber in the empty building. When he was gone, Randy turned to Ace. He extended his hand to her. "No hard feelings whichever way this goes. You're one hell of a driver, Ace."

She shook his hand. "Apparently you are too, although I wish I had gotten to see you." She offered him a small smile.

He chuckled. "Rumor has it you've never been out here before."

"Nope, I didn't even know about it until a couple weeks ago."

He glanced at her in disbelief. "How long have you been racing?"

"A few years at home."

"Years?" He repeated. "You're not very old as it is. When did you start, as soon as you got your license?"

"My boyfriend made me start when I was fourteen."

Randy's eyes widened. "You … fourteen? Wow. And this is your first time here?"

She nodded. "First and last."

"You can't mean that. You obviously love it."

She shrugged. "It comes with too many strings. I just need the money so I can pay off my medical bills."

"Medical bills?" He smiled and shook his head. "Oh, you are so good. You play the game well."

She smiled weakly. "Funny, now that I'm here at the end, I'm not even playing anymore."

"Are you serious? Really? This is it for you?" He looked at her deeply, in the eye, searching for the truth.

A single tear fell from her eye as she answered. "Yes, I'm completely serious. This is my last race."

She turned and started back to her car and the reality of it all sank in. She was done. Ace was throwing in the white towel, and Jez could feel it. As she slid behind the wheel, she pulled her crimson lipstick out and looked at herself in the rearview mirror. The door was still open as she looked at herself and started to sing. "I'll have one for my baby, and one more for the road."

When she was done, she applied the red color to her lips and put the tube in her pocket. Pulling the door closed, she started the engine. Randy was already waiting for her at the line. As they pulled out together to the start line, Ace looked at the sky. She hadn't realized how fast the day had gotten away from her. But the sun was already being pulled to the western sky signaling the late afternoon. A heaviness sank into her and a tear fell from her eye. She brushed it away and turned on the stereo one last time as the flag girl climbed the stairs to the platform. As Lemmy's voice started the iconic lyrics, she dropped the flag and they were off.

Ace wasn't sure why, but the entire race seemed to slow down. Every other race she had ever driven had been over in the blink of an eye, but this one was moving in slow motion. She popped the clutch and hit the gas in perfect unison, as they jumped from the line. Randy was matching Ace for every shift of gears and every turn of the wheel. They were bumper to bumper the entire stretch until the last ten feet. For some reason, he dragged back a half a foot, allowing her to cross the finish line first. The two cars slowed and pulled to a stop just as they had the entire race, in unison. Randy jumped out of his car and walked over to where Ace sat stone still behind the wheel. He waited for a moment then pulled open the door. Her song spilled out into the air and he took a step back at the loudness of it. He offered her his hand and she stepped out.

"Congratulations. It was a great race."

She wrapped him in a hug and whispered into his ear. "Thank you. I don't know why you did it, but thank you."

He stepped back and gave her an odd look, but when he opened his mouth to speak, the rush of people flooded into them. Boone came from nowhere and grabbed her up into his arms. He spun her around and held her tight. When he stopped he kissed her deeply, and she melted into him. Drinking in every touch, taste, and scent she could get. Skye and Mel were there too, and when Boone broke the kiss, they scooped her up and handed her around. Ace laughed and smiled. But as she was being held up, she realized that this really was it for her. She wasn't happy about the win like she should be. It tasted bittersweet in her mouth. As she was set back down, Boone was there next to her. The crowd was singing the chorus to Ace of Spade loudly around her, so he had to lean down next to her ear to be heard.

"Are you OK?"

She nodded and offered him a smile. But she could tell he wasn't buying it.

He took her arm and moved her back over to the car. She climbed in but then climbed into the passenger's seat as Boone climbed behind the wheel. Before he closed the door, Boone lowered the radio. Once they were locked in the semi-quiet car, he looked at her again. "What's wrong?"

"Not a thing."

"You don't look happy. You just won and yet you don't look happy. What is it?"

She rolled her eyes. "It's surreal. Did I really win?"

He looked at her, and while she was trying hard to make him believe it, he still wasn't. "You'd tell me if something happened right?"

"Of course." She said. "Nothing happened. Everything's fine. Wow, I won." She repeated and leaned back in the seat as if the news was just sinking in. She giggled and covered her face with her hands. Boone put a hand on her leg and started the car. It took quite a while for the crowd to move out of the way enough for them to get through, but eventually he made it. He got them back to the bus, where Skye and Mel were waiting anxiously.

They pulled her from the car and danced around with her, making her laugh. Just watching the three of them together was enough to help her mood. Skye and Boone soon left her dancing with Mel and went to take care of the car. Grey approached from the other side and laughed as he watched Ace and Mel jump around in the dirt.

"Congratulations Ace." He said making her and Mel stop. "I have to say, I don't think I would have believed it if I hadn't seen it with my own eyes. Guess Boone finally picked a winner."

Mel stiffened but Ace let it slide. "What do you need, Grey?"

"Just wanted to make sure you knew what to do now, since you've never been here." His attitude was thick. "In an hour, you get to meet tonight's headlining band in a personal meet and greet. You get front row seats to the show. And at the end of the show, you'll be presented with your prize."

"Ok, thanks." She said as Boone and Skye stepped up behind her.

Grey's eyes flashed up to Boone's. "Finally picked a winner, huh Boone?"

Boone's hand landed on Ace's shoulder. "In more ways than one."

Grey glanced down at Ace. "We'll see you, and your friends, at the show."

She watched as he turned and walked off. Mel called him an asshole under his breath and Skye mumbled something under his breath as well. Boone just gripped her shoulder tightly. When Grey was far enough away, Ace turned and looked at the guys, a smile spreading across her lips. "Well, I guess I should go change and get ready."

"I thought you'd be more excited." Skye said. He turned to look at Boone. "You did say her favorite band was Stone Cold right?"

"As far as I was told."

Ace blushed and put a hand over her mouth. "Really? It's really Stone Cold?"

Boone chuckled. "I told you before we came."

"I thought, I guess I just assumed, ..." she couldn't speak she was so flustered.

Without another word, she rushed into the bus to get ready. As she darted up the steps, she heard Boone say, "I thought that's how she'd be at winning the race."

Chapter 50

She ripped off her clothes as she rushed to the bathroom, only stopping when her hand touched the white bandage on her rib below her breast. Shame rose in her and she stopped her forward motion. Her excitement dimmed as she once again remembered the reality around her. Jez pulled off the white gauze and started the shower water. The voices in her head started up. You know he let you win. You didn't really deserve any of this.

She tried to ignore them, but they grew louder the more Ace was washed away. Jez grew weaker and weaker, and when she had finished washing, she had to sit on the toilet and rest. A knock came at the door pulling her from her harsh thoughts.

"Come on, Ace, we need to shower too." Skye called in a happy voice.

Jez took in a breath and stood up. Making sure the towel was wrapped around her, she pulled the door open. "All yours."

She forced a happy smile as she stepped around him to clear the way. He reached out and touched her arm, "You OK?"

She smiled. "Absolutely." She moved quickly back into the bedroom and away from his looks. She shut the door and turned around. Boone sat on the bed, he looked troubled. She walked over and smiled at him. "Are you OK?"

"I could ask you the same thing."

She held the same fake smile and took a seat next to him on the bed. "I'm fine."

He looked over at her. "Are you? Really?"

She nodded. "I won the race. I'm getting to meet Stone Cold. I've got the best boyfriend ever. Why wouldn't I be fine?"

He reached out and pulled her closer, wrapping his arms around her. He rested his head against her breasts. She hugged him back, feeling the weight between them. "We have a lot to talk about."

"Shh," She turned his head up, leaned over, and pressed her lips to his. At first, he tried to pull away, but she kept at him and eventually he gave in. His kisses became deep and needy as did hers. She knew, in the back of her mind, that this wasn't the best way to handle this. But she didn't have another option. She needed to feel him again. She wanted to let him know she was alright. She wanted to make him believe that she was his. Tomorrow, when they went home, he had to know that she loved him, no matter what. She owed him that much.

Giving in to her desires, Jez twisted and slid onto his lap straddling him. His hand held her firm as he kissed her with as much passion as he usually did. When she had to pull away to catch her breath, he kissed his way down her neck.

She felt him growing beneath her and her desire grew with his firmness. She tugged at his shirt wanting nothing between them as his hands moved to cup her ass. He stood up, lifting her easily. He turned around and set her back on the bed. While his eyes were locked on her, he pulled off his shirt. She looked down at his muscular chest. It was as if she had never seen him before. She saw all the tiny scars and all the black tattoos in the dimmed light that filtered through the large window. As her eyes lifted to his, she shuttered.

He had stopped undressing and watched her as she looked upon him. She couldn't take not having him near. She reached out and grabbed at his waistband, pulling him forward. He took the two steps as she fought the button and zipper. He popped free and she smiled that he wasn't wearing anything but his jeans. It was hot. She felt the heat and need growing wetter between her legs. Before he could stop her, she took his large cock in her mouth and swallowed as much of him as she could. He tasted like sweat and smelled like man. It was raw and real and completely washed everything away. In that moment, all she wanted to do was please him.

Jez work him, up and down, licking and tickling him. His sounds were music to her ears and only encouraged her. It wasn't long before he twitched in her mouth and he grabbed the sides of her head, "Jez."

She fought against his hands though and continued doing what he seemed to enjoy. He moaned again. She took him just a little deeper and when she pulled back, he took a step away pulling free of her. She looked up at him. His look was dark, and she wondered for a moment if she had upset him.

"I won't be satisfied until you are." He said softly. In a smooth motion, he knelt before her and grabbed her knees. He moved his hands up her legs and grabbed her ass. Pulling her to the edge of the bed, he buried his face between her thighs. She felt his hot breath on her tender places. Just that simple sensation was enough to undo her. As his tongue touched her, she shuttered and fell back on the bed.

He laughed, "Well that was easy."

She convulsed in pleasure as he rose on his knees and pressed his still hard dick into her. She tightened around him and came again almost instantly.

"God you're fucking gorgeous when you do that." He whispered as he pushed into her. She whimpered in pleasure at his movements. At some point, he leaned down and sucked on her breasts that had come free from her towel. It wasn't too much later when he worked her harder and finished as well, by then, Jez was completely spent. He collapsed onto her, resting his head on her chest. "I love you so much, Jez."

"I love you too, Boone." The words hurt to say but not because they weren't true.

A bang came at the door. "Hey love birds, we're going to be late if you don't hurry up."

Boone smiled up at her. "Wouldn't want you to miss the highlight of your trip."

She smiled and knew that she hadn't. Meeting Stone Cold was going to be amazing, but not nearly as amazing as being here in Boone's arms.

He got up and pulled the towel off her. As he wrapped it around his waist, he noticed she wrapped her arm around her stomach. He smiled at first, thinking that she was covering herself against him, but then he realized that she was only covering her cuts and scars. His smile faded. He opened his mouth to say something, but thought better of it. He turned quickly and left the room, closing the door behind him.

She didn't waste one second of being alone. She quickly found the first aid kit that sat on the floor near her suit case. She pulled free a clean gauze pad and tape. After applying some healing ointment, she taped the clean pad to her ribs, then got dressed. By the time, Boone came back from his shower, she was dressed in the short lace skirt and off the shoulder matching top. Her legs were covered with shimmering stockings that ended in a lacey band that hugged her leg just below the skirt's hemline. She wore baby doll socks and high heels. Her Spade hoops dangled from her ears. She was covered in red with black lace from head to toe, just like her car.

She was just putting on her mascara when he came into the room and stopped suddenly. She looked over at him, "what?"

His open mouth closed and his jaw worked.

She finished what she was doing, and looked back up at him. "What?"

He pushed away whatever thought he had and turned to his duffle bag. She got up and left him to change, while she stepped into the bathroom to do her hair. Leaving the door open, she called to Skye. "Hey Skye, I think I left my cup in the car. Could you get it for me?"

"I'll get it. I need a smoke anyway." Mel called and she heard him leave the bus. A second set of footsteps came her way and Skye appeared in the doorway.

"Wow." He said and she looked at his reflection in the mirror. "Does it look alright?"

He smiled. "Boone's going to have a hard time tonight." "Why?"

"Well, he's going to be hard all night with you looking like that." Skye chuckled.

"Not if guys like you keep looking at her." Boone's dark voice spoke from the bedroom doorway. While his words were threatening, his face held a thin smile.

Mel pounded back into the bus and called. "Got it."

"Thanks." She had finished, not doing much with her hair aside form parting it and tousling her natural waved into it. She waved for Skye and Boone to move out of her way. Skye turned and headed back to the front of the bus, and Boone followed. Jez watched him, a familiar desire growing in her. He looked good, and she realized she was going to have just as hard a time tonight, if not worse. He was dressed in all black and his shirt was just tight enough to show all his muscles. The girls were sure to be all over him. While part of that was upsetting, a little voice told her that maybe it was for the best. Maybe he'd find someone more worthy of him.

She pushed the voice aside as he looked back at her. He seemed to feel the conflict in her and gave her a small smile. But as his eyes drifted over her, his smile faded and he closed his eyes. She used that moment to escape to the bedroom. Finding a new bottle, she returned to the kitchen. The guys all waited, fairly impatiently, for her. She smiled and rinsed the cup. Quickly adding ice, she poured the purple liquid in the cup.

"What'cha doing Ace?" Skye asked watching her.

"Just getting something to drink." She smiled.

Screwing on the lid, she joined the guys. They moved out of the bus and down the packed dirt road. Boone held one of her hands, and Skye walked on the other side of her. Mel followed behind smoking a cigarette, and glancing down at her ass.

"Look at my girl's ass one more time, Mel, and you'll spend all your winnings on hospital bills." Boone said out of nowhere.

Mel and Skye both chuckled, and Jez blushed. "Never noticed what a nice ass it was. Maybe it's the skirt or the stockings."

"Or the fact she just won you a ton of money." Skye added.

Boone tightened his grip on her hand, and she pulled her cup to her lips to hide her smiled.

"What are you drinking?" Skye asked and grabbed the cup from her lips. He took a sip from the straw and his face contorted into disgust. He spit the liquid out and looked over at her. "What the fuck is that?"

She giggled. "What did you think it was?"

"I don't know. Moonshine or something. Isn't that your drink?"

She laughed. "You think I've been drunk this whole time?"

He shrugged.

"It's a hydration drink." Boone said softly and seriously. "Like G2 but without the sugar."

"Like that crap that you drink when you're hung over or sick?" Mel asked from behind them.

Jez nodded.

"Well if you're drinking Moonshine all the time, I guess I can see why you'd have to drink that crap." Skye replied trying to piece it all together.

Boone glanced over at him. "She's sick, you idiot. She drinks it because she has to."

"So.. the Moonshine?" Mel asked, stepping up closer to them.

Jez dropped her head. She didn't like them knowing all this. "I use to drink it to help make me numb before the races. Molly and the others ... well, it helped. I don't drink it much anymore though. Aside from a few sips here and there to calm my nerves, I can't."

"Just Moonshine or any alcohol?" Skye seemed curious.

"Anything really. I'm not supposed to at least. It makes my symptoms worse."

"So what kind of sick are we talking about, Ace?" Mel asked softly. "You don't have cancer, right?"

"No, I don't have cancer." She gave Boone a dark look for even bringing it up, but he didn't seem to notice. They were approaching the stage and the crowd was growing thicker around them. He pulled her a little closer and the people around them moved out of her way. There were stares, glares, and smiles as people noticed her. She pulled on the purple liquid nervously.

Boone held her close and tight as they walked up to security. They didn't even have to say anything as they were ushered into through the gates. Grey walked up as they followed the yellow jacketed security guard. "Well, about time you got here."

"Sorry, it's my fault." Jez said with a small smile.

"It was worth the wait." A smooth voice spoke and the group turned to look at who had spoken. Connor Cory, lead singer for Stone Cold was coming up behind them. His eyes looked over Jez. "So which one of you is Ace?"

Boone stiffened and Skye stood just a little taller too. But Jez smiled. "That would be me."

His cocky smile brightened. "Beautiful and fast. My kind of girl."

He stepped a little closer and raised his hand to her. Without a second thought, she took it and stepped away from the guys. Boone clung to her hand but when she gave him a look he dropped it.

"Relax, man. She just a little star struck." Skye said softly.

Boone let her hand go, and Jez walked with Connor across the open area. The guys followed and Jez could feel the weight of their eyes on her. As they moved, Connor looked down at her. "So, you kicked some serious ass out there today."

"You saw it?" She asked amazed.

"Sure." He laughed. "I use to race a little back in the day. That's why we agreed to play here."

"Cool." She smiled. He led them into a large tent where the other band members sat around on patio styled furniture. There were the four other guys she recognized from the videos and posters, as well as several girls.

"Guys, this is Ace." Connor presented her. They all smiled or waved. Connor made the introductions. "Eddie, Tyler, Seth, and Max."

Boone stepped up close behind her, and Ace felt his hand on her shoulder. "This is Boone, Skye, and Mel." She said smiling back at her guys.

"Pit crew?" Max smiled.

"Boyfriend." Boone replied making his presence known loud and clear.

Everyone smiled and Connor dropped her hand, moving away. He used the offer of a drink as an excuse to his quick retreat. "You guys want a beer?"

Skye and Mel nodded and stepped over to where Connor was grabbing one for himself. Skye pulled one out for Boone and brought it over to him.

"How about you, Ace? You want something?" Connor asked, motioning to the ice chest.

"I'm good. Thanks." She smiled and held up her cup.

"Bring your own? Are you that worried?" Eddie asked, looking her over.

She shook her head, but it was Mel that spoke. "Most people don't carry her drink of choice."

"And what would that be?" Seth, who had been leaning back lazily, leaned up and rest his elbows on his knees showing his interest.

"Moonshine." She smirked.

There was a collective chuckle and a few comments. Seth laughed outright. "What else would the fastest girl on the west coast drink, but white lightning?"

"Have a seat, get comfy." Connor said waving them to a few empty chairs.

As they sat, Ace smiled and giggled. "I can't believe I'm meeting you. I am a huge fan."

"What's your favorite song?" Tyler asked, shoving the girl who had been sitting on his lap off.

"Um, I like a lot of them." She rambled off several she enjoyed but her eyes fell as she avoided the question.

"Wow, she doesn't have a very good poker face, does she?" Eddie laughed out right.

She looked up a little surprised. Boone nudged her. "Tell them your favorite one, Ace. They don't believe that you're a fan."

She licked her lips and swallowed her nerves. "My favorite is Cut." She said softly.

"Cut?" The room instantly sobered. She had all their attention now. "That's not one we hear often. What makes you like that one?"

She shrugged. "I can relate to it, I guess." She dropped her eyes, as the pain in her ribs throbbed knowingly.

Jez's eyes were caste down in humiliation so she didn't see the curious looked that Skye and Mel gave to Boone, or the dark look that painted his face. The moment passed, Connor cleared his throat and changed the subject. "So, where'd you learn to drive like that?"

Another touchy subject, but Ace was ready. "My ex taught me."

Boone stiffened and reached out to put his hand on her back. "He may have taught you the basics, Ace, but your talent is all natural."

"That car of yours' is sweet." Eddie commented.

"That's all them." She motioned to the guys around her with a smile. "I just drive it, they built her."

And then the conversation took off. The eight guys spent the better part of an hour chatting about cars and engines. Jez sipped her drink and sat silently. When her cup was empty, she looked around for the bathroom. One of the scantily clad girls waved to her, and Jez followed her just outside the tent. Boone watched her, but didn't move. He could see her head to the trailer with the dark blue lettering.

After using the facilities and washing her hands, Jez made her way out of the trailer. On her way back to the tent, Eddie was headed towards her. She smiled but he stopped her completely. "Cut, huh? That's a hardcore song."

She nodded and swallowed down her nerves.

"What makes you like it so much?"

"It's honest and true. It says what some people can't." She admitted, looking up to him. His long black hair blew in the wind. "I can relate to it."

His eyes narrowed as he looked at her. "It's nothing to be ashamed of, you know. It's not healthy, but it's an illness, like depression. If you're struggling with it, you really need to get some help. Don't be ashamed."

She swallowed down the tears that threatened. "I've been better, and I'm going to be better now that all this is over."

"That guy in there really cares about you. You owe it to him, and to yourself too, to get help." Eddie sighed. He reached out and put a hand on her cheek. "A pretty girl like you shouldn't hurt so much."

"I'm not pretty." She replied instantly.

"Ace?" Boone called to her, and she turned away from Eddie. She smiled at Boone who stood rigid in the doorway of the tent. Without a word, she turned from Eddie and rushed back to Boone's side.

He wrapped her up in his arm. "What did he say to you?"

"Nothing important." She smiled up at him.

"Did he hit on you?" Angry flamed in his eyes.

She smiled and rolled her eyes. "No, we were talking about the song. You know, not every guy wants to fuck me."

He tensed under her hands at her sharp words. He reached around and placed his hands on either side of her face, tilting it up. "I don't know whether to be pissed at your naivety or love you more for it."

She smiled and pushed up on her tip toes to place a kiss on his lips.

"Hey Ace!" Connor's voice called to her. "This is supposed to be about you, come here and tell us about yourself."

Boone rolled his eyes, obviously displeased by Connor's attention, but Ace just smiled. He took her hand and led her back into the room where he took a seat and moved her onto his leg. "What do you want to know?"

"What do you do in real life?" Someone asked.

She shrugged but Boone wasn't so quiet. "She works with her brother at her dad's auto parts store and she goes to school."

"Image a racer working at an auto parts store." Tyler smirked. "Can't imagine where her love of cars came from."

"She doesn't know a damn thing about cars though." Skye laughed.

"Are your dad and brother here?" Connor asked curiously.

She shook her head and dropped her eyes. "No, they don't know about any of this."

"You're kidding? How do you keep it all hidden from them?" Eddie asked.

She looked up at him and locked eyes. "It's easy once the lies start. People only see what they want to, don't they?"

"Skye was just saying you've never been out here before. I think he's lying. No way someone as good as you has never run here before." Connor changed the subject quickly.

She looked to Skye who waved a hand, indicating she should tell him, with a pleased smirk. "Tell him, kiddo."

"No, I've never been here before. I've never done anything like this before. First and last." She smiled.

Skye and Mel spun their heads to her, but their questions were cut off by Tyler. "So, you've never raced like this?"

"Not like this. I'd run the small street track at home. Mostly just the locals, but every few weeks or months someone from out of town would come in. It wasn't anything like this though."

They shook their heads. "Fuck girl." Seth said, "First time and you dominate."

She smiled. "I wouldn't say I dominated. Randy gave me quite a run. I wasn't sure I was going to win that last one."

"What goes through your mind out there?" One of the girls asked softly, seeming impressed. "I'd be so scared."

"I don't really think." Ace admitted. "I just turn up my song and it all falls away. It's just me and the car." She smiled. "I can't even tell you who I raced against, accept for Hector and Randy."

Boone looked at her. "You play with them at all?"

"Oh, she played with them, she just didn't know it." Skye laughed. "You should have seen her that first day. All giggles and smiles, never seen Ace like that." He smiled and shook his head. "Like a damn five-year-old."

"It was exciting." She defended herself with a giggle.

"Well, she had them right where she wanted them. Should have heard them. Beginners luck only lasted until she ran the second time." Skye replied.

"I hear some drivers get pissed. Any issues?" Seth asked.

She looked at him wide eyed with surprise. "No, I expected some. Half expected Hector to come after me, but if they were pissed, they didn't let me know."

"Even Randy?" Mel asked. He had been unusually quiet this whole time.

She nodded. "Even Randy. He was really nice. We talked a little before the race. He wished me luck and shook my hand."

Boone chuckled. "He thought he had you."

"I'm not surprised. He almost did." Her mind flashed back to the race and to the specific moment when he lagged for just a second. "But he was really nice after I won. He even congratulated me."

"He won't be so nice next year." Grey said from the doorway.

"There won't be a next year, at least not for me." She smiled. All the eyes returned to her, and Boone's leg tensed beneath her.

"It's a little early to be saying that." Grey smiled. "Just ride the high for a while. And speaking of, it's almost show time. I've come to show you to your seats."

Ace nodded and stood up. Everyone else did too. She stepped over and the guys all shook hand with each other. She gave each of the band members a hug and thanked them for their time. They each laughed at her and said the pleasure was all theirs. Eddie held her just a little tighter and a little longer though. In her ear, he whispered, "Be careful, Ace. You're too pretty to keep hiding the pain. Stop lying to those who love you and let them help."

She pulled away, fighting down the tears. He placed a hand on her cheek and she nodded. "I'll try."

Boone was suddenly there, pulling her away from Eddie. "It was nice to meet you." Boone said thrusting his hand at Eddie, making his presence known.

Eddie smiled and shook his hand. "You too. Keep a close eye on this one," his smile faded a little. "She needs a lot more love and protection than most."

"Don't I know it." Boone replied. The two men shared a look that Ace didn't understand, and nodded to each other.

The quartet, led by Grey, moved through the back stage area and then out a side gate, and into a smaller area that was wrapped in a small fence. The large crowd was already gathered for the show but they would be just in front of them.

"VIP area." Grey chuckled.

There were four seats and nothing else. She looked up and saw they were right at the edge of the stage. "Front row."

"As promised." He smiled. "Now at the end of the show, someone will come out and get you, Ace. He'll take you around so that we can bring you up on stage to get your prize."

"I have to go on stage?" She felt her knees grow weak.

Grey just laughed and walked away. "See you later. Enjoy the show."

She turned to look at Boone, her eyes showing all the fear she felt.

"It'll be fine, Ace." He soothed her. "Just keep your eyes on me, and you'll get through this."

She nodded and felt her head grow light. She swooned and Boone grabbed her arm. "Have a seat, Ace."

She allowed him to help her to the hot metal seat. Mel caught the eye of one of the security guards. "Hey, do you think we could get her some water?"

The guy nodded and spoke into a walkie talkie. Two minutes later, a roadie rushed out on the stage and dropped a cold bottle of water into Skye's hands. He cracked the lid and handed it to Ace. She smiled weakly. "Thanks."

After a few sips, she started to feel a little better. The three guys were all watching her closely though. "You OK, Jez?" Mel asked softly.

She nodded. "Sure. It's just all a little overwhelming." She offered as strong a smile as she could.

It wasn't five minutes later when a guitar chord vibrated through the speakers. The crowd went wild and Jez forgot she wasn't feeling well. As the band walked onto the stage, she stood up. Boone and Skye both moved a little closer to her sides. Stone Cold smiled and pointed to Ace as they started their first song. It was one that she knew well, and she began to sing along with a broad smile. Ten songs later, Jez was just about as tired as the band was. She had sung along, danced, and jumped up and down to every beat of every song. As the band ended the song, she sagged against Boone. He looked down a little worried, but her excited smile made him relax. He pulled her close and wrapped an arm around her.

"OK, so are you all having a great fucking time?" Connor yelled into the mic. The crowd roared. "OK, so, as you all know; Ace is the big winner this weekend." He pointed at her and she blushed stupidly.

"We got the chance to meet her a little while ago, and I want you all to know she's as sweet as she is fast." This got mixed reactions from the crowd, but Jez was too embarrassed to care. Connor must have though, because he laughed, "Shut the fuck up, losers."

"This next song is for her." Eddie said as the crowd quieted. He looked right at her and she swallowed. She knew before the first chord what song it was. She didn't know if she should smile or cry. It was haunting and hard, and every word was sung directly to her. With mixed emotions, she sang them right along. Her hand came to rest on her side where the newest cut was still sore. Rubbing it as she sang about the blade that brought freedom brought tears to her eyes. Eddie's eyes looked watery as well. Boone pulled her close and intertwined his fingers into hers. He was so rigid she knew he was hearing every word. She felt his head rest on hers as the song ended. Suddenly needing to held, she turned in his arms and wrapped her arms around him. Tears dripped from her eyes as he held her tight.

Skye leaned over and spoke. "What the fuck is that all about?"

"Later." Boone replied and Jez looked up at him. He leaned down and placed a kiss on her lips as the band went into their next song, which was all about holding on to what you love. It took a few seconds before Jez recognized it, but when she did, she turned and looked at Eddie. He was smiling at her. She rolled her eyes and nodded. A smile spread across her face, and she looked up at Boone. Happy to see her smile, he knelt down and pulled her onto his back, piggyback style. She wrapped her arms around his neck and he held her legs. She sang the lyrics along with Connor and the guys laughed.

It was a couple hours later when they finished their last song. They had played every song from every album and the crowd still wanted more. Connor got them quieted down and said that it was time to bring Ace up. The guy who had given directions in the hangar was suddenly waving for Ace. She gave a small kiss to Boone before walking over to head up to the stage.

When they got backstage the guy smiled at her. "Have to say, I never thought it'd be you."

She smiled and shrugged. Eddie reached out and grabbed her hand and drug her out in front of the crowd. She covered her open mouth and giggled as Connor introduced her. "Here is your Desert Run Champion. Ace MacIntosh!"

The crowd erupted into cheers. She knew there were some people out there booing, but she couldn't hear them, and she didn't really care. Connor pulled her to center stage and she looked down at Boone, Skye, and Mel who all cheered and whistled. She blushed in embarrassment as Connor wrapped an arm around her shoulders. "So, Ace," He said in his sexy on-stage voice. "This is a whole lot of money. What is a young little thing like you going to do with it?"

Jez bit her lip. A piece of her wanted to be honest, but she just couldn't, not with all those eyes on her. Ace appeared behind her eyes, and she said in an innocent filled voice, "I think I'm going to lay it all out on my bed and fuck my boyfriend on it."

Her comment was so different from person that the band had just met backstage that it blew them away. Connor flew away from her as if her words had caused an electric shock between them, and almost fell over with laughter. The other band members' expressions ranged from shock to lust filled jealousy. Connor pointed to Boone, who was laughing as well. Skye and Mel both stood dumb-founded by her comment. "You are one fucking lucky guy, Boone!"

He raised his hands helplessly. He said something but she didn't catch it. Connor must have because he started laughing and pointed to Boone. "He just said anything to keep her happy."

The crowd laughed and cheered. Jez covered her face with her hands laughing.

"OK, ok," Connor said trying to quiet them. "Let's bring out the person who puts this thing together every year, Mr. Grey Loacher."

Grey walked out and waved. He thanked Connor as he took the mic and stepped up next to Ace. "Hey, what a fucking amazing weekend!" The crowd cheered and he waited for them to quiet. "Good luck to those of you who are racing tomorrow. Now, on to the matter at hand. This has been a weekend of firsts. It's the first time a rookie has taken the title, it's the first time someone under the age of 21 has taken it. Yes, she's a young one." He pointed to the audience in a mock warning. "And it's the first time a woman has taken it. So Ace MacIntosh, you will be written in the history books as a legend."

She looked at Boone, Skye, and Mel who were all beaming proudly at her. Grey grabbed her hand and placed a kiss on it.

"You will forever be known as the Princess of the Desert Run."

She rolled her eyes and giggled.

"Now, normally we give you a trophy and your prize money, plus the bragging rights. But since this is such a historical moment, someone recommended we get you something else also." He turned and Jez watched as a tall, beautiful brunette pranced out holding the trophy. She was followed by a blond, holding a large check, and finally a red head who held a square pillow with a tiara on it. Ace turned as red as her under skirt as the woman stood behind her. She watched as Grey lifted the tiara and moved to place it on her head. He then handed her the trophy and the check. When he was done, he turned back to the crowd. "I present to you, Ace MacIntosh, Princess of the Desert Run!"

The crowd started to cheer and yell. She heard whistles and shouts. Embarrassed beyond comfort, she looked over at Eddie, who stood just a few feet from her. "How do I get off?"

He grinned, and glanced at Boone. "That's a question for your boyfriend, Princess, not me."

It took a minute for her to register what he had said and then the question she had asked. She flushed even more embarrassed. He laughed and stepped over to nudge her in the shoulder. The three girls were all moving off the stage, Grey followed them. Jez took that as her hint to go also but Connor stopped her. "Where do you think you're going, Princess?"

She looked back at him nervously.

"Get back over here." He said. A roadie came out and helped her hand down the check and trophy to Mel and Skye. When her hands were empty, Connor pulled her closer. "So, since it's a weekend of firsts. We thought we'd do something extra special. Everyone knows this girl has a theme song, right?"

She looked over at him, then down at Boone confused. He just smiled and chuckled.

Connor saw her confusion. "Come on now, what song do you listen to when you race?"

"Ace of Spades." She said softly. "But how do you know?"

"Ace of Spades." He shouted. The crowd erupted. "So as our closing number, in honor of our own Ace of Spades, we'd like to play a special closing song for you."

Jez's head spun as the heavy riff echoed out of the speakers and Ace didn't know what to do. She smiled so brightly her cheeks hurt, and tears of happiness stung her eyes. Connor pulled her off to the side so she was still on stage but not in the way. As the lyrics echoed in her head, she began to sing along, bouncing to the rapid beat.

When it came to an end, Jez moved to the edge and stepped just off stage while Connor and the rest of Stone Cold took their bows. When they came off, they looked tired but each gave her a quick hug. She thanked each of them again. Eddie was the last one and he held her just a little tighter again.

"Please think about what I said." He touched her stomach and felt the bandage under her shirt. "If anyone is not helping you, cut them off. You deserve to be happy, and pain isn't going to get you there."

She flinched and nodded. "Message received, loud and clear."

He placed a kiss on her forehead, then turned and walked away. With a sigh, she felt the adrenaline start to come down. A security guard stepped over and offered to take her back to her friends, but they were rushing at her. Boone wrapped her in his arms and lifted her off the ground. She laughed and grabbed for the tiara that was falling off her head.

"Fuck!" Skye said excitedly.

"Wow!" She giggled still in shock. She let out her breath and staggered. Boone and Skye both reached for her.

"Ok, I think it's time to get you back to rest for a bit." Boone said still smiling.

Mel took the check and the trophy, so Skye could walk close to Jez and Boone, whose arm was wrapped tightly around her.

Grey called to them before they got too far, and rushed over carrying a plain file box. He looked down at Jez with concerned eyes. "Are you alright?"

She smiled and nodded. "A little tired."

He didn't look convenience, but he handed over the box to her. "Here, this is yours."

"What is it?"

"It's the rest of your prizes. Guard it with your life, it's worth a lot." He winked at her. "See you next year."

As he walked away, a peaceful sadness settled in her. "Good-bye Grey."

Boone kissed the top of her head. "Want me to carry that?"

She looked up at him horrified. "Absolutely not! He said to guard it with my life."

At first, Boone looked shocked, but then he laughed and shook his head.

"So, what do we call you now?" Mel asked out of the blue. They had made it out of the concert area and were crossing the hard-packed dirt. "Bels? Ace? Pickle? Jez? Princess?"

"Not Bels." Boone and Jez said in unison.

"And not Pickle, that's the dumbest thing I've ever heard." Skye said.

"I think we need to leave Ace here too, and maybe Princess as well." Jez said. With a shrug she said, "Looks like it's back to just Jez."

"But I like Princess." Skye said. "I think it fits you."

"Me too." Mel agreed. "I'm sticking with Princess. Princess Ace."

Skye nodded and Boone laughed. "Princess Ace."

"That's stupid." She rolled her eyes and giggled.

They rounded the corner of the last row where they had parked the bus and continued to walk toward it. But as they got closer, Jez looked up and saw three figures standing by a familiar car. Her heart sank into her feet and tears sprang into her eyes. She slowed her gate, and it was only then that Boone and the others grew aware that something was wrong. Boone pulled her closer and whispered. "It's going to be fine."

She shook her head as the got closer. The trio turned and faced them. Jez's heart started to slam in her chest. Skye smiled weakly. "Hey Jordy, Ty, OB. What are you all doing here?"

Jordy's eyes fixed on Jez's. She hadn't seen him that angry, ever.

"Funny thing," OB said darkly. "Jordy got a text that said Jez was out here racing. Of course, we know that Jez don't race, so we didn't believe it. But Jordy here was worried. We tried to tell him that Boone would never put her in that kind of danger. After all, he promised to keep her safe. But he wouldn't let it go, so we closed up shop and came out to prove him wrong. Imagine our surprise when we get here and see our little Jez racing under a different name."

"She didn't race." Mel tried to lie even though it was no use.

Their dark looks fell on him. "She was on stage receiving her prize."

"How long have you been here?" She asked softly.

"All day." Jordy's voice was just as soft. But where hers was in fear, his was hushed in anger. "Get in the car, we're going home."

She took a step but Boone stopped her. "She's not a child, Jordy. She can make her own decisions."

Two steps. Two steps and one raised fist, Boone was on his ass on the dirt. "Fuck you. Stay away from her."

Jez trembled, tears spilling down her cheeks. Jordy grabbed her arm and pulled her back to the car. He tossed her into the backseat of the old green Buick and climbed in after her. Ty and OB climbed in the front and tore off. Jez tried to look back, but Jordy raised a finger to stop her. Instead, she pulled the tiara off her head and slid it into the box, not lifting the lid any more than necessary. She gripped the box tightly and tilted her head down. Tears fell on the paper top, dotting it.

Thank you so much for reading the first part of Wrong Things Right. I hope you enjoyed meeting Jez, Boone, Skye, and the others as much as I did. Jez and Boone's story does not end here. It continues in the next sections Wrong Things Right: Losing Hand and Wrong Things Right: Straight Shot. I hope you'll come along for the ride ....

Printed in Great Britain
by Amazon

66901192R00203